THE PREY

Also by Yrsa Sigurdardóttir

The Thóra Gudmundsdóttir novels

Last Rituals

My Soul to Take

Ashes to Dust

The Day is Dark

Someone to Watch Over Me

The Silence of the Sea

Standalones

I Remember You

The Undesired

Why Did You Lie?

The Freyja and Huldar Series

The Legacy

The Reckoning

The Absolution

Gallows Rock

The Doll

The Fallout

About the Author

Yrsa Sigurdardóttir works as a civil engineer in Reykjavík. She made her crime fiction debut in 2005 with *Last Rituals*, the first instalment in the Thóra Gudmundsdóttir series, and has been translated into more than thirty languages. *The Silence of the Sea* won the Petrona Award in 2015. *The Prey* is her sixteenth adult novel.

About the Translator

Victoria Cribb studied and worked in Iceland for many years. She has translated more than forty books by Icelandic authors including Arnaldur Indridason, Ragnar Jónasson and Sjón. In 2017 she received the Ordstír honorary translation award for her services to Icelandic literature.

THE PREY

Yrsa Sigurdardóttir

Translated from the Icelandic by Victoria Cribb

HODDER &
STOUGHTON

First published in Great Britain in 2023 by Hodder & Stoughton
An Hachette UK company

First published with the title *Bráðin* in 2020 by
Veröld Publishing, Reykjavík

I

A CIP catalogue record for this title is available from the British Library

Hardback ISBN 978 1 529 37743 9
Trade Paperback ISBN 978 1 529 37744 6
eBook ISBN 978 1 529 37745 3

Typeset in Sabon MT Std by Manipal Technologies Limited

Printed and bound in Great Britain by Clays Ltd, Elcograf S.p.A.

Hodder & Stoughton policy is to use papers that are natural, renewable
and recyclable products and made from wood grown in sustainable forests.
The logging and manufacturing processes are expected to conform
to the environmental regulations of the country of origin.

Hodder & Stoughton Ltd
Carmelite House
50 Victoria Embankment
London EC4Y 0DZ

www.hodder.co.uk

This book is dedicated to my father,
Sigurdur B. Thorsteinsson

Pronunciation guide for character and place names

Agnes (as in English)

Ágústa – OW-goost-a

Andrés – AN-dryes

Bjólfur – BYOHL-vur

Dröfn – DRERBN

Erlingur – AIR-ling-ur

Geiri – GYAY-ree

Haukur – HOH-kur

Hjörvar – HYER-var

Höfn í Hornafirdi – HERBN ee HORD-na-FIRTH-ee

Hornafjördur – HORD-na-FYERTH-ur

Ívan – EE-van

Jóhanna – YOH-han-na

Keflavík – KEB-la-veek

Kolbeinn – KOLL-baydn

Kollumúli – KODL-loo-MOO-lee

Lón – LOHN

Lónsöræfi – LOHNS-er-RYE-vee

Morri – MORR-ree

Múlaskáli – MOOL-a-SKOW-lee

Neskaupstadur – NESS-kohps-STAATH-ur

Njördur Hjörvarsson – NYER-thur HYER-vars-sson

Rannveig – RANN-vayg

Reykjavík – RAYK-ya-veek

Salvör – SAAL-ver

Selfoss – SELL-foss

Sigvaldi – SIK-val-dee

Stokksnes – STOKKS-ness

Styrmir – STIRM-eer

Thórir – THOHR-eer

Tjörvi – TYER-vee

Vatnajökull – VAT-na-YER-kudl

Vík í Mýrdal – VEEK ee MEER-dal

PROLOGUE

The woman on the doorstep looked nothing like Kolbeinn had pictured her when they'd spoken on the phone. Her deep, husky voice seemed at odds with her slim figure and cheerful demeanour. He had been expecting someone far more world-weary, with a cigarette dangling from the corner of her mouth and a miniature of vodka in her pocket. The woman standing at his door looked more likely to drink spinach juice than alcohol, and there was no way she could be a smoker. But the moment she introduced herself, her voice removed all doubt that she was the woman who had phoned.

'Sorry it's taken so long. I just didn't have any reason to come to Reykjavík before now.' She held out a cardboard box. As Kolbeinn took it, he registered the weight of the contents. Books, he guessed. 'Like I said, we found this box in the loft,' the woman went on. 'Behind a pile of old insulation off-cuts. I expect that's why it got left behind when you cleared out the house.'

Kolbeinn apologised that he and his brother hadn't done a better job of emptying the loft. The woman replied that there was no need; it didn't matter. She herself had accidentally left a bike in the cycle shed when she and her husband had moved out of their flat and into Kolbeinn's father's house. These things happened.

The box was covered in dust. Kolbeinn put it down. It was marked back and front with a brand of margarine that was no longer on the market, a brand he couldn't even remember seeing in the shops. The box must date from decades ago.

The woman suddenly seemed struck by a thought. 'Oh, yes, I nearly forgot: I've brought something else too. I don't know if it'll be of any interest to you but I didn't like to just throw it away.' She pulled a clear plastic bag from her coat pocket and handed it to him. Inside, there was a small brown object that he couldn't immediately identify. 'It's a shoe. We found it back in the autumn when we were digging the foundations for our deck. I expect it belonged to you or your brother.'

Now that she'd said it, Kolbeinn could see that it was a shoe. A small child's lace-up shoe, made of brown leather, he thought, though it was hard to guess the original colour. It could have been white for all Kolbeinn knew. The laces at least must have changed colour over the years and were now as brown as the soil the shoe had been lying in.

Whatever its original appearance, Kolbeinn was sure that, like the brand of margarine on the box, he had never seen it before. Not that this was necessarily significant. The shoe couldn't have belonged to a child older than about three or four, and he had absolutely no memories from that age, so for all he knew it could have been his. In any case, it must have belonged to a member of his family, or perhaps a visiting child, because his parents had built the house and the shoe was unlikely to have been lying in the ground when they bought the plot.

Kolbeinn raised his eyes to the woman's. 'Thanks. That's interesting.' She seemed disappointed that he had nothing else to say about the relic. Perhaps she'd been hoping to hear the story of how the shoe had come to be lost, but he had no idea what that story might be. He tried to make up for the fact:

'I bet we searched high and low for it at the time. We didn't have an endless supply of clothes and shoes in those days.' He turned the bag over in his hands, examining the shoe. 'I wonder how on earth it came to be buried under the lawn. The garden was already well established by the time my brother and I would have been wearing shoes this size.'

The woman nodded. 'Yes. It is rather odd. Mind you, it did turn up right beside the flagpole, so I'm guessing it might have fallen into the hole when the foundation was being dug and no one noticed.' She looked at him a little anxiously. 'We took the flagpole down – I hope you don't mind.'

He smiled. 'No, of course not. It's your house now and you can do what you like with it. The flagpole was never particularly popular. Not with my mother, anyway. She told me they'd only ever raised a flag once, and then only to half mast. She didn't say what the occasion was, but she did say she'd nagged Dad for years to get rid of it.'

The woman appeared relieved. 'If he was responsible for putting it up, I can understand why he didn't want to take it down. It was embedded in an oil barrel full of concrete. We had to hire a small crane to remove it.'

This didn't surprise Kolbeinn. His father had never done things by halves – on land or sea. If he installed a flagpole, you could be sure it would withstand anything the elements chose to fling at it.

They exchanged a bit more small talk. He asked how she was enjoying life in the small town of Höfn í Hornafirdi, in the south-east of the country, some 450 kilometres from Reykjavík. She said it was great. She asked in return if he ever thought about moving back there, and he said he couldn't see it happening. He was too much of a city boy now, having come to live in the capital as a child, following his parents' divorce.

After this, they ran out of things to say. Their paths had only crossed through the sale of his father's house, after all. Kolbeinn and his brother hadn't met the woman or her husband at any stage in the process, leaving it to the estate agent in Höfn to take care of all communication with the buyers. Actually, things might have moved faster if the brothers had got more involved, but neither had been that fussed. Their father had died a well-off man and once his estate had been wound up, there was no particular urgency about releasing the capital tied up in the house. Their part in the process had merely been to agree to the sale and sign the papers. Although their mother had survived their father, she hadn't inherited the house. Not that it would have made much difference if she had, since she was incapacitated by dementia. If she'd been required to sign the contract, she wouldn't have known which way round to hold the pen, let alone how to write her name.

After a brief, awkward silence, Kolbeinn blurted out an offer of coffee, which the woman declined, saying she had a long drive ahead of her and needed to get going while it was still light. He thanked her again for the box and the shoe, and they said goodbye.

Kolbeinn watched her walking away and waved to her as she got in the car. Then he closed the front door, still holding the plastic bag. It was kind of her not to have simply thrown the shoe away, but really it was only a matter of time before he did so himself. He wasn't the type to hang on to old junk, and a child's shoe that had been buried in the ground for donkey's years definitely fell into that category.

Still, maybe his brother would like it. Especially if it had belonged to him. Neither of them had kept much from their father's estate. Since moving to Reykjavík with their mother, they'd had only sporadic contact with their dad, so there were few memories attached to any of his things. When the brothers travelled east together to empty the house, they had soon realised that none of the furniture or other belongings held any sentimental value for them, and decided to sell or throw away the bulk of the contents.

The stuff they had chosen to keep amounted to barely any more than this box and the child's shoe.

Kolbeinn removed the shoe from the bag. The dried-out leather smelt faintly of earth. It was so hard to the touch and the laces were so stiff that it was more like the cast of a shoe. He turned it over in his hands but there was nothing familiar about it. When he looked inside, though, he saw something that triggered a childhood memory.

Above the heel he could make out a name tag of the type his mother used to glue or sew into all the brothers' clothing until they were well into their teens. The labels were supposed to ensure that their belongings would be returned if they ever forgot or mislaid them.

The shoe must have belonged to Kolbeinn or his brother, then. He scratched at the label in a vain attempt to clean the dirt off the red embroidered lettering. In doing so, he inadvertently dislodged one of the laces, revealing the original colour of the leather underneath.

Kolbeinn was a little taken aback. As far as he could tell, the shoe had once been pink. It couldn't possibly have belonged to him or his brother. Although nowadays children's clothes were no longer strictly colour-coded according to gender, it had been different in his parents' day – especially his father's. He had been a bit older than their mother and even more old-fashioned in his views. There was no way he would ever have agreed to let his sons wear pink shoes.

But why would his mother have sewn a name tag in the shoe of someone else's daughter? It was almost unthinkable that anyone else could have done it. His mother had been the only person who labelled clothes that way: other mothers had made do with marking their children's things in ink, if they bothered labelling them at all. He remembered this because he and his brother had been teased about it at school. Other mothers apparently had better things to do with their time than sit there painstakingly embroidering their children's names onto small fabric tags.

Kolbeinn's curiosity was aroused. He decided to wet the tag in an attempt to wash off the dirt and see if he could read the name. There was no danger the letters would run and become illegible since they were embroidered onto the label.

The water in the kitchen sink turned brown as he rubbed the shoe under the tap. By the time he could finally make out some of the raised letters his fingers were sore.

The first letter was clearly an 'S'. This was followed by something that could have been an 'a', an 'e' or an 'o'. Then there was an 'l', followed by two illegible letters and finally an 'r'. It didn't take him long to look up Icelandic girls' names of six letters that began with an 'S' and ended with an 'r', and there were only two on the list he found online: Salvör and Sólvör.

Kolbeinn put the shoe down.

Salvör.

The name nudged at something in his past. But the harder he tried to recall it, the more elusive the memory became. It was like trying to grab hold of smoke. In the end he gave up.

Putting the shoe on the draining board, he watched the brown water trickling down the sink, aware of strange feelings stirring inside him. He tried to empty his mind, pushing away anything that could conceivably be connected to the name. Not thinking about things you couldn't remember was often the most effective way of retrieving them. You could be sure the memory would pop to the surface, like a child who wants nothing to do with you until you pretend to ignore them.

Before his theory could be put to the test, the phone rang. It was a member of staff from his mother's nursing home, calling to tell him to hurry over as his mother had had a suspected heart attack and the outcome was touch and go.

It was a long time since his mother had enjoyed anything like a normal existence, and her health had been going downhill rapidly in recent months. Even so, this was a distressing phone call to receive. He spluttered something while he was recovering from the initial shock, then said he was on his way.

'Will you let your brother know?'

Kolbeinn said he would. Before the nurse rang off, she added: 'And your sister. It matters a lot to your mother to have her here too. Though it's very difficult to understand her, she's been asking for her repeatedly ever since she had her attack. So please could you make sure she gets the message.'

'My sister?'

'Yes,' the nurse said, sounding a little flustered. 'Salvör. She wants to see her daughter, Salvör.'

Chapter 1

There were no tracks to suggest anyone had ever been there, just pristine white snow as far as the eye could see. No living creature moved in the landscape, but then few animals could scratch out an existence in the depths of winter in such a barren waste. They had come across stark evidence of this on the way there in the form of a dead sheep. The carcass had been buried in a drift, apart from a patch of exposed fleece, encrusted with clumps of snow. Clearly, a grim fate awaited any animal that wasn't rounded up in the autumn and taken down to the farms to wait out the winter. It had been a dispiriting sight and they hadn't lingered. There was nothing they could do for the poor beast now.

In the midst of the desolate, treeless landscape stood a large wooden hut. The faded paint must once have been much brighter, the texture less matt, but in spite of its weathered appearance, the hut stood out in sharp relief, moss green and rust red against an otherwise white backdrop.

Jóhanna paused to listen. There were no sounds coming from the hut. Apart from the squeaking of the snow under her companion Thórir's feet, the silence was absolute. Even the wind seemed to be holding its breath, as if exhausted by the recent storms. For the last few weeks, the depressions had formed an orderly queue across the Atlantic, one following inexorably on the heels of the other. In the end, Jóhanna had taken to switching off the radio before the forecast, as there was no point getting depressed about it. The weather came and went, behaving exactly as it pleased, and there wasn't a thing she could do to change it.

'There isn't a soul here.' Thórir, a member of a Reykjavík search and rescue team, came to stand beside her. 'No tracks. Total silence.'

Jóhanna didn't reply. After all, it was self-evident. She pointed up one of the snowy slopes that formed a deep bowl around the valley floor on which the hut stood. 'What do you make of that?' Jutting out of the snow near the top of the slope was a pair of reindeer antlers – or at least that's what it looked like to her. 'Are those antlers or branches?'

Thórir shrugged, the movement barely visible under his thickly padded snowsuit. Jóhanna was wearing identical survival gear, marked back and front with the logo of the Hornafjördur Search and Rescue Team. 'Can't tell,' he said. 'It's not a person, though.'

Jóhanna had nothing to add. She turned her attention back to the hut. 'Let's take a look inside, anyway, now that we've come all this way. Who knows? They could be in there, even though we can't hear anything. Asleep, maybe.'

'Or exhausted.'

Neither mentioned the third possibility. Instead, they set off over the frozen snow-crust towards the hut. They both knew when to keep quiet and for that Jóhanna was grateful. On previous searches she had often been paired with team members who yakked away nonstop. It didn't seem to matter whether she answered curtly or not at all; the person in question would simply talk all the more to make up for her silence. By the time she got home after a day like that her ears would be aching. No doubt the chatterer's jaws would be too – not that this was any compensation.

Jóhanna was aware that her teammates thought she'd drawn the short straw when she was paired with Thórir. He had been seconded from a Reykjavík rescue team to assist with the search, along with a handful of people from other parts of Iceland. As he was from the big city and specially trained in disaster management, he was suspected of being a know-all who would look down on the local volunteers. This suspicion was based on nothing more substantial than the man's apparent assumption, when he first arrived, that his expertise would be required at the team's headquarters in Höfn. But because of the shortage of available manpower, he had been lent a snowsuit and packed off to join the searchers. This misunderstanding aside, Jóhanna hadn't been aware of anything in his demeanour to justify the others' prejudice. After all, the man had let her take charge and followed her lead without comment or criticism. Yet in spite of that, she couldn't shake off the feeling that everything she did was being carefully observed and judged.

They stepped up onto the raised wooden platform in front of the hut. Like everything else, it was covered in a deep layer of snow. Untouched snow. Jóhanna inspected the front of the building, noting the winter shutters nailed over the windows. This wasn't necessarily significant. If the trekkers had taken refuge here, they were unlikely to have bothered to remove the shutters. Who would care about the view from the windows if they had just made it to safety after an ordeal in the wilderness? Besides, the shutters provided additional protection against the blizzards that raged almost constantly at this time of year, nowadays especially. Jóhanna couldn't remember the storms having been this bad when she was a child, or at least not as relentlessly regular.

Above the door was a wooden board bearing the name of the hut: *Thule*. They stared at it, neither voicing aloud what they were doubtless both thinking: that the American sign seemed totally out of place up here in the Icelandic highlands. As if by tacit agreement, they began scraping the accumulated drifts away from the door. Even after they had cleared a sufficiently large area, they continued brushing away bits of snow and ice, delaying the moment of truth. Because although there were no indications that the party they were looking for were inside, they were both conscious of one thing: if the missing walkers were in there, they were very unlikely to be alive.

When their brushing and scraping had gone on so long that it was becoming embarrassing, Jóhanna drew a deep breath. There was no excuse not to open the door. The icy air flooding into her lungs did nothing to revive her, but at least she could blame her sudden shiver on that and tell herself that it had nothing to do with the ominous silence inside the hut.

'Have you ever come across a dead body?' Thórir seemed to read her mind.

This was the last thing Jóhanna wanted to think about now – or indeed ever. She always did her best to push the memories back down when they threatened to surface. 'Yes, unfortunately.'

Thórir paused, then asked: 'Many?'

Jóhanna sighed inwardly. If this was a test, it was a lousy one. 'Three. And I've witnessed plenty of bad injuries too.' Her mind presented her with images from the scene of a bus crash on the Hellisheidi mountain road outside Reykjavík, which she had attended two years earlier when she still lived in the capital. Three of the passengers had ended their journey among the jagged lava flows after being thrown from the vehicle by the force of the impact. This was followed, inevitably, by images from the accident she herself had been involved in, the accident that had left her lying like a rag doll, maimed and barely conscious, on the side of the road. It had been a narrow escape. She tried to focus on that thought: perhaps these missing people would be as lucky as she had been; perhaps they too would be saved, although the outlook seemed bleak. But it didn't work. Closing her eyes, she grimaced, then forced her mind back to the present. 'What about you?'

'Yes. Unfortunately.' The man seemed no more eager to talk about it than she was. Maybe he had wanted to find out how experienced she was, so as to gauge what response he could expect from her if they encountered a scene of horror inside.

Well, he needn't worry that she would freak out. Jóhanna opened her eyes again and squared her shoulders. 'I reckon the hut's as empty now as it was when the door closed behind the warden last autumn. I very much doubt we're going to be faced with anything grim.' Her words ran contrary to her gut instinct. There was something hostile about this godforsaken spot. People didn't belong here. Neither did the hut. Nature should have been left undisturbed.

Concealed under the snow, on the level ground surrounding the hut, there was a patchy meadow. The grass had been sown by volunteer conservationists in a vain attempt to soften the harsh terrain. Every summer they had to re-seed the large bare patches to prevent them from spreading. She herself had come here with her husband last summer to help with the task.

The trip had been a unique experience. Nature had pulled out all the stops, and the array of colours in this once active volcanic area had been unlike anything Jóhanna had seen before. In places, the mountains were literally blue; there was no need for distance to create the effect, the rhyolitic rocks had seen to that. Some of the slopes had combined every colour of the rainbow. She and her husband had visited not only this hut but also several others in the south-eastern highlands, as part of a fundraiser for the Hornafjördur Search and Rescue Team. Most of the hut owners in the region had been willing to pay for their greening services. As a result, they had travelled the length and breadth of the nature reserve with a relaxed team of volunteers. But the sense of wellbeing and spiritual uplift that Jóhanna had experienced on that trip now seemed remote, replaced by dread and a presentiment of doom.

Her despondent mood was only partly caused by the uniform blanket of snow that obscured the unearthly beauty of the bare rocks. It had more to do with the purpose of their mission. There was little reason for optimism, despite the attempts of the rescue-team leaders to raise morale before the team left base. No one had been convinced. Information about the missing travellers was thin on the ground, but the little the searchers had been told was decidedly odd.

They were looking for four or five individuals, all Icelanders, who had last been heard from more than a week ago. No one had noticed they were missing for five days, and severe weather conditions had prevented a search from being launched until this morning. While the blizzard was raging, the police had used the enforced wait to track the group as far as they could via their mobile phones, which had all last connected to the GSM network on the Kollumúli mountain road, heading into the Lónsöræfi wilderness. After that, all four had dropped off the grid.

It was unclear whether there had been a fifth member of the party. Signals had been picked up from only four mobile phones, but that alone was no guarantee of the number of travellers. The fifth person might not have been carrying a phone or might have switched it off. What suggested there could have been five people was that the two missing couples had flown to Hornafjördur but didn't appear to have hired or borrowed a car for their onward journey. They had spent one night at a hotel in Höfn, and the receptionist who checked them out had been under the impression that there was some-one waiting outside to collect them, though whether that per-son was a man or a woman, she hadn't a clue.

Even more puzzling was the fact that no vehicle had yet been spotted parked by the Kollumúli track or any of the other access routes to the area that were passable at this time of year. Of course, if it had been a big mountain jeep with raised suspension, it could have driven off-road, further into the nature reserve, which meant it might still be found. Equally, it was possible that the party had arranged for a driver to give them a lift into the highlands and that the per-son in question had gone home afterwards. In that case, the driver would presumably come forward once the search was reported on the news.

Tourists going missing in the wilderness was nothing new. Nor was it unusual for them to blunder off into the unknown, in defiance of a bad weather forecast. But for a party of Ice-landers to take it into their heads to go on a tourist jaunt in the wilds at this time of year was highly unusual. On the rare occasions that locals went missing in winter, it tended to be two or three friends who'd taken off on snowmobiles or cross-country skis. If it was autumn, you might also get a few ptarmigan hunters going astray.

But that wasn't the case this time. As far as anyone was aware, the missing people – two couples from Reykjavík, in their early thirties – weren't winter sports enthusiasts. In fact, they weren't known to be big outdoors types or particularly adventurous at all. The two men had apparently gone on a couple of organised reindeer shoots in the past, but the season was long over and the herds had all abandoned the area for their winter pastures in the lowlands. And neither of the women had ever applied for any type of hunting or fishing licence. No one knew why they had taken it into their heads to travel into the area. Perhaps they had simply been after that perfect Instagram shot.

Even this explanation seemed far-fetched, though. Picturesque white winters weren't confined to south-east Iceland; if they'd wanted to encounter a snowy landscape, they wouldn't have had to jump on a plane. There were plenty to choose from on Reykjavík's doorstep.

According to their next of kin, the couples had notified their families and workplaces that they would be away for just under a week: they were going on an adventure tour in the interior and would be without phone or internet reception. Beyond that, they had given away nothing about how they were planning to travel – whether they meant to walk or use cross-country skis or even snowmobiles – or where exactly they were heading. Some people said they had described it as a mystery tour. Their families were mostly under the impression that they must have paid for an organised trip that had been sold to them under that description.

So far, however, the police had had no success in tracking down any travel companies that sold mystery tours into the Lónsöræfi wilderness out of season. They'd have been surprised if they had. No serious tour operator would plan a rash undertaking like that, let alone sell it to members of the public.

The police did, however, establish that the East Skaftafell Touring Association had received an enquiry about accommodation in the Múlaskáli hut, which could have come from this group. They had explained to the caller that the hut was closed for the season. Although it was left unlocked in case it was required as an emergency shelter, it was not rented out to tour groups in winter. But the warden who spoke to the man had got the feeling he wasn't going to take no for an answer. After all, the hut was open, so there was nothing to stop him staying there.

As a result of this information, the largest party of searchers had been detailed to head straight to Múlaskáli. They would check in and around the hut, as well as visiting the mountain cabin at Múlakot, which in summer was used as a base by rangers of the Vatnajökull Ice Cap National Park.

The rest of the team had split up into smaller groups to check the other huts in the area. In common with other uninhabited parts of Iceland, there was a sprinkling of such cabins in Lónsöræfi. A couple belonged to local walking clubs, there was a privately owned cabin at Eskifell, and then there was the hut that Jóhanna and Thórir had been tasked with searching. Although none of the owners had received any enquiries about renting their properties, that didn't rule out the possibility that the lost party might have taken refuge in one of them. As an afterthought, two men had been sent up the Víðidalur valley in case the travellers had sought shelter in one of the derelict farmhouses at Eskifell or Grund.

This type of scattergun approach was necessary when nothing was known for certain about a missing party's movements. The extra volunteers had come in useful too, since although the local rescue team was well manned, they couldn't cover an area of some three hundred and twenty square kilometres without support.

The Thule hut that Jóhanna and Thórir had been assigned to search had originally been built by a US Army unit based at the Stokksnes radar station on the coast, some twenty kilometres east of Höfn by road. Later, when the Icelandic Coast

Guard had taken over the radar station, the hut had been thrown in, though from what Jóhanna had heard, the gift hadn't been particularly welcome. The Coast Guard staff had little use for it. No doubt they got their fill of outdoor adventures during their day job and weren't that eager to spend their summer holidays travelling in the Icelandic interior.

Jóhanna now took a step towards the door but Thórir got there first. Perhaps he wanted to uphold the honour of his Reykjavík rescue team. Or maybe he was afraid she'd despise him as a coward if he displayed any nerves about what they might discover inside. If he thought that, he was badly mistaken. Anyone who didn't dread coming across a tragic scene had no place on a search operation of this kind.

Jóhanna was content to let him go ahead. She watched him drag open the door and peer into the gloomy interior. From the expression of wonder that crossed his face, she gathered that he had seen something unexpected, but that it wasn't a dead body. He looked surprised, not saddened.

Jóhanna pushed the door wider and saw what it was. Just inside the entrance lay a heap of clothes. She thought she could see a thick padded jacket, a pair of over-trousers, a glove and a couple of snow boots, as well as the other bits of trekking gear you'd expect. The inner door was open into a dark hallway that appeared to be empty. Jóhanna fished out her torch, switched it on and directed the beam at the floor beyond the heap of clothes. There were signs of considerable activity in the layer of dust on the floorboards. The number of footprints indicated that several people had tramped in and out, though there was no way of telling how many or when.

'Do you think the tracks could have been made by our guys?' Thórir turned to her. 'And that the clothes are theirs too? Or could they have been left behind in the autumn?'

Jóhanna couldn't answer that. But if the coat and boots had belonged to one of the party they were looking for, the individual in question couldn't be far away. No one in their right mind would have gone outside in the snow without them.

The silence was growing oppressive. Jóhanna stuck her head inside and sniffed warily. To her relief, the smell gave no indication that they were about to enter some kind of charnel house, though since it was as cold inside as it was outside, that indication might not be accurate.

They examined the brightly coloured clothes. Instinct told Jóhanna that they had been dropped there recently. Perhaps it was the absence of dust on them. There was nothing for it but to go inside and search the hut from top to bottom. It was the reason why they had gone to all the trouble of getting here, after all; first enduring the rough jolting in the back of a mountain truck, then being dropped off at the head of the trail and slogging along it for two hours, clambering over drifts, slipping and sliding, losing their footing, and ploughing through narrow gullies. Turning back now was out of the question.

'Let's have a look inside.' Jóhanna squeezed past Thórir, who made way for her. She didn't know if he did so out of politeness or because he was reluctant to go first. Not that it mattered. She bent down to examine the clothes. 'Judging by the size, I'd say they belonged to a woman. Or more than one woman.' She blew out a breath. 'Come on. Let's do this systematically. We'll start upstairs and work our way down.'

The air inside was stale. Thórir closed the door behind him, plunging everything beyond Jóhanna's torch beam into darkness. The weak winter light couldn't penetrate the heavy shutters. Hastily, he opened the door again, but even then the daylight didn't extend beyond the hall, and the hut was large, with rooms on two floors.

When Thórir switched on his torch as well, the situation improved slightly. Jóhanna would have liked the beams to be stronger and illuminate a larger area, but it couldn't be helped. They would have to do their best with what light they had. They picked their way into the central space, then split up.

Twenty minutes later they were standing outside on the platform again, as mystified as before. They had found various signs of occupation. In one room, a pair of socks was lying inside out under a bed – free of dust, unlike the floor. In the kitchen, empty food packaging had been sorted into the relevant bins and it was clear that someone had cooked a meal there. Judging from the dates on the wrappers, they had been thrown away recently. In the toilet, they found a toothbrush and a tube of toothpaste in a glass, and an almost empty packet of wet wipes on the shelf above the sink. The open waste bin on the floor beside the lavatory turned out to contain used dental floss and a scrunched-up wet wipe that looked as if it had been used to clean off mascara. A small towel hung by the sink. It was dry to the touch, as was the tea towel that had been draped over the handle of the oven door. Dry but not dusty. Almost everywhere they looked they could see evidence that people had been here.

Yet, despite searching high and low, they hadn't found the people themselves.

Jóhanna surveyed the surrounding landscape from the platform. White snow, white snow and more white snow. And then those reindeer antlers at the top of the slope. Shielding her eyes with one hand, she decided she had been right: they were antlers, not the twisted branches of a dwarf birch. They reminded her ominously of a skeletal hand, reaching its bony fingers towards the sky. A hump under the snow where they were protruding suggested it wasn't just antlers but an entire animal. Jóhanna lowered her hand and looked away. The reindeer couldn't have anything to do with the missing people. 'Where the hell can they have got to?'

Thórir knotted his dark eyebrows. 'Perhaps they set off on a hike and got caught by a blizzard. It's been snowing nonstop for several days, so their tracks will have disappeared. Apparently, the recent snowfall has broken all records.'

He was right: it was the most likely explanation. The party had ventured out on a walk and ended up dying of exposure. The Lónsöræfi nature reserve covered a huge area and numerous hiking trails converged on the hut. It would be no easy task to find the missing walkers if their bodies had been buried under the snow. To make the job even more difficult, yet another storm was forecast, accompanied by several days of sub-zero temperatures.

She just hoped against hope that the couples had sought shelter in one of the other huts. Perhaps another group of searchers had already found them.

But this thought failed to comfort Jóhanna for long. A hike wouldn't explain why a coat, boots and other cold-weather gear had been left behind in the hall.

'We'd better head back before the light goes.' Jóhanna's eyes strayed to the antlers again. Their presence at the top of the slope troubled her. The men in the party had been hunters. If the animal had been shot, that might be relevant somehow. Pressed for time though she and Thórir were, they couldn't leave without making sure. It would look bad if the purpose of the trip turned out to have been poaching and they had failed to spot the fact. Besides, Jóhanna had a reputation for being thorough. 'But first we'd better take a look at that reindeer.'

As Thórir made no objection, they plunged off across the deep snow, moving as fast as they dared. In places the crust was paper thin and they sank halfway up their calves with every step. Their progress became even more of a struggle once they began to climb the slope. Just before they reached the antlers, Jóhanna came to an abrupt halt. 'I trod on something.' She looked down at her right leg.

'A rock maybe?' Thórir paused with his hands on his hips, grimacing.

'No. It wasn't a rock.' Jóhanna extracted her foot and peered down the hole. Then she gave a sharp intake of breath, staggered and nearly fell over backwards down the slope. 'Jesus. Jesus Christ.'

Thórir came over to where she was standing and nearly fell over backwards himself. At the bottom of the hole, part of a face could be seen, its wide-open eye staring blankly back at them.

Chapter 2

Lónsöræfi, the previous week

Dröfn was beginning to enjoy herself. At long last. She'd woken up feeling queasy from the acidic churning in her stomach, but the strenuous trek in the pure winter air had taken the edge off her discomfort. True, her calves were aching, the rucksack was weighing heavily on her shoulders and her thigh muscles were on fire, but compared to her earlier suffering this was a breeze.

There were five of them strung out along the trail, with her bringing up the rear. Haukur, their guide, led the way; the others followed in a line. Since the route was arduous and they were unsure of themselves, it was safer for everyone to pick their way along in Haukur's footsteps than to bunch up behind him. In any case, according to him the path was so narrow that for much of the way people could only traverse it in single file, even at the height of summer. One false step could end in disaster.

Dröfn's husband, Tjörvi, was following on Haukur's heels, determined not to be outdone. Behind him came Bjólfur, then his wife, Agnes. They had both been as grey in the face as Dröfn when they'd met up in the hotel lobby that morning.

It had been a while since they'd glanced behind them, so Dröfn didn't know if a healthier colour had returned to their cheeks. She guessed it had from the way their shoulders were no longer sagging as they had been at the outset. She couldn't see past them to her husband, but experience taught her he would have shaken off his hangover long before the other three, if only because he would resolutely ignore it. They had been together eight years and in all that time he had never once admitted to being hung-over. Even when he was throwing his guts up or popping painkillers like Smarties, he always insisted that there was nothing wrong.

The only member of the group who hadn't overdone the boozing was Haukur. He'd booked a room at a guesthouse, which was cheaper than their hotel, though this was glossed over. He had stopped drinking after a single glass of red wine, and said goodnight shortly after dinner. The other four had carried on partying. Not content with knocking back several glasses of red with the main course, dessert wine with pudding, and brandy with their coffee, they had thought it was an excellent idea to drop by the hotel bar for a nightcap once they got back. In hindsight, maybe that last part had been a mistake.

When they'd met up this morning, Haukur had made no attempt to hide his disapproval. He had bawled them out for sleeping in until nearly midday instead of gathering at the agreed time. Unused to being scolded like naughty kids, they had remained sheepishly silent during his tirade. Being hung-over didn't equip one for arguing back or making excuses at the best of times, and it was even harder when they were well aware that they were in the wrong.

Dröfn didn't know about the others but she had resorted to counting under her breath during Haukur's diatribe. He hadn't been raging at them for long before she realised that it was making her headache worse. 'What were you thinking? . . . Leaving me hanging around like an idiot . . . I've half a mind to . . .' The repetitive recriminations only intensified the throbbing in her head, making the pain ever more unbearable. Whereas if she distracted herself by counting, it provided some relief.

Because of this, she hadn't taken in everything he said, though she did hear enough to gather that their fecklessness had put them all in danger. Haukur was seriously considering retracting his offer and going it alone. The daylight wouldn't last long and they were inexperienced. This was followed by a rant about how he couldn't understand what he'd been thinking of, taking them along in the first place.

The truth was that it hadn't been his idea. If anything, they had forced him to take them. It had sounded like such a great way to shake up their dull routine. Although they would never admit it, their lives had become pretty monotonous. Perhaps the reason why none of them discussed this, though, was that it was such a first-world problem. On social media, at least, they appeared to have a fabulous life. They were forever eating out, cooking gourmet meals, drinking fine wine, travelling, going to gigs or the theatre or the gym. All right, they couldn't exactly claim to be influencers, but they were quick to adopt all the latest trends, always ahead of the pack. Viewed from the outside, their lives were enviable. They were financially comfortable, well educated, healthy and intelligent. But even good fortune has a tendency to lose its lustre over time.

So they had jumped at the chance to do something new and completely different. They'd first met Haukur at a dinner party given by another couple they knew. He hadn't said much, but when he did open his mouth, he'd come out with some pretty interesting stuff. Like the fact that he was about to go on a crazy solo mission into the Lónsöræfi wilderness in the south-east of the country. The purpose of the expedition was to collect readings from some kind of measuring instrument located on the edge of Vatnajökull, Europe's largest ice cap. He needed the results to finish his doctoral dissertation. Apparently it was such a long time since the readings had last been taken that he had given up waiting for anyone else to do it.

By this stage of the evening they had all been drinking for several hours and alcohol had expanded the horizon of possibility. It felt like the sky was the limit; nothing was beyond them. Their hosts had already made their excuses and gone into the kitchen to wash up, as a polite hint that it was time to go home. But their 'Anyway . . .' had gone unnoticed; the guests had simply passed the wine round again and continued to listen with rapt attention to what Haukur had to say.

Admittedly, no one at the table had the slightest interest in Haukur's research or the subject of his PhD: it was the idea of a journey into a wilderness that few people ever visited in winter that had fired their imaginations. It would be a breathtaking, once-in-a-lifetime experience. An adventure you could brag about for years to come:

'Oh, really? You've been to Everest Base Camp? Tjörvi and I were thinking of doing that but we made the decision a while ago to avoid taking unnecessary flights. Global warming and all that – you know how it is. Instead, we did this epic trek into the Lónsöræfi nature reserve in the middle of winter. An awesome experience – tough, but worth it. So totally worth it. You know, when it comes to outdoor adventures, Iceland's actually pretty hard to beat.'

Of course, they wouldn't be able to talk like this if Haukur were present, but there wasn't much risk of that. He was new to their circle of friends and hadn't yet earned a place as a regular – if he was even interested in being one. By his own account, he was so busy with his research that he hardly had any time for a social life. He'd met their dinner hosts at the gym, but apparently that was the one luxury he allowed himself, regardless of the pressure of work. The dinner party was the first he'd attended in six months or so and would probably be the last for the next six months. No one could accuse him of being a party animal – as last night had proved. Party poopers like him had little sympathy with those who enjoyed a good night out, and his furious reaction had made that abundantly clear.

In the end, Tjörvi had lost patience. Raising his voice in turn, he'd reminded Haukur that he was wasting precious minutes on pointless moaning. They should just hit the road and stop arguing about what was too late to change. Besides, it was Haukur's own fault. He should have had the sense to give them a wake-up call instead of sulking outside in his car, waiting for them to surface on their own.

This had the desired effect: Haukur had fallen silent, but it did nothing to improve his mood. Dröfn guessed he was probably still simmering with resentment, though they'd driven for more than two hours and been hiking for another two. During the couple of rest stops they'd taken, he had stood on the edge of the group in moody silence, avoiding eye contact. It had been the same on the drive there. They had left Höfn on its narrow, low-lying peninsula and headed east along the ring road, with steep, scree-skirted mountainsides to their left and the sea to their right. Apart from the occasional red-roofed farmhouse, they had seen little but the big golf-ball-like structure marking the radar station on the Stokksnes peninsula. Almost immediately after that, they had entered the Almannaskard tunnel and emerged in the farming district of Lón. Another twenty kilometres or so and they had reached the junction where the Kollumúli mountain track turned off inland towards their destination. All their attempts to make conversation had fallen flat. Not that it mattered much, since from the moment they left the main road, any talk would have been impossible.

The snow had not been ploughed there and the super-jeep with its raised suspension lurched about all over the place as it negotiated the almost impassable track. This was a picnic, though, compared to what followed once they drove out onto the gravel flats of the Jökulsá á Lón river. The route crossed frequent streambeds, carved out by the glacial torrent during the wet summer months but dry now except for a trickle. It was a challenging job for the driver: one minute the jeep seemed to be plunging almost vertically down into a watercourse, the next it was rearing up, again almost vertically, on the other side. It felt more like being tossed about on a rough sea than driving. The slow-motion pitching and rocking put a strain on their necks as their heads whipped back and forth. Even without the frosty atmosphere, it would have been hard to conduct a conversation when it took half their energy just to hang on, and the other half not to throw up.

Really, it was a miracle none of them had succumbed to carsickness.

Now, thank God, Dröfn's hangover was nothing but a bad memory. Physical exercise, oxygen, fresh air and the bracing cold had all helped her to shake it off. There was no feeling in the world to beat a release from suffering, she thought, whether it had been caused by flu, a stomach bug, a headache – or the ill effects of too much booze.

In the end, the jeep had come to a standstill on the brow of a hill after a dramatic ascent during which Dröfn had mostly kept her eyes shut. Haukur had announced that from then on they would have to rely on their own two feet, as the descent ahead was too steep, slippery and dangerous for any vehicle. No one had protested or pestered him to give it a try: they were all too attached to their necks. So Haukur had eased the jeep off the track, killed the engine and jumped out. The four passengers silently followed his example.

The sun had dropped behind the mountains and a blue shadow was stealing down the slopes, but no one drew attention to the fact. It would only reignite the quarrel about their laziness and general irresponsibility. If they'd just woken up at the right time, they would still have had a couple of hours of full daylight left for their hike.

The scenery was different from what Dröfn had been expecting, but it was spectacular nonetheless. The photos she had found online in preparation for the trip had all been taken in summer and featured the incredible spectrum of colours that characterised the rhyolitic rocks here, the legacy of long-extinct volcanoes, but these were now invisible under an obliterating layer of snow. Apart from the precipitous belts of crags on the mountainsides, which were bare and black in places, and here and there a jagged outcrop of rock, their surroundings were a uniform white. Yet, even so, they were extraordinary. It was a pity that all their attention had to be fixed on the ground at their feet, giving them little opportunity to enjoy the views.

During the Ice Age, glaciers had scoured the landscape, gouging out gullies and cavernous gorges, through which they now threaded their way. The sheer rock walls rising to meet the sky on either side made Dröfn feel as insignificant as an ant. She was filled with a mixture of fear and awe for this wild, alien world. They climbed screes, passed countless waterfalls bound in massive fetters of ice, and picked their way across rocks and stones, all without being able to see clearly what the terrain was like underfoot. Here and there, bare twigs poking through the snow-crust testified to the presence of pockets of birch scrub and they made a careful detour to avoid damaging the sensitive vegetation that lay under the ice, dreaming of summer. Now, though, they were toiling across a flat snow-field and there was less risk of slipping and falling than there had been on the earlier sections of the path. So it was a welcome break to be able to relax a little and take a proper look around. As Dröfn drank in the beauty of their surroundings, everything else seemed to recede.

The landscape may have looked more dramatic in its summer incarnation, but it still took her breath away. The gleaming, near-vertical mountains, screes and crags were beautiful but forbidding. It was a view full of paradoxes. In less challenging circumstances, the immaculate white might have seemed symbolic of purity and innocence, but now it seemed inhuman, a symbol of their powerlessness in the face of the elements. Without the appropriate equipment, they wouldn't stand a chance. And if anything were to go wrong . . .

The shiver that ran through Dröfn had nothing to do with the cold. Shrugging it off, she quickened her pace to catch up with the others, who hadn't slowed down to admire the view like her. They were probably postponing the moment until they were standing safely on the platform outside the hut – their night's lodgings. That would be sensible, of course, were it not for the rapidly dwindling light.

It couldn't be far now. When they'd abandoned the car, Haukur had said curtly that it was at least two hours' walk to the hut. So there shouldn't be more than half an hour left, give or take.

Tomorrow's trek would be longer, assuming they stuck to their plan of accompanying him. They had the option of staying behind in the warmth while Haukur went to the glacier alone to collect the readings he was after. But they hadn't tagged along on his expedition just to spend their time kicking their heels in some grotty old hut.

Dröfn noticed that Haukur had come to a halt. The line of walkers closed up behind him, with her bringing up the rear. This was unexpected. Haukur didn't seem the type to stop for a breather when they were this close to their goal. Perhaps he wanted to say a few words to them before they reached the hut. Make his peace with them, so they could cover the last stretch reconciled and in better humour. She hoped so.

This thought lasted until she saw why they had stopped. There was a dark object on the snow. When she got closer, she saw in the last rays of daylight that it was red. Bright red. After hours of having nothing but whiteness before her eyes, the colour seemed unreal, as incongruous as stumbling across a hothouse flower in the middle of the frozen wastes.

Tjörvi crouched down and scraped at the snow with his gloved hands. When he had cleared away enough to get a grip, he tugged the red material free and straightened up.

It was a hat. Haukur held out his hand and Tjörvi passed it to him. Haukur turned it over, examining it inside and out.

As far as Dröfn could see, it was a perfectly ordinary woollen beanie. Nothing like the smart designer skiwear they themselves had bought for the trip. Yet Haukur seemed strangely fascinated by it.

Dröfn broke the silence. 'Could it have been left behind in the summer or autumn?'

Haukur shook his head. The little of his face that could be seen between his hat and his scarf was flushed. 'No. There wasn't enough snow on it. If it had been lying here since last summer, it would have been completely buried. It's been an unbelievably harsh winter and the snow's a couple of metres thick here, so it must have been lost recently. Strange.'

Bjólfur and Tjörvi were silent, obviously still in a huff, but Agnes spoke up. She worked in human resources and it took a lot to upset her composure. 'You're not saying there's another tour group out here? I thought we'd have the hut to ourselves.'

'We'll definitely have it to ourselves.' Haukur didn't look at Agnes as he answered. 'There shouldn't be any other group in the area. None that I've heard about, anyway. Only lunatics like me. And you lot.' His bad mood obviously hadn't lifted.

Tjörvi rolled his eyes but bit back a snarky response. 'Can we get a move on? It's too cold to hang about.' He jerked his chin at the beanie. 'What kind of nutter would take their hat off in this temperature?'

They all stared mutely at the hat until Haukur stuffed it in his pocket and they moved off again.

As she trudged along, Dröfn couldn't get her husband's words out of her head. What kind of nutter would drop their hat in the highlands in the middle of winter? Who would even be out here at this time of year? She couldn't come up with any answers. She was still wrestling with the problem when they entered a narrow cleft between two ridges that led into a sort of bowl or cirque, carved out by a glacier. And there, before them, was the hut.

Twilight was a hair's breadth from dissolving into darkness but their eyes had had time to adjust. As they were walking, heavy clouds had piled up, blocking out the sun and rolling in a thick pall across the sky, leaving not even a chink for the moon. There wasn't even a soft glow backlighting the clouds to give an idea of where the moon had reached on its journey across the firmament.

They paused to survey the hut and its surroundings. Now that the snow-crust was no longer squeaking under their feet, there was no sound at all. No wind, no birdsong, nothing. It was as if someone had muted nature's volume.

Here, too, snow blurred every feature and landmark. Not even the steep sides of the bowl-like valley were marred by a single protruding rock. Nothing could have been more wintry than the monochrome scene before them. It was perfectly still. There was no smell in the air. The only thing that impinged on their senses was the cold. No one could fail to notice it now that they had stopped moving. It bit into their cheeks and penetrated the soles of their shoes and their gloves, tightening its merciless grip on their fingers and toes.

This made the hut appear in a much more welcome light than it would have done otherwise. In spite of its dilapidated air and the shutters nailed across all the windows, its four walls held out the promise of warmth and that was all that mattered to them at that moment.

Haukur turned to his weary but satisfied companions. 'You did well.'

Dröfn smiled. He was extending a hand of reconciliation. It seemed to work – Tjörvi and Bjólfur each slapped Haukur on the shoulder and muttered that they'd done nothing but follow his lead. Quietly relieved, Dröfn adjusted the heavy rucksack on her back, longing to be free of its weight so she could flop down on a sofa or chair.

Only Agnes seemed unwilling to enter into the spirit of friendliness, which was unlike her. She just stood there, staring hard at the hut, as if unaware of her companions. Then she looked round at them and asked: 'Is the door open?'

All heads turned to the hut. She was right: the door was ajar. The happy mood instantly evaporated and they covered the remaining ground without exchanging another word. The wooden platform surrounding the hut emitted a hollow boom as they stepped up onto it, then Haukur dragged the door fully open and called inside to ask if there was anyone there. He received no answer. But then, as Dröfn had noticed, there were no footprints on the snowy deck.

Haukur got out his torch and they filed one by one into the freezing gloom. In the entrance hall, there was a coat hanging on a peg.

A red anorak to match the hat they had found.

The last shreds of Dröfn's good mood vanished and her stomach twisted with sudden apprehension. Judging by the expression on Haukur's face, he shared her concern.

Without a hat or coat, no one would stand a chance out there. If their owner wasn't in the hut, it wouldn't be hard to guess their fate.

The oppressive silence and darkness inside gave no cause for optimism.

Chapter 3

Hjörvar's new job at the radar station on Stokksnes wouldn't be everyone's cup of tea. The isolated location would be totally unsuitable for those who enjoyed the sociable bustle of a busy workplace. Here, no one strutted about with entry passes dangling from their necks, waving reports or clustering around the coffee machine to moan about how swamped they were. Instead, there was perfect peace and quiet in which to concentrate. As a rule, the station was manned by only two employees at a time and on rare occasions by one. Apart from other Coast Guard staff, the engineers who came to take care of maintenance and the odd visit from NATO inspectors, the two-man team hardly met a soul. Almost the only time they saw another human face was when tourists strayed off the well-marked footpaths on the peninsula and tried to get inside the compound. In winter, though, tourists were few and far between, and visits from managers were kept to a minimum. The station staff might as well have been alone in the world. And that was just the way Hjörvar liked it.

It was quite a change from the days when more than a hundred US Army personnel had been based at the station. They had experienced isolation too, though of a different kind. Thanks to the insular mindset at the time, contact between Icelanders and the foreign staff at the station had been discouraged. As a result, the military personnel living within the perimeter wire were forced to be self-sufficient as far as company and entertainment were concerned. Once a year, schoolchildren from the neighbouring Hornafjördur district were invited to visit, but the most left-wing parents kept their sons and daughters at home. They were afraid that their off-spring would come back brainwashed, wearing baseball caps, chomping American gum, blathering on about the freedom of the individual and dreaming of joining the army.

Since then, the army base had been torn down. The gym had vanished, along with the cinema that had so enchanted the visiting schoolchildren, leaving only concrete foundations as a testament to the once lively community on the site. Apart from a scattering of small outhouses, the only buildings that remained were the radar station itself and a house containing staff accommodation and a workshop.

There was no need for any more. Advances in computer technology and positioning equipment meant that a couple of employees could now perform the tasks that had once occupied a workforce a hundred-strong. Data was no longer processed on site; instead, the base had been converted into a relay station, where signals were collected and forwarded, either scrambled or in clear, depending on the recipient. Rows of communication masts were arranged across the site, with the radio antenna itself, in its spherical protective shield, tak-ing prime position. This radome looked like nothing so much as a giant golf ball perched on a tee, waiting for the trolls to come down from the mountains and hit it out to sea. Inside the dome, the huge antenna revolved in infinite circles, scanning the airwaves for signals from aircraft and other flying objects invisible to the naked eye or to secondary surveillance radar.

The solitude agreed with Hjörvar. He didn't miss the city at all. As a rule, he worked normal office hours, but there were times when he couldn't leave the site due to impassable roads, equipment failure or high winds. This was fine as far as he was concerned. He had nothing waiting for him in the little town of Höfn, where he hadn't yet settled in or made any friends – which was partly his own fault as he hadn't made any attempt to socialise. On his good days, he spent his evenings and other free time slumped mindlessly in front of the TV, not really taking in anything he watched. On his bad days, he made do with staring at the blank walls or ceiling of his poky flat.

Höfn had an extraordinary setting on a low-lying peninsula that jutted out into the Atlantic off the south coast of Iceland, protected from the ferocity of the sea by two sandbars that almost closed off the lagoons on either side. To the north, the horizon was dominated by the Vatnajökull ice cap with its tumbling glacial tongues; to the south, by sandy spits and islands. In fact, you'd be hard pressed to find a window in the entire Hornafjördur district that didn't boast a stunning view, but Hjörvar's rabbit hutch was the exception. It had three windows, all of which faced onto the yard behind the house that appeared to be mainly used as a dump for scrap metal. His landlord hadn't been able to hide his surprise when Hjörvar didn't lose interest immediately after seeing the place. Hjörvar had felt compelled to make excuses, saying that he wasn't after any kind of luxury as he was only in Höfn for work. The man had nodded, still looking vaguely bemused. Hjörvar hadn't tried to convince him further as he knew from experience that over-explaining would only make the situation more awkward.

In any case, he had more than his fair share of incredible views from Stokksnes. He still hadn't got bored of them and doubted he ever would: the surroundings were too awe-inspiring for that. The prize for most picturesque view of all was a toss-up between the black sand beach with its peculiar wave-like hummocks crowned with grass; the angry sea; and Mount Vestrahorn, with its near-vertical walls towering almost half a kilometre into the sky, stoically withstanding the violence of the surf crashing at its foot. Hjörvar marvelled at its fortitude and would have given anything to be able to cultivate the same quality in himself. His own response to conflict and scenes was to run away. This had cost him all his friends, one after another, and – which was worse – his family as well.

But there were no scenes or conflict at the radar station. His co-worker, Erlingur, was an impassive character who never let himself get worked up. He was about as sociable as Hjörvar, and said little beyond any necessary communication regarding the job. This suited Hjörvar down to the ground. He had never been any good at keeping up a flow of small talk.

The company Hjörvar derived the most pleasure from at work was not, however, that of his co-worker. Nor was it the company of those he spoke to on the phone at Coast Guard HQ in Reykjavík or at Keflavík Airport. No, the one whose company he valued most was the least communicative of all.

It was a cat. The animal had appeared at the station some two months previously. Where he had come from was anybody's guess. He could have strayed all the way from Höfn, or trotted through the road tunnel from the Lón district, or run away from one of the handful of farms that still clung on in the neighbouring countryside. Possibly. Although bedraggled and collarless, he didn't appear to be a stray. Not from the way he had immediately attached himself to Hjörvar and kept getting underfoot during his tours of inspection around the site. This had initially led Erlingur to suspect that the animal belonged to him, despite his denials. In the end, though, Erlingur seemed to believe Hjörvar, and as a result decided to accept the animal.

They had delayed too long in giving the black-and-white tom a name. By the time they finally decided he needed one, it was too late. They'd been calling him puss for three weeks and the name had stuck. He became Puss with a capital P, not that this made any difference to the poor creature.

At first, Puss had lived in a nook by the station building, within the perimeter fence that was supposed to be secure but clearly proved no obstacle for a cat. Hjörvar, taking pity on him, had started putting out bowls of food by the wall. To begin with, this consisted of leftovers from his own lunch, not all of which were appreciated by his furry friend. But he soon swapped them for dry cat food that he bought in Höfn.

The nook provided shelter from the worst of the storms, but when the wind was coming from the wrong direction, snow had a tendency to collect there. So, without even discussing it, they started letting the poor creature come inside, in tacit agreement that this was for the best. They'd simply opened the door one day and Puss had darted in. Since then he had rarely gone out alone, except to do his business and, when the weather was good, to perform a patrol of the area. Otherwise, he spent his days snoozing on a table next to the computer equipment. Puss had no interest in the priceless gear beyond the fact that it generated warmth.

In between sleeping, Puss sometimes sat up, yawned and watched Hjörvar and Erlingur going about their business. He seemed as unimpressed by their work as he was by the hi-tech gadgetry that provided him with a snug bed. When they were alone, Hjörvar used to explain to the cat how vital the instruments were, not just for Iceland but for the whole of NATO. Puss stared at him sceptically. The cat's superior expression only softened when Hjörvar started talking about himself, about his upbringing and the circumstances that had led him here, to the back of beyond.

It was extraordinary how easy he found it to open up to the animal, given the problems he had talking to his fellow human beings. Perhaps it was because he knew there would be no reply. There was no risk of Puss giving him good advice or pitying him or demanding that he pull himself together. Or hectoring him about toughening up, taking his eye off the rear-view mirror and facing the road ahead. Or reminding him that he was still in his prime. No, Puss just gazed at him, giving every impression of listening attentively. Hjörvar had half convinced himself that the cat could absorb his problems, digest them and make them disappear. The idea worked as long as they were together. But on Hjörvar's days off, the depression would descend again with its familiar crushing weight.

There was no point taking Puss home with him to his lonely flat after work, as he had discovered to his cost. Three times he had kidnapped the reluctant animal and taken him back to Höfn, and each time Puss had done nothing but yowl and run around, refusing to eat or drink. His distress had been so evident that Hjörvar had abandoned the attempt.

Given the choice, Hjörvar would have preferred to spend all his time at work, forgoing his days off and sleeping there overnight, together with his furry friend. But he knew that if he so much as aired the possibility to his managers, he would be instantly transferred. Or fired. The Coast Guard was keen to discourage unstable weirdoes from working in its ranks. Even the faintest hint of eccentricity could make his bosses start doubting his mental health, despite the fact he had worked for the Coast Guard for more than a decade with a good record.

When the position at Stokksnes became available, he had immediately let his interest be known in-house. The job had come up the previous year too but at the time Hjörvar hadn't even considered applying. It just went to show how quickly circumstances could change – particularly for his predecessor in the position, who had died in an accident before the year was out.

Hjörvar's enquiries had been well received, since there were few other applicants. But the clincher had been his willingness to move at short notice. The job was his and such was the urgency that within two days he was on his way east. No doubt his superiors had been keen to ensure that he didn't have time to get cold feet. Certainly, they had been careful in all the interviews for the post to say as little as possible about his predecessor's accident, for fear it might deter would-be applicants. The only time the subject had come up, they had implied that the employee in question had been suffering from mental health issues. The accident needn't have happened – but then that was the nature of accidents.

Hjörvar's predecessor had fallen down the blowhole or *stokkur* in the rocks, from which the peninsula derived its name. The accident had happened on a Friday and the man's disappearance had only been discovered when he'd failed to turn up for work the following Monday morning. His co-worker had gone home early on the day of the accident and so hadn't been on hand to come to his rescue or witness the tragedy.

Every time the station staff left the site, they were supposed to notify HQ in Reykjavík. Their work vehicle was equipped with a Tetra radio for reporting their departure and subsequent arrival back in Höfn. But this time no notifications had been received. Due to an audit that was being conducted at headquarters, no one had followed up on the failure to report. It was thought that the co-worker's notifications had mistakenly been assumed to apply to both men. The body had been washed up eight days later on the Hafnartangi spit, two kilometres to the north-east.

The blowhole, a phenomenon also known as a marine geyser, was a tunnel-like shaft in the flat rocks lining the shore just below the radar station. It ended in an opening, through which the sea would surge and boil, sending up a column of spray when the wind was coming from the right direction. No one knew why the man had ventured onto the rocks in the first place, since they were outside the perimeter fence and unconnected to the station. Presumably it was this that had given rise to the suspicion that it hadn't been a straight-forward accident. Although no one said so in as many words, the implication was that the man had taken his own life.

The last thing Hjörvar wanted was for his managers to be afraid that he was going the same way. Of course, there was no danger of that. But if he announced that he wanted to spend all his free time at work, it might lead to misunderstandings. So he resisted the impulse to ask and obediently took his days off like Erlingur.

There were times, though, when he got his wish. Whenever a storm was imminent, someone had to stay on site in case of damage. On these occasions, he could volunteer for the job, safe in the knowledge that, far from attracting suspicion, it would make him appear responsible; an exemplary employee, in fact. As Erlingur always accepted his offer gratefully, every-one was happy. Happiest of all, though, was Hjörvar. To his delight, the winter had been particularly severe since he'd started his job, with a relentless succession of storms, which meant he had got to spend more time out at Stokksnes than he would have dreamed possible.

Hjörvar watched Puss hoover up what was left in his bowl. Since the cat had gone from being puss to Puss with a capital P, Hjörvar had taken to giving him prawns or poached had-dock instead of dry food. He cooked especially for the cat, happy to make the effort.

Puss raised his head and licked his lips hopefully. But he was out of luck. 'Come on. You don't want to get any rounder than you are already.' Hjörvar gave Puss an affectionate nudge with his toe. He needed to go out and patrol the site to make sure that all the equipment was properly secured before the next storm hit.

It had begun to snow gently, the small flakes falling vertically in the still air. The moment the wind picked up, they would start whirling in every direction, so it would be as well to complete his inspection before conditions deteriorated. Puss needed to be let out too. Although he had litter trays in the office and staff quarters, the cat preferred to do his business outside, which suited Hjörvar and Erlingur just fine.

As Hjörvar dressed himself in a thick down jacket and boots, Puss wound himself round and round Hjörvar's legs. He didn't know much about cats, but interpreted this as thanks for the meal. Come to think of it, though, Puss did exactly the same when he was hungry, so perhaps Hjörvar had got it wrong. Perhaps it meant something quite different.

At that moment, the entryphone rang to indicate that someone was outside the gate, wanting to come in. Startled, Hjörvar went over to answer. It was the first time he could remember hearing it ring. He picked up the receiver and said his name, expecting the person on the other end to be some outdoor enthusiast who'd rashly underestimated the conditions, or a driver whose car had got stuck. But there was no answer. Hjörvar said 'Hello' several times, but the only response was silence. Then there was a crackle and he thought he heard the faint echo of a voice saying words he couldn't make out. He called 'Hello' again and asked the person to speak into the microphone. Nothing.

Hjörvar hung up and thought he'd better go and see what was happening. He was on his way out anyway and the person at the gate might be in trouble. He went to the door and stepped outside into the bitter cold with Puss on his heels.

The first thing he noticed was the absolute silence. The breeze that usually blew in off the sea or down from the mountains was absent and everything was perfectly still. Even the waves appeared to be slumbering. The sky was overcast and the snow was already coming down more heavily. Yet, despite the poor visibility, Hjörvar could make out the gate.

There was nobody there. He walked towards it, scanning the surrounding area in case the person hadn't heard him and had wandered away. But there wasn't a soul to be seen. What's more, when he got to the gate and peered through the wire, there were no footprints in the snow by the entryphone. However thick and fast the flakes were falling now, there was no way any tracks could have been completely obliterated in the short time it had taken him to walk from the door to the gate.

Hjörvar frowned. What the hell was going on? All he could think of was a fault or short circuit in the phone system. It was the only rational explanation. He must have imagined the voice he thought he'd heard. Or been confused by the crackling static. Of course, that was it. Anything else was unthinkable.

Puss seemed to sense that something was wrong. Normally he bounded ahead on these little outings, pausing briefly here and there, pretending to ignore Hjörvar, while actually keeping a careful eye on him. But this time the cat stayed so close to his side that Hjörvar had to be careful not to tread on him when he started moving again. 'Come on, nitwit. The inspection awaits.'

Their gazes met. The cat's yellow eyes darted away, then he mewed and hissed as if he was aware of something out there in the falling snow. He bristled all over, his back arched, his tail like a bottle-brush.

'What's the matter, Puss?' Hjörvar peered through the haze of white but it was getting too thick for him to see. He looked down again at the cat, then added: 'Can you smell a fox?'

He got no answer.

Hjörvar continued his patrol, with Puss clinging close to his heels, still behaving oddly. After walking around the perimeter fence, they checked every single mast before finally doing a circuit of the giant radome. Everything seemed in order and there was no sign of any object that the wind could snatch away: no loose panels or gaps in the cladding, or any build-up of ice on the equipment.

And no fox.

Or any human presence.

So Hjörvar could safely escort Puss back to the station building where the cat could make himself comfortable. Hjörvar meant to do one more tour of inspection before going home, but he had already decided to leave Puss inside for that. It wasn't only that the cat was obviously unsettled, its fear was infectious. Again and again, Hjörvar caught himself looking over his shoulder and feeling uncomfortable whenever his back was turned to the shore. Although he regarded himself as pretty down to earth, he couldn't help thinking about his predecessor in the job. He kept imagining that if the snowfall eased, he would see the dark outline of a figure standing on the rocks, staring down the black blowhole.

'Come on, Puss. That'll do for now.'

He received a loud miaow in reply, which he interpreted as relief. But the cat didn't seem reassured on the short walk back to the building. If anything, he appeared even more scared and slunk along close to Hjörvar's feet. Perhaps this was partly because the wind had started to show its claws. When they'd first ventured out, it must have been the calm before the storm.

As they reached the door, Hjörvar heard a sound he recognised inside. The entryphone was ringing. He turned and peered through the curtain of white towards the gate. There was nobody there.

He hurried inside and snatched up the receiver. He could hear the same crackling static as before but also that strange, faint voice. He could have sworn it was a child. Hjörvar hung up.

The ringing immediately began again. Hjörvar stood there, rigid with fright, staring at the receiver but making no move to pick it up. He didn't want to hear the creepy noises, though they must be caused by an electrical fault or crossed wires. There could be no other explanation. It couldn't really be a child. Kids had no business out here in this remote spot in the dead of winter.

The ringing stopped for a few moments, then the shrill sound started echoing round the station again. Puss hissed, pressing against Hjörvar's leg, his back arched as the hackles rose along his spine.

Chapter 4

The peace and quiet around the hut were a distant memory. There was noise coming from all sides now, from the crowd of helpers who had arrived to search for the missing trekkers and to excavate the body that Jóhanna and Thórir had quite literally stumbled upon in the snow.

Searchers fanned out over the valley floor and up the surrounding slopes. Most conspicuous among them were the brightly coloured snowsuits of the rescue team, whose members walked in orderly rows, carrying avalanche probes that they prodded into the snow at regular intervals. But apart from the single body near the reindeer, nothing else had been found.

In addition to the rescue volunteers, there were two police officers from the local force in Höfn and their boss, the Police Commissioner for South Iceland. Although based in the town of Selfoss, four hundred kilometres away in the south-west of the country, he had travelled over due to the seriousness of the case, bringing a detective with him. There were a couple of forensic technicians from Reykjavík too. Having completed their examination of the area around the corpse, they had turned their attention to the hut. Also present, on behalf of the National Identification Commission, were a pathologist and another man whose role was unclear to Jóhanna. He seemed to do nothing but get in the way.

To avoid being accused of the same thing, Jóhanna and Thórir had withdrawn to the lee of the hut, where they could shelter from the biting wind while watching what was going on. At first, they'd been kept busy answering the barrage of questions fired at them by the police, the leaders of the rescue team and the representatives of the Identification Commission. Basically the same questions, endlessly repeated, only phrased slightly differently according to who was doing the asking. Their answers were almost always, word for word, identical. They described in detail everything they had done from the moment they had entered the bowl-like valley in which the hut stood until they had returned to civilisation. The most exhaustive questions concerned the discovery of the body, their reasons for deciding to climb up the slope to the reindeer carcass and what had led them to realise that there was a body under the snow. Jóhanna was also asked repeatedly why she had placed her scarf over the corpse's face, a decision she now bitterly regretted, since it seemed so peculiar. For a while, she had started to get rattled, believing that she and Thórir were suspects. As if they had done away with the person themselves, covered the body in snow, then pretended to find it. But of course that was nonsense. They weren't suspected of any wrongdoing. It was only that the gravity of the case was reflected in the faces and voices of those questioning them.

It hadn't helped that one of the two police officers from Höfn was her husband, Geiri. Since he was the only detective on the local force, there was no possibility of his stepping back because of her involvement in the discovery of the body. Presumably he would have had to take himself off the case if she and Thórir had really been suspects. Nevertheless, Geiri had stood aside while she was being grilled about the sequence of events. She had struggled to avoid looking over at him during the interrogation. Not because she was hoping he would betray some hint of how she was doing, but because he was the person she always turned to in times of trouble – and vice versa. One smile from him was enough to make even the most difficult day bearable.

When it was over and the torrent of questions had finally dried up, Geiri had given her a brief nod, then escorted the group to the makeshift base beside the helicopter that had been used to transport some of the personnel and equipment to the site. What looked like a small marquee had been erected after the helicopter had landed. Inside was a table that had been used for drawing up the action plan and organising the search. The tent would also serve as a temporary storeroom for any evidence they uncovered.

Once out of the firing line, Jóhanna and Thórir had made desultory attempts at conversation, which soon petered out. It was hard to hit on a subject that wasn't in such glaring contradiction to the circumstances that it seemed inappropriate. Having quickly exhausted the possibilities of the latest weather forecast, they had lapsed into silence – except when Thórir had enquired out of the blue whether she'd hurt herself the day before. Jóhanna had looked at him in surprise and asked what he meant. In reply, he'd gestured to her leg and said he'd noticed her limping. He was quite right: she did have a tendency to limp whenever she overdid things, but it wasn't something she gave much thought to these days. To ease the momentary awkwardness, she explained to Thórir that it was the result of an old injury; nothing to worry about. He wouldn't take the hint and drop the subject, though, so in the end she had been forced to tell him what had happened. She'd related the story as briefly as possible, letting her annoyance show but stopping just on the right side of being downright rude. When he'd finally picked up on this, he had fallen silent.

That silence still hadn't been broken.

Jóhanna's gaze kept wandering back to the slope where they were digging out the body. Despite her reluctance to see it lifted out of its snowy grave, she found it almost impossible to tear her eyes away. Even when she did, they would be inexorably drawn back to the scene a moment later.

The previous day, she and Thórir had stood there, rooted to the spot, staring at the blank, frozen eye, unable to speak. The experience had been so surreal, so disturbing, that there were no words to express their emotions. Eventually, Jóhanna had steeled herself to break the silence. As a representative of the local rescue team, she'd felt it was her duty to take the lead. She couldn't just stand there, gawping like an idiot, leaving the newcomer to deal with the situation. Thórir may have been a bit older than her, and more highly trained and experienced, but he mustn't be allowed to go back to Reykjavík and spread it around that the Hornafjördur Rescue Team were a bunch of wimps.

Jóhanna had proposed that they carefully retrace their steps, walking backwards and placing their feet in their own tracks, so as to disturb the scene as little as possible. It didn't for a second occur to her that anything could be done for the owner of the eye. She had seen enough dead bodies to feel sure that there was no point checking for vital signs. Even an amateur would have realised that it was too late.

But once she had backed away and recovered her composure slightly, Jóhanna had changed her mind. How was she supposed to answer when they got back to base and she was asked if she had made certain that the person was dead? Would she be as confident when forced to admit that she'd drawn her conclusion from the little that was visible of the face? No, probably not. Picturing the sceptical looks, she had decided to overcome her reluctance and make absolutely sure.

Thórir had offered to do it for her but Jóhanna had declined.

It had taken guts to make her way back up the slope to the hole in the snow, to bend down and dig out more of the face. But she had done it. She had scraped the snow and ice from the throat, trying not to dwell on the sight, then tugged off her gloves and fumbled for a pulse. There was no sign of life.

She would never forget the chill of the frozen flesh under her fingertips. Afterwards, she hadn't been able to get the warmth back into her hands. The feeling was purely psychological, of course, because it persisted even after she got home to her cosy house. Her fingers felt as icy under the duvet in bed as they had on the tough route march back from the hut. As freezing under the hot shower as they had when she and Thórir had stood, mute with shock, by the mountain track, waiting to be picked up. As cold in the back seat of the heated vehicle on the way back to Höfn as when she had straightened up, loosened her scarf and laid it gently over the deep-frozen face.

When Thórir asked why she had done it, she had answered truthfully that it had been to prevent any animals from getting at the face. Although predators were rare in the highlands in the dead of winter, there was the odd creature on the prowl – Arctic foxes, ravens . . . Any that hadn't left the area when autumn arrived would be starving by now.

To Jóhanna's relief, Thórir hadn't pursued the matter or asked why she hadn't simply filled in the hole again with snow. She didn't want to have to tell him that she couldn't bring herself to. She was well aware of how foolish this was. A body was nothing but an empty husk. The person had departed. A body didn't have feelings, couldn't mourn its fate, wouldn't care whether it was lying under ice or a soft scarf. But none of this altered the fact that she couldn't make herself heap snow onto the face.

Jóhanna closed her eyes, making an effort to distract herself by picturing something associated with life: flowers, animals, summer, children. But it was no good. Her imagination wouldn't fire up, even when she tried to focus on thinking about her neighbours' precocious little daughter, who never normally failed to bring a smile to her face. Giving up, she made another attempt at conversation with Thórir. 'Maybe we should move. I'm not sure it's a good idea to watch when they lift out the body.'

But Thórir kept his gaze fixed on the figures who were working around the hole high on the snowy slope. 'In my experience, it's better to confront unpleasant things than to leave it to the imagination. Usually, the reality isn't as bad as what your mind can conjure up. Well, at least in my case it could hardly be worse.'

Jóhanna knew what he meant, though that wasn't to say she agreed with him. Still, what was she supposed to do? She couldn't physically drag him behind the hut.

It had been a mistake to force them to return to the scene, especially when they weren't allowed to join the searchers. She knew the leaders of the operation shared her opinion. They had a large area to cover and there were more than enough jobs that needed doing. But it hadn't been the rescue team's decision; it had been police orders. Geiri's boss from Selfoss had wanted Jóhanna and Thórir on hand so they could talk the police through their actions prior to discovering the body. Since they had done this as soon as everyone had arrived, Jóhanna couldn't really see what their continued presence was achieving.

Thórir was still staring up at the slope. 'You're sure it was a woman?'

Jóhanna nodded. 'Yes. Quite sure.'

Thórir's expression suggested he had been hoping for a different answer, but to Jóhanna, the victim's sex was irrelevant. The fact of their death was terrible, whoever it was.

Up on the slope, something appeared to be happening. One of the distant figures beckoned to the men from the Identification Commission, who had been standing, conferring, beside a row of snowmobiles that had been used to transport some of the personnel to the site. The two men began to clamber hurriedly up the steep slope towards the hole, accompanied by a pair of drones that had been hovering over the area. There was no question: the moment had come.

Jóhanna drew a sharp breath. Assailed by a sudden fit of shivering, she hugged herself. She darted a quick glance at Thórir, whose jaws were working as if he was grinding his teeth. Again, she suggested they move, but he shook his head. Hard though it was to admit to herself, she was relieved. His comment that the reality wouldn't be as bad as anything they might imagine had stayed with her. She expected he was right. As she watched, though, she recalled various things she had seen over the years that she could have done without remembering. Her imagination couldn't have invented the horrific news images on her TV screen, showing the victims of war, terrorism and famine.

They had one such victim of starvation before their eyes right now. The reindeer had been uncovered first, as the job didn't require the same care as the excavation of the human remains, and its emaciated carcass suggested that it had died of hunger. Once the police had established that the animal hadn't been shot or killed with a knife, they had left it lying there. An open pocket knife had been found beside the human body and forensics had originally thought it might have been connected somehow to the animal's death, but clearly that wasn't the case.

The group on the slope bent down in unison. Jóhanna took off her goggles and strained to see. Thórir followed suit. Side by side they watched as the body was lifted out of its icy grave.

Their view was impeded by all the people around the hole, which only made their apprehension worse. They got a glimpse of something resembling a statue. Jóhanna saw enough to realise that the body was unnaturally stiff: the head wasn't drooping from the neck and the arms and legs weren't dangling as you'd expect. Bodies became rigid due to rigor mortis, she knew, but that stage only lasted a short time. Judging by the depth of the snow, the woman must have been lying there for several days, at least. It couldn't be rigor mortis, then. Her body must be frozen solid.

What shocked Jóhanna far more, though, was the discovery that, as far as she could see, the woman was virtually naked. Recently, temperatures in this area had plummeted so low that it was hard to believe anyone would have voluntarily removed so much as a mitten, let alone stripped off every garment she was wearing until she was standing there in nothing but her underwear. The clothes in the entrance hall of the hut must have belonged to her.

'Is she naked?' Thórir had noticed too. He seemed as dumbfounded as Jóhanna.

'Pretty much.' Jóhanna grimaced involuntarily as she peered over at the group. They were laying the body on a stretcher and they stepped aside for long enough to afford her an almost unhindered view. Now it was clear that the dead woman was indeed wearing nothing but her underwear. It was also clear that her body was deep frozen, with one arm at a peculiar angle and both legs bent slightly at the knee. The colour of her bare flesh was hardly distinguishable from the snow. Jóhanna dropped her gaze. It would have been easy to kid herself that it was an alabaster statue, were it not for the fact that no sculptor in their right mind would create anything that macabre.

'That explains the clothes, then. Did you realise she was almost naked when you checked for her pulse?' Thórir had looked away too. Jóhanna thought she detected a hint of accusation in his voice, as if she had been deliberately with-holding the information from him, which was absurd.

'No. I uncovered as little as possible. And I wasn't thinking about anything except trying to find a pulse. I didn't want to drag out the experience.'

There was a shout from one of the lines of searchers. Like everyone else, Jóhanna turned and looked in their direction. The man who'd shouted had put down his avalanche probe and was sweeping away snow from the ground at his feet. Raising his head, he called out again: 'Blood! There's a big patch of blood under the snow.'

Chapter 5

Lónsöræfi, the previous week

They had managed to get the stove going in the hut. While it was nowhere near as warm as their flats in town, at least they were no longer shivering. When they first entered, it had felt even colder inside than outside, though of course that had been an illusion. It was as if, like a cornered beast, the cold bit harder in the confined space than it had out in the open air.

Once the worst of the chill had been banished, Dröfn's uneasy feeling that something was wrong had also faded away without a trace, leaving only a sense of wellbeing. It helped that peace seemed to have been restored between the four feckless slobs and their responsible guide.

Tjörvi and Bjólfur had set to work, helping Haukur connect the cooker to the half-empty gas bottle, track down a stack of firewood and light the old stove in the common room. After this, the three men had tinkered unsuccessfully with the lighting system powered by the solar roof panels before giving up, concluding that the snow was to blame. If the solar panels were covered, naturally they wouldn't be able to produce any electricity. As climbing on the roof to clear away the snow and ice was out of the question, they would have to do without the hut's small quota of electric lights. Once the men had dealt with these technical tasks, they offered to do the cooking, and neither Dröfn nor Agnes raised any objections. Tjörvi and Bjólfur were both pretty competent in the kitchen but there was no opportunity to show off their skills here: the supplies they'd brought along wouldn't exactly call for flambéing, fine chopping, slow-cooking something in its own broth or serving it on a bed of anything.

Still, it sounded as if the three men were enjoying having something practical to do, and this left Dröfn and Agnes free to rest their weary bones. If anything, the men seemed relieved to have them out of the way.

While they were heaving around gas cylinders and checking the supply situation, the two women hunted around for candles. The store cupboard they found turned out to contain nothing but a few loo rolls and a bottle of washing-up liquid. But luck was with them when they opened the badly painted kitchen cupboards and discovered two candle stubs, which they stuck into empty wine bottles. Judging by the thick layer of dust on the bottles, they must have been standing on the kitchen counter for months. Left behind by the last summer visitors, perhaps. But instead of making Dröfn think of barbecues on the deck under a sunny sky, they reminded her of the state the four of them had been in that morning. She pushed the thought away.

She and Agnes carried the primitive candlesticks into the common room. In addition to the dining table and chairs, there were a couple of sofas that had clearly been gathering dust for months. Before flopping down on them, the two women beat the cushions vigorously, sending up great clouds of dust to glitter in the soft radiance of the candles.

'It's a bugger that we can't crack open a window.' Agnes collapsed onto one of the sofas once the dust had settled.

Although she was the biggest neat freak Dröfn knew, she was obviously too tired from their long walk to throw a wobbly about the dirt. Dröfn followed her example, trying to make herself comfortable on the other sofa. As soon as she lay down, her nose started itching but it couldn't be helped. They had known this wasn't exactly going to be a glamping trip.

Dröfn turned to look at one of the windows, staring at the shutter that was dimly visible through the filthy glass. The men had temporarily fallen quiet in the kitchen and the creaking of the timbers in the hut seemed suddenly more noticeable. The wind was gathering strength outside, heralding the onset of the storm that had been forecast. 'I reckon we'll soon be grateful that they're nailed shut.' Dröfn turned back to her friend. 'Who do you think the hat belonged to? The same person who owned the coat in the hall?'

The dancing candle flames cast odd shadows, making Agnes appear unnaturally pale and heavy-browed, her eyes sunken in dark circles. Dröfn assumed she herself looked no better.

When Agnes replied, she sounded surprised, as if she hadn't been giving any thought to the fate of the clothes' owner. 'I don't know. I doubt it. The coat's probably been hanging there since last summer. You always get lost property in huts like this. The hat must have just blown here from somewhere.'

Agnes had always been the down-to-earth one. She'd never been the type to over-dramatise things. Usually, her common-sense attitude had a reassuring effect on Dröfn, but this time the magic failed to work. Although Dröfn didn't say anything, she continued to brood over the problem.

The anorak hadn't been covered in the layer of dust that lay over everything else inside the hut. And the hat couldn't have been blown here by the wind. Not without looking a lot more battered than it did. The nearest habitation must be more than twenty kilometres away. Then again, what did she know about it? Perhaps hats could blow from one end of the country to the other without being ripped to shreds. And now that she thought about it, the draught from the open door could have blown the dust off the coat.

But who had opened the door? It couldn't possibly have been standing ajar since the autumn. If it had been, the door wouldn't still be hanging on its hinges. The countless gales that had raged across the country in the intervening months would have torn it off. By now it would have been lying a hundred metres away on the valley floor, or halfway up the nearest slope. The other three had simply shrugged and dismissed the problem from their minds, but Dröfn had been disturbed and she had noticed from Haukur's expression that it had given him pause, too.

'It looked like a woman's coat to me.' The moment she had spoken, Dröfn regretted it. If Agnes didn't share her concerns, harping on about them wouldn't achieve anything.

'So? Don't you think women come here in summer as much as men do?' Agnes rolled her eyes, then closed them and gave a great yawn. Folding her arms across her chest, she settled down for a nap.

Dröfn shifted about on the uncomfortable sofa. Agnes's question had been rhetorical. The gender of the coat's owner was irrelevant. If it had been left here recently, a coatless man would be no better off than a woman in the lethal cold.

'Christ. I can't remember getting from the bar to our room last night,' Agnes said suddenly. 'I can hardly even remember the bar. Did you see the look that girl gave us when she was checking us out this morning? We must have disgraced ourselves.' Agnes blew out a breath. 'Shit.'

'My memory's extremely hazy.' Dröfn couldn't recall any more than Agnes. 'But you can be sure Tjörvi would have told me if we'd disgraced ourselves. He always remembers everything. So I expect we didn't do anything too cringe-worthy.' Dröfn didn't want to dwell on the previous evening's excesses or this morning's embarrassment. She was too preoccupied with the mystery of the coat, the hat and the open door.

'Well, I for one am never drinking again,' Agnes groaned, her eyes still closed. As far as she was concerned, the other subject was closed. 'At least, not cheap stuff like that paint-stripper last night.' She tried to stretch out her legs but the armrest got in the way, so she turned onto her side. 'Only the finest wines from now on.'

Her hangover had more to do with quantity than quality, Dröfn thought, but there was no point saying so. 'You'll feel better once you've eaten.'

Agnes murmured drowsily in reply. Hearing her breathing becoming heavy and even, Dröfn tried to copy her. But it was no good. In spite of her tiredness and her earlier hangover, she simply couldn't switch off.

After a while, she got up. The cheerful sound of the men talking in the kitchen seemed out of place in the dark, airless hut, but it was comforting anyway.

Taking one of the candles from the coffee table, Dröfn padded in her socks towards the entrance hall. She wanted to get a closer look at that coat and now was her chance. Agnes would only be irritated if she caught her at it. Tjörvi too. She knew they believed there was no point deliberately looking for problems.

Dröfn and Tjörvi were almost always on the same page as a couple. Or at least on the same double-page spread. But there were times when they might as well have been in different books, from different genres. Because this happened so rarely, it left them a bit flummoxed when it did. Dröfn had the feeling that the coat would turn out to be one of those points of contention and that Tjörvi would quickly lose patience if she didn't immediately come round to his viewpoint. He was a division manager at a large pharmaceuticals company and spent his days working with figures, results and performance – in other words, with easily quantifiable facts. There was no place in his job for anything vague or open-ended. Gradually this had come to affect his attitude to life in general. In his opinion, if a subject didn't lend itself to concrete conclusions, there was no point even discussing it. And they were unlikely to solve the mystery of who had left the door open or owned the coat – not to mention the hat.

Being careful not to knock into anything with the candle, Dröfn opened the door to the small entrance hall. It was horribly cold and damp out there and the flame started flickering wildly in the draught from the cracks around the front door. She quickly closed the inner door behind her so she wouldn't be scolded for letting out the precious heat.

There was no shelf or surface in the hall where she could put down the candle. When she tried placing it on the floor, the light from the small flame was too feeble to reach high enough, so she had no choice but to hold the bottle in her left hand while searching the anorak with her right.

She began by taking it off the peg and holding it up to inspect it. It was definitely a woman's coat. She managed to read the label inside but didn't recognise the brand name. Judging by the finish and material, it must be cheap. Replacing it on the peg, she managed to slip her free hand into each of the pockets.

She found a lighter, a hundred-krónur coin, a menthol sweet in a wrapper, and a credit-card receipt for petrol. The receipt was only around two months old. Dröfn felt her heart sink. That put paid to the theory that the anorak had been left behind in the autumn. The pockets contained nothing else.

Suddenly, out of nowhere, Dröfn was hit by a feeling of pure dread. Her hand fell to her side and she stood there, rooted to the spot, staring at the shadows dancing on the wall in front of her. She didn't know if she was even breathing. But her heart certainly hadn't stopped: she could hear the blood booming in her ears.

The crippling fear must be something she had summoned herself by letting her imagination run wild. There had been no warning. One minute she was studying the coat, the next she was gripped by panic, convinced that its owner was standing outside the door. There had been no uncanny noises, no glimpses of any movement out of the corner of her eye. She had just been seized by a strange conviction that there was somebody out there. Standing just the other side of the door.

In spite of her terror, her mind was clear. If there had been any shreds of hangover still fogging her brain, they had been swept away. The rational thing to do would be to open the door. To take a peek outside and prove to herself that there was nobody there. Because of course there wasn't.

Yet despite telling herself it was ridiculous, she couldn't get up the nerve to open that door. Couldn't even turn her head to look at it.

Perhaps this was a waking nightmare, the kind that makes people believe there's someone sitting on their chest or looming over them. She'd heard talk of something similar at work, and the woman who experienced it had described exactly the same kind of paralysis that now had Dröfn in its grip.

She tried counting up to ten but couldn't get beyond five. The image of a frozen woman, staring fixedly at the door of the hut through the falling snow, forced its way past the numbers. Dröfn tried instead to focus on steadying her breathing. This helped enough to let her turn her head away, towards the inner door that led back into the warmth, to the others.

Swallowing the constriction in her throat, Dröfn heaved in several more deep breaths, and concentrated on emptying her mind. Only then, moving as if on autopilot, did she manage to leave the hall. In frantic haste, she shut the inner door behind her, put her back to it and fought to get her breathing under control.

What the hell had come over her? Admittedly she did sometimes let her imagination run away with her – as anyone would. Like the times she had convinced herself that there was a burglar in the house, although all the doors were locked and the windows securely fastened. But the feeling just now had been far worse, far more powerful. Normally she was aware that she was being irrational. This time she felt a creeping doubt. Could she genuinely have sensed a presence?

Dröfn paused. What was wrong with her? Was she losing it? On top of her racing heart, prickling skin and ragged breathing, she was seized by a panicky thought. Could someone really tip over the edge from one minute to the next? Was that what was happening to her?

Next moment she felt angry with herself for even contemplating such a thing. Of course not. There was nothing wrong with her, damn it! Her anger had the effect of dispelling her fear a little, enough to allow her to move away from the door and walk back into the common room on shaky legs.

All was peaceful. The wood crackled in the stove. In the kitchen she could hear the comfortingly normal sound of the men's voices. Agnes was still asleep on the sofa. No one had noticed her brief absence. Just as well, because she was reluctant to discuss with the others what had just happened. Returning to the sofa, she sank down and lay there, wide awake, staring up at the wooden ceiling.

Chapter 6

It was getting on for one in the morning when Geiri finally came home. Once the search had been called off for the day, he had gone back with the other police officers, the leader of the rescue team and the representatives of the Identification Commission to Höfn's small police station, where Jóhanna assumed they'd held a progress meeting. She and Thórir, meanwhile, had returned to Höfn with the other rescue-team members. Then everyone had dispersed homewards, leaving Thórir to go to his guesthouse.

As they said their goodbyes, the local volunteers had all carefully avoided catching the eye of the out-of-towners, since no one wanted to have to invite them back for supper. Everyone except Thórir had got the message and made alternative arrangements. Only he had remained standing with the group of locals, apparently oblivious. Jóhanna's teammates kept shooting her glances, clearly thinking it would be most natural for her to offer – after all, she and Thórir had been partnered two days running. But, like them, she was too physically and mentally drained to play host. The man would just have to go to a restaurant. If he ended up staying longer in town, she might take pity on him, if only because she didn't want her teammates to think her inhospitable.

This time, though, she had behaved like the rest of them, muttering goodbye, her eyes sliding over Thórir's shoulder.

Then she headed home to the empty house. Perhaps one of her teammates had done the generous thing, she thought, but she doubted it.

It wasn't the first time Jóhanna had waited alone at home for Geiri. The police station in Höfn covered a large chunk of rural south Iceland, extending as far as the village of Vík í Mýrdal, some two hundred and seventy kilometres to the west, and taking in half the immense Vatnajökull ice cap, where its jurisdiction met that of the North Iceland police. So it was no wonder that her husband sometimes got home late, often much later than tonight. But she had never been involved in any of those cases, and somehow that had made the waiting easier. It was always lonely, though, because she was a newcomer to the town and their social circle was still made up of Geiri's friends rather than hers. Inevitably, she was drifting apart from the people she had left behind in Reykjavík too. She had more or less stopped following them regularly on social media.

On the rare occasions she did ring her old friends these days, it only brought home to her how far apart they had grown. There was so little left to bond over. Stories of scandals or amusing incidents weren't nearly as juicy or funny when you only heard about them second-hand. Although she laughed and expressed outrage in the right places, her laughter was hollow and her outrage insincere.

She would get to know people in Höfn eventually. The rescue team was part of her bid to be independent rather than having to rely on the kindness of Geiri's friends' wives. The decision to join had not been a random one: she had belonged to a search and rescue team in Reykjavík and enjoyed it. Thanks to her experience, she had immediately been accepted into the Hornafjördur team without having to prove herself first. So far, though, her contact with the other members had been limited to team operations. They already had their established social circles and didn't need the acquaintance of a young woman from Reykjavík to complete their lives. She hoped that in time the situation would change and she would be able to ease her way into a good group of friends. If not, too bad.

Since coming home at eight, she had eaten some toast, taken a shower, tried to watch TV, surfed the net and read a few chapters of the book on her bedside table. Up to now, she had been finding it hard to put down, but this evening she could hardly follow the plot. This wasn't surprising, since she kept standing up, going to the sitting-room window and staring out at the police station. She was checking to see if the lights were still on, because if they were off, it would mean that Geiri had finished work. Her constant trips to the window were pretty pointless, though. Höfn was such a small town that it was only a few minutes' walk from the station to their house. By the time she noticed the lights were off, he would be stepping in through the front door.

When Geiri did finally walk in, she wasn't at the window. She was lying on the sofa in the sitting room in a last-ditch attempt to immerse herself in her novel. The instant she heard the door, she threw down the book and hurried into the hall.

He gave her a tired smile and emitted a heavy sigh. Instead of immediately pestering him for news, she kissed him and held back her questions until he had finished eating. Or nearly finished eating. He still had a few bites left of the odds and ends he had taken out of the fridge when, unable to restrain her curiosity any longer, Jóhanna asked him about the dead woman.

Geiri swallowed his mouthful. 'Well, the Commission still have to make their formal identification, but we're confident it's one of the two missing women. The clothes found in the hut were almost certainly hers. Why she took them off and went outside in her underwear in those conditions is something we'll probably never know.'

Jóhanna was silenced by this and Geiri was able to finish his meal while she was pondering the news. He stood up and cleared away his plate. 'They found two phones in the coat pockets, which is a bit odd, but only one glove. That fits with the frostbite on one of the hands of the dead woman. I don't imagine we'll ever find out what happened to her other glove, but the phones will be sent to Reykjavík for analysis. I doubt they can both have been hers. I mean, who needs two phones?'

Not many people, in Jóhanna's view. 'What about the blood? Did they find any explanation for that?' Despite a thorough search, the team hadn't been able to find any other bodies near the large red stain.

Geiri shook his head. 'No. That's another thing they'll be looking into in Reykjavík. It can hardly have come from an animal. There were no feathers or fur or wool to suggest that a predator had been at work. Only the sheer amount of blood. But that could be misleading. It had seeped into the surrounding snow, which may have made the patch look bigger than it actually was.'

Jóhanna hadn't been able to see any obvious wounds on the woman's body when they lifted her up, but then she hadn't got a very close look at her. 'Was the woman injured? Could the blood have been hers?'

'She didn't have so much as a scratch on her. Nor did the reindeer. So there has to be some other explanation. All I can think of is that a fight must have broken out between members of the group and ended in bloodshed. During the night, maybe. That could explain why the woman was almost naked and carrying a pocket knife. Maybe she ran out of the hut with no time to get dressed, and grabbed the knife to defend herself.' Geiri sighed. 'It doesn't make sense, though. Surely she'd have fled with her clothes in her arms instead of dropping them in the hall? Even if she was in shock, she must have realised it was suicidal to go out there without a coat on. And who did the blood belong to? Could she have stabbed someone? Did she go crazy and attack one of her companions with the knife?'

'If someone was stabbed, I just hope they're still alive.' Jóhanna knew how unrealistic this was. An injured person would have even less chance of surviving in the wilderness than someone who was unharmed. But that didn't stop her from sending up a fervent prayer.

Geiri looked sceptical. 'Then there's the car. Where is it? The helicopter did a sweep of the surrounding area but found no sign of it. So it's possible that at least one member of the group got away. But, in that case, I can't understand why he or she hasn't come forward. Unless the driver was to blame for the whole mess.'

'I'm sure the car will turn up. The driver too.' Jóhanna rubbed her aching back. 'It must have been a pretty big vehicle if it was capable of getting them to the trail head in those conditions, with four or five people on board.'

'And don't forget all the gear they had with them when they checked out of the hotel.' Geiri rinsed his plate. 'That hasn't turned up either.'

'Perhaps they weren't intending to stay the night. Perhaps it was only meant to be a day trip and their stuff is still in the car.' Then Jóhanna remembered the toothbrush and toothpaste left in the toilet at the hut. People didn't usually take a toothbrush along on day trips. 'When will we know which of the women it is?'

'The Identification Commission are going to start their investigation first thing tomorrow morning. The body was taken to Reykjavík by helicopter. That sort of thing takes time, though you'd have thought it would be easy enough to work out. I'm guessing we'll have a name by lunchtime, even if the formal identification isn't complete.'

Somewhere in the country, the woman's family were waiting, clinging to the hope that she would be found alive. 'If there were five of them,' Jóhanna said, 'why has no one been in touch to report the fifth person missing? Or has a report been received?'

'There are always missing people, but no one's disappeared in the last week or so.' Geiri sighed. 'Of course, it's possible that no one's noticed their absence yet. Or that there were only ever four of them.'

'Isn't that the most likely explanation? I don't know anyone who could vanish without somebody noticing. Even if it was only their workmates.' Jóhanna didn't say so, but she was thinking of her own situation. If she didn't have Geiri, her absence would only be noticed if she failed to turn up for work. She had a job in quality control at the largest fish-processing factory in Höfn and regarded herself as an indispensable member of the value chain. Or, at least, as indispensable as any other member of the team. If she didn't turn up, it would be noticed. As it was, she'd had to ask for time off to take part in the search and, although permission had been granted, she had been left in no doubt that her absence was inconvenient. Jóhanna was the most experienced member of the quality-control team now that the woman she used to work with had left. Which wasn't bad going, given that Jóhanna had only been with the company a few months.

Geiri yawned. 'The four people known to be missing managed to take a week off work without the world ending. So why not the fifth person too – if there was one? Not everyone has a typical nine-to-five job. Or a job at all. If they don't have much contact with the outside world, they might well not be missed immediately. But somehow I don't think that's the case here. I mean, if the fifth person was such a loner, why would they be travelling with the two couples? No, on balance it's far more likely that it was only ever the four of them.'

Jóhanna agreed. 'Has it become any clearer what exactly they were doing up there?'

'That's being looked into. So far no one seems to have a clue about the purpose of the trip. Anyway, the Reykjavík police are taking care of that side of things.' Geiri was overtaken by another huge yawn, which lasted even longer this time. 'I need to hit the sack. We've got another early start tomorrow. You too, I expect. They've drawn up new search areas.'

So much for the weekend. She and Geiri had been planning to go out for a meal as well as tackling various chores they'd been putting off. Including painting the guest bathroom and visiting Geiri's brother, who lived in the Lón district and was always asking when they were going to drop by. She didn't envy Geiri having to break the news that they were cancelling at short notice.

'Do you think I'll be allowed to take part?' Jóhanna asked. No one had told her and Thórir directly that they were cleared of any wrongdoing. Perhaps because it was so blindingly obvious. And neither of them had asked.

'Sure. Today's business was just a formality. You're not under any suspicion. Unless, of course, you don't feel up to going? It can't have been a very pleasant experience.' Geiri looked suddenly contrite. 'Has no one talked to you about it?'

Jóhanna shook her head. 'No. Only the other members of the rescue team.'

'I'm sorry.' Geiri reached out and took her hand. 'Of course I should have talked to you. I just—'

She interrupted him. 'You don't have to apologise for anything.' It was true. She could understand. Geiri had been on duty and it was awkward when one's private life spilt over into work, particularly when his superior from Selfoss and other colleagues he barely knew were present.

She saw that her words had failed to put his mind at rest. Not wanting him to feel bad on her account, she quickly changed the subject to something else she had been intending to share with him. 'Thórir mentioned that when people get hypothermia, they sometimes have the delusion that they're boiling hot and start stripping their clothes off. He's an expert in that sort of thing, so he must know what he's talking about – unlikely though it sounds. Could that explain why the woman was almost naked?'

Geiri shook his head. 'No. I doubt it.' He met her gaze. 'I mean, I'm sure it happens, but in this case it looks like she took all her clothes off inside the hut. She can hardly have got hypothermia inside, even if the hut wasn't heated. As long as you're indoors, you can always curl up in a ball or wrap yourself up warmly to conserve your body heat. Hypothermia's normally caused by windy or wet conditions, but you wouldn't experience either of those indoors. Mind you, I'm sure it would be possible to die of cold if you were in there for a long time without any form of heating.'

72

Jóhanna nodded. She'd had trouble accepting Thórir's explanation too. It was so hard to get one's head round the idea that anyone would resort to stripping off if they were dying of cold. Jóhanna had often got so badly chilled that she'd felt as if she were freezing, but she had never experienced the slightest desire to rip off the clothes that were the only thing between her and certain death. Then again, she had never been in the same desperate straits as the dead woman.

If you could call it desperate, when the hut had been within reach.

Geiri watched her, his mind apparently working along the same lines. 'You're positive the hut wasn't locked when you got there?' He didn't meet her eye, as this was something of a sore subject. They had recently quarrelled over some trivial items they suspected each other of having lost or mislaid. She'd been convinced he was to blame and vice versa. They had never got to the bottom of the mystery and ended up quietly dropping it.

'Yes.' Jóhanna smiled to show that she hadn't taken the question personally. 'Those huts are usually left unlocked. Besides, we didn't have any keys, so if it had been locked, we couldn't have got in.'

'No. Of course not.' Geiri grabbed her hand again and squeezed it. 'I just can't understand why she didn't take refuge inside. If I try to put myself in her situation, I can't think of anything inside the hut that could be more frightening than the idea of freezing to death. Unless I was running away from one of the others, who was trying to murder me. The fact she took a knife with her would make sense in a scenario like that.'

Jóhanna agreed. She reckoned she'd have a better chance of surviving an encounter with a would-be murderer than with the brutal winter weather. But she and Geiri were in no state to solve the puzzle now, bone-weary as they both were. 'Let's hope it'll all become clear in the end.'

Before going upstairs to bed, Jóhanna went over to the sitting-room window. Geiri was in the habit of going down to the kitchen in his underpants to make their morning coffee and she didn't want any passers-by to get an eyeful. Especially when his boss from Selfoss and his Reykjavík colleagues might be out and about. The path to the police station ran right past the bottom of their garden.

You had to be careful when drawing the curtains as the poles were cheap and flimsy, and couldn't take much strain. The curtains were only a temporary solution, so they hadn't wanted to spend much money on them. The plan was to plant a hedge to shelter the house from the path, then dispense with the curtains as soon as the hedge was sufficiently tall and thick. Jóhanna drew them slowly and carefully across the glass. As she was doing so, Geiri switched off the lights. With the room suddenly plunged into darkness, she could see the garden more clearly.

There was something out there – a large shadow, blacker than the night. It moved. Startled, she let go of the curtain.

Then she gave a sigh of relief. The shadow was Morri, the neighbours' black Labrador. He was a well-trained dog, familiar enough with her and Geiri to wag his tail when he saw them. Now, though, he was standing stock still, staring intently. Since he was facing slightly away from the window, it couldn't be her he was looking at.

'What's wrong?' Geiri had come over to stand beside her. 'Is there somebody in the garden?' Jóhanna saw him stiffen all over, his muscles tensing. She attributed it to the job, this instant watchfulness.

'It's only Morri. I don't know what he's doing in our garden.' As far as she was aware, the dog had never come onto their property before. He seemed to be kept quite busy enough guarding his own territory from birds and the odd trespassing cat. What's more, their properties were separated by a high fence, which meant the dog would have had to come by a circuitous route to get into their back garden. Unless the fence had blown down? That wouldn't have surprised Jóhanna. It was looking pretty dilapidated and was near the top of their list of repairs that needed doing. But when she peered towards it, she saw that the fence was still standing. 'I expect he chased some animal over here. He seems to be staring into the bushes.'

Geiri bent closer to the glass, straining his eyes to see what it was that had captured the dog's attention. If there was something in the bushes, they should be able to spot it since at this time of year the shrubs were little more than skeletal twigs.

Geiri straightened up. 'There's nothing there. Nothing I can see, anyway. Maybe it's a mouse or some other small creature.' He opened the window to order Morri to go home. But as he did so, they became aware of a low noise.

'Is that him growling?' Jóhanna couldn't remember ever hearing the good-natured Labrador growl before. Even Morri's bark always had a happy note.

'Sounds like it. Maybe it's a rat.' Geiri called the dog's name but Morri didn't look round. Geiri repeated it and whistled. Morri still didn't react. He just stood there, staring fixedly ahead and keeping up that continuous low, angry growling.

Jóhanna hugged herself against the icy air that was pouring through the open window. 'Shall I ring next door? What if he's locked out?'

Before Geiri could answer, Morri let out a yelp, spun round and fled.

Jóhanna and Geiri stood there for a moment or two, staring into the empty garden. Nothing scurried out from under the bushes now that Morri had gone. For some strange reason, this seemed worse to Jóhanna than if a rat had just sauntered across their snowy lawn.

Chapter 7

It was one of those winter days that really meant business. The morning was dark, overcast, windy and cold, with a fifty-fifty chance of snow. On their way out to the Stokksnes peninsula, they saw a river of cloud cascading down over the Almannaskard pass. It was a magnificent sight, which was supposedly useful in predicting the weather too, though Hjörvar didn't know if it was a good or bad sign. Erlingur, who was driving, could have enlightened him, as he was the one who had told him about it the first time Hjörvar had witnessed the phenomenon. But as Hjörvar hadn't got round to asking him then, he felt it was too late now. It was a bit like failing to ask someone their name at the beginning of a conversation. There's a moment for that, but if you miss the opening it's too late.

They turned right onto the dirt road to Stokksnes, stopping to open and close the first barrier, intended to deter tourists from continuing onto the peninsula without paying an entrance fee. It was situated by the solitary Viking Café, which was named for the Viking Village just out of sight over a rise. This was an abandoned Hollywood film set, built for a blockbuster that had never been made. It was a picturesque spot, the cluster of wooden, turf-roofed houses so convincing that you could easily imagine men in tunics and fur cloaks, girded with swords, practising for their raids on the British Isles and mainland Europe. The café, too, was built of wood and decorated with reindeer antlers – though the vikings would hardly have had access to those, Hjörvar thought critically, since reindeer had only been brought to Iceland from Norway in the late eighteenth century, hundreds of years after the vikings had laid down their weapons and become a race of peaceful farmers and fishermen.

The only time the two men spoke was when Erlingur started grumbling as usual about the battered old estate car that had been sitting there for ages, half hidden by the Viking Café. For some reason, the car's presence seemed to irritate the hell out of Erlingur. Anyone would have thought it had been left cluttering up the landscape purely to annoy him.

They continued across the narrow causeway to the radar station, then parked in one of the gravel spaces beside the perimeter fence and stepped out of the car. Erlingur said he'd go in and put the coffee on while Hjörvar did a circuit of the site to check for any storm damage during the night. The instant Erlingur opened the door, Puss came flying out. After nosing about for a bit, conducting his own brief inspection, he trotted after Hjörvar and accompanied him on his.

As soon as they got back to the building, Puss started mewing pathetically and winding himself around Hjörvar's legs. This little routine was intended to remind him that the cat needed feeding. If he didn't attend to this urgent matter before sitting down to his coffee, the mewing would get progressively louder and the circling of his legs more frantic. So Hjörvar made it his first job on entering the little kitchen attached to the canteen to fill his bowl. Only when Puss was contentedly crunching up his food could Hjörvar take a seat.

He took a sip of coffee, then put down his mug. 'There's something wrong with the entryphone. The one by the main gate.' He was careful to keep his voice casual, betraying no hint of the fear he had felt the previous evening. But then the crawling sense of dread had diminished now that it was morning. Yesterday he had been alone, with the black night pressing in on him. Today, it was nothing more than a bizarre memory. 'Maybe we should check it out. It could be an electrical fault.'

Erlingur's expression suggested that he'd seen through Hjörvar's faked nonchalance. 'I already know about it,' he said.

'Oh?' Hjörvar raised his eyebrows. 'Has it happened to you as well?'

'No.' Erlingur took a mouthful of coffee, then stared down at his mug. 'Not that I can remember, anyway. But I got a phone call yesterday. From Reykjavík. They told me about your little adventure.'

'My adventure?' This struck Hjörvar as an odd way of putting it, to say the least. He had rung and reported the business with the entryphone, offering to stay overnight in case there really was someone prowling around outside the compound. His offer had been swiftly and definitively turned down. Hjörvar had got the impression that the man on the other end felt he was wasting their time on a trivial matter. But he must have got that wrong if they'd thought it worth bothering Erlingur about it. 'Why did they contact you?' he asked, puzzled.

Erlingur shrugged. 'They have their reasons.' He shook his mug gently, watching ripples form on the surface of his coffee. 'Look, I wouldn't call anyone if it happens again. Except me, maybe. It would be better if you just tried to shrug it off.'

'Why?'

'Long story.'

It wasn't as if they didn't have plenty of time on their hands. 'Go on. Spit it out.'

Judging by the way Erlingur's mouth turned down, he wasn't keen. But after a brief pause he began to talk, still without looking at Hjörvar. 'Ívan, the guy who did your job before you, was always ringing up headquarters with the same story. He complained that someone kept messing around with the bell, even though there was nobody at the gate. He actually claimed he heard a voice over the phone. A girl. Or a woman.' Raising his eyes suddenly, Erlingur caught and held Hjörvar's gaze. 'But you didn't hear anything like that, did you?'

'No.' Some information was better kept to yourself. Hjörvar hadn't mentioned the voice when he'd spoken to the man at headquarters yesterday, and now he was glad. He had merely described a crackling noise. On second thoughts, that was all it had been, perhaps. Static. He hadn't heard any actual words, just an echo that resembled a voice. An odd kind of static – but static all the same.

Erlingur nodded and glanced over at the window. It faced the sea and he appeared to be watching the surf breaking on the rocks just beyond the security fence. 'Good. It would have been a bit weird if two station employees in a row had started hearing things.'

'Don't worry about me. I just thought there might be something wrong.' Hjörvar added hastily: 'With the entryphone system, I mean.'

'Yeah, well, the entryphone can't have developed a fault for the simple reason that it's not connected. It hasn't been used since the army left.'

The news left Hjörvar momentarily speechless. Realising that his mouth was hanging open, he snapped it shut. 'Oh? Why wasn't I told?'

Avoiding his eye, Erlingur studied his clasped hands. 'I didn't think there was any need. You knew the copper-wire telephone system had been disconnected. The wires have been pulled out. I told you that when I showed you round the station on your first day. The entryphone was part of that network.'

'I didn't connect the two.' Hjörvar felt deeply uncomfortable. No wonder the guy he'd talked to yesterday had reacted oddly. And no wonder he had got straight on to Erlingur. What the hell could have happened? 'But I heard a ringing,' he insisted. 'Where it came from, I don't know. Come to think of it, maybe it was just a notification from my phone. Some app that hasn't pinged before.' Hjörvar didn't believe this for one minute. The ringing hadn't come from his phone – of that he was certain.

'Yeah. Maybe.' Erlingur looked sceptical. They finished their coffee, then got down to work without any further conversation.

Their job was to keep an eye on the station operations, particularly those involving the mechanical and electronic instruments. When necessary, they also cleared away snow. There was a set procedure for everything and their checks varied in thoroughness according to whether they were done on a daily, weekly or monthly basis. The latter included testing the fire-extinguisher system and starting up the reserve generators. While they were performing their tasks, they said nothing more about the entryphone but stuck strictly to the jobs in hand. Towards midday, they returned to the canteen where Puss was asleep on the windowsill. He got up when he noticed them and stretched luxuriously, right down to his claws. Then he jumped onto the floor and started demanding food again.

Once the priority of feeding the cat had been taken care of, the two men sat down with their own lunches. As always, Erlingur's food was considerably more appetising than Hjörvar's, but then Erlingur's wife worked in catering, while Hjörvar lived alone. Despite leading a bachelor existence for many years now, he had never bothered to learn to cook properly. There was nothing appealing about the idea of preparing gourmet treats for one.

Erlingur was still enjoying his lamb chop and potato salad as Hjörvar swallowed the last mouthful of his dry sandwich. He sought out something to focus on while his co-worker was finishing his lunch, but there was little to distract him. He ended up staring at the screen on the shelf, which showed the radar antenna revolving ceaselessly in its dome. Every time the transmitter on the antenna passed the recording device it caused a ripple of interference. Not exactly gripping viewing but strangely hypnotic nonetheless. While Hjörvar was mesmerised by the black antenna, he didn't have to think about the entryphone.

In the end, his concentration was broken by the radio. The announcer read the lunchtime news summary, then moved on to the first item. A search was under way for a trekking party who were believed to have gone missing in the Lónsöræfi wilderness. Apparently, one member of the group had been found but there was no information as yet about their condition. This didn't bode well. If the person had been found safe and sound, there would have been no reason to withhold the information. It would be another matter, of course, if they were in a critical condition or dead.

It was possible they would get to hear more later today, as the radar station served as a refuelling stop for the Coast Guard helicopter. Mercifully, it was rare for the helicopter to land there, since on the occasions when it did, it was generally in connection with a disaster of some kind. As it happened, the chopper had stopped there to take on fuel the previous day, but Erlingur and Hjörvar had not been told the reason for its presence in the east. Now, though, they understood why the crew had been in such a hurry.

Erlingur listened attentively, then shook his head. 'Hell of a thing.'

Hjörvar agreed. He was still trying to think of an appropriate follow-up when Erlingur spoke again. 'I've been thinking about that business with the entryphone. Did someone tell you that your predecessor had complained about it?'

Hjörvar shook his head. 'No. This is the first I've heard about it.'

'Hmm.' Erlingur put down his knife and fork. He had finished eating and his plate was almost spotless. 'I'm beginning to think it might not have been disconnected after all. They could have forgotten to do it. That didn't occur to me at the time.'

'Why not?'

'Because the ringing only happened when Ívan was alone here. It didn't happen once when I was at work. At first I thought there was something wrong with Ívan's ears. But after he started behaving oddly, I came to the conclusion that he must have been hearing things – you know, hallucinating or something.'

'So the entryphone system was never checked?' Hjörvar felt a rush of relief. There was no question in his mind that the phone had rung. After all, there was nothing wrong with his ears and he was confident that he hadn't been hearing things. Then again, wasn't that the point about hallucinations? To the person experiencing them, they seemed perfectly real.

'Of course the phone was checked. It was dead. I tried it myself. I went out and rang the bell and there was no sound, either outside or inside. But I didn't check if the wires had been pulled out,' Erlingur added. 'Like I said, they could still be in place. So I'm not trying to imply that you're crazy.'

Hjörvar didn't know whether to be grateful for this vote of confidence or offended by it. Best not to rock the boat. Erlingur had meant well. 'Thanks. I'm not.'

Erlingur nodded. 'I realise that. You can relax.' He got to his feet. 'There's something you need to see. The coffee can wait.'

Their office opened off the canteen, and Erlingur went over to his desk and sat down at his computer. Hjörvar followed and took up position behind him, watching as his colleague searched for a folder on the hard drive. When he found it, the name left the contents in no doubt: Ívan – recordings.

The files in the folder turned out to be the same kind as the recordings from the station's CCTV system. There were numerous security cameras on the site, monitoring everything both inside and outside the buildings. 'These are recordings from when Ívan was alone here – including from the day he fell down the blowhole. It's blindingly obvious that he's seeing things, and hearing them too probably. These files are made up of clips that have been run together. They cut all the bits where he's out of shot, to make it easier to get an overview of his behaviour. Originally, they only meant to view the footage from the day of his accident, but when they saw how strangely he'd been behaving, they decided to examine the recordings from over a longer period. That's why there are so many files. These are the ones that show him acting oddly. There were days in between when his behaviour seemed perfectly normal. And he was always normal when I was here. Which is strange in itself.'

Erlingur started the first video. It consisted of footage from a camera located just inside the front door of the station building. A man Hjörvar had never seen before walked past the two big steel containers in the centre of the room that housed the radar equipment. Heading straight to the entryphone, he picked up the receiver. Although there was no sound on the recording, his mouth could be seen moving. Hjörvar assumed he was saying what people usually do when they answer the phone: 'Hello.'

After repeating this several times, Ívan hung up. He went to the front door and opened it. Then the view changed to a clip from the camera outside the door, which showed the man peering towards the gate where the bell was located. After looking all around, he disappeared inside again. The action repeated itself in the next clip. The man went to the phone, answered it, hung up, peered outside, then went back in. This pattern of behaviour was horribly familiar to Hjörvar. Swap Ívan for him, and the recording could have been made yesterday.

'This on its own wouldn't seem that strange, especially if the entryphone turns out to have been connected after all.' Erlingur closed the file and selected another. 'But there are about a dozen identical recordings where he keeps going in and out, and picking up the phone. His behaviour becomes more and more erratic. All this happened over a period of just under a month. Towards the end, he seems to be having great long conversations with someone at the other end of the phone. But the recordings from the cameras mounted outside show that there was no one by the gate at the time.'

Hjörvar wondered uneasily if someone in Reykjavík was now sitting there, assembling a similar montage of his own behaviour the day before. Feeling his cheeks grow hot, he vowed to himself that he would ignore the entryphone if it ever rang again.

Erlingur now started a video that he explained showed the last time Ívan had answered the phone. As Hjörvar watched, he noticed immediately that the man seemed far more agitated and distressed than he had been in the first clip. He appeared to be screaming into the receiver and kept spinning round as if he expected to see someone behind him. Then he slammed the phone down so hard he was lucky not to break it. But then, like everything else in the station building, it had probably been designed to withstand a minor nuclear attack.

'You say this was on the day he died?'

Erlingur nodded. He was peering at his computer screen, hunting for another file. Explaining to Hjörvar that this was the very last recording of Ívan, he pressed 'Play'. Then he looked round and asked if Hjörvar was sure he wanted to see it: he wasn't under any obligation.

Hjörvar said he was sure. What else could he do? He had taken the bait and now he was well and truly hooked. If he didn't watch it with Erlingur, he would only be drawn back to the computer later. The file would be like Pandora's box: in the end, his curiosity would get the better of him.

The screen showed Ívan crossing the canteen, presumably on his way to the very office they were sitting in now.

Abruptly, he stopped and turned to the window. Eyes widening and mouth opening as if in shock, he went over to the glass and banged on it. As in the previous video, he appeared distressed and agitated. He spun round, shouting something, then retreated until he was standing with his back pressed to the wall that was at right angles to the window. As if that way he could see outside without losing his view of the canteen. He stood there for several minutes, repeatedly banging on the glass and shouting at the window, until eventually he stepped away from the wall and exited the canteen. What followed was a series of clips of Ívan running through the station to the gate in the perimeter fence, then out of it and on towards the sea and the rocks.

They could see him climbing down the slope until he was only visible from the waist up, the shore ridge blocking their view of his legs. Even so, it was obvious that he was taking great care as he picked his way over the slippery, flat rocks. Hjörvar didn't think this looked like someone who was planning to kill himself. Surely a man in that state wouldn't care if he slipped and fell into the rough sea? After all, that would be the plan.

If anything, Hjörvar thought it looked much more like the behaviour of a man who had seen something or someone out there who needed help.

'Watch, now. He stops and . . .'

A huge, foaming wave erupted from the rocks right in front of Ívan, like a spouting geyser. Hjörvar had often observed this phenomenon from the canteen window. But what happened next was something he had never seen before and hoped never to witness again. As it fell back, the wave caught hold of Ívan and dragged him down the blowhole.

Neither of the watching men said a word. Although Hjörvar had no idea what was going through Erlingur's mind, his own thoughts were clear: what had it been like to die like that? Had Ívan got stuck in the shaft or had he slid right through it and fallen, still alive, into the sea? Which fate would be worse?

Hjörvar couldn't decide. Because either way, you would drown.

Chapter 8

The storm reached the peak of its ferocity while they were sitting over their no-frills supper. The wooden hut creaked and groaned around them, as if in pitiful protest at the battering it was receiving from the elements. Dröfn kept having to remind herself that it must have withstood much worse punishment over the years: there was no chance of it blowing away from over their heads.

Having the shutters there, blocking their view of the outside world, somehow made it more alarming than if they had been able to see the curtains of snow being driven across the landscape. And the flickering candlelight only made things worse, the flames guttering wildly every time the hut shuddered. Black shadows danced in time to the gusts, giving the impression that the whole room was on the move. In the eerie illumination, their faces looked ghoulish, their eye sockets like black pits in their skulls.

Yet in defiance of the gloomy setting, everyone was in quite good spirits. Everyone except Dröfn, that is. The others didn't seem to notice how subdued she was. They were too busy wolfing down their pasta in tomato sauce with bread, the kind of thing they would normally have turned their noses up at, calling it nursery-school food. Even Dröfn, who usually lost her appetite in a crisis, polished off her share in record time. Perhaps that was why nobody was paying her any attention.

Nobody except Haukur, anyway, whose gaze periodically wandered to her face and lingered there longer than necessary. She looked away hurriedly, grateful for the dim light that would hopefully conceal her heightened colour. He was the only one who seemed to suspect that something was up – which was odd, considering that he knew her the least well of anyone there. But Tjörvi was too focused on the constant stream of stories and anecdotes that Agnes and Bjólfur were regaling them with to take any notice of her. Dröfn just couldn't take the stories in. Her thoughts kept slipping back to the entrance hall and that overwhelming sensation of terror.

She did manage briefly to switch off her fears. The sound of the others' conversation washed over her in the way she assumed animals must experience human voices; an incomprehensible jumble of noises that didn't convey anything to her beyond the odd word that penetrated her consciousness. She had sunk into a reverie by concentrating on the details of the interior, such as the panelling that covered every vertical surface. In the gloom, the wood appeared darker than it really was: cheap pine, full of knots, converted by the shadows into rosewood.

The furniture was also pine, of a dated design that you only came across these days in mountain huts and old holiday cottages. There was a clunky dresser, with a decorative vase that looked totally out of place. The vase contained a sad, withered bunch of what must once have been dandelions, picked, presumably, in late summer. Against one wall was a bookcase containing a poor selection of titles left behind by visitors over the years. Everything else in the hut seemed to have found its way there by the same route. Apart from the wobbly table and matching set of rickety chairs, the only other furniture was the two uncomfortable sofas and the coffee table between them.

Dröfn turned her attention to the walls, which were hung with faded photos of young men in uniform. Always in groups, posing, straight-backed. Bjólfur had wandered round the room, holding up a candle to examine them, then turned to Haukur and asked what was with all the weird pictures of soldiers. Haukur had explained that the hut had been built by the US Army. They were the ones who had called it Thule, after the legendary land in the north.

Dröfn thought the military connection explained a lot about the spartan furnishings. In normal circumstances, she would have amused herself by wondering how to improve the hut, as she reckoned she had quite a good eye for interior design. She pictured the place painted white, and without all that tasteless pine. But that was as far as she got. The thoughts she was doing her best to shut out kept coming back to haunt her.

She was so wrapped up in her reverie that she didn't notice when Agnes spoke to her until she'd repeated her name twice. Then the fog lifted and she shook herself slightly, turning, flustered, to her friend. 'Sorry. What were you saying?'

Agnes locked eyes with Dröfn, frowning. 'Is everything OK?'

Dröfn smiled weakly. 'Yes, sure. Sorry, I was miles away.' Her words may have satisfied the rest of them, but Agnes wasn't fooled. They had been best friends ever since they'd met, aged six, in Year 1, and had seen each other through every stage of development, every formative experience since then: exam revision, sports practice, boy trouble and fashion trends. They had been there for each other in the bad times and celebrated together in the good. Cried on each other's shoulders, laughed, whispered and shared their secrets. They knew each other inside out. Dröfn couldn't deceive Agnes, any more than Agnes could fool her.

But Agnes seemed to shrug off her momentary concern. She smiled and repeated the question that Dröfn had failed to hear. 'Aren't you having kittens at the thought of roughing it in a tent in the middle of winter?' Agnes's gaze shifted briefly to their surroundings, then back to her: 'This hut may not exactly be the last word in luxury, but I reckon we'll be missing it by tomorrow evening.'

Dröfn forced her features into what she hoped was a normal expression and tried to sound like her usual self. 'I'm not exactly dreading it. But, if I'm honest, I'm not hugely looking forward to it either.'

'You two are such wusses.' Bjólfur put down his knife and fork on his empty plate. 'I can't wait. It's going to be epic.'

Tjörvi immediately seconded this, though it rang a bit hollow in his case. The fact was that much as he loved the great outdoors, he was a terrible baby about the cold. Especially at night. One of the few bones of contention in his marriage to Dröfn was whether or not to sleep with the window open. Dröfn kept tactfully silent and squeezed out another half-hearted smile when their eyes met. If Tjörvi and Bjólfur wanted to pose as intrepid outdoorsmen, she wasn't about to ruin it for them. Though even they must realise deep down that going on a couple of reindeer shoots didn't make them Bear Grylls. Especially when those 'expeditions' had involved staying in a hotel and being chauffeured to the hunting grounds in a four-by-four. That had absolutely nothing in common with their present foolhardy undertaking.

'I don't think *epic* is quite the right word.' Haukur was looking distinctly unamused. 'It's going to be a cold and challenging ordeal. Like I told you right at the beginning.'

'Cold and challenging.' Bjólfur's face split into a wide grin. 'Like I said: epic.'

Agnes gave him a friendly nudge. 'Better not tempt fate.'

She was right. Dröfn was extremely fond of Bjólfur but his over-confidence had a way of getting him – and them – into some sticky situations. Come to think of it, this trip was a classic example. He was the one who had suggested at that dinner party that they should tag along on the expedition, airily dismissing Haukur's protests, and then followed up on the idea over the next few days by bombarding Haukur with phone calls and messages.

As far as Dröfn could gather, Haukur had been keen to back out. He fully intended to go himself, but not with them. They had no business on a trip like that. He said he could get into all kinds of trouble if it emerged that he had dragged a bunch of amateurs into the highlands with him on a journey connected to his research. He risked losing his grant and could even be reported to the ethics committee if something went wrong. But Bjólfur had refused to take no for an answer, swearing that they wouldn't tell a soul about the expedition.

The trouble was that he could be so persuasive. Bjólfur had been to drama school, though he had never made a living as an actor. Instead, he had started an advertising agency and now used his innate talents and training to flog slogans, brands and adverts to companies. Needless to say, his business was thriving. Poor Haukur hadn't stood a chance.

If it hadn't been for Bjólfur's insistence, the idea would have been quietly dropped, as most ideas hatched under the influence of alcohol deserve to be. Normally, common sense, temporarily caught napping, reasserts itself the next day, preventing them from ever being realised.

It was too late to start getting cold feet now, though. Soon they would go to bed in their sleeping bags on the dusty old bunks in the dark, airless rooms upstairs. Then wake up

– with headaches, no doubt – and head off on another route march, the moment the weather let up enough for it to be safe. Tomorrow's task was to hike to the measuring instrument that the whole trip revolved around. Apparently it would take Haukur a bit of time to record the necessary readings, so they wouldn't be able to return the same day to the hut – or to any other hut in the area. Instead, they would have to pitch their tents and spend the night beside the glacier. Although Bjólfur had learnt this detail early on in his conversations with Haukur, he hadn't immediately shared it with the others, but waited until he'd sold them the idea. Only after that had he casually announced that they would have to invest in a couple of tents. By then, it had been too late to back out.

Dröfn suspected that the real reason why she, Tjörvi and Agnes had got so pissed at the bar was that none of them really wanted to be here. Unlike Bjólfur, they were prepared to admit to themselves that Haukur wasn't like them. The three men's facial hair was enough of a giveaway. Haukur seemed to have grown his simply to avoid the hassle of shaving, whereas Tjörvi's and Bjólfur's fussily trimmed beards were even more time-consuming to care for than if they'd been clean shaven. Haukur was the genuine article; he was at home in this primitive hut. They weren't.

Still, one night out there in a tent would be enough to teach them not to despise the hut, Dröfn thought. Though, on second thoughts, she'd have to be pretty bloody cold, miserable and fed up with cooking on a primus to make her think more favourably of being shut up in this claustrophobic, creaking box with its blanked-out windows.

At that point it occurred to her that not being able to see outside might be an advantage. She might not like what she saw.

Of course, there was nothing to stop her from getting up, going into the hall and poking her head out of the front door. But Dröfn couldn't shake off the foolish notion that the woman who owned that anorak would be standing outside. Standing there, staring at the door, her face blue with cold, unable to knock. Dröfn's imagination had abandoned all reason now. She knew that if she allowed her thoughts to stray down this path, she would soon be picturing the woman dead: a frozen figure, looming out of the dark, her blank eyes boring into Dröfn's. She didn't know why but she imagined the woman's eyes as pitch black, as if the pupils had burst in the frost and leaked into the whites.

The candles had almost burnt down, which brought the meal to a natural close after a brief discussion of the next day's schedule. They pilfered two more candle stubs from the kitchen cupboard so they could see to wash up and put away the dishes. Agnes and Dröfn offered to take care of this while the men went upstairs to decide who should sleep where and to bang as much dust as possible from the mattresses.

Haukur had turned on the water for the washing-up, saying he would drain the system immediately afterwards so the pipes didn't freeze in the night. Clearly, this was taking a risk, as the water that ran out of the tap was so bone-numbingly cold that Agnes and Dröfn could only keep their hands under it for a few seconds at a time. They had to take it in turns to wash up. To make matters worse, there was no washing-up liquid or brush, and the icy water made little impact on the greasy plates. All they could find in the store cupboard was toilet cleaner. The old pair of yellow rubber gloves they discovered under the sink provided little insulation but they put them on anyway.

Dröfn peeled off the unpleasantly clammy gloves and passed them to Agnes. Rubbing her hands together, she blew into her cupped palms.

Agnes made a face as she pulled on the gloves and stuck them under the trickle of water. They had spoken little since starting the washing-up, beyond exchanging a few words about the next day, but now Agnes asked abruptly: 'Come on, what's up, Dröfn? Don't fob me off with that crap about everything being fine. I know something's wrong.'

Carefully avoiding her eye, Dröfn stared at the plate she was drying with unnecessary thoroughness. 'I'm just feeling a bit apprehensive. About tomorrow. I'm afraid of falling over and breaking my leg – or worse.'

Agnes seemed relieved. 'Hey, don't worry about it. Nothing like that's going to happen. And even if it does, we'll sort it out. There's absolutely no need to stress about it.'

Although Dröfn had not in fact been worrying about the walk and had simply made this up on the spot to hide what was really on her mind, she suddenly felt a stab of genuine anxiety. 'How? How would we sort it out?' She looked up, still rubbing the plate, though it was already dry.

Agnes removed her hands from under the cold tap and turned to look at her. 'Oh, I don't know. We'd make a splint for your leg and rig up some kind of sledge to get you back to safety.' She smiled, her face radiant. The look suited her. Even the shadows under her eyes in the flickering candlelight couldn't detract from the happiness in her expression. She pushed a lock of hair out of her eyes with a finger encased in yellow rubber, then contorted her mouth to blow it away when it wouldn't stay put. 'It'll be a piece of cake.'

Dröfn couldn't agree but she bit back any further concerns she had about this or any other aspect of the trip – the mystery woman, the weather, the suffocatingly airless hut. Instead, she smiled back at Agnes, who apparently interpreted this as meaning that everything was fine now. Which couldn't have been further from the truth. A smile couldn't magically make everything better. Not now.

After they'd finished washing-up, the two women went upstairs. Neither they nor their husbands usually went to bed early or would describe themselves as morning types, but they were in no mood to make a night of it now. The strenuous hike from the car, which had included wading through long stretches of deep snow, had taxed their thigh and calf muscles and left them all exhausted. And, if Haukur was to be believed, tomorrow's trek to the measuring equipment would be no less challenging.

He'd forbidden them to take any candles upstairs, citing the fire hazard, so they'd have to fall back on the torches he'd insisted they bring along. When packing for the trip, Dröfn had considered leaving theirs behind to lighten their loads. They already had more than enough weight by the time they'd packed the essentials. And Tjörvi's rucksack also contained the tent and a hip flask of brandy that she had spotted him slipping into it just before they'd left the flat. She was relieved he hadn't brought it out after supper. Haukur would not have been amused.

What a good thing Tjörvi had refused to leave the torches behind. As usual, he had insisted on following the instructions to a T. And as usual this had paid off. Dröfn wouldn't have wanted to fumble around blindly in the little bedroom while they were undressing and wriggling into their sleeping bags.

It was important to spare the batteries, though, so Tjörvi switched the torches off as soon as they were lying down with their bags zipped up. They had both crammed onto one of the room's two single beds, reluctant to sleep alone. Dröfn cuddled up against Tjörvi, her nose in the nape of his neck to avoid breathing in the dust. When he conked out almost immediately, she had to fight back the urge to prod him and force him to keep her company until she herself had dozed off.

Squeezing her eyes tightly shut, she did her best to forget where she was and surrender to the power of fickle sleep. But as always when she needed it most, sleep proved elusive. Ironically, the one time she found it really easy to drop off was when she was determined to stay awake.

All of a sudden, she surfaced with a gasp. There was no way of telling how late it was or how long she had been asleep. The shuttered windows would make the room as dark by day as it was by night. The roof was still creaking and rattling above them, and Dröfn tried to convince herself that she had been disturbed by an unusually loud groan from the timbers. That must be it. That had to be it.

Tjörvi snored away, totally oblivious, while Dröfn's heart pounded frantically in her chest. Keeping her eyes shut, she pressed even closer to her husband, until her nose was bent against his neck. Nothing would induce her to sit up and look around.

Because, in spite of the enveloping darkness, Dröfn was convinced she would be able to see. See well enough to make out the shape of a woman standing at the foot of the bed, blue with cold, her black eyes fixed on Dröfn and Tjörvi.

Chapter 9

They had spotted two tents with the aid of the rescue-team drone. Judging from the photos, one was a new-looking, bright yellow trekking tent, while the other was smaller, and, from what could be seen of its dull green canvas, it appeared to be older and shabbier. There had been no sign of human figures on the drone footage, but that didn't rule out the possibility that the people they were searching for were lying inside the tents. This did nothing to boost the searchers' optimism about finding anyone alive, though, as the tents had collapsed and were half buried by snow.

Having radioed the police to let them know that the missing party had possibly been located, Jóhanna and her fellow volunteers set out for the site on foot. They wouldn't necessarily get there first, though, as the police and other investigators had a fleet of snowmobiles and the Coast Guard chopper at their disposal.

When the throbbing of helicopter blades reached Jóhanna's ears, she craned her head back to look up at the sky. The blue-and-white colossus was still some way off but moving fast and would be over them before they knew it. She envied the people on board, sitting snugly in the warmth, spared the need to battle their way through snowdrifts or worry about slipping and injuring themselves. This last was a real concern as none of the volunteers wanted to risk breaking or spraining anything and have to be rescued themselves, thereby reducing the number of people out looking. The search took priority, even though few – if any – believed that the missing walkers were still alive. It was significant that those heading the operation hadn't sent to Vík í Mýrdal for the special police drone, which was equipped with a heat sensor and could be used to communicate with stranded people spotted on the footage. Nobody thought that either of these features would be of any use in this case.

Nevertheless, Jóhanna allowed herself to nurse a faint spark of hope, because you never knew – stranger things had happened. In the best-case scenario, the lost walkers could all be huddled together in one of the tents, their combined body heat keeping them alive, even if they hadn't had the strength to put it back up after the wind knocked it down.

She was walking somewhere in the middle of the column, taking care to match her pace with the man in front of her. Thórir was immediately behind her. Like most of her companions, she had barely spoken a word since setting out. Only the drone operator had broken the silence when he came back with news of the tents. He had been riding ahead on a snowmobile, stopping frequently to scan the area for any signs of human presence.

With his help, the team leader had worked out the best, least hazardous route to the tents, after which the drone operator had roared off again on his snowmobile. It wasn't that long or difficult a trek from their current location, and they all realised how lucky they were, as the potential search area was so enormous that the odds had been against their finding any trace of the missing party at all.

The team had picked up their pace on hearing the good news, and Jóhanna was having to push herself hard not to lag behind. Her legs were killing her after the previous day's efforts, and she was out of condition following a couple of inactive winter months. Although she used the police-station gym when she could be bothered, those exercises did little to improve one's stamina on hikes. Her damaged legs didn't help either. She wasn't supposed to overdo it like this, but she just couldn't accept the necessity of living within the limits set by her accident. Every time she over-stretched herself, she hoped she had set the bar a little higher for the next occasion. But every time she was disappointed. If anything, the bar seemed to get lower.

To make matters worse, Jóhanna had slept fitfully. The rest she needed to restore her aching muscles had refused to come. She had tossed and turned, and rearranged her pillow, to no avail. It seemed ridiculous, thinking about it now, but she hadn't been able to stop obsessing over Morri's strange behaviour and the mystery of what it was that had drawn him into their garden.

She had a habit of doing this, of lying awake, fretting over things that ceased to matter the moment the sun came up. Normally, this only happened when Geiri was on night shift. When he was lying beside her, his warm body and deep, regular breathing were usually enough to keep such worries at bay. But not this time.

The lace had come undone on one of Jóhanna's boots. She stepped out of the line to re-tie it. The men behind her didn't wait but overtook her one by one while she was bending over her foot with her glove in her mouth. Even Thórir chose to follow the others rather than waiting until she had sorted herself out. Perhaps he was fed up of being sidelined with her. No doubt he felt he was too important to be one of the ordinary foot soldiers. But if he hoped to find someone higher up in the pecking order who would take him under their wing, he'd be disappointed. The locals' attitude to him hadn't changed. He was still suspected of being the know-all from the big city.

Jóhanna didn't share this view, perhaps because she was from Reykjavík herself. Thórir seemed like a decent bloke who behaved himself and gave no hint of looking down on anyone. Actually, she was fairly sure that the reason he was avoiding her had to do with her limp. Ever since she'd told him about the accident, he had kept his distance. She assumed this was because he didn't want to get stuck with a companion who would hold him back – which was rubbish. She could move just as fast as the others when required. She simply gritted her teeth and got on with it.

When she straightened up again, she found herself at the back of the column. In some ways this was fine, as it meant the group had trodden down the snow as far as that was possible. On the other hand, it felt uncomfortable having no one behind her. If she dropped out of the line, there was no one to notice.

Jóhanna hurriedly closed the gap with the others, but remained in the rear for the rest of the way. They were nearly there when they were overtaken by several snowmobiles. Jóhanna thought she recognised Geiri on one but she couldn't be sure. The drivers wore helmets and were as thickly bundled up as astronauts; it was hardly possible to tell whether they were male or female, let alone recognise individuals. No one slowed down or waved to her, but then she wouldn't expect that from Geiri. For as long as the search lasted, he would remain as aloof as he had been the day before. That was fine with her. They had the evening and the rest of their lives to behave normally around each other.

As the back marker, Jóhanna was the last person to spot the helicopter and snowmobiles when their destination finally came into view. The moment she did, she felt a renewed burst of energy and her tiredness fell away. Not everyone reacted like this; many people succumbed to exhaustion when they

saw the finishing line. It was a quality that had taken her far
in her athletics days, when she had been regarded as Iceland's
brightest hope in the long-distance category. She still held a
national record in the juvenile division and a Nordic record
too. Not that dwelling on these former glories gave her any
pleasure. If anything, it made her miserable to be reminded
of what could have been and what she had lost; the bright
future she had been deprived of by the driver who'd knocked
her down. She was aware that these thoughts were unedifying
and served no purpose; walking around burdened with sorrow
and loss for something you couldn't change was like filling
your pockets with rocks every morning. She would get over
these negative thoughts one day. After all, she had found it in
herself to forgive the driver, although the woman had tried to
shift the blame onto the man who had repaired her car instead
of shouldering the responsibility herself.

Jóhanna's mother had encouraged her to take her old
medals and cups with her when she'd moved east to Höfn, but
they were the last things she wanted to be confronted with
every morning. They were guaranteed to make her depressed.

Jóhanna filled her lungs, ignoring the pain in her leg, and
powered forwards. She started overtaking people, Thórir
included, and by the time they came to a halt she was third
in line. She could easily have been first but saw no reason to
annoy the two men in the lead. The rest of the team couldn't
care less where they finished. They were just glad of a chance
to catch their breath at last. It wasn't a competition, after
all; there were no prizes to be had: no honour, points, cups,
medals or bunches of flowers.

Now that they had reached their destination, the rescue
team took a moment to survey the area and assess what they
saw. Stretching north as far as the eye could see, dominating

the view, was the dirty-grey glacier, criss-crossed with crevasses. Here at the edge, the ice cap bore no resemblance to the vast, pure-white expanse it presented from the air. It looked almost as if it had been turned upside down to reveal its grubby underside. The camp lay some distance from the edge of the ice, chosen presumably because the ground there was free from rocks and stones.

Apart from the looming mass of the ice cap, the blue-and-white helicopter was the most conspicuous object in the landscape. The snowmobiles, on the other hand, being mostly white, blended into the background. The police officers and other personnel who had already reached the scene were standing around in two groups, one larger than the other, and paid little attention to the rescuers now arriving on foot. One member of the larger group waved to them, before turning straight back to his companions and continuing to talk. From time to time, all heads would swivel towards the two tents that were pitched a short way apart, near a drift so large that there must have been a small hillock underneath it. The campsite had been sensibly chosen, in Jóhanna's opinion. And the tents didn't give the impression of having been hastily thrown up in the middle of a storm, when no one could see what they were doing. She herself would have pitched them closer together, but that was a question of preference.

Jóhanna had once seen the personal effects left behind by a walker who had got lost in a blizzard. The tent had almost torn itself loose from its moorings, as only about a third of the pegs had been used and even those had been poorly secured. The site had been badly chosen too, on an exposed piece of ground with no shelter nearby. The owner's backpack had lain open beside it, most of its contents blown away by the gale. Jóhanna hadn't been with the group who'd initially found the tent but she had been in one of the search parties that had combed an ever-expanding area around it, hunting for the owner. The body had never been found. She just hoped it wouldn't be the same story here.

Just then a gust whirled up the loose snow and Jóhanna noticed that the canvas on one of the tents was flapping. It appeared to be torn – by the wind, she guessed. What else could it have been? She couldn't imagine anyone deciding to slash a hole in the only shelter they had. Unless a wild animal had clawed the canvas in search of food?

Something Geiri had said came back to her: he'd wondered if one or more members of the party could have cracked up and gone berserk. Someone with a very feeble grip on reality, perhaps, who had been destabilised by the extreme environment. Certainly, there was little out here for a city dweller to latch onto: no shops, tarmac, streetlights or shelter. Just endless snow, lethal cold and the savage wind. Anyone venturing into these parts would be deprived of all the security and physical wellbeing they took for granted. A person who was already teetering on the brink of some kind of breakdown might well tip over the edge in an unforgiving place like this. Perhaps the crazed individual who had slashed at the tent had also been responsible for driving the woman out of the hut to her death. Maybe the aim had been to destroy the only available refuge.

The leader of the rescue team walked over to the assembled investigators and spoke to a man Jóhanna knew to be Geiri's boss from Selfoss, as well as one of the men from the Identification Commission. Their conversation was unusually animated, involving exaggerated gestures and arm-waving that presumably related to the organisation of the search but looked absurdly as if they were playing charades.

When the leader returned, they learnt that the tents were deserted but the missing couples' gear was inside. One contained three backpacks, four sleeping bags, a mobile phone and, ominously, coats and other outdoor clothes belonging to two people. It seemed highly unlikely that there would be any survivors. The second tent had been empty apart from a few scraps of food. The plan now was to comb the surrounding area for the people themselves, whose bodies were presumably lying under the snow, though it was anybody's guess exactly where. As a result, the rescue team was split up into three parties; one to cover the ground to the east of the tents, the second the area to the west and the third the area north towards the edge of the glacier. Since they had approached the camp from the south without spotting anything suspicious along the way, that direction was not considered a priority. While they were working, the drone operator would fly his device systematically over the landscape, which had been divided up into sectors, trying to spot something that might allow them to narrow the search area.

Jóhanna was assigned to the party covering the northern route. Thórir was also ordered to join it. While it made no difference to her which group she was in, she thought she caught a brief look of disappointment cross Thórir's face. Yet more confirmation, she thought, that he didn't want to be lumbered with her company.

Personally, she reckoned all the search areas offered similar conditions; none looked noticeably easier than the others. And as she knew all the team members equally well, she didn't mind who she was put with.

They hadn't walked far, though, before Jóhanna found herself wishing with every fibre of her being that she had been assigned to a different group.

Chapter 10

Hjörvar was alone on duty again. He and Erlingur had had to split up the day between them to ensure that one of them was on hand when the helicopter landed to refuel. Although many tasks at the radar station could be performed remotely from their laptops, this wasn't one of them. And since they didn't know when to expect the helicopter, the station would have to be manned until evening, maybe even into the early hours. When Hjörvar offered to take the later shift, Erlingur had agreed, albeit reluctantly. Hjörvar suspected Erlingur wasn't entirely convinced of his mental stability, though he hadn't said so in as many words. But the prospect of getting home earlier to his wife, and spending the evening with her rather than Puss, had overcome Erlingur's reservations.

In fact, Erlingur's concerns seemed likely to prove groundless. So far, nothing out of the ordinary had occurred. The entryphone remained silent, though Hjörvar felt a slight contraction of the heart every time he walked past it. In other respects, he felt perfectly normal. That is, as long as he carefully avoided dwelling on his solitude in this desolate place. No one had any business out here this late on a dark winter's evening. He also kept his eyes firmly averted from the canteen window with its view of the seashore and the blowhole in the rocks.

Still, he couldn't deny that he was feeling a tad less relaxed now that it was pitch dark outside than he had been when there had still been a lingering trace of the short-lived winter daylight. When his gaze accidentally fell on the window, he realised that the shore ridge above the rocks was no longer visible. The world outside was black. He reflected that it was actually better to be able to make out something, even if it was something he didn't want to see. As it was, anyone could be on the prowl out there, unseen in the gloom. Anyone – or anything. He could hardly see a metre beyond the window now. Better not to look.

This feeling of uneasiness must be because he had nothing to occupy him. Once he had completed his duties, all he had left to do was kick his heels while he waited for the helicopter. He sat down at his desk, intending to surf the net, but the moment he took hold of the mouse, he changed his mind. Instead, he navigated to the area on the server where Erlingur had accessed the recordings of Ívan, the man who used to do his job. Hjörvar felt a little ashamed of his curiosity but he wanted to see more, and he could only do that while he was alone at work. The last thing he wanted was for Erlingur to catch him at it.

Hjörvar wouldn't get a better opportunity than this. Yet although he had all the time in the world, he only managed to get through a third of the recordings. They made for such disturbing viewing that he had to break off and stand up. The footage didn't only show scenes of the man running to the entryphone, then out to the gate. Numerous clips also showed him starting and twitching in the middle of his duties, raising his head as if someone had called his name. He kept glancing over his shoulder as if expecting to see someone standing there, though the footage showed plainly that he was alone. At times he ran in and out of the station, at others he charged around the site, flinging open doors and peering into the various outhouses. He checked behind the cupboards containing the operating equipment, climbed the spiral staircase to the radome, opened storerooms, went outside and peered into his car, and generally behaved as if he was the seeker in a game of hide-and-seek. The only problem was that there was nobody hiding: he was alone on the site. It was noticeable how few of the recordings seemed to be from times when Erlingur was also present.

Watching a man apparently suffering from advanced paranoia was a profoundly uncomfortable experience. The recordings varied in quality but in some Hjörvar thought he could read the terror in the eyes of the gaunt figure as he jerked and spun round. It occurred to Hjörvar that he must have looked pretty haunted himself when the entryphone had kept ringing like that the other day. The thought of people at headquarters watching the footage drove him to his feet.

He hovered by his desk for a while, wondering how to occupy himself. Eventually, feeling an uncharacteristic need to talk to another human being, he took his phone out of his pocket. But who should he ring? The few people close to him would either be so surprised to receive a call from him that they would guess something was up, or they wouldn't answer. He had burnt too many bridges by cutting himself off.

As a case in point, he didn't feel he could call his son Njördur or his daughter Ágústa. It would only be a source of more misery for all of them. Their problems were too numerous and too complicated, and Ágústa was vocal in her belief that they could all be traced back to him. He had let their mother down, let them down. She was right, of course. He had failed as a husband and a father, but there was little to be gained from constantly reminding him of the fact. The past wasn't some half-finished Lego castle that could be taken apart, brick by brick, and rebuilt. There was nothing he could say or do to change what had already happened. Besides, his apathy and indifference couldn't be the only things to blame. There must have been other factors behind the breakdown in their relationship.

The ball lay in their court too. He had invited his kids to visit him in Höfn and planned all sorts of outings to show them the sights. Ágústa had cancelled with two days' notice, saying she couldn't face it as the trip was bound to end in a quarrel. Njördur hadn't shown up at all, just sent him a message some time later with a fabricated excuse. It would be a while before Hjörvar invited either of them again. Come to think of it, though, that had been four months ago and his anger was cooling. If only his daughter's resentment wasn't so implacable.

So the kids were both sulking and the few people he could call his friends probably felt the same. He had recently ignored all their messages and phone calls, guessing that they were getting in touch about his birthday. When he'd turned fifty, he'd bought himself five years' grace by promising to throw a big party to celebrate being fifty-five instead. But when the day of reckoning arrived, he was no more enthusiastic about the idea of making any sort of fuss than he had been before. He didn't want to celebrate his fifty-fifth birthday and couldn't be bothered to explain or defend his decision. So he had avoided returning their calls straight away, preferring to wait until after the date had passed. But as time had gone on, he still hadn't got round to it, and he doubted they would be pleased to hear from him now – if they bothered to pick up in the first place. Hjörvar knew they felt sorry for him but there were limits to how far he could push their sympathy.

Nor could he ring his brother, although their calls were generally brief in a way that was perfectly natural to them. Neither enjoyed talking on the phone, unlike his friends who seemed content to yak away endlessly and were reluctant to be the first to ring off, or his daughter who couldn't stop venting her rage at him. Or his son who was always so full of bullshit. His brother, in contrast, got straight to the point, said what he wanted to say, then said goodbye – unless Hjörvar had something to contribute to the conversation, which he rarely did. He was closer to his brother than anyone else in the world. It was his name Hjörvar had given the office as his next of kin, although he was 'blessed' with kids. If anything happened to him at work, his brother would be the first to hear.

The trouble was that because they knew each other so well, his brother was too good at interpreting Hjörvar's voice. He would immediately clock that something was up, and Hjörvar was reluctant to discuss how he was feeling with him or anyone else.

Erlingur's name was also on his short list of phone contacts, but any conversation with him was bound to be embarrassing and awkward.

Hjörvar could have gone over to the staff quarters and watched a film. It would have satisfied his need to hear the sound of human voices. But that was out of the question because, to be on the safe side, he needed to be in the station building when the helicopter announced its arrival. If there really was a fault in the entryphone system, he couldn't be sure that the radio in the staff quarters would work, and the last thing he wanted was to screw up the one job he was here to do.

Hjörvar had no idea whether the rescue mission in the highlands had been successful. Erlingur had spoken to the pilot before Hjörvar had got in to work that day, but there had been no news then. The long delay in the chopper's return could mean one of two things: either the search was still in progress, or the missing people had been found and their bodies were being prepared for transport.

Hjörvar wasn't getting his hopes up that there would be any survivors. Although he had never visited the Lónsöræfi wilderness himself, he believed Erlingur when he said flatly that if the walkers hadn't been found in one of the huts, they would have zero chance of making it out of there alive.

The internet was silent about the search, as was to be expected. The only news was from midday, when they had reported that the rescue effort was continuing but that no information had been released as yet about the status of the person found yesterday. For once, Hjörvar knew more than the news sites because Erlingur had told him that it was a woman and that she was dead. He'd got the information out of the helicopter pilot.

Puss chose that moment to jump onto the windowsill, startling Hjörvar so much that he almost spilt coffee all over himself. He was sitting at the small kitchen table and had just raised the mug to his lips. He hadn't noticed the cat come in. Puss seemed totally indifferent to the shock he'd caused. He sat there, staring out into the night and mewing.

'Stop making that racket.' Hjörvar's voice sounded odd to his own ears after he had been silent for so long. The same couldn't be said of Puss, who had kept up a continual plaintive miaowing ever since they had been left alone together this afternoon. For once, though, it didn't seem to be about food. The cat was restless. He yowled at the front door, only to pause in the gap when Hjörvar opened it for him. Then he started yowling by one of the spiral staircases that led up into the radome, but made no move to go up there. After that he had yowled around Hjörvar's legs, but Hjörvar couldn't see any indication of what might be wrong. And now he was yowling at the darkness outside.

Perhaps the poor creature was ill. Or sensed that something was brewing. According to Erlingur, Puss had been very alarmed when the helicopter had landed that morning on its way to the nature reserve. That must be it.

Hjörvar slurped his rather watery coffee, turning away from the cat. The human eye is naturally drawn to screens and Hjörvar's was no exception. His gaze drifted to the monitor showing the giant antenna revolving in its protective dome, and lingered there, though there was nothing of interest to see.

The antenna went on turning as usual. Although the recording had no audio, the noise travelled down the stairs from the dome, along the corridor and in through the open door of the canteen.

Hjörvar frowned. As he watched the regular waves of interference caused by the powerful transmitter, he could have sworn they were out of sync with the antenna's revolutions. He squinted to focus better, then, sure he wasn't imagining it, he got up and moved closer to the screen. He was right: the interference was distorting the picture a little after the trans-mitter had pointed directly at the camera.

There had to be an explanation. A fault in the camera, maybe. Or with the connection to the screen. Perhaps there was a short circuit somewhere in the system that had also been responsible for the ringing of the entryphone.

Hjörvar felt a surge of relief. He wasn't going mad. It was a technical glitch. An old-fashioned problem with the electrics. The engineers would no doubt have a nightmare diagnosing the fault but they'd find it in the end. Then they'd have the headache of replacing the station wiring and resetting the operating system. Hjörvar was just glad this wouldn't be his job. He was a car mechanic and pretty clueless when it came to electronics. All major repairs and maintenance were handled by specialist contractors, whose presence would at least liven the place up. Normally,

Hjörvar would have dreaded the disruption, but now he actively welcomed it.

Puss mewed again. When Hjörvar turned his head, he saw that the cat too was staring at the screen, its yellow eyes fixed on the antenna transmission. Hjörvar couldn't remember the animal ever showing any interest in it before. Suddenly, Puss hissed, leapt down from the windowsill and shot out of the room as if the devil was on his heels.

Hjörvar became aware of the same, skin-crawling unease as he'd experienced when he'd first noticed the odd pattern of interference. Overcoming his reluctance, he looked at the screen, then took an involuntary step backwards when he thought he saw a dark shadow appear just as the wave of interference rippled the screen. The distortion made it hard to see what it was. Hjörvar moved a step closer again but couldn't see anything out of the ordinary. The antenna went on revolving as usual and there was no sign of anything that didn't belong in the dome. But when the interference started up again, the same shadow appeared.

Hjörvar stood stock still, his heart racing. Fuzzy though the shape had been, it had resembled a human figure. Could someone be hiding in the radome? Had Puss been yowling by the stairs because he knew?

The station had been built at the beginning of the Cold War and was supposed to be able to withstand anything bar a direct hit from a bomb. The concrete walls were the thickest Hjörvar had ever seen and heavy steel doors closed off the various rooms. At the heart of the station was a nuclear bunker with a double-door system that worked like an airlock. It was designed to protect the radar and the reserve power generators, as well as any personnel who might have to shut themselves in there to keep the station going in the event of a nuclear attack. Hjörvar assumed that none of the Icelanders who had been employed here since the US Army left had imagined that this would ever be put to the test.

The most important spaces were the best protected, while those that were of minor relevance for the defence of the country were more conventional in their design. These included the canteen and the office, both of which had windows to the outside world and normal internal doors. If an intruder had got in, they must have done so through one of the windows. There was no way they could have broken in via the reinforced front door. It hadn't been left open at any point either. Hjörvar had left and re-entered by the front door when he'd gone on his patrol, but he had locked it conscientiously behind him. He had also opened it three times when he thought Puss wanted to go out, but he'd stood waiting while the cat hovered on the threshold, not leaving the door unattended at any point.

But what about this morning, when Erlingur had been alone on duty? Unlikely though it seemed, he could conceivably have left the door open while he stepped out briefly. Though for what purpose it was hard to imagine. Both men always closed and locked the door. Their orders were clear. Still, Hjörvar supposed there was a possibility that Erlingur might have left it slightly ajar for the cat, if Puss had been acting as strangely this morning as he was now.

There was nothing for it but to climb up into the radome and check what was going on. Hjörvar could hardly think of a worse cock-up than to go home that night leaving an intruder locked inside the station. The only question was whether he should inspect it now or wait until the helicopter crew had radioed their approach. It was probably best to get it over with. It would only take him a minute as there was nowhere to hide up there.

The dome was empty. Hjörvar walked quickly round the antenna, afraid he wouldn't hear the radio while he was up there. But that wasn't the only reason. The truth was he didn't feel comfortable there, a sensation he had never experienced before. Previously, the only cause of stress in the radome had been health-and-safety related: the awareness that he mustn't injure himself. His disquiet now was quite different in nature: a vague, yet powerful sensation that he wasn't alone. That he was being watched. Which was completely irrational as he was the only person up there.

He descended the steel stairs, two at a time. When he got to the bottom, he heard Puss's pathetic mewing from somewhere inside the station building, but when he tried calling him, the cat didn't appear. That was a pity, as Hjörvar could have done with his company. He paused, about to call the cat again, then, hearing the radio, he dashed into the office.

Hjörvar needn't have worried about trying to disguise his breathlessness when he talked to the pilot, as it was drowned out by the thunder of the rotary blades. But he caught every word of the pilot's brief message. The helicopter would be there in ten minutes to refuel, then it would continue straight on to Reykjavík. No further search was scheduled for the next day as the operation was almost certainly over. Before ending his call, the man added that there were three bodies on board: one young woman and two men of a similar age.

All four members of the missing party had been found.

Having assured the pilot that he was on standby, Hjörvar ended the call. He put on his coat and switched on the floodlighting around the fuel pump. Then he went outside into the freezing night, heading for the illuminated helipad. The door to the station building was shut and there was no chance of any sound carrying through the thick doors and walls, yet he fancied he could still hear the radar antenna, revolving ceaselessly in its dome.

Chapter 11

Lónsöræfi, the previous week

When Dröfn awoke, the darkness was as impenetrable as when she had gone to bed. At this time of year it wouldn't get properly light outside until nearly midday and, according to her phone, it wasn't yet seven. Even if the moon was shining, the heavy shutters would ensure that no gleam could find its way inside.

Despite the unrelieved gloom, there had at least been one improvement. The storm had died down. The wooden walls and roof of the hut were no longer creaking, and the howling of the wind had fallen silent.

Dröfn put down her phone and groped for the torch on the bedside table. The metal tube felt icy to the touch, sending goose pimples up her arms. She wasn't looking forward to getting out of her sleeping bag and easing herself into her clothes.

Tjörvi was snoring beside her, the sound muffled as he had buried his head inside his sleeping bag. She guessed she would have to hand him his clothes so he could get dressed in his bag, or the freezing temperature would be the death of him. For the first time, it struck her how odd his aversion to the cold was. She had never given it any thought before, just taken it for granted. But now it struck her as so inconsistent with the rest of his behaviour. Because, despite approaching everything with caution, Tjörvi was unusually tough and resilient. He never flinched or spared himself, and would put up with a lot without complaint.

His hatred of the cold was completely out of character.

Had her grandmother been alive, she would have said that the explanation was to be sought in his past life. Mind you, that's where she used to believe all answers were to be found. Tjörvi must have died of cold in a previous incarnation, an experience so traumatic that it had accompanied him into his next life.

For once, Dröfn couldn't bring herself to smile at the memory of her grandmother's nonsense. It was as if the absence of electricity, heating, phone and internet connections had shaken the foundations of her world, forcing her to question all her assumptions. Now that she was thinking about her grandmother, she recalled what the old lady used to say about outdoors types. Whenever there was news of missing ptarmigan hunters, snowmobilers or hikers, she would mutter: *What's the matter with these people; why can't they just stay at home?*

Her words seemed horribly appropriate at this moment.

Shrugging off these negative thoughts, Dröfn switched on her torch. Heartened by the brightness, she counted up to ten, then forced herself out of her cosy sleeping bag. The glacial floorboards burnt the soles of her feet and she started dressing as fast as she could. This hurt too, as she was agonisingly stiff after the previous day's efforts. Reaching down painfully, she pulled on her socks, then a long-sleeved woollen vest and long johns. The garments were as chilly as everything else in the room, but quickly warmed up once she had them on. Only then did she stop feeling as if she was about to die of cold. But the feeling didn't last long, so she gritted her teeth and hastily pulled on the rest of her clothes.

While she was getting dressed, she heard sounds from downstairs that suggested someone was already up and making breakfast. Agnes, probably. Or Haukur. She'd better hurry down and help, just in case it was Haukur. It wouldn't do for him to get up long before the rest of them for the second day in a row. Gathering up Tjörvi's clothes, she stuffed them inside the neck of his sleeping bag. He stirred and muttered a protest but Dröfn cut him off, telling him to get dressed once they'd warmed up. She added that he should be grateful as it was bloody freezing in the room.

Leaving the torch with Tjörvi, she picked up her phone. Although it was as cold to the touch as the torch, the weight of it in her hand made Dröfn feel warm inside. It was a link to everything they'd left behind when they'd embarked on this expedition. Top of the list were their expensive coffee machine and the underfloor heating that almost kissed her feet when she got out of bed in the mornings.

Dröfn used the phone to illuminate her way from the bedroom to the stairs, then descended one step at a time, partly because she couldn't see properly and partly because she was so stiff. The steps felt slippery, too, and she didn't want to add a bruised bum to her list of aching body parts.

The low echo of a woman's voice reached her from behind the closed kitchen door. Agnes must be up. Either she was talking to herself or Bjólfur was there too. Or Haukur. Maybe both. Dröfn had hoped Haukur would come down last, preferably once breakfast was on the table. Then they would more or less have made up for yesterday.

She groped her way through the common room, past the dining table where they had eaten supper, and narrowly avoided banging her hip against a chair that had been pulled out or hadn't been pushed back under the table last night. She couldn't remember how they had left things.

The glow from her phone screen was so weak that she was relieved to reach the kitchen door without colliding with the corner of the dresser or stepping on a mouse. Of course, she had no idea whether there were any rodents in the hut, but there were bound to be lots of cracks and holes that mice could enter through. They certainly wouldn't survive the winter outside, if any actually lived up here in the highlands.

Happily anticipating the aroma of freshly made coffee, she lifted her hand to the door knob, but as she did so she finally made out what Agnes was saying; she seemed to be repeating: 'Let me in, let me in. Please, let me in.' Dröfn thought she sounded desperate. But what could Agnes mean? Had the kitchen door jammed? And if so, why was she murmuring like that rather than shouting to rouse the others?

To Dröfn's surprise, the door opened perfectly easily. Inside, the kitchen was as dark and deserted as the common room. There was no lit candle, no steaming coffee, no pan of porridge on the stove. She raised her phone and swept the room with its faint glow. Everything was just as she and Agnes had left it the previous night.

The voice had fallen silent too. It had gone quiet the moment Dröfn turned the door handle.

Standing rooted to the spot, she licked her dry lips and swallowed. Her ears must have been playing tricks on her. She had decided yesterday evening that she couldn't be going mad. No way. There had to be another explanation. Perhaps she was still half asleep. Or she was suffering from tinnitus that sounded like a human voice. That had to be it.

The floorboards creaked behind her and Dröfn tensed. She couldn't turn, couldn't breathe.

'Did you sleep well?'

It was such a relief to hear Haukur's voice that for a moment she felt tears welling in her eyes.

Dröfn cleared her throat silently before looking round and saying: 'Yes. Like a log.' Then she turned away, grateful for the gloom that would conceal her momentary shock. 'And you?'

Haukur nodded. 'Yes, sure. Though I thought I'd never be able to drift off, the wind was making such a racket.' He paused for a beat, then added: 'Is everything OK?'

It obviously wasn't dark enough to hide Dröfn's fright. She opened her mouth to say that everything was fine, then changed her mind. This man was a scientist. A person who lived and worked entirely in the material world and thrived on finding rational explanations for everything. Who better to calm her jangling nerves?

Dröfn said in a rush: 'I thought I heard a woman in the kitchen. It gave me such a shock when there was nobody in there. Totally ridiculous, I know. I expect I'm just not used to the silence out here. My brain must have started inventing noises to make up for it, or something.' She stopped, giving Haukur a chance to weigh in with an intelligent reaction; something to make her smile at her own foolishness.

'A woman, you say?' Haukur frowned. 'What made you think it was a woman? Rather than a man, I mean.'

It was a reasonable enough question but Dröfn had been hoping for answers. That there was a problem with the plumbing, say, which sometimes made it sound as if people were moving around in the kitchen. She wasn't that fussed about the plausibility of his suggestion. Whatever he said, she would seize on it gratefully. 'I thought I heard a voice,' she explained. 'A female voice.'

His next question was even more unexpected. 'What did you think she was saying?'

'*Let me in.* I thought she kept repeating "let me in".' Dröfn was surprised her words didn't sound as idiotic as she'd expected.

Haukur looked at her, his expression seeming to reflect what she was feeling. She could have been mistaken in the dim light but she didn't think there was any mockery in his face. Far from throwing her a lifeline, though, in the form of a rational explanation for her experience, what he said next made Dröfn feel even worse.

'I never sleep well in this hut. I don't know what it is. Its history, maybe.'

'Its history?' A prickle down her spine made Dröfn suddenly acutely aware that she had her back turned to the kitchen.

'The place doesn't have a very good reputation. I've heard various tales, most of them complete rubbish. But I know that at least one of them is true, if my grandfather wasn't lying to me.' He smiled at Dröfn. 'A woman died outside the hut. Froze to death, right on the doorstep.'

A chill ran through Dröfn's body, making her feel as cold as when she had first emerged from her sleeping bag. 'Was she here like us? In the middle of winter?'

Haukur nodded. 'Yes, but not for the same reason. She was brought here against her will – by a crazy husband who locked her out without her coat on. She died of exposure right there on the deck.'

'Seriously?' Dröfn wished she knew Haukur better. She couldn't tell from his face whether he found the story gruesomely entertaining or sad. 'Why here?'

'He thought she was cheating on him with a soldier from the radar station.'

Dröfn couldn't see the connection. 'What did her cheating have to do with this hut?'

'It's not quite clear but the story is he believed his wife had been meeting her lover here. At the time it was frowned on for locals to fraternise with American soldiers. But the idea that she would have trekked all the way out here to meet her lover is obviously nuts. The hut's not exactly accessible. The husband wasn't in his right mind. He was crazy enough to listen to his wife pleading for mercy as she died of cold on the other side of the door, without lifting a finger to help her. So she died. With the hut and its life-saving warmth right in front of her eyes.'

'What happened to the husband?'

She thought Haukur grimaced, though the deceptive light had a way of turning every expression into a scowl. 'He was never found. It's believed he died of exposure too. Either on his way back to civilisation or from suicide. That he just went on walking further into the wilderness, knowing he wouldn't survive.'

Dröfn's shivering intensified and she wrapped her arms around herself. 'How do they know? Did he leave a note behind?'

Haukur nodded. 'Yes. They found it in his car. He probably parked in more or less the same place I did.' He broke off and met her eye. 'It was my grandfather who found the woman's body. He was a farmer in the Lón district and was up here looking for lost sheep when he came across her. It's not a story for children but I first heard it when I was a kid. And many times since then. There are other stories, too. Perhaps not as tragic – but grim enough. No doubt that's why I never feel comfortable in this hut.' He broke off again, then added belatedly: 'But don't let it get to you. Or the business of the coat in the hall. It must have been left behind when the farmers were here for the sheep round-up in the autumn. They sometimes use the hut as a base.'

But Dröfn knew better and decided to share the information with him. She had kept it to herself yesterday evening so as not to spoil the mood, but she saw no reason to spare Haukur – he was so glum by nature that he had no good mood to spoil. 'I found a petrol receipt in the pocket. It's more recent than that – from only two months ago.'

Finally, Haukur said something designed to banish her fears. 'Oh, that doesn't mean anything. They never manage to round up all the sheep the first time. The farmers often take advantage of lulls in the storms to search for the ewes that got left behind. I'm sure that's the explanation. The coat may have been hanging there and someone borrowed it while their own was drying out, for example. The receipt must have ended up in the pocket by accident. I wouldn't worry about it, trust me. If someone had gone missing out here recently, I'd have heard about it.'

Feeling slightly reassured, Dröfn quickly changed the subject before he could tell her any more horror stories about the area. All she wanted now was for them to get packed and out of here as quickly as possible. 'Shall we sort out breakfast, then hit the road?' She didn't offer to cook it herself as she didn't want to spend a minute alone in that kitchen. When Haukur agreed, she gave a half-hearted smile and moved aside to let him go in first.

The lazybones upstairs eventually wandered down while Dröfn and Haukur were getting things ready in the kitchen. Haukur had raised his eyebrows when she'd propped her phone up over the worktop, to enhance the light of the candles he had lit, but he didn't comment and neither did she. She didn't care if her phone battery ran out. It wasn't like she could make any calls or go online as they had no signal out here. Apart from using it as a torch, all she could do was take pictures with it. But as Tjörvi always took millions of photos, she could share his when they got back to town.

That's assuming she actually wanted any visual reminders of this trip. So far, she thought it unlikely.

Having stuffed themselves with breakfast, they made sandwiches for the next stage, then tidied up the hut and sorted out their gear. Dröfn was hopping with impatience to get outside in the open. Out into the natural darkness and fresh air. Only then would she cease to be constantly on the alert for the woman's pleading voice behind her. She was the first to leave the hut. If any of the others were surprised by how fast she strode through the cramped hall and past the red anorak, they didn't mention it.

Outside they were confronted by the same wintry world as they had left behind the previous evening. It had snowed heavily during the night, obliterating their tracks and making it look almost as if they had flown there. Dröfn realised too late that she had forgotten to go into the little loo to fetch her toothbrush and toiletries. But it didn't occur to her to go back for them. She could survive without brushing her teeth for twenty-four hours. Anything was better than going back inside that horrible hut.

Haukur led the way as he had the day before. And Dröfn brought up the rear. She felt her spirits rising with every step they put between them and the hut. Despite the heavy going, she wasn't even aware of the lingering stiffness in her legs.

It wasn't long, though, before her sense of wellbeing began to ebb. Her discomfort wasn't physical, since any muscle cramps had swiftly faded as her leg muscles warmed up. And they hadn't gone far enough yet for her shoulders to start protesting at the weight of her rucksack.

The discomfort was psychological. No matter how hard she tried to concentrate on the magnificent scenery or sporadic conversation of her companions, she couldn't shake off the absurd feeling that they were being followed. Not by just anyone, but by the imaginary woman. The woman who, it seemed, might be connected not to the anorak but to the hut itself. Dröfn caught herself constantly glancing over her shoulder, but every time she was met by the same sight: steep mountainsides, black belts of crags, endless snow and their own tracks.

The winding path hampered Dröfn's view, but as far as she could see, there was no human figure on their trail. No one pursuing them.

Yet this didn't alter the fact that every time she turned round to reassure herself, she caught sight of a shadow. It was only visible while her head was moving, disappearing as soon as she had turned.

After a while of this, Dröfn eventually spotted a movement at the edge of her vision without even turning her head. When she looked towards it, she felt dizzy with relief. A lone reindeer was standing on a ridge, curiously watching these interlopers, ready to bound away if they changed direction and started coming towards it. The beast was a wretched sight, the skin hanging off its bones. Presumably there was hardly anything for it to eat in these barren, snow-covered wastes. Dröfn called out to the others and the line stopped moving as everyone turned to get a look at the animal.

Tjörvi and Bjólfur immediately started showing off on the strength of their two hunting trips and agreeing that the animal wasn't even worth shooting. Dröfn was pissed off by their callous tone, and grateful when Haukur shut them up with a more well-informed take. He told them the reindeer was almost certainly a cow since mature bulls would have shed their antlers by now. He added that cows sometimes became separated from the herd when the animals migrated down to the lowlands in autumn. Usually this was because they were injured or too ill to follow the others. If they survived the harsh winter up here, they would be reunited with the herd when it returned to the highlands in the spring.

Dröfn's smile quickly faded when Haukur added that it was more usual for the cows to collapse and die of starvation.

The same fate befell most of the ewes that evaded the autumn sheep round-up.

The reindeer slowly swung her large horned head to the side, looking away from the humans. Then she moved off unhurriedly, presumably too weak to flee. Once she had vanished from sight behind the ridge, the landscape was deserted again. Dröfn hoped that by some magic the cow would find a patch of vegetation, bare of snow. Her mood was depressed enough already without worrying about the poor creature as well.

The others didn't seem to share her concern. When Dröfn turned back, they had already started moving again. Even though she had an explanation now for the mysterious movements she'd glimpsed, she was afraid of being left behind and reluctant to walk in the rear, with no one behind her.

She quickened her pace until she had caught up with Agnes, then asked if she could overtake her. She did the same with Tjörvi and felt a little less jittery once she was walking in the middle of the column. When Tjörvi asked why she wanted to change places, she answered that she was afraid of falling and wanted him there to catch her if she lost her footing. He seemed to believe her – or at least, he didn't ask any further questions.

Perhaps – just perhaps – in a few days' time she would feel able to tell him how spooked she had been. She might even, unlikely though it seemed, be capable of laughing at her fears once they were safely back at the hotel in Höfn, sitting in the bar with drinks in their hands. Until then, she would just have to get on with it. She sent up a silent prayer that the time would pass quickly.

Chapter 12

The snow showed no signs of letting up, the thick flakes floating lazily down to earth as if they were weightless. The town looked as if it had been upholstered with a thick layer of white that smoothed out all its sharp outlines and contours. It was very quiet; lights were on in every house but at this late hour the streets were empty.

Far from bringing Jóhanna any inner peace, the snow served as a reminder of the bleak, icy wastes and the horror of the bodies they had discovered that day.

The chill in her bones had stayed with her all the way down to the lowlands and home. She had only managed to expel it by taking a hot bath. The water had also soothed her weary, aching muscles. And the reheated soup had helped with her nausea. She was almost feeling human by the time she threw all her clothes into the washing machine and nearly broke the drier by stuffing her heavy, wet snowsuit into it. The snowsuit hadn't exactly been dirty but she'd felt a compulsion to wash everything she'd been wearing, as if to rinse the memory of the day's events out of her clothes. She had even been on the verge of chucking her hiking boots into the washing machine but had stopped herself just in time.

Yet none of this had helped to combat her mental fatigue.

There was little consolation in the knowledge that she wasn't the only one to have been badly affected by the day's events. On the way back to town, the mood of the rescuers had been sombre. They had sat in the ice truck, heads drooping, none of them making any effort to fake indifference. Although it had been clear to most of them from the beginning of the mission that there would be no survivors, they had only now received the final confirmation. The missing party were all accounted for, all dead. One body had been found near the glacier's edge and two in the vicinity of the tents, and then there was the woman who had already been dug out of the snow near the hut.

The party Jóhanna and Thórir were in had located the first body. Unlike the one near the hut, it hadn't been completely buried in drifts since it lay on a piece of exposed ground that had been scoured by the wind.

Part of the man's back and head had been visible. He had died lying face down. Almost naked, like the woman they had originally found. As far as they could tell, he must have removed his clothes just before he expired. His shoes and phone lay nearby. A little further off they spotted his coat, almost covered by snow. His lighter garments must have been carried off by the wind because the searchers could find no trace of them.

Once the snow had been scraped away from the frozen body, they discovered that the man had been trying to crawl on hands and knees when he'd taken his last breath. Where he'd been going they would never know for sure, though it was easy enough to guess. He must have been making for where he thought he would find warmth and shelter. The odd thing was that he wasn't facing in the direction of the tents.

Unless he hadn't been crawling *towards* something but *away* from something. The terror imprinted on his frozen features had lent support to that theory.

It was no wonder the man's end had been far from peaceful. His fingers, toes and face showed unmistakable signs of frostbite, indicating that he had been out in the open for some considerable time before he died. Jóhanna noticed that her companions' reaction on seeing his damaged flesh was, like her own, to zip up their snowsuits more tightly.

The other man's body, found by another group, also showed evidence of severe frostbite. The woman's body displayed none, but that wasn't to say she'd escaped injury entirely. Her right wrist was swollen and bruised, and jutted out at an odd angle, suggesting that it was broken.

Like the others, these bodies had hardly any clothes on. The woman wore a long-sleeved thermal vest, knickers and socks, while the man wore nothing but a pair of long johns and his feet were bare. The glove lying beside the woman was said to be identical to the one discovered in the pile of clothes in the hut. A scarf appeared to have been draped over the man's head. The rest of their clothes and shoes were presumably among the gear that had been found in one of the tents, several dozen metres away from the spot where the couple had succumbed to the elements.

Strangely enough, these two seemed to have been heading away from the camp as well. The door flaps of both tents were shut, the zips firmly closed, indicating that they hadn't been abandoned in a hurry. But the newer-looking tent had been slashed with a knife, possibly from the inside, if the rumours circulating among the rescuers were to be believed. In addition to the clothes, sleeping bags and rucksacks with rations in them had been found in there, and a primus as well. Everyone Jóhanna had spoken to while they were watching the police forensics team at work agreed that if the people had stayed put inside the tents, they would almost certainly have survived. It was a grim thought.

Since the presence of four sleeping bags seemed to confirm that the party had only consisted of the two couples who had been reported missing, the search had been called off for now. If there had been a fifth person, they must have got away. At least, there was still no sign of any vehicle. If new evidence emerged on that point, the search would be resumed.

As if the situation wasn't already strange enough, none of the three bodies displayed any injuries that could explain the large blood stain found in the vicinity of the hut.

Jóhanna pulled the hood of her coat lower over her face to stop the weightless snowflakes constantly getting in her eyes. Although she had only walked a relatively short distance, her forehead was already aching with the cold. It occurred to her how pathetic her discomfort was compared to the ordeal the doomed trekking party must have suffered.

Even more pathetic was the fact that she hadn't been able to face waiting alone at home. She yearned for Geiri's company, or at least his presence. He didn't have to say anything or entertain her with conversation, just be there.

The instant Jóhanna had seen the lights go on in the little police station, she had pulled on her coat and set off on foot. Normally, she would have rung ahead to let him know she was coming but she had been afraid Geiri would tell her to wait as he would be home soon. She didn't want to wait. Especially since she knew from experience that it always took him longer than anticipated to sort things out at the station.

As far as she had been able to tell from the sitting-room window, his car was the only one parked outside the station, so she assumed he was alone. The investigation team must have returned to their hotel, apart from those who had already hitched a lift back to Reykjavík with the helicopter. Exactly who had gone and who had remained behind, she didn't know. But the chopper had gone, that much was certain. She had heard the throbbing of its blades as she wallowed in her hot bath.

Jóhanna rang the bell and waited for Geiri to open the door. He looked tired, but if he was surprised to see her there, he didn't show it.

The police station was an unassuming building that had once housed the town library. No hint remained of its previous incarnation; there wasn't a book, magazine or bookcase to be seen, let alone a children's play corner.

A desk behind a glass screen separated the reception from the rest of the station. There were only two seats in the waiting area as the crime rate in the region served by the Höfn force was low and few people had formal business at the station. Jóhanna doubted there were many occasions when both chairs were occupied at once.

Round the back, there were various rooms: offices, a meeting room, store cupboards, toilets, an interview room that resembled a small lounge, a kitchen and the cells. There were two of these, in addition to one especially equipped for prisoners detained in custody. Generally, prisoners in this category were transferred across the country to Hólmsheidi, the prison a few kilometres east of Reykjavík, as soon as a verdict was available, but sometimes the move was prevented by bad weather or some other unforeseen eventuality. Jóhanna didn't think the cell had been used once since Geiri had started work there.

'Do you want a coffee? I'm nearly done here. I just need to send a couple of emails.'

Jóhanna declined the offer. She didn't want to wait on her own in the kitchen, let alone endure a night of caffeine-induced insomnia. It wasn't hard to guess what images would haunt her in the darkness. 'I'll just take a seat in your office. I promise not to disturb you.'

Geiri nodded. He seemed to know intuitively how she was feeling, without her needing to put it into words. She was so grateful to him for that. She realised that if she were forced to describe her thoughts aloud, they would sound foolish. Not that Geiri would judge her or belittle her worries; a more understanding man would be hard to find. This quality must make him a good policeman – for the victims of crimes, at least.

While Geiri was hammering at his keyboard, Jóhanna sat in the visitor's chair facing his desk. She enjoyed being in his company without needing to talk. At times like this she hated being alone with her thoughts. Even their cosy house hadn't had its usual soothing effect on her when she had got home, dog-tired. She felt more at ease in this impersonal office, thanks to Geiri's presence, and experienced no urge to pick up her phone as she often did while she was waiting.

The tapping fell silent at last and Geiri leant back in his chair. He looked at her with a ghost of a smile. 'This is a hell of a situation.'

She nodded, filling her cheeks with air and exhaling gloomily.

'Tell me something. Does the rescue team teach you anything about how people behave when they're dying of hypothermia? I'm trying to get my head round the scene . . . and the other one by the hut . . . but I can't for the life of me work out what can have happened. Do people go crazy?'

Jóhanna didn't need to think about her reply. The rescuers had discussed little else. No matter how the conversation started, it had invariably ended with the same question: why had the trekkers left their tents?

'People get disorientated. That's clear. In a blizzard, when they can't see anything but snow and everything's a blur, they can totally lose their bearings. Even those who should know better have a tendency to blunder off at random instead of staying put. And it's well known that hypothermia can make people confused. Cause them to react the wrong way.' Jóhanna smiled at her husband. 'But you know all that already.'

Geiri didn't confirm or deny it. 'I'd understand if they'd been out walking and got caught in a storm, but only one of them seems to have gone any distance. The others had shelter within reach. The fact that all four of them were almost naked like that . . . I'm pretty sure the two found near the tents had been lying in their sleeping bags when they suddenly took it into their heads to rush outside. And that they left in such a panic that they slashed their way out through the canvas instead of opening the tent door. They hadn't been out walking, they were inside the tent. I'm absolutely sure of that. And the woman who turned up first had been in the hut. What's more, she was carrying a knife that was almost certainly the same one that was used to cut through the tent canvas. At least, no other knife has turned up in either of the tents or near the bodies. So, the question is, did she spot the reindeer and mistake it for a member of the group? Did she run outside, intending to help? If not, it seems a pretty odd coincidence that she was lying so close to the animal.' Geiri shook his head, frowning. 'She charges out of the hut, with hardly any clothes on; the other two rush out of their tents with a scarf and one glove. All of them going straight to their deaths. What the hell would have made them do it?'

'Could they have been off their heads on something? Or terrified? Maybe there was a gas leak? Or it was a cry for help? There could have been somebody else there. If the fifth person was injured, that would explain the blood.' Jóhanna stopped; she had run out of theories.

'Then where is this person? No, I just can't picture it.'

'An injured animal, then? It could have wandered between the two sites.'

He smiled at her. 'An injured animal? What, they were such animal lovers that they rushed out naked to help it?'

Jóhanna had to admit that this didn't sound very convincing. 'No. That can't be it.'

Geiri slapped his hands on the arms of his chair, then got to his feet. 'Maybe something will come to light during the post-mortems. All I can think of is that they must have been on drugs. That would explain a lot. So far, we don't even know if they all died on the same day or some time apart. Or if they definitely died of hypothermia. Perhaps the cause of death was poison or something else altogether. Their belongings were taken to Reykjavík with the bodies and they'll be examined as well. It's frustrating that it's going to take such a long time – we won't get any answers for a few days, I expect. But poison or drugs is my bet.'

Neither of them spoke for a while. Jóhanna guessed they were both picturing the frozen faces. Do people grimace in their death throes when they're poisoned? It sounded plausible.

There was no let-up in the snow when they emerged from the police station. If anything, it was coming down more thickly now. Jóhanna pulled up her hood again while Geiri was locking the door. Seeing all the snow that had piled up on the car, they decided to walk home: they were both too tired to scrape the roof and windows.

Jóhanna leant against Geiri's shoulder as they walked the short stretch, feeling as if they were alone in the world. The only tracks still faintly visible were her own, from when she had come to the station. Apart from that, the pavement was covered in a smooth, white quilt. The streets, too; no one had driven along them for a while.

Everything appeared pristine in the glow of the streetlights. But underneath the sparkling surface, she thought, nothing had changed: the lumps of chewing gum on the paving stones, the loose grit on the tarmac, the rotting leaves and bits of litter blown there by the wind. Although Höfn was a pretty, well-kept little town, it had its fair share of ugliness. The moment the temperature rose above zero, the imperfections would reappear, like a cloth being removed from a scratched dining table.

They only had a few steps left to the house when Geiri abruptly halted. 'Did you leave the front door open?'

Jóhanna straightened up from his shoulder and stared at the gaping dark doorway. 'Er . . . no. I closed it. Definitely.' When she started speaking she was sure of herself but by the time she finished she felt a sneaking doubt. Could she have gone out without checking that the lock had clicked?

Dropping her eyes to the pavement, she noticed that there were no footprints other than hers approaching or leaving the house. Since her own tracks were already half filled with fresh flakes, clearly no one could have been there after her.

Geiri looked at her and shrugged. He was too tired to discuss it any further. He had so much else on his mind.

But Jóhanna couldn't just shrug it off. She tried in vain to recall the moment when she had left the house. Common sense told her she must have forgotten to shut the door. Everything pointed to that explanation. But once they were in bed and she was on the point of dropping off, she found she could clearly picture not only closing it but locking it too.

Instantly, she was wide awake. For a long time afterwards she lay there, unable to sleep. The scar that ran down her back ached and the other ones criss-crossing her legs itched in sympathy. They reminded her of cracks in clay or concrete and she didn't like to look at them. She never wore shorts, however good the weather. When Geiri suggested a foreign holiday, she was careful to choose somewhere northerly. They had made more trips to Finland and Norway than any other couple they knew. Yet although Geiri must have suspected the reason for her cold-weather fetish, he had never referred to it, a fact for which she was eternally grateful. She didn't want to have to discuss how she felt when she saw strangers surreptitiously eyeing her injuries and wondering what the hell had happened to her. It was a conversation she'd been forced to have once too often when she lived at home with her parents. Their repeated mantra that other people's opinions didn't matter had been no comfort at all.

Jóhanna rolled over onto her back. She had already tried that position, as well as lying on her stomach and on both sides. Several times. The new position would work well for a few minutes before she felt the need to shift again. Her weary mind tried to persuade her that it would be easier to get to sleep if she just turned over one more time. Geiri, in contrast, had gone out like a light the moment his head touched the pillow. All she could do was lie there staring into the darkness while she waited for sleep to come. Listening to the familiar night-time noises.

Noises that up till now had always seemed comforting and homely.

Chapter 13

Lónsöræfi, the previous week

'Have they been away an unnaturally long time?' Dröfn had been biting back the question for a good half-hour, but she could no longer stop herself; she had to ask.

'Nah.' Agnes shook her head inside the capacious hood of her coat. 'I don't think so. I swear the time just passes more sluggishly when it's freezing. Like it's oozing along, thick as slush.'

They were sitting in Dröfn and Tjörvi's tent, still in their down jackets and over-trousers, wrapped in their sleeping bags. It was the only way they could convince themselves they weren't about to perish from the cold. The feeling had to be psychological, because they were no longer shivering or breathing out clouds of steam. It was prompted by the realisation that there was nothing but a thin sheet of canvas between them and the freezing conditions outside.

If the candlelight in the hut had given them all black hollows around their eyes, the torchlight in the tent, turned a bilious yellow by the canvas, made the two women look as if they had jaundice. Agnes and Bjólfur's tent was identical, as they had purchased it at the same time in the same shop, especially for this trip. Haukur's, in contrast, was a dull green colour – like a military tent, Dröfn thought. She hadn't been inside it but couldn't imagine that a green filter would make them look any better.

When Haukur reckoned they were close enough to the edge of the ice cap, he had proposed setting up camp. At that point, Agnes had still been feeling energetic enough to suggest a race to see who could put their tent up first. She'd divided them into three teams – Dröfn and Tjörvi, Agnes and Bjólfur, and Haukur – then whistled the starting signal. This was typical of Agnes in HR manager mode. Dröfn had lost count of the times she'd heard her talking about all the games and competitions she organised for team-building at work. Tjörvi and Bjólfur, who were both competitive by nature, were immediately on board; Haukur and Dröfn were less keen. In spite of this, Dröfn had worked as fast as her husband to erect their tent, though it had nothing to do with any desire to win; she just wanted its shelter.

Agnes and Bjólfur had finished first with a great deal of crowing, much to Tjörvi's annoyance. Haukur didn't seem bothered: he had simply put up his tent at his own speed, making little more than a pretence of taking part in the race.

Once the tents were up and they had unrolled their sleeping bags, there was no way Dröfn could be persuaded to abandon this newly acquired refuge and traipse off through the snow to the measuring instrument with Haukur. She could see in Tjörvi's eyes that he was no more eager to go than she was, but the moment he heard that Bjólfur was game, Tjörvi started faking an equal amount of enthusiasm. The upshot was that the three men had set off soon afterwards, leaving Agnes and Dröfn to get into one of the tents together and wriggle down inside their sleeping bags.

They had sat there, listening to the squeaking of the snow under the men's boots as it faded into the distance, until all they could hear was their own breathing. At that moment

Dröfn was seized by the sensation she always had on a roller-coaster, when it reached the top and was on the point of plunging down the biggest drop: *What the hell am I doing here?* On the rollercoaster, she could close her eyes and scream at the top of her voice, but of course she couldn't do that here in the tent.

Instead, she smiled weakly at Agnes, hoping to see the same doubts reflected in her face. But Agnes was looking perfectly happy and almost immediately began chatting to Dröfn as if they were curled up on the sofa at home and their husbands had just popped out to fetch a Chinese takeaway.

Their conversation quickly petered out. As soon as the warmth crept back into their bodies, they began to yawn and before they knew it they were asleep. The length of their nap suggested that they had been more tired than they realised, which was saying something. But the rest had done nothing to restore Dröfn's weary limbs, and when she woke up she was even more aware of the cramps in her legs than she had been before she'd nodded off.

It wasn't long before she forgot about her stiffness and started to fret about Tjörvi instead. She did her best to conceal her anxiety and keep up her side of the conversation with Agnes, which had picked up where it had left off earlier, once they'd rubbed the sleep from their eyes. Yet all the time Dröfn was wondering where Tjörvi was, how far the men had gone and whether they were OK. She envied Agnes her casual confidence but didn't want to infect her friend with her own anxiety. Not that that was likely to happen, as Agnes seemed almost impervious to fear. Her default setting had always been that everything would turn out fine. And this was, admittedly, usually the case. No one could avoid misfortune forever, though, however unevenly it was doled out.

Dröfn had given in to the temptation to keep an eye on the time, despite the drain on her phone battery. She kept stealing glances at the screen, tricky though it was in the cramped conditions to do it without Agnes seeing. Every time she checked, she grew more jittery. And now that it was more than four hours since the men had left, she could no longer keep her worries to herself.

Agnes poured cold water on her fears, of course: 'They'll be back. Stop worrying. It's not achieving anything.'

Dröfn gnawed at the inside of her cheek, her eyes on the closed tent flap. 'But they said they wouldn't be long.'

'Oh, please. That's what Bjólfur said. How much do you think he knows about how long it'll take to find the equipment and read off the measurements? Anyway, if he says something will take five minutes, you can be sure it'll be anything from fifteen minutes to an hour. His sense of time isn't exactly his strong point. Besides, it's perfectly possible they encountered a hitch. Haukur did say it wasn't unlikely.' Agnes gave her a reassuring smile. 'And you can bet it'll take longer than Haukur anticipated, with those two tagging along. He didn't seem particularly pleased to have their company. I can just picture them standing over him, pestering him with endless questions about the bloody instrument. There's nothing worse than trying to work when someone's breathing down your neck. Except when it's two people breathing down your neck.'

Agnes was right. Dröfn felt a little better. 'What's he measuring, anyway?'

'I don't know. The glacial retreat, maybe.'

Dröfn considered this. 'But couldn't you see that from the air? Take photos and do the measurements that way?'

'Probably. But you wouldn't be able to measure the thickness from the air. Or the temperature. Anyway, it's probably monitoring something quite different. I suppose it's kind of bad that we didn't ask.' Agnes reached for the water bottle that was propped between them. She took a good swig, shaking herself a little to conquer her shivers as the icy liquid trickled down her throat. 'The trouble is, I find the whole subject so incredibly boring.'

She wasn't alone there. The only thing Dröfn wanted to know about Haukur's research was how soon he could finish collecting the information he needed, so they could all hurry back to civilisation. The thought that she had abandoned a heated house, decent food and her personal safety in order to sit here in the arse end of nowhere, bundled up in a sleeping bag and all her clothes, was enough to make her cry.

There was a sudden creaking outside, like footsteps in the snow. 'There!' Agnes beamed at Dröfn. 'They're back.' Then she made a face. 'Whoops. Should we have got a hot drink ready for them or something?'

Dröfn didn't answer, just shuffled on her knees to the tent door to unzip the flap. She couldn't wait to see Tjörvi, ruddy-cheeked and weary but in one piece. Behind her, Agnes warned in a low voice: 'Careful. They're probably planning to surprise us. Why else would they be sneaking up on the tent like this?'

That was true. And it was a little odd that the two women hadn't heard the men exchange a single word. Surely they couldn't be too exhausted to speak? 'Tjörvi!' Dröfn took hold of the zip, ready to pull it up the moment he replied. There was no answering call from outside. Nothing but that creaking of the snow. Dröfn let go of the zip and shrank back from the tent door.

'What?' Agnes looked astonished. 'Aren't you going to open it?'

'It's not them.' Dröfn's voice was devoid of emotion, almost robotic. She couldn't explain why but she was suddenly sure that it wasn't their husbands outside. Someone else was making that sound. Since entering the tent, she had managed to banish all thoughts of the frozen woman but now they crashed over her with renewed force. 'I'm telling you: it's not them.'

Agnes wasn't having any of it. 'Rubbish.' She made her way to the door and unzipped the flap, then stuck out her head. 'Bjólfur! Tjörvi! Haukur!'

Nobody answered. She pulled her head back inside and closed the flap again. 'That's weird.' She turned to Dröfn, making a visible effort to appear unconcerned. 'Probably some animal. There must be animals out there. Like that reindeer.'

Dröfn nodded, forcing herself to accept the explanation. Perhaps the reindeer cow had turned up. It must be a lonely, monotonous existence roaming around in this empty landscape. Perhaps the tents had looked interesting in comparison to the endless expanse of snow.

But Dröfn wasn't convinced and Agnes didn't seem sure either. They sat there, holding their breath, listening to the creaking and crunching that seemed one minute to be getting further away, the next to be coming closer.

'What are we going to do if they don't come back? Would you be able to find your way to the hut?' Dröfn had retreated as far as she could from the door, although she knew the canvas was no protection and that it didn't really make any difference where she sat.

'They'll be back. There's no need to lose your shit just because some animal's wandering around outside.'

Agnes hadn't answered Dröfn's second question, so she repeated it. 'Would you be able to find your way back to the hut?'

'Sure. Of course.'

Agnes wasn't fooling either of them. Few people had as poor a sense of direction as she did. Dröfn had lost count of the times she'd had to intervene when they'd been on their way from the Kringlan shopping centre to the car and her friend had taken off in completely the wrong direction. When they were abroad, you'd have thought she'd been spun in circles deliberately to disorientate her. You could almost use her as a compass. If Agnes thought they should turn right, you could be sure they should turn left. There was zero chance she could lead them back to the hut – and Dröfn was equally unlikely to manage it. She couldn't for the life of her remember the route. Snow, snow and more snow was all she could recall from their trek.

The absurdity of the situation struck her with renewed force. She should be at work now, just about packing up to go home. She had a degree in the geography of education, and worked for a small start-up that developed software for distance learning. Most of the crises they experienced at the office were digital in nature and never involved genuine danger to the employees. In the worst case it might be touch and go whether their salaries would be paid at the beginning of the month. But somehow things always turned out OK. She would gladly sacrifice a month's pay, she thought, to be sitting at her desk right now.

What kind of idiots were they to have rushed off into the unknown like this?

Yet even as she was thinking this, Dröfn realised that she was becoming resigned to the situation. She couldn't simply magic herself home again. She had to face the fact that she was here. The realisation lifted a heavy burden from her shoulders; so heavy that once she was free of it, she felt ridiculously light-hearted. The sensation reminded her of the time she had tried smoking a joint back when she was a student.

Ignoring the noises outside, she turned to look at Agnes in her bulky orange coat. Even the hood was so oversized that it resembled a helmet.

Dröfn broke the silence. 'You look like Tintin in his spacesuit in *Explorers on the Moon*.'

'What?' Agnes glanced down at her thickly padded jacket. 'Oh, yes. You're right.' She grinned. 'Pretty damn cool, in other words.'

'Yes. Very cool.'

They smiled at each other. But their smiles vanished when the creaking stopped and was replaced by a sound that couldn't possibly have been made by any wild animal.

'It's just the wind,' Agnes said quickly. But there was a tremor in her voice, her eyes were stretched wide and her face seemed even yellower than before.

She didn't believe it any more than Dröfn did.

They sat there, rigid with fear, listening to the low muttering outside. Dröfn didn't dare ask if Agnes could make out the words that seemed to be repeated again and again. She didn't want confirmation that she had heard right. Because she could have sworn that the voice outside was muttering over and over, *Let me in, let me in, let me in . . .*

Chapter 14

Hjörvar hadn't meant to answer the phone to his brother Kolbeinn. He had meant to check who it was first but had got so flustered that he pressed the wrong button. And once he'd done that, there was no way he could end the call.

To begin with, he thought it was going to be one of those easy conversations that would soon be over. Kolbeinn had a reason for calling: he was asking about the search for the missing walkers, on the off chance that Hjörvar knew more than the sketchy information the police had released so far. His brother was obviously as gripped by the story as the rest of the nation.

Before leaving the radar station the night before, Hjörvar had received an email from his boss, addressed to him and Erlingur, ordering them not to talk to the media about the rescue mission. Reporters had got wind of something strange going on and were desperate for information. Although the news outlets had agreed for the moment not to publish anything but the official press releases, they were unlikely to hold back for long. And when the dam finally burst, the leak must on no account be traceable back to the Coast Guard.

Hjörvar had replied simply: *Message received.*

With this email in mind, he had told his brother that he knew little beyond what had already been reported in the news. Kolbeinn was the last person to gossip, but it was better to err on the safe side. Especially when Hjörvar knew there must be question marks at HQ about his own mental stability.

Not very serious ones, perhaps, but in the circumstances he was determined to avoid putting a foot wrong.

In hindsight, it might have been more sensible to slip Kolbeinn a tiny nugget of information. He could have confided in him, for instance, that there were no survivors. His brother wouldn't have spread it any further, and in any case an official announcement was about to be made. Then the brothers could have spent the rest of the phone call discussing the fate of the walkers, and expressing disapproval of their recklessness. Once that topic had been exhausted, the conversation would have petered out naturally. Kolbeinn would have asked if Hjörvar was still enjoying life in Höfn and he would have asked in return if the new metal roofing plates on Kolbeinn's house had survived the latest gales. After that, one of them would have said: 'Any other news?' The other would have said no, then they'd have rung off.

But now that Hjörvar had given him the brush-off about the search, Kolbeinn had felt compelled to cast around for a new topic. He couldn't simply end the call after such a brief question and an even briefer answer. Unfortunately, the topic Kolbeinn had seized on was the very one Hjörvar was desperate to avoid. The fact was, he had neglected to do any of the things he'd promised, and he wasn't particularly eager to own up to the fact. He was even less eager to explain why he hadn't got round to them, but luckily he managed to dodge that particular topic – although he was forced to admit that he hadn't achieved anything in the five months he'd been living in Höfn.

Before ringing off, Hjörvar had promised his little brother that he would pull his finger out. They agreed to talk again later in the week, by which time Hjörvar should have some answers for him. After that, Kolbeinn passed on a message from Hjörvar's daughter Ágústa that she would appreciate a call from him. But one unwelcome phone conversation was quite enough for the evening, so she would just have to wait. Hjörvar assured Kolbeinn that he would get in touch with her soon, though. He had been worn out when they spoke, having just got home to his poky little flat, still badly shaken by the uncanny events of his evening shift.

It was morning now. Hjörvar had slept soundly and was feeling positively invigorated after a refreshing shower, even though the shower cubicle was junk, like everything else in the flat. It rattled and threatened to fall apart, so Hjörvar always emerged feeling relieved that at least it was still hanging together.

Last night he had been too tired and strung out to ring Ágústa; now he was in too good a mood. A phone conversation with her would only ruin it. He would ring her when he was neither happy nor sad.

For once, he had a bit of time off, on a weekday, during office hours, awarded as compensation for putting in an evening shift yesterday. He had accepted it gratefully; he needed the rest. It also meant that he was in a position to put his promise to his brother into action. Best get it over with, he thought. It wasn't as if it required much effort on his part. All he had to do was ask a few questions in one or two quarters and then the matter could be put to bed. He would ring Kolbeinn in a few days and tell him what he'd found out. Then they need never talk about it again.

All this made his reluctance to get on with it even odder. Ever since his brother had rung and told him about the shoe, he'd had a sinking feeling in the pit of his stomach that he couldn't explain – to himself or Kolbeinn. The name alone – Salvör – had stirred up something from his past that left a bad taste in his mouth. He hadn't managed to dredge up any concrete memories, though, only that strange bad taste and an inexplicable feeling of dread. His brother had admitted to him that he had felt the same.

Kolbeinn had got confirmation that the girl had definitely existed. She was listed as their parents' daughter in the National Registry, which meant she must have been their full sister, though they had been unaware of her existence. She had been younger than them, born a year after Kolbeinn and two and a half years after Hjörvar. Kolbeinn had also established that she had died in an accident just before the age of three. At the time Kolbeinn would have been just four, and Hjörvar five and a half.

Kolbeinn hadn't left it at that. He had rung their maternal uncle, the only surviving relative who could possibly tell them anything about their parents, but had learnt little from him. Their uncle had said it was all so long ago; it had happened after their mother had moved east to Höfn, and he'd been taken up with his own affairs at the time. He did recall, though, that the little girl had been given a quiet funeral out east. He knew almost nothing about the accident but had a feeling she'd drowned. There had also been some vague talk about there being something wrong with the child – that she hadn't been right in the head. But then he'd backtracked and said it could have been something completely different.

The brothers had agreed that their uncle was probably going gaga like their mother, as dementia was known to run in the family.

It was frustrating not to have got any clear answers from him, since they didn't have any other surviving relatives and they themselves remembered nothing as they had been so young when their sister had died. That said, Hjörvar had been five and a half. Old enough, he'd have thought, to recall something, yet he drew a blank. Perhaps he had the same faulty gene as his mother. He could remember almost nothing about the years before he'd started school at seven. Just hazy fragments: his mother putting up the Christmas tree; his father going for a walk with him on the beach; a trip to Reykjavík when he had appendicitis, and the soreness of the wound after the operation. Kolbeinn with a cut on his knee after falling on a rock; the scent of the bath oil his mother used to like; cigarette smoke in the car. Apart from that, he might as well have been born at seven or eight.

Nowhere in these brief snatches of memory was there any glimpse of a little girl. Was she fair? Dark? Skinny or plump? He hadn't a clue.

Hjörvar had done a quick online search on the subject of children's memories and was reassured by what he read. It seemed that the brothers' experience was consistent with expert opinion. Few people recall anything except fragments from the first six years of their life. The memories from this time gather dust and are lost, especially if they aren't re-inforced. In other words, it was entirely their parents' fault that the brothers could remember nothing about Salvör. Neither could recall ever hearing their mother or father mention her, either when they were boys or later, after they had grown up.

The box his brother had been given along with the shoe had contained photo albums dating back to the years when their mysterious sister was alive. Yet there wasn't a single picture of her. That said, they did contain a number of blank spaces where photos had obviously been removed. There were snap-shots of Hjörvar and Kolbeinn as babies and toddlers; of their parents and other adults they didn't recognise. The photos had been taken on a variety of occasions, both indoors and outdoors, in winter and summer. Most were from Höfn, some from a camping trip to the countryside that could have been anywhere in Iceland, and others from a sledging slope that was equally hard to locate. Two pictures showed their mother lying in a hospital bed with a newborn Kolbeinn in her arms. The only thing these moments from their past had in common was that their sister was nowhere to be seen. It was peculiar.

The only explanation the brothers could come up with was that the little daughter's sudden death had affected their parents so badly that they couldn't bear to be reminded of her. As neither Hjörvar nor Kolbeinn was blessed with much emotional insight, this was a shot in the dark. Kolbeinn's wife had pointed to another possible explanation, which was that the photos had been removed for the funeral or the obituary in the papers. After all, even young children were given lengthy obituaries in Iceland. Their parents could have taken them out when trying to choose suitable pictures for the death notice, then forgotten to put them back afterwards. Presumably they would have been distracted by the terrible tragedy.

This seemed a sensible suggestion to Hjörvar, although the brothers had had no luck in tracking down an obituary or death notice. Kolbeinn, on the other hand, believed that another, more interesting motive might have been behind the decision to remove the photos, such as the idea that their sister had been deformed and their parents hadn't wanted to see any pictures of her. That was obviously ludicrous, Hjörvar thought. In that case, why would they have taken photos of her in the first place? Another, equally ridiculous suggestion was that their mother had had Salvör with another man and that their father couldn't bear to be reminded that she'd betrayed him. Kolbeinn had got carried away, spinning a tale about a dark-skinned lover, which would have made it impossible to disguise the child's paternity.

Hjörvar didn't believe for a minute that their sister had had a different father. Their mother had been such a cold type that he couldn't imagine her taking a lover. He based this belief on the fact that she hadn't jumped into anyone else's arms after the divorce or indeed in later life. Not as far as he knew, at any rate.

It was probably doomed to remain a mystery. Hjörvar could live with that. It was Kolbeinn who couldn't. He was curious to know more. What had happened? Why had their parents never mentioned their sister to them? For a while, Kolbeinn had even managed to spark Hjörvar's interest, enough to motivate him to apply for the job at Stokksnes when it came up. He'd thought that once he was out there he could ask around, as some of their parents' contemporaries must still live in the area. They couldn't all be suffering from the same patchy memory as his uncle. Hjörvar could also drop by the police station and ask if he could see the files on their sister's accident.

So far he hadn't got round to any of this. It was Kolbeinn who had gathered the small amount of information they had so far. The only thing Hjörvar had done off his own bat was to go through two small boxes of his father's stuff. These were bits and bobs that Hjörvar had hung on to when they cleared out the house, just so he didn't walk away empty-handed. The boxes turned out to contain nothing of any interest, apart from a black film cartridge that he discovered in a small case containing some cufflinks and his father's watch. Of course, Hjörvar had then failed to take the film to the developer's, and the cartridge had travelled out east with the rest of his belongings. Unfortunately, there was no film developer's in Höfn any more, not that the locals lost any sleep over the fact. In the end, Hjörvar had posted the cartridge to Kolbeinn in Reykjavík, for him to deal with – and he hadn't taken it to the developer's yet either. Hjörvar suspected that his brother was deliberately waiting until he himself got round to some of the enquiries he had promised to make in Höfn. And now, belatedly, he was on the case.

At first, he had simply been too tired after work, from the strain of getting used to his new job. But as time went on, he had succumbed to the usual reluctance that built up inside him every time he postponed something. The longer he delayed taking action, the more insurmountable the task appeared to him. This was one of the reasons why his wife had left him. He dragged his feet about far too many things, according to her. Including telling her that maybe they should split up. Instead, he had waited for her to come to the same conclusion and act on it. Which she had.

The memory of the conversation in which she had told him she was leaving had an unusually galvanising effect on him. He would go to the police station today, right now, and on the way he would keep an eye out for elderly people who were the right sort of age to have known his parents. He was still stinging from his ex-wife's litany of his faults. It was up to him to prove her wrong. No one else could do it for him.

Who knows? Maybe the knowledge would help lift his mood. It wasn't inconceivable that the strange events at the radar station were connected somehow to the mystery that had been weighing on him all these months. Perhaps it was the nagging sense of guilt at his own apathy that had caused him to hear and see things that weren't there. Perhaps a bad conscience on top of all his other worries and failures had been more than he could take.

Hjörvar put on his coat, scarf and hat, and left the house. He drew a sharp breath outside and set off with a new sense of purpose, certain that from now on everything would be better. He'd stop feeling jumpy the whole time at work. Start sleeping properly again.

And stop jerking awake in the night with his dead sister's name ringing in his ears.

Chapter 15

Jóhanna's legs and back were killing her. The drugs she had taken that morning seemed to have had little effect. They did dull the agony a bit but only enough to prevent her from wincing at every step. There were stronger tablets available, strong enough to confuse the messages to her brain and trick her body into believing that nothing was wrong, but Jóhanna didn't like the drowsiness they caused. Or the risk that the magic solution they provided would become a permanent fixture in her life. That wasn't an option. It was better to grit her teeth and console herself with the thought that the pain would eventually pass. The more gently she took it, the sooner that would happen.

This wasn't a good moment to take it easy, though. And there rarely was a good moment; life couldn't be put on hold just because she happened to be suffering from her old injuries. Life wouldn't even slow down. She could have stayed home, called in sick. Her boss would have been understanding, as up to now she had taken very little sick leave. But she wanted to do her job, and she preferred not to have to explain what was wrong with her, let alone lie that she had a fever or a bug of some kind – particularly because her co-worker in quality control was fairly new and didn't know the ropes yet. The woman who used to do the job had met the captain of a fishing boat and moved to the East Fjords to join him, and Jóhanna missed her a lot. She'd been a really hard worker, and, as she came from Poland, she had been able to talk to the Polish workers on the factory floor without having to resort to broken English like the rest of them. With her there, Jóhanna's days at work had been much less hectic and more manageable. It had also been handy that the woman had an evening job in one of the town's hotel bars and used to give Jóhanna a good discount on the rare occasions that she and Geiri dropped in for a drink.

Still, in spite of the pain and having too much to do, Jóhanna was glad she had made herself go into work. It was a relief to have something to distract her from dwelling on the horrible events in the highlands. The job of quality control in one of Höfn's biggest fish factories was about as drama-free as it got. Her working day revolved around form filling, random sampling, testing, assessment and the preparation of documents relating to production. All these tasks were clearly defined, leaving no room for speculation or doubt. Everything was done according to established procedures and no allowances were made. The total absence of anything strange or inexplicable was a blessed relief.

Jóhanna had almost succeeded in pushing the discovery of the bodies to the back of her mind, though occasionally images of the dead would surface without warning. She blamed the ubiquitous white of her surroundings for that. White overalls, white aprons, white tiles, white boots, white polystyrene and white walls. White fish fillets. Everywhere she looked it was the same. The all-pervasive colour had never really struck her before, but now it was a constant reminder of snow, ice and frozen corpses.

It wasn't the only reminder, either: her co-workers talked of little else during their coffee breaks. It was no secret that Jóhanna was in the local rescue team, and the other employees kept throwing her sideways glances. Luckily, though, she wasn't the only team member to work there, so she wasn't alone in having to field questions from curious colleagues.

Almost the only people to show no interest were the foreign workers. As far as they were concerned, it was just another tragic accident caused by the brutal Icelandic climate. It wasn't the first and wouldn't be the last time that the winter here proved fatal. Their attitude wasn't a sign of callous indifference so much as realism and a degree of detachment. Their roots did not lie as deep in Icelandic society. Unlike the locals, they weren't worried that those who died might be people they knew. As the victims' names hadn't been released yet, there was a good deal of suspense among the Icelanders about who they might be. But, despite being repeatedly asked, neither Jóhanna nor the other rescue volunteers employed at the factory gave anything away. It wasn't their place to report the fate of the walkers. Iceland was such a small country that there was a risk they might be revealing the death of someone who had a close relative in the canteen.

It was getting on for midday and Jóhanna realised she wouldn't get any peace if she ate lunch at work. Since her boss often sat at the same table, she decided the most tactful thing to do would be to make herself scarce. The thought of having to rebuff his questions with the reply that she wasn't at liberty to reveal any information was not one she relished. And, even if he didn't ask, she'd rather not have to listen to her fellow diners discussing the search. Besides, the pain had affected her appetite.

She changed out of her white coat and wellies into a down jacket and snow boots. After leaving the factory, she went to stand on the docks for a while. The fresh salty air was so invigorating that she could feel the ache receding a little, though that probably had more to do with the change of footwear than the oxygen. Her orthopaedic surgeon wouldn't have approved of her white work wellies.

She gazed out over the mirror-like surface of the sea at the islands dotting the lagoon. There were said to be seventy-two of them in all but Jóhanna had never managed to count them. Her eyes lingered on the island where Geiri had told her the locals used to hunt seals in the old days. The hunters used to lay hooks, then drive the frightened animals onto them. She looked away, wishing Geiri hadn't told her this story. Such depressing thoughts were the last thing she needed at the moment; her mood was low enough already.

Her decision to avoid the canteen had gone no further than that. She hadn't given any thought to where she should eat instead. Should she go home, to a restaurant, or look in on Geiri at the police station? The town was so small that these options were all within walking distance. Of course, the most sensible thing would be to nip home. It would be cheaper than eating at a restaurant and she wouldn't be disturbing Geiri at work.

But she didn't want to go home to the empty house, even though the daylight was as bright as it got at this time of year. She didn't know why this was, as up to now she had always felt comfortable in their home, had seen it as a place where she could relax and recharge her batteries.

Yet she had woken up that morning with the same sense of disquiet as when she had gone to bed. It wasn't until she'd left the house for work that the feeling had lifted a little. Perhaps the neighbours' small daughter had helped with that, as she had come outside with her mother at the same time. The child had waved to Jóhanna and she had waved back. The mother had smiled and said good morning, and then the three of them had walked along the pavement together until their paths diverged. The little girl chattered away nonstop, telling Jóhanna that it was her first day at nursery school and she was going to make friends. Lots of friends. She didn't have any yet. Only Morri, and he didn't count.

The family were recent arrivals in Höfn, which explained the child's loneliness. Jóhanna told her she wouldn't have any problems: everyone would want to be friends with her, she could be sure of that. The girl's mother gave Jóhanna another friendly smile and they said goodbye. Jóhanna watched the two figures walking hand in hand down the road, and the sight of the child's brightly coloured little backpack with the picture of the pony on it brought a smile to her face. How wonderful it must be to have no worries, only a positive goal: to make loads of friends.

After they had vanished from sight, Jóhanna's despondent mood returned. She wasn't usually prone to depression, not since she had reconciled herself to the fact that her days as a sporting champion were over. The only possible explanation for her low spirits was that she was still in shock after finding the bodies. But then, she reminded herself, it would be unnatural if she wasn't.

All the rescue volunteers had been offered trauma counselling but no one had accepted it. Jóhanna belatedly regretted this decision, and guessed that she wasn't the only one, but there was little point requesting it now. She would just have to deal with it. The memory would fade over time and everything would return to normal.

She started walking, not in the direction of the town centre with its restaurants and cafés, but towards the police station. It wasn't a conscious decision so much as her body obeying a deep need to be near Geiri. Just like last night. She couldn't care less about the limited food on offer at the station – a dry crispbread would do. Geiri wouldn't have to share the food tray that was delivered to the officers on duty. The helpings weren't generous enough, anyway.

She could have sworn she was limping less with every step that brought her closer to her husband. By the time she entered the station, her gait was almost normal again. The young uniformed officer on reception greeted her with a smile – although he had only just started working there, he recognised Jóhanna and admitted her straight away. 'He's in a meeting but happy to be disturbed, he made that clear. Any distraction welcome.' The young man winked.

Before Jóhanna could object and say it wasn't important, he had marched over to the meeting-room door and knocked. After announcing Jóhanna, he stepped aside and Geiri appeared in the doorway. Behind him, she could see a large map of the search area on the overhead projector screen, with the hut, the place where the tents had been found and the location of the bodies marked on it. Between the markers, lines had been drawn that she assumed were possible walking routes.

To Jóhanna's relief, Geiri's face brightened on seeing her. Her momentary anxiety was ridiculous, she realised: there was nothing in their relationship to suggest she should doubt his affection in any way. Her apprehension was entirely due to the low self-esteem she had been wrestling with ever since she'd finished rehabilitation. She worried constantly about holding him back.

'Lucky you didn't arrive ten minutes later. We're about to take a short break and we were planning to go out for a bite to eat. You'll come too, won't you?'

Jóhanna hadn't been expecting this. She'd hoped for a chance to sit quietly with Geiri in his office while he was finishing his lunch tray. 'Who's going?' she asked.

'The DI from Selfoss, the woman from forensics in Reykjavík, a member of the Coast Guard and two guys seconded from other rescue teams. You know one of them: Thórir.'

'Why are they still here?' Jóhanna asked, adding quickly: 'I thought the rescue team's job was finished.'

'Oh, they offered to stay on and help out, and their expertise is certainly coming in handy. We've got a huge number of photos and a ton of data about the area, which we're trying to piece together so we can work out the sequence of events. None of us at the station are particularly clued up about that kind of thing, so we're lucky to have their assistance. One's an expert, the other's got a lot of experience under his belt.'

So Thórir had managed to talk his way into the innermost circle after all. Jóhanna nodded, trying to think of an excuse not to go to lunch with them. Something other than the real reason, which was that she stank of fish. She herself had long ago become inured to the smell and so had Geiri, but these people were unlikely to be familiar with the inside of a fish factory. She was too late, though. Geiri clapped his hands and said he'd fetch the others.

The group filed out, their faces betraying how badly they needed a break from the stuffy room. Geiri introduced her, and she nodded and smiled. She recognised all of them from the weekend, but she could tell from their expressions that most of them weren't aware they had seen her before. It wasn't surprising: in the highlands, they'd had clearly defined roles to perform, whereas she had merely been part of an amorphous group, just one more local in an orange snowsuit whose face was barely visible. Only those who had interviewed her and Thórir after the discovery of the first body were likely to remember her, but they had returned to Reykjavík or to Selfoss, in the case of Geiri's boss.

Everyone broke into smiles as they emerged into the beautiful winter weather. Some of them seized the chance to fill their lungs with fresh air as Jóhanna had on the docks earlier. She shrank back a little in case they wrinkled their noses when they smelt the fish on her clothes. The group included the kind of suits who looked as if they were happiest behind a desk and didn't like to get their shoes dirty.

As they set off on foot, Jóhanna was careful to stay downwind of them. They were practically retracing her steps of a few minutes earlier, but instead of continuing right out to the fish factory, they turned off towards a restaurant that offered a suitably varied menu for such a large group.

The only woman among them, the forensics technician from Reykjavík, seemed to go out of her way to avoid sitting next to Jóhanna when they were shown to the table. At first Jóhanna put this down to the stench, but then she realised that the woman probably didn't want to get stuck having a stilted exchange with her while the men, relieved that someone else was taking care of the guest, discussed more interesting topics.

Thórir took the seat beside her. Leaning over, he said in a low voice: 'I couldn't help noticing that your limp seems worse. Yesterday too. Is that because of the accident you told me about?'

Jóhanna coughed. 'No. I've just pulled a muscle.'

Thórir smiled in embarrassment. 'Oh. Sorry. Only, I wanted to tell you that I've got a friend who's an orthopaedic specialist. You know, in case you happened to be on the lookout for one. He's the best in his field.'

'Thanks, but I'm not.' Jóhanna tried to come across as grateful, though she resented his interference. It was kindly meant, that was obvious, but inappropriate. Forcing her features into a smile, she handed him a menu. 'I recommend the lobster.' Then she turned to the other rescue team guy who was sitting opposite her. 'How are you getting on? Are things becoming any clearer?'

'Not much, to be perfectly honest. There's no way of telling what they thought they were doing out there. Let's hope the guys handling the investigation in Reykjavík are making better progress. The couples must have mentioned the purpose of their trip to someone before they set out.'

Thórir put down the menu without looking at it. Perhaps he was planning to go with Jóhanna's recommendation. 'You never know, the post-mortem might reveal something too. Perhaps they were on drugs. Or they'd been drinking. Intoxicants and wintry conditions are a lethal combination.'

Thórir went on to tell them about a mountain-rescue operation he had been involved in while studying in Britain. A group of young people had got lost in the Scottish Highlands after wandering away from their car, all of them off their heads. Three of the four had been found dead, but the last had never been found and was assumed to have succumbed to the elements.

The case was almost identical to the one they were confronted with now. But in Jóhanna's view, the similarity ended there. The people they had been searching for had shown no signs of being addicts. She had sneaked a look at their social media pages and thought they seemed to have their lives sorted, if you discounted the unnaturally large number of pictures in which wineglasses could be glimpsed. On the other hand, the glasses had been deliberately included in the frame, which suggested they weren't trying to hide an alcohol problem, though of course that didn't rule out the possibility that they drank too much.

They could have been dabbling in drugs, too, but the picture their social media accounts provided gave no hint that they were users. Far from it. They were preoccupied with whatever was trending, and came across as well-meaning liberals, with both feet firmly planted on the ground. They had posted considered opinions about global warming, animal welfare, energy exchange, public transport, a new constitution and the refugee question. These weren't agitated outbursts, just comments that showed they cared.

When Thórir finally shut up, Jóhanna asked a question: 'Were there any bottles of booze or evidence of drugs in their luggage?'

Overhearing the question, Geiri replied: 'A hip flask of brandy in one of the tents and several empty wine bottles in the hut. But they were dusty and had been used as candlesticks, so they probably didn't belong to the group. There was no trace of drug use.'

One flask of brandy among four – that would hardly be enough to make the group lose their grip on reality.

That left the question Jóhanna was beginning to think they would never be able to answer: what the hell had they thought they were doing out there?

A waiter appeared at the end of the table to take their orders and they all focused their attention on the menu. Thórir went for a burger, not the lobster.

Chapter 16

Lónsöræfi, the previous week

When the men finally got back, Dröfn broke down in tears. She didn't sob noisily, just wept in silence. The tears rolling down her cheeks were a combination of relief and hysteria; relief that Tjörvi had returned safe and sound, hysteria at what she and Agnes had gone through while the men had been away.

The creaking footsteps and the muttering had gone quiet shortly before they heard the men returning. Dröfn had no idea how long they had been sitting there, rigid with terror, listening to the sounds repeatedly moving closer, then further away. It felt as if it had lasted for hours but she was sure that if she checked her phone, she would discover it had only been a few minutes. Perhaps that was one way to slow down time and live forever, she thought wryly – to exist in a permanent state of terror.

Well, in that case she had absolutely no desire for longevity and would be entirely reconciled to death when the moment came.

'What, no coffee or anything?' Bjólfur pushed his head through the tent flap next to Tjörvi, who had got there first. Their cheeks were a fiery red from the cold and they both looked exhausted. The moment he saw the women's faces, Bjólfur stopped short, just as Tjörvi had a moment before. 'What's wrong?'

While Agnes was stammering out a brief description of what had happened, Dröfn sat there listening, her whole body tense, the tears still pouring down her face. She felt Agnes was totally failing to capture the true horror of their experience. If anything, the account made them sound like idiots; like children trying to persuade their parents there was a monster under the bed. When Agnes had finished, Tjörvi and Bjólfur exchanged glances, then withdrew their heads. A few seconds later, they reappeared, looking no less bemused than when they had been listening to Agnes's story.

'There are no tracks outside.' Bjólfur's face suddenly split into a grin. 'Are you two pulling our legs?'

Tjörvi didn't smile. His gaze locked with Dröfn's. He knew she wasn't capable of faking tears. 'It must have been an animal,' he said. 'We came across a dead sheep on the way. I expect it was a sheep or a fox. Or that reindeer we saw earlier.'

Dröfn shook her head mutely. It hadn't been a sheep, or the reindeer or a fox. Or any other wild animal. But after Agnes's clumsy attempt to describe it, she knew the men wouldn't believe them. And if Agnes couldn't convince them, it was pointless for Dröfn even to try.

They heard Haukur asking outside the tent: 'Is everything OK?'

'No,' Agnes answered curtly.

Tjörvi opened his mouth to say something, then shut it again. He withdrew his head and they heard him talking to Haukur, every word audible through the thin canvas. Although Tjörvi did his best to repeat their story without dismissing the women's fears, the gist of the message was clear: they had freaked out. Affected by spending hours alone in that hostile environment, they had misinterpreted the noises around them. Haukur's only comment was that it wouldn't be the first time that had happened. It wasn't clear whether he was referring to them or to someone else, but Dröfn had the feeling it was the latter, since Haukur barely knew them.

Dröfn was a little cheered by this. She realised that her flow of tears had finally dried up. Perhaps Tjörvi was right: they *had* freaked out, as many people would in the circumstances, according to Haukur. Maybe it was a common occurrence. The best thing she could do right now was to persuade herself that all her spooky experiences in the tent and hut could be put down to the alien surroundings and the strangeness of their situation. It was a bit of a stretch to accept it but, if she could, she knew she'd feel better. Temporarily, at least.

Dröfn turned to Agnes, removing a hand from her sleeping bag and reaching out to her. Agnes looked away from Bjólfur and met her eye. 'I'm satisfied with that explanation, Agnes. I'll feel happier if it's true.'

Agnes heaved a deep breath, thought for a moment, then nodded. 'Yes, that must be what happened.' She nodded again and repeated, as if trying to convince herself: 'That must be what happened.'

'Of course it is.' Bjólfur couldn't hide his relief that the drama appeared to be over. He had never been good at handling this kind of situation and had a tendency to sulk if people didn't immediately snap out of whatever was bothering them. 'I mean, obviously.'

The two women got out of their sleeping bags and went to join the men outside, careful not to meet each other's eye. They knew that if they did they would be able to read in the other's gaze that neither of them really believed they had been imagining it. But that discussion could wait until they were safely back in town, far away from this place.

It was pitch black outside, as Dröfn and Agnes hadn't failed to notice inside the tent. When the last of the feeble daylight had abandoned them, Dröfn had rooted around for her torch and switched it on, not caring a damn about preserving the batteries. She couldn't think of a better time to use them. Feeble though the torch beam was, anything was better than sitting there blindly in the dark, their ears straining for eerie noises outside.

Dröfn brought the torch with her as she emerged from the tent behind Agnes. The heft of the metal cylinder in her hand gave her a sense of security. The torch was a link to civilisation and to the safe world they had left behind; a weak and tenuous link, but a link nonetheless. She reminded herself that they would soon be back in town, surrounded by the roar of traffic and the other comfortingly mundane sounds that accompanied real people going about their lives.

The first thing she did once she was standing under the overcast night sky was to illuminate the snow around the tent. Bjólfur hadn't been telling the truth when he'd claimed that there were no tracks. In fact, the snow had been trampled down, but whether by them alone it was impossible to say. They had all been milling around out there earlier and of course they had walked round the tents when they were pitching them.

Shining the torch beam further away, Dröfn spotted the tracks they had made when they'd arrived at this spot, and the men's trail leading off in the direction of the glacier. There were no other visible footprints. Dröfn tried to remember where she and Agnes had originally heard the creaking coming from; she had a feeling it was behind the tents. But when she walked round and examined the snow there, there was nothing to see. The frozen white crust was as unspoilt there as when they had first arrived.

Dröfn returned to the others. 'When are we leaving?'

Tjörvi and Bjólfur both looked at Haukur. It was obvious from his expression that he realised he would have to answer. When he opened his mouth, though, it wasn't to say what Dröfn longed to hear. If she had her way, she would head home right now. If not in the darkness, then at first light tomorrow.

'We didn't find the measuring instrument.' Haukur kept his eyes lowered as he spoke. He was wearing a head-torch that turned the snow blue at his feet. 'I'm going back tomorrow to have another stab at finding it. I don't understand what's happened.'

No one spoke for a moment, then Agnes weighed in. Since Haukur barely knew her, her exaggeratedly level tone probably misled him at first into believing that she was taking the news well. The other three knew better: Agnes was as angry as she ever got. 'You mean it's gone missing? How can a piece of measuring equipment go missing? In the middle of nowhere? It's not like someone can have been passing and taken a fancy to it, surely? Or did you by any chance forget to check its exact location before leaving home?'

By the end of this speech, Haukur was left in no doubt that Agnes was furious. He grew defensive. 'I know exactly where it's supposed to be. It wasn't there. Perhaps it's been moved without anyone bothering to inform me. I'm not the only person taking readings from it. But if so, it can't have been moved far. If I head out first thing in the morning, I'll find it and take the necessary readings, then we can go home straight after that. Tomorrow – I promise.'

Tomorrow. There was no way Dröfn could face another day sitting, waiting in that tent. Absolutely no way. Either they started back now or at the crack of dawn tomorrow. 'How about *we* leave now and you follow tomorrow?' she suggested in an acid tone.

Haukur shrugged as if he didn't care either way, but Tjörvi objected. 'We're not going anywhere now. That would be crazy. Let's have supper, get some sleep, then work out the rest tomorrow morning. We're all tired, thirsty and hungry.'

By 'we', Tjörvi really meant 'you'. And Dröfn knew that 'you' referred to her and Agnes. The choice of pronoun was deliberate: if everyone was lumped together, his suggestion was more likely to be accepted. It wasn't the first time he had resorted to this trick. She suspected that he had learnt the technique on one of the endless management courses they sent him on at work.

Bjólfur backed him up. 'It's the only sensible solution. Let's eat, then get some kip. We'll decide what to do in the morning. Don't forget that us three have been walking all day. While you two have been putting your feet up in the tent, we've been slogging through the snow for hours on a wild-goose chase. I for one am completely knackered.' He glanced at Tjörvi for support and got it.

'Same here. I couldn't walk another step. And I'm too hungry to waste any more time discussing it.'

So that was that. There was no point arguing. From Tjörvi and Bjólfur's haggard faces and the way their teeth were chattering, they weren't exaggerating their exhaustion. Haukur was shivering too, not as badly but enough to make the light from his head-torch quiver. He looked so despondent that Dröfn couldn't help feeling a little sorry for him. He'd come all this way, with them in tow, only to fail in the purpose of his mission.

His clothes were probably partly responsible for her pity. Next to the four of them, he looked like a pauper. They were all kitted out in brand-new, brightly coloured trekking gear, made from the latest hi-tech manmade fabrics, and their hiking boots were waterproof and warmly lined – with a breathable coating and ankle support, according to the salesman. All their garments and footwear featured the word 'pro' somewhere in their names, though clearly this wasn't sufficient to turn them into the professional outdoors types they were so desperate to pass as.

Haukur, in contrast, wore scuffed leather hiking boots, a down jacket and trousers that might have been warm but looked shabby. Under his jacket he wore a woollen jumper – a traditional Icelandic *lopapeysa*. Yet, amazingly, he didn't seem to be suffering from the cold as badly as they were. If Dröfn had been asked to picture a geologist with a passionate interest in glaciers, she would have come up with an image exactly like the man standing in front of her. Presumably experts like him didn't dress like that by chance – or from lack of cash. His outfit seemed to do the job of keeping him warm far better than their fancy kit.

Following their discussion, Agnes and Dröfn made supper while the men got into their sleeping bags and tried to alleviate their shivering. The women lit the primus, placing it as close to the tents as they dared without risking sending the whole camp up in smoke. Since the meal was basic, all it involved was standing there, watching the aluminium pan as they waited for the water to boil. Everything else was ready: they'd taken the sandwiches from their rucksacks and emptied the sachets of dried soup into plastic bowls. The only drink served with supper would be water.

A dismal meal perfectly suited to their dismal situation.

The tents were too small for everyone to crowd inside one. At a pinch, four could have fitted, but not five. Tempting though it was to leave Haukur out, none of them could bring themselves to suggest it. In the end they split into couples, with Agnes and Bjólfur eating in their tent, Dröfn and Tjörvi in theirs, and Haukur alone in his. Apart from

Agnes calling '*Bon appétit!*' at the beginning of the meal, they ate in silence. All Dröfn could hear was Tjörvi's quiet slurping and lip-smacking beside her.

Once they had finished, they all congregated outside the tents again for a chat. But in contrast to the previous evening's seamless flow of stories, no one seemed to have anything to say. None of them wanted to discuss their plans for the following day, so that subject was off the table. The same went for the mysterious noises by the tents.

Since all other subjects appeared trivial in comparison, conversation soon faltered. By the time everyone had contributed one comment on any given topic, they found they had exhausted it. Then they would cast around for something else to talk about, only for that conversation to fall flat as well. Before long, they were all back in their tents, preparing to get into their sleeping bags.

The tents were pitched in a row. The echo of Agnes and Bjólfur's low voices reached Dröfn and Tjörvi, but understandably nothing could be heard from Haukur, who had no one to talk to. Agnes was saying a lot more than Bjólfur, in an emphatic tone. If Dröfn had wanted to, she could have eavesdropped on their conversation, but she made an effort not to listen. Besides, she didn't need to: she knew Agnes was talking about what had happened earlier. And no doubt about their plans for tomorrow as well.

Dröfn needed to have the same conversation with Tjörvi. There were things she had to get straight before they went to sleep or there was a danger that when she woke up, rested, she would have lost some of her resolve. They were lying huddled together in their sleeping bags. She had her back to Tjörvi and his mouth was resting against the nape of her neck, his warm breath on her skin making it seem almost cosy. Almost. 'Let's get one thing clear, Tjörvi. You're not going with Haukur tomorrow to find that measuring thingy.'

He murmured something, on the verge of dropping off. She shook him. 'Tjörvi! You've got to promise me you won't go with him tomorrow in search of that bloody equipment. I'm serious.'

'Mm, right. We'll see.'

We'll see almost invariably means the opposite of what the person asking wants to hear. 'Don't say "we'll see", Tjörvi. You're not going. End of.'

The murmuring against the back of her neck was unintelligible. Tjörvi had answered in his sleep.

Dröfn shut her eyes tightly, grateful that she could still hear Agnes and Bjólfur's voices. The rising and falling murmur was comforting and familiar, reassuring her that they were still there.

But the feeling of reassurance didn't last. Their voices grew quieter and quieter until they ceased. Dröfn couldn't hear a thing now. Even Tjörvi, who usually snored, might as well have stopped breathing altogether.

There was nothing to muffle or drown out the noises outside if the creaking footsteps started up again. Dröfn resorted to clamping her mittened hands over her ears. The only way to get a wink of sleep would be if she couldn't hear a thing.

It worked. Dröfn drifted off into a deep slumber.

So she didn't hear the creaking when it began again outside.

Chapter 17

Hjörvar ended up alone at Stokksnes, although as the helicopter wasn't due back, there was no need for a double shift. He'd come in expecting them both to be on duty, only to learn that Erlingur had been given the afternoon off, just as he himself had been given the morning. At the time, the news hadn't disturbed Hjörvar; he'd been in too good a mood. A half-day at work would be easy. Some of their duties still remained to be done, as they were designed to be performed by two members of staff. But when Hjörvar arrived and Erlingur handed over a list of the remaining jobs, he saw that Erlingur had dealt with the most demanding tasks himself, leaving only the lighter ones.

They were both too reserved by nature to comment on the fact. After running his eyes down the list, Hjörvar merely nodded.

'Call me if anything comes up.' Erlingur paused by the front door. 'Whatever it is.'

Hjörvar realised what the other man was implying. 'Nothing will come up,' he said firmly.

'No. Right.' Erlingur took hold of the door handle but didn't turn it. He seemed to have something on his mind, but in the end he just said goodbye.

Hjörvar watched Erlingur walking to his car, then closed the front door. The familiar hum of machinery inside the building sounded louder now that he was alone. Well, apart from Puss, of course. The cat was sitting on the spiral staircase leading up to the radome, watching Hjörvar with half-closed eyes. He didn't look too impressed by what the men had said. Silly though it was to think that way, Hjörvar suspected that Puss was particularly dubious about his airy assertion that nothing would come up. A conclusion probably based on the fact that now he was alone, he was beginning to have doubts himself.

On the drive to Stokksnes he had been feeling positively chipper, pleased with his morning's work. Earlier that day he had gone to the police station and extracted a promise that his sister's case would be looked into. Admittedly, he hadn't been given the information on the spot or told explicitly that it would be provided, only that the matter would be looked into. When, exactly, he hadn't been told, but then the police were rushed off their feet because of the unfolding tragedy in Lónsöræfi. Hjörvar was assured they wouldn't forget, though; they'd get round to it in due course and give him a call.

If and when they got in touch wasn't really the point. The point was that he could now ring his brother and tell him that he had actually pulled his finger out and done something. Kolbeinn was the one who wanted to get to the bottom of the family mystery. In Hjörvar's view, the most likely explanation was that their sister's story had been so tragic that their parents had just wanted to bury the memory. It's what people used to do in those days. Besides, sometimes it was better not to go raking up the past. Hjörvar knew that from personal experience.

Maybe he had more in common with his parents than he'd realised. Cold, distant and taciturn – just like his mother. He could tick those three boxes with a good conscience. But not the character traits he associated with his father: harsh, stern, angry. Luckily, none of those applied to him, which was just as well, because Hjörvar's relationship with his children was strained enough already without these sins being added to

Ágústa's litany of complaints or Njördur's excuses for repeatedly screwing up his life.

Hjörvar called to Puss, hoping the cat would keep him company while he went about his tasks. Puss's presence was reassuring. For one thing, it allowed Hjörvar to attribute any unexpected noises behind him to the cat. But Puss wasn't interested. He looked away, showing no sign of budging from the metal stairs.

Hjörvar shrugged, trying not to mind. As he made a start on the remaining jobs, he patted his pocket to make sure his phone was there in case anyone called. He hadn't bumped into any senior citizens on his walk to the police station that morning, so he had decided to pay a visit to the old people's home. It had made sense to exploit his sudden burst of enthusiasm since it wasn't often he had the energy to do anything more than drag himself through the day. Fortunately, the home was only a ten-minute walk from the police station. If it had been any further, his enthusiasm might well have waned. Certainly, the closer he got, the more it had ebbed away.

The reason for this was obvious: the route from the police station to the old people's home had taken him along a path with a view of his childhood home. The moment he saw the house, he had been assailed by the same waves of negativity that had afflicted him when he and Kolbeinn had gone to clear the place out after their father's death. And it hadn't been just him: that first evening, when the brothers were eating supper at the hotel, Kolbeinn had mentioned the feeling too.

In spite of this, Hjörvar had managed to shake off his momentary gloom, recover his good mood, and continue on his way.

At the old people's home he had encountered a carer who had listened patiently to his story. Once he had stammered it out, privately cursing himself for not having rehearsed it before-hand, the woman told him it wasn't a good moment. Not because they were too busy, but because it was coffee time, and after that they were going to take advantage of the good weather to get a bit of fresh air. So it was up to him: either he could come back later with the names of the residents he wanted to talk to, or she could ask around on his behalf and see if anyone remembered his parents. There was no question of him being allowed to waltz around the place asking questions on his own, though.

He opted to let the carer speak to the residents for him. She promised to phone him but didn't commit to a time or tell him when he could visit in person.

At least this had the advantage of giving him more time to work out what questions to ask whichever senior citizen was unfortunate enough to remember his family. Hjörvar was under no illusions; he knew he wouldn't be the most entertaining visitor in the world. If the talk touched on anything other than his errand, he would find it hard to keep up his end of the conversation. That's what it had been like on his visits to his mother at her nursing home. By the end, conversations with her had been like talking to a stranger. He had struggled to find anything to say.

The best way to distract himself from this nonsense was to focus on the tasks Erlingur had left for him. There would be no room for brooding if his mind was taken up with his job.

Slowly and methodically he worked his way down the list. One task after another was completed without a single strange incident. The entryphone remained silent and the screen showing the antenna behaved as it should. The interference was perfectly in sync with the moment when the transmitter passed the camera. If there had been an electrical fault, it must have corrected itself. On the other hand, maybe it had been a figment of his imagination, his bad conscience causing him to see things that weren't there. He didn't know if such a thing was possible, but it dawned on him now that he had been racked with guilt before he finally made the effort to do what his brother had asked.

Whatever the truth of this theory, he seemed to have put all that behind him now. When he passed the canteen window and noticed that the daylight was fading, he felt no twinge of apprehension. He didn't avert his eyes from the shore where the rocks and the blowhole were for fear of glimpsing the silhouette of his dead predecessor.

Clearly, things were looking up.

The phone rang in his pocket. Hjörvar didn't recognise the number that flashed up on screen. It could be the police, the old people's home or his daughter, hoping that he would pick up if she rang from an unfamiliar number.

It turned out to be the carer from the old people's home on the other end, who told him that one of their residents used to live next door to his parents. He was eager to talk to Hjörvar and, if it was convenient, she could pass the phone to him now. Hjörvar was wrong-footed by this speedy response. He had been expecting things to move slowly at the home. Agreeing to talk to the man, he sat down at the table in the canteen, ready to ask the few questions he had prepared so far.

The old man introduced himself as Sigvaldi. He also volunteered the information that his late wife had been called Björk. Neither name rang any bells but Hjörvar covered up the fact by hastily introducing himself.

'Are you the elder or the younger brother?' The frail voice reminded Hjörvar of the old men he had exchanged the odd word with on his visits to his mother at her nursing home. Time had softened its timbre.

'I'm the elder.'

'Right you are.' The man cleared his throat before continuing. 'Then you owe me a living-room window. Your brother owes my wife a rosebush. But since she's no longer with us, I expect that debt is now void.' Apparently sensing Hjörvar's confusion, Sigvaldi went on: 'Only joking. You brothers were a couple of tearaways, though. Before the fence was put up between our gardens, your younger brother kicked a football into a small rosebush Björk had been nurturing. Then he finished it off completely when he came over to fetch his ball. Your achievement was to fancy yourself a baseball player and smash a ball right into our living room. But don't worry – I blame the bloody US Army. And your dad paid for the damage at the time, so I'm only teasing you.' The old man paused for breath. 'You and your brother are both doing well, I hope?'

'Oh, yes. Fine.' Hjörvar debated whether to mention that he had moved back to Höfn but thought better of it. The fact was irrelevant and risked diverting the conversation into a discussion of his workplace, the history of the radar station and so on. Besides, it didn't sound as if Sigvaldi was any great fan of the army or, by extension, of NATO. Better not get him started on that.

'I was sorry to hear about your mother. I saw the obituary. My condolences to you both.' Before Hjörvar could thank him, Sigvaldi continued: 'To be honest, I wasn't expecting to hear from you or your brother. It got me curious. Were you wanting to know more about your parents' life here? Interest in the past and your family tree increases as you get older, as I expect you've noticed. But sometimes it's too late and there's no one left to ask.'

'Yes. You're right there.' There was no point explaining that his mother had been in no fit state to communicate properly for several years before she died. Of course, it didn't really matter now, but he knew she wouldn't have liked him discussing her illness with just anybody. She had gone to great lengths to hang on to her dignity and hide the evidence of her dementia for as long as she could. But her attempts had become increasingly desperate until it had become clear to anyone who cared to see which way things were heading. 'That's exactly why I wanted to talk to you. I didn't get a chance to ask my mother before she died. Or my dad back in the day.'

'Let's just hope I can dust off my memories. Luckily for you, I'm much better at remembering the distant past than what happened yesterday.' Sigvaldi chuckled. 'Well, you know what I mean.'

'I wanted to ask you about my sister, Salvör. My parents didn't really talk about her much.' Hjörvar had decided not to let on that they'd kept her existence secret. It would sound better to pretend they had just been reluctant to speak about her.

The old man on the other end was silent, for long enough for Hjörvar to glance at his phone screen to check if the connection had been lost. 'Salvör. Yes. It's a long time since I heard her name.'

'But you do remember her?'

'Yes, I do. Sadly, it tends to be the good memories that go and the bad ones that stick. And that business with your sister was awfully sad.' Sigvaldi paused again but only for an instant. 'Life was always a struggle for her. But to die like that. It was terrible. Your parents were never the same again. Well, I lost touch with your mother after the divorce, of course, because she moved away with you boys, but I know your father never got over it. I hope she did.'

Hjörvar didn't know what to say. As far back as he could remember, his mother had been the same: depressed and cold. But his memories didn't reach back to the years before his sister's accident, so for all he knew she could have been a cheerful, happy woman in those days. 'You say Salvör didn't have it easy. Can I ask in what way?'

'Well, you know she wasn't quite right?' Sigvaldi's tone suggested he thought Hjörvar might be messing with him. Leading him into a trap, perhaps.

'Sadly, my brother and I know very little about Salvör.' Hjörvar felt he had no alternative but to tell the truth. If he didn't, he might never find out what his sister's problem had been. He was clumsy in his dealings with people and incapable of using cunning to elicit the information he wanted. 'Could you maybe tell me what was wrong with her?'

'Oh. You'll have to ask somebody else, I'm afraid. As far as I know, she never got any kind of diagnosis. She just seemed to find life so difficult. She was always misbehaving, always screaming and crying. She couldn't talk and she was backward in other ways too. I felt sorry for the poor little mite. For your mother too. She was left on her own a lot to cope with the three of you while your dad was away at sea, and it was awful. You could hear the poor little girl screaming from next door. The noise was deafening when your mother put her outside to play in the garden. But like I say, I don't know what was up with her. Only that something was very wrong. My wife and I had four children, some of them more difficult than others. But your sister was on a different scale. There was something very wrong there,' he repeated.

Sigvaldi's mention of screaming dislodged something in Hjörvar's memory. An ear-splitting screech that cut through flesh and bone. But nothing else. No picture emerged from the dark corners of his mind. Not of a helpless little girl. Or his exhausted mother.

'Maybe the health service can give me some information. Salvör must have been examined and diagnosed by a doctor.'

Although he said this, Hjörvar didn't expect the girl's records to be released. The data protection laws would prevent that. He asked himself as well if he really needed to know. After all, what would be the point? It wasn't as though he could do anything to help his sister now. 'I'll have to see.'

'Yes, you do that. But if I were you, I wouldn't get your hopes up. Your parents tried to kid themselves that she would grow out of it. As far as I know, she was never taken to Reykjavík for a proper examination. They were in denial. Especially your mother. She'd been longing for a girl, after having two boys. She was radiant with happiness when she first brought her home. But that didn't last long. She soon had shadows under her eyes and looked worn out, poor thing. If the little girl had lived, they'd have gone looking for help in the end. That was obvious.'

Hjörvar had rehearsed various ways of asking a stranger about Salvör's death without giving away the fact that he and his brother were totally in the dark. He had come to the conclusion that it was best to be honest. To tell the simple truth. 'My parents never told us how she died. You couldn't help us out there, could you? All I know is that it was an accident. Then I won't take up any more of your time.'

'You're not taking up my time, believe me.' Sigvaldi cleared his throat again and coughed. 'Sorry. I've been a bit under the weather lately. Anyhow. An accident, you say. I suppose I can understand why they didn't talk about it. It's not something any parent would want to share with their kids.'

Hjörvar didn't like to point out that their parents had had many years to tell him and Kolbeinn about it after they'd reached adulthood. He supposed it had been difficult to find the right – or at least a suitable – moment. And before their parents knew it, perhaps the moment had passed. The more time went by, the harder it must have been to broach the subject. If they had, the brothers would only have demanded to know why they hadn't been told earlier.

'Your sister drowned. Your father was on shore leave and he took her down to the beach to give your mother a rest. Salvör ran off and the rest is history. Absolutely terrible.'

This struck Hjörvar as a bit odd. His father had always been fit and healthy, right up to the end. Surely he could easily have caught up with a small child? Hjörvar would have thought so. If Salvör ran off, his father would have overtaken her immediately. It takes more than a few seconds for someone to drown, and the beaches around Höfn were mostly gently shelving. At low tide it was possible to walk out to some of the islands in the lagoon to collect eiderdown, so it was hard to see how a child could have drowned there if they were accompanied by an adult. Unless Salvör had fallen off the jetty where the water was deep and been sucked underneath it, so her father couldn't find her. Or it had happened after dark when the sea was black. 'Where did it happen?' he asked.

'Oh. It was out at Stokksnes. Right by the radar station. On the rocks just below it. She fell down the blowhole.'

Hjörvar turned with inexorable slowness to the window. He stared out to where he knew the rocks – and the blowhole – were hidden by the gloom.

He was sitting only about a hundred metres from the hole that had swallowed up his sister.

Somewhere in the building, Puss began to yowl.

Chapter 18

Jóhanna's jaw ached from smiling. This never happened when her smile was natural, but throughout the meal her face had been set in a polite rictus to hide her boredom. She still felt wrung out from all the physical and emotional strain of the previous weekend and would gladly have flopped on the sofa after work and watched TV, rather than hosting dinner for a bunch of people she didn't know.

She did it anyway, for Geiri's sake. It wasn't often that he asked her a favour like this. All the same, she had hesitated a little too long when he rang. Instead of instantly replying, 'No problem,' she had been silent, racking her brain for a plausible excuse. Geiri had felt compelled to explain that the investigators were fed up with eating at restaurants, then admitted that he had already invited them. Jóhanna wasn't angry; she just wished she'd said yes straight away.

After asking what time to expect them, she had said goodbye and hurried out to the supermarket to buy something suitable for supper. They had a freezer full of fish and lobster, but she didn't want to serve seafood. At lunch, no one from the group had ordered it. The men had gone for burgers or other meat, the woman for chicken salad. No surprises there.

Jóhanna returned from the supermarket with twice as much meat and salad as they needed. She and Geiri would be eating leftovers for the rest of the week. But she didn't have time to worry about that. She had to roll up her sleeves and get cooking. Lay the table, grab a quick shower and change. By the time the guests turned up, she'd had everything ready for ten whole minutes, yet she found herself pretending she'd flung the meal together at a moment's notice. God knows why.

Everyone was wearing the same clothes as they had been at lunchtime and looked distinctly crumpled and dishevelled after their long meeting. As a result, Jóhanna felt as if the tables had been turned: she was more smartly dressed than them now, in contrast to earlier that day when she had felt as scruffy as a restaurant washer-upper in their company. It gave her the confidence to contribute more to the conversation and feel like a proper part of the group. Yet despite getting to know some of the others as well as the two rescue-team members she'd sat with at lunchtime, she hadn't really enjoyed herself. Smart clothes were no cure for tiredness.

There were only four of them left now. She and Geiri, the detective from Selfoss and Thórir. The rest had excused themselves after dinner and gone back to their hotel. Jóhanna had struggled to hide her disappointment when the two men didn't go with them. They had even accepted Jóhanna's offer of coffee, which she feared would give them a second wind. As if that wasn't bad enough, they hadn't said no Geiri's brandy either. That had really put a strain on her smile.

'Is it any clearer when you'll be able to go home?' Jóhanna took a sip of coffee. She'd poured a cup for herself as well, reckoning that she was so tired even caffeine wouldn't be able to keep her awake once she finally got to bed.

The detective from Selfoss said he thought it would be tomorrow or the next day, depending on when they got the results of the post-mortems, and various other factors.

Thórir said he expected the same. Tomorrow. Or the next day. He could stay as long as he was needed.

It occurred to Jóhanna that she didn't know what Thórir did for a living. She had heard all about his training but not what he used it for, apart from his volunteer work for the rescue team. His employer must have an unusually strong sense of social responsibility. True, workplaces were generally understanding when rescue volunteers had to answer callouts, but the operation was finished and most bosses would raise their eyebrows if an employee of theirs said he was planning to stay on indefinitely to help with the investigation. 'By the way, Thórir, what do you do for a living?' The moment she'd said it, she wished she hadn't. What if he was unemployed?

Fortunately, it turned out he wasn't. 'I'm a consultant. On safety issues. There isn't a big market for that here in Iceland, so most of my jobs are abroad. Mainly in Norway, in connection with the oil industry. Drilling platforms – you know.' Thórir sipped his brandy. 'I'm currently between assignments, so I'm not in any hurry. Not until next week when I'm due to go abroad again.'

Perhaps that explained his odd fascination with Jóhanna's accident. If he worked in health and safety, he was bound to be interested in that sort of thing. She wished she'd asked before. If she had, she might have liked him better.

Geiri interrupted with a question about oil rigs. While Thórir was reeling off anecdotes, Jóhanna fought back a yawn. As she had absolutely zero interest in the subject, it worked on her like a sleeping pill. Not that Thórir's stories were lacking in drama: he seemed to have had more than his fair share of adventures and witnessed some pretty harrowing incidents.

She got up to make more coffee. Once out of sight in the kitchen, she gave in to the urge for a huge yawn. In the middle of it, she became aware of an icy touch, of freezing fingers slipping under her jumper and stealing up the small of her back. She let out a yelp of shock. She couldn't stand it when Geiri surprised her like that, and was just about to whip round and give him a piece of her mind when she heard his voice calling from the sitting room: 'Is everything OK?'

Adrenaline coursing through her veins, she turned, expecting to find Thórir or the detective behind her. Much as she dreaded having to lose her temper with one of her husband's guests, she wasn't putting up with behaviour like that. MeToo hadn't passed her by.

There was nobody there.

Jóhanna's heart began to pound as she stood there, staring around the empty kitchen. Geiri called out again. 'Is everything OK, Jóhanna?'

She drew a deep, shaky breath. 'Yes, sure. I just banged into something.' As she listened to the coffee trickling into the jug, she tried to recover her composure. There must be some perfectly natural explanation for what she had felt. She was tired out. She'd overdone it. The damaged nerves in her back must be sending garbled messages to her brain. She'd had odd sensations before.

As she concentrated on getting her breathing under control, Jóhanna felt her ragged heartbeat beginning to slow and the heat in her hands and feet ebbing away. She had imagined it. That's all it was. But in spite of her conviction, she couldn't help recalling the kind of confused neural messages she had suffered from previously. She'd itched in places supposedly left numb by nerve damage. She'd experienced heat or cold around the scars, out of all sync with the actual conditions. But never before had she felt anything like fingertips touching her skin. Tiny fingers.

Jóhanna wrapped her arms around herself, feeling suddenly chilled. It was warm in the house but a shudder ran through her just as it had when she had watched the bodies being dug out of the snow. As if cold air were being blown down her neck.

The trickle of coffee had slowed to a drip. Jóhanna took the jug and hurried back into the sitting room. A few minutes ago she had been grateful for the excuse to leave her guests; now she couldn't wait to rejoin them. To sit there listening to a string of dramatic yet tedious tales about oil rigs was better than standing in the kitchen, panicking that she wasn't alone.

The coffee did the rounds, followed by the brandy. Again, Jóhanna declined a glass, though a shot of brandy might have calmed her jangling nerves. She was no fan of spirits and worried that it might simply add fuel to her imagination.

She managed to sit through the tales being swapped by Thórir and the detective from Selfoss, behaving as if nothing was wrong. The men's conversation was turning into a contest, each of them vying to top the other's stories. If things carried on like this, Jóhanna's money would be on Thórir to win, as it went without saying that there was more drama to be netted from the North Sea than from policing the quiet little town of Selfoss.

Geiri caught her eye and winked conspiratorially. She winked back, rolling her eyes to say that enough was enough. She hadn't decided whether to tell him about her creepy experience in the kitchen but thought she'd probably keep it to herself. He had quite enough on his plate without having to worry about her as well.

The doorbell rang just as she thought Geiri was about to fake a yawn to convey the message that it was late. They didn't often have guests for supper on a weekday. It was getting on for eleven and most of the town's inhabitants would be relaxing at home by now. Even at weekends there wasn't much entertaining done in Höfn.

Jóhanna suppressed a sigh, fearing that the other guests had returned and that supper was going to develop into a party. Geiri went to the door and came back with a man from the rescue team who Jóhanna knew quite well. One of the old hands – Andrés. An earnest type, who was extremely unlikely to have just been passing, seen the light on and decided to drop in for a coffee – and brandy.

'Sorry to disturb you. I didn't realise you had guests.' Andrés shifted from foot to foot in the sitting-room doorway, then turned to Geiri. 'I tried calling but I couldn't get through. So when I saw the lights on . . .'

'Don't worry. You're not disturbing us. I just forgot to turn my phone back on after the meeting.' Geiri offered the man a seat. To Jóhanna's relief, he declined. He didn't plan to stay long. With any luck, she thought, the other two guests would be drawn into leaving with him when he went.

'There's something I need to show you.' Andrés held up a laptop he had been carrying under his arm. 'Something that can't really wait. I wouldn't have intruded otherwise.'

The detective from Selfoss looked up. 'Is it connected to the search?'

Andrés nodded. He went to the dining table and moved a dirty plate to make room for the laptop. Jóhanna immediately felt a stab of guilt for not having cleared the table. Really, she had to do something about these constant feelings of inadequacy. It wasn't her job to make sure that everything was always perfect.

In any case, none of the men even seemed to notice that the dishes were still on the table. All their attention was focused on the computer. The two guests got up from the sofa and came over to stand beside Geiri and Andrés. Jóhanna joined them.

'I was going over the drone footage. You can't always spot everything at the time, what with the small screen and the tricky light conditions, so I always try to go over the footage again once the operation's finished. I didn't get round to it until this evening, but then I wasn't really expecting anything to crop up. It rarely pays off, but this time I reckon it just might.' Andrés clicked on a video in a folder containing a large number of similar files. He pressed play towards the end of the clip, then stood back, folding his arms across his chest and waiting. 'You'll see it in a moment. At the sixteen-minute point. The rest is just snow. No point wasting time on that.'

They all stared, jostling against each other to see the small screen. Jóhanna forgot about the cold fingers creeping up her spine, all her attention fixed on the featureless white expanse captured by the drone on its journey over the snowy wastes.

'Here it comes.' Andrés leant forwards again, ready to pause the video. The others watched more intently. Andrés stopped the playback. 'There it is.' He pointed to the lower right-hand corner of the screen. 'There.'

They all bent closer, inevitably bumping heads, but no one winced or drew back. Geiri was the first to voice what the others were thinking. 'Hang on, what are we looking at? As far as I can see it's a rock. Rhyolite, maybe. There's enough of that around there.'

'It's not a rock. You'll see if I zoom in.' Andrés blew up the image as far as the resolution would allow. 'Really, it's sheer luck that I noticed it and took a closer look. But then I was working on a very big screen.'

He fell silent and they all peered at the grainy image of what looked like a hand protruding from the snow.

'There's another body there.' Andrés released the breath he had been holding. 'There were five of them.'

Geiri straightened up. The carefree manner that he had gradually been relaxing into during the evening had vanished. He had snapped back into the professional police officer mode that Jóhanna had seen when she'd dropped by the station earlier: straight-backed, his jaw clenched, his eyes narrowed. 'Where was this taken? Near the tents?'

'No.' Andrés called up a map of the area and pointed. 'Here. More or less. Closer to the hut. But not as close as the first body we found. A bit less than five hundred metres away, as the crow flies. Further on foot.' He closed the map. 'Clearly, we'll have to go back to the scene.'

The mood was transformed. Neither Thórir nor the detective returned to their competitive storytelling. Instead, they checked the time and finally made a move to leave, after arranging to meet first thing the following morning. The detective from Selfoss volunteered to contact their boss, while Geiri was going to talk to the Coast Guard. Andrés said he'd get in touch with the rescue team and put them on alert. All this had to happen before they went to bed tonight, to give those taking part in the mission to retrieve the body sufficient time to organise themselves in the morning. If they were lucky, the search could be launched by midday.

After the men had left, Geiri picked up his phone to ring the duty officer at the Coast Guard HQ, hoping he would be able to put him in touch with someone who had the power to author-ise another search. The moment the phone was answered, Geiri stepped aside. He was in the habit of doing this when making a phone call, as if he found it uncomfortable talking in front of an audience, even when the only other person present was his wife. This didn't bother Jóhanna, as much of what he discussed was police business that had nothing to do with her. But he did it even if the call was to his brother or a tradesman or to order a pizza.

Jóhanna stacked the dishes on the dining table but didn't take them through to the kitchen. That could wait until morning. She couldn't face going back in there now, but her fear would have vanished by the time she woke up tomorrow morning.

As soon as Geiri had finished his phone calls, they went up to bed. Geiri was muttering to himself that it had been a mistake to serve wine and brandy. Neither he nor their guests could afford to be hung-over tomorrow. When Jóhanna pointed out that no one could have foreseen that the search would be relaunched, he fell silent. Not long afterwards his breathing grew regular and heavy. He was asleep.

Although Jóhanna hadn't touched any booze, the coffee had been a mistake. It had taken the edge off the tiredness that had almost overwhelmed her earlier in the evening. She kept tossing and turning, searching in vain for a comfortable position. Then she realised that she needed to go for a pee. Pushing back the duvet, she went into their little en-suite toilet.

As she sat there, emptying her bladder, she heard Geiri mumbling, his words too thick with sleep to make out – if he was actually saying anything. Usually when he talked in his sleep, his words were too incoherent to make sense. They lacked a beginning or an end and sometimes merged together into new words that could mean just about anything.

When she came back into the bedroom, however, she heard what he was saying. Frowning, she noticed that Geiri was batting a hand behind him as he protested. He could no longer be sound asleep, because his words made perfect sense: 'Don't do that. Your hands are freezing. Stop it.'

But there was nobody lying in the bed beside him.

Chapter 19

Lónsöræfi, the previous week

They had woken up, one after the other, to darkness, cold and perfect stillness. Individual noises no longer had to compete for attention with the loud roaring of the wind, and the sounds of movements and scrabbling about in the two neighbouring tents carried over to Dröfn and Tjörvi. They could hear Agnes and Bjólfur daring each other to get out of their sleeping bags. This had a demotivating effect on Dröfn and Tjörvi, who were struggling with the same reluctance to emerge into the cold. Clouds of steam accompanied every breath they took and Dröfn didn't think she had any feeling left in the tip of her nose. The temptation to duck down into her cosy cocoon was irresistible. Given a choice, she would happily have hibernated until spring. But from what Haukur had told them about the weather in these parts, she would have to wait until midsummer before the wintry conditions relented.

There was no point waiting for the sun to come up either. Its rays wouldn't have much impact on the temperature. It would only be like moving from a deep freeze to the freezer compartment of a fridge. Dröfn gritted her teeth and began to pull on her clothes. She was in a hurry and the tent was cramped, so Tjörvi could hardly have failed to notice, but he pretended to be oblivious.

'We've got to get up.' Dröfn shook her husband. His mumbled complaint was muffled by the sleeping bag. Tucking his head inside like that was a big mistake. If your head was cold, it was easier to get up; less of a shock to the system.

The tent smelt of sandwiches. Tjörvi had collected up the wrappers from yesterday's supper and put them in here with them, forgetting to tie a knot in the rubbish bag. Before they came on this trip, he had gone on about how great it was waking up in a tent: the first thing you noticed in the morning was the scent of unspoilt nature. Not last night's prawn sandwiches.

Dröfn poked him again. 'Bjólfur will be out of his tent before you. Haukur too. Do you want me to tell them you're too chicken to get up?'

That did it. Tjörvi reared up out of his bag. One of the strangest bonds of friendship between him and Bjólfur was their competitiveness. They could compete over literally anything. In addition to all the conventional stuff like computer games, cycling races or weight-lifting, their rivalry extended to the ridiculous, like who could quote lines from films more accurately or who had the better phone. And then there was the time Dröfn had caught them each closing one eye and vying as to who could see further. She didn't know if they'd ever settled that particular question.

The remarkable thing about this constant rivalry was that it never caused them to fall out. The loser was simply convinced that he would win next time. And so it went on. They entered into every contest as if a world championship was at stake. This expedition was typical. Everything they did was motivated by the same spirit of competition. If Haukur proposed a ten-hour trek in a blizzard, they would both nod and agree, equally determined not to be the first to quit. In fact, quitting was out of the question. It had never happened.

Their stubbornness wasn't so much of a problem in the city, but out here the consequences could be deadly. Dröfn suddenly regretted having appealed to Tjörvi's competitive nature to force him out of bed. It wasn't the first time she had resorted to that trick, but this was neither the time nor the place to encourage a spirit of recklessness.

'Could you hand me my jumper?' Tjörvi jerked his chin at the pile of clothes he had taken off the night before.

Dröfn grabbed it and was about to pass it over when she snatched back her hand. 'You're not going with Haukur to look for the instrument. Promise me. We've got to persuade him to turn back. Straight away.'

The answer she received was ambiguous. One of those 'let's see' answers. Tjörvi's teeth were chattering so loudly that she saw no point in attempting to bargain with him. She merely repeated: 'You're not going with him.'

Tjörvi said nothing, just carried on getting dressed. She noticed that he was avoiding her eye. A bad sign.

He was searching for his socks when Dröfn scrambled out of the tent, saying she was going to heat up water for coffee. The truth was, she had another motive. As well as boiling water on the primus and spooning instant coffee into plastic cups, she was planning to get Agnes on her side. Together they'd have more chance of stopping their husbands from deserting them than they would on their own. She didn't doubt for a minute that Agnes was as eager to head for home as she was.

It was still dark outside, but not as impenetrably black as it had been in the middle of the night. It held out a promise that soon everything would take a turn for the better. The sun was on its way. Dröfn tilted back her head to look up at the sky. A star twinkled faintly in a rare gap, and in one place the thick mass of cloud was backlit by a pale glow, suggesting that the moon was hiding there. But nowhere could she see any sign that the cloud cover was dispersing enough for the moon to break through. Of course not, she thought sourly. Knowing their luck, the sky would only become more overcast as the morning wore on, so that even the sun wouldn't be able to make any impression on it.

All the more reason to hit the trail as soon as possible.

The bumping and rustling coming from Haukur's tent suggested he would emerge shortly, so Dröfn hurried behind the tents for a pee. She had to overcome a sense of reluctance as sleep had done nothing to cure her jumpiness. Keeping her back to the tent, she faced the empty wastes as she squatted to relieve herself. That way she would be able to see if there was anything sinister lurking out there. Even so, the darkness had her so spooked that she reckoned she had set a personal record for speed and was still fumbling with trembling fingers to do up her trousers as she dashed round to the front of the tent.

Glad to have got that over with, Dröfn went to the door of the neighbouring tent and asked if Agnes would help her make coffee. It was absurd to pretend she couldn't manage on her own, but too bad. Agnes responded by pulling up the zip and forcing her way out, hampered by her bulky orange coat.

'What's with this cold? Can't it just bugger off somewhere else?' Agnes stamped her feet and hugged herself. 'Can you remember – is there a sauna at the hotel? If there is, I swear I'm going to bed down in there when we get back. I'll take the duvet and pillow from my room and sleep in the bloody oven.'

'There was no sauna.' Instantly regretting having ruined Agnes's fantasy, Dröfn added quickly: 'But there were radiators. Hot showers and proper beds.' She crouched by the primus. 'Speaking of the hotel, I vote we head back straight away. Are you with me?'

'What, and abandon all this luxury? What do you think? Duh . . . yes. No-brainer.' Agnes scooped snow into the saucepan. 'But you have a go at talking to Bjólfur, will you? He's determined to find that measuring equipment even if it means walking right round the bloody ice cap.'

Dröfn was hit by a paralysing sense of hopelessness. There would be no talking Bjólfur round, and, if he refused to go back now, Tjörvi could be relied on to take his side. Her best bet would be to persuade Haukur to give up on finding the instrument – the entire purpose of his mission. She knew she was unlikely to succeed and anyway it would be unfair, but she would have to try. Dröfn took the pan from Agnes, put it on the primus, then stood up and crunched over to Haukur's tent. Now was her chance, while Tjörvi and Bjólfur were still bracing themselves to step out into the icy air. Of course they would hear the whole conversation, but protests from inside their tents would be less effective than if they were standing beside her.

'Haukur.'

The sound of bumbling inside the tent ceased and there was the sharp tearing noise of a zip. Haukur's head poked out and said good morning, then the rest of him followed. He was already fully dressed apart from his gloves, which he pulled on as he stood up.

'We were just wondering if it wouldn't be best to head straight home.' Dröfn made it sound like a group decision, rather than just hers and Agnes's. 'A blizzard could blow up any minute and you wouldn't be able to find the measuring instrument anyway.'

Although it was hard to make out Haukur's features in the gloom, Dröfn thought he looked undecided, and felt a faint spark of hope. But this was immediately snuffed out by Bjólfur, who shouted from his tent: 'You must be fucking kidding!' They were going to find that bloody meter. This was followed almost at once by a declaration of support from Tjörvi in the other tent.

Haukur seemed embarrassed. He shifted from one foot to the other in front of her. 'I'm afraid I've got to go on looking, but there's nothing stopping you lot from leaving. You can wait for me at the hut. You'll be more comfortable there, with the heating on.'

To his credit, he didn't remind her of all the times he had tried to discourage them from gatecrashing his expedition. He had been straight with them about the hardship involved but they had refused to take the hint, and now here they were, planning to ruin things for him. No one would have blamed him if he had lost his temper, but he didn't.

'What's going on?' Bjólfur was halfway out of his tent but already in full gear. 'We'll find that instrument. Don't talk crap. We didn't come all this way just to crawl back with our tails between our legs.'

At that moment, Tjörvi put in an appearance too, as warmly bundled up as Agnes. He had his hood up, his hat pulled down over his forehead and a scarf covering the lower part of his face. Only his blue eyes, his nose and a bit of moustache were visible. When he spoke, his voice sounded as muffled as it had from halfway down his sleeping bag, but there was no mistaking what he was saying. 'I'm with Bjólfur. We're not throwing in the towel now.' Again, Dröfn noticed that he was avoiding her eye.

Haukur had donned his head-torch and switched it on. The dazzling glare made it impossible to see from his expression how he felt about these declarations of support from Tjörvi and Bjólfur. It was easy to guess, though: he must be hugely relieved. Yet Dröfn had him down as the conciliatory type, who couldn't be entirely happy unless everyone around him was in harmony. And she was right: Haukur started trying to come up with a compromise. 'How about I go by myself, hunt for the instrument until around midday, but make sure I'm back here in time for us to make it to the hut before sundown?'

This well-meaning suggestion suffered the fate of most compromises – it left both sides dissatisfied. The women wanted to leave immediately but weren't going to get their way; Bjólfur and Tjörvi wanted to go on looking until they found the equipment, even if it meant spending another night at the camp. Now, though, the search would be limited to a few hours.

Dröfn quickly answered Haukur: 'Fine. Agreed. You three have until midday. But we're coming too.' She would rather spend hours trekking in icy conditions than wait inside the tent again.

Agnes backed her up, adding that she was ready whenever; she just needed to pop behind the tent for a wee. The sooner they started, the sooner they could go home.

She hadn't been out of sight for more than a few seconds when she let out a scream. It was the kind of sound that Dröfn had wanted to make when her mind had conjured up the image of the frozen woman standing outside the hut. Or when she had been cowering next to Agnes, listening to that ominous creaking, like footsteps in the snow. She had bitten it back for fear that once she started screaming, she wouldn't be able to stop.

Agnes yelled: 'There's something out there!' This was followed by another shriek, then the noise of her blundering about, accompanied by what sounded like a sharp yelp of pain.

Bjólfur set off at a run with the others on his heels. Behind the tent, Agnes was sitting in the snow, her trousers round her ankles, clutching her right wrist. From the way she was facing, it was clear that, like Dröfn earlier, she'd wanted to keep her back to the safety of the tents. Haukur averted his eyes when he saw her state of undress, and the beam from his head-torch slanted away, plunging the scene into the same darkness as before he had emerged from his tent.

When Bjólfur bent down to Agnes, she let go of her wrist and gestured with her left hand into the blackness beyond. 'There, look! There's something moving.'

They all turned to look where she was pointing. At first, they couldn't make out a thing, then Bjólfur recoiled in shock. 'Whoa!'

Dröfn grabbed Tjörvi's arm, pinching it hard in her fright. Reluctant as she was to see what was out there, she couldn't tear her gaze away. She felt Tjörvi flinch, then spotted a movement, but couldn't see what had caused it or how far away it was. It was impossible to judge distances accurately in the dark.

'What the fuck is that?' Bjólfur broke the silence. 'Did you see it?'

Before the others could answer, the movement became clearer. A deeper shadow appeared to be drawing closer. Dröfn, concentrating hard on breathing, realised her entire body had seized up with fear. Her mind was screaming at her to get the tents between her and whatever it was, but her limbs refused to obey. Not that it mattered. If that thing meant them harm, their tents wouldn't provide any protection.

Tjörvi was the first to work out what it was. Perhaps, after all, his eyesight was better than Bjólfur's. 'Christ. It's a reindeer.'

Once he had pointed this out, it was obvious. Dröfn's eyes had adjusted too.

Dimly she made out the shape of a big head and antlers. It must be the cow they had spotted the day before. Dröfn felt a slight pang. Tjörvi had told her that reindeer were timid and avoided people. The fact the cow seemed to be following them must be a sign that she was starving; desperate enough to risk approaching them in the hope of finding food.

'Well, that explains the footsteps you heard.' Bjólfur raised an imaginary rifle to his shoulder. Closing one eye, he pretended to shoot. 'Bang! Bang!'

No one laughed, least of all Agnes. 'Stop messing about and help me,' she snapped.

Bjólfur dropped his arms. He hauled Agnes to her feet and helped her do up her trousers. She whimpered, clutching her wrist and saying she had landed on it awkwardly when she'd fallen over backwards.

Dröfn was just relieved that Agnes hadn't injured her ankle. Having to carry her back to the car would be the final straw. But she didn't like the way Agnes continued to whimper as Bjólfur helped her past them and back round to the front of the tent.

They had to get out of here.

The reindeer came warily closer and, although she halted a little way off, she was close enough for Dröfn to make out the gleam of her large, dark eyes. 'Can't we give her the crusts from our sandwiches?' Dröfn asked Tjörvi.

'No. She just needs to find a spot where she can scratch through the snow down to some grass. There must be one. The drifts aren't as deep everywhere as they are here.'

In spite of his assurance, Dröfn felt almost like a traitor as they followed Agnes and Bjólfur, leaving the cow alone in the dark. When Dröfn glanced round, she thought the animal was watching them walk away. The desire to get as far from this miserable place as possible surged through her more strongly than ever.

They drank their coffee largely in silence, handing around a bag of nuts and raisins. Dröfn, unable to eat, passed it on. This could have been a bad mistake, but as they started making preparations to leave in search of Haukur's elusive instrument, it became clear that Agnes wasn't up to it. With a horrible inevitability, since she couldn't be expected to wait alone, it was decided that Dröfn should stay behind with her. Dröfn didn't protest. Seeing the poor reindeer had gone a long way towards dispelling her fear that there was something evil on the prowl out there.

True, there hadn't been any reindeer tracks near the tent, but the noises could have been coming from further away than they'd realised. Dröfn firmly quashed the thought that reindeer didn't ask to be let in, however desperate they were.

For whatever reason – because the women were feeling reassured, or the animal had wandered off in pursuit of the men – they didn't hear any unexplained noises while they were waiting. Yet Dröfn felt a deepening disquiet. Far from improving, Agnes's wrist was looking blue and swollen. Dröfn didn't like to say anything but she was afraid the injury was serious, that Agnes had broken it or torn a ligament. Both, maybe. Certainly, the painkillers she made her swallow didn't seem to have helped much.

The pills did at least send Agnes to sleep. Dröfn couldn't bring herself to poke her and selfishly force her to stay awake to keep her company. It was a great relief when Agnes finally stirred, but the pain in her wrist turned out to be no better.

By then it was well past noon.

The plan that the men would return by midday at the latest seemed to have fallen by the wayside. Dröfn was livid, although she concealed the fact from Agnes.

But she did nothing to hide her anger when they weren't back by afternoon coffee time. Or her trepidation when the light failed, it was getting on for suppertime and there was still no sign of them.

The hours dragged by.

As if things weren't bad enough, it started to snow.

Then a whistling, followed a moment later by a rippling of the canvas, heralded the arrival of the wind.

The two women assured each other that the weather wasn't so bad and that it would be all right. Their husbands and Haukur had simply been delayed. But in the end they had to admit to themselves that conditions outside were serious. Things weren't looking good.

By nine o'clock, Dröfn began to be afraid she was having a heart attack. Her chest felt tight and she couldn't speak. Oh God, what was she supposed to do? Should she go out and look for them? Maybe she should have done that hours ago. Where had the men gone after they'd passed out of sight? Their tracks would have been filled in by the fresh snow long ago and the most likely outcome, if she went in search of them now, was that she would die of exposure too.

The word *too* lingered in her mind, as unwelcome as a hair on a dinner plate. Up to now, she had carefully avoided letting herself think about exactly what might have happened to Tjörvi, Bjólfur and Haukur. She had killed any speculation as soon as her mind strayed close to the logical conclusion. But that one little 'too' betrayed what her subconscious was saying: that the three men must have succumbed to the cold.

Suddenly, without warning, Dröfn opened her mouth and screamed, a loud, raw cry tearing from her throat. After the first shocked glance, Agnes didn't react, just carried on her endless rocking back and forth, cradling her right arm.

Now that she had given in to the urge, Dröfn couldn't stop. She screamed until she was hoarse and her vocal cords were aching. The hush that followed was eerie, as if the remnants of the scream were still hanging in the air. As if the noise had stained it, like a red sock in white laundry.

Why couldn't they rewind? Start again?

The harsh noise of the zip tore into the strange hush.

Dröfn and Agnes both stared, paralysed with fear, at the door of the tent. When Tjörvi's head appeared, Dröfn's relief was like a punch to the stomach. He looked terrible, his face a fiery red, his lips white and flaking, his beard caked with ice – but he was alive.

Dröfn released her breath and, despite her worn-out vocal cords, emitted another croaking cry. She started gabbling incoherently as Tjörvi forced his way into the tent.

A moment later, realisation struck her dumb.

Agnes was staring at the open flap, her eyes wide with hope and dread. After a moment, she turned slowly to look at Tjörvi and their eyes briefly met. He was the first to drop his gaze. As he started struggling with frozen hands to close the zip again, the tears began to trickle down Agnes's cheeks.

There was nobody else outside. Tjörvi was alone.

Chapter 20

The cemetery gate creaked as Hjörvar undid the latch and pushed it open. If he came back here, he would bring a can of oil to lubricate the hinges. But he wasn't expecting to come back. He wasn't the type to bother with maintaining family graves. To his shame, he hadn't once visited his mother's grave since her funeral. Or his father's, for that matter, but in that case he'd had an excuse – until recently, at least. His father was buried in the churchyard here in Höfn and Hjörvar would have had a six-hour drive from Reykjavík to visit his grave – twelve if you included the return journey. Few people would go to all that effort just to lay a bunch of flowers on a pile of earth, even if they'd had a closer relationship with the deceased than Hjörvar had had with his father.

He closed the gate behind him. There was a superb view across the Hornafjördur lagoon to the south coast and the towering ice cap, which looked impossibly beautiful in the soft winter light. Few cemeteries could boast such picturesque surroundings, though of course they were lost on those who rested here. Only the living could appreciate the splendour, so Hjörvar might as well make the most of the opportunity. He had the morning off again, this time because they were expecting the helicopter back in connection with the continuing search effort in Lónsöræfi. Erlingur had taken the early shift, he would take the late one. The arrangement was settling into a habit.

When Hjörvar had had his fill of the view, he turned to survey the cemetery itself, trying to reconcile what he saw with the plan he had studied online. It wasn't easy, as the plan had shown neatly demarcated graves, tightly arranged in rows, whereas the reality was rather more haphazard, perhaps due to the graves that were harder to spot because they weren't marked by a cross or a conventional headstone.

The cemetery homepage had not only provided a map, it also had a search function for looking up where people were buried. Among them, his sister Salvör. His father's grave was there as well, but Hjörvar could find that without help; it was only two years since he and Kolbeinn had stood there watching his coffin being lowered into the ground. There had been no other mourners. The funeral had been a private affair, not through any expressed wish of their father's but because the brothers had thought it would be less embarrassing that way. Their father had died without a friend in the world.

During the funeral, they had paid no attention to the neighbouring graves. Not unreasonably, Hjörvar had assumed that Salvör's plot would be next to their father's, so he had been surprised to discover, when searching online, that they were some distance apart. He didn't know much about burial customs but he did know that it was possible to reserve a plot for close relatives beside the person who died first. Clearly, this hadn't been done in Salvör's case.

He guessed it hadn't even occurred to his parents at the time. They must have been far too distraught to think about the future. After all, no one should have to bury their child.

Hjörvar decided to begin by visiting his father's grave. He might as well, since he wasn't planning to come back here and he had plenty of time on his hands. He found it without much difficulty. The grave was conspicuous, though not for a good reason: despite the covering of snow, it was obvious that his father's plot was neglected in comparison to the neighbouring ones.

The cross that he and his brother had chosen with a minimum of thought was leaning at an angle, and the snow lay perfectly smooth on the grave, betraying the lack of any flowers or vases or other loving offerings of the type that adorned the surrounding plots. In his father's case there were no attentive relatives or good friends to remedy this lack. He had chosen to live like a recluse, shunning almost all contact with other people.

It was depressing to think that this description could equally well apply to Hjörvar. He could look forward to the same kind of lonely, unvisited grave. As he stood there, contemplating the dreary plot, it occurred to him that he would actually prefer it that way. He didn't like to think of his children standing there, shedding tears of regret. The strained relationship wasn't their fault. He hoped they would realise that once he'd gone. Mind you, judging by Ágústa's resentful anger and Njördur's nonsense, there was no danger of their forgetting.

Not if he went by his feelings towards his own father. He felt no urge to blame himself for the estrangement as he stood here. No, it was clear to him that his father had stood in the way of their ever having a closer relationship. He had applied for captain's jobs on the kind of ships that would require him to be away on long tours of duty. After the divorce, even when he was on shore leave, he'd done everything he could to avoid inviting his sons to stay with him in Höfn, his excuses becoming ever more far-fetched. In time, the boys had grown used to the fact that the only contact they had with their father was gifts of money for birthdays and Christmas. Apart from that, they were barely aware of his existence. Nor did they know of any relatives on his side of the family.

A neglectful father and a distant mother. Hjörvar had to admit that he owed Kolbeinn a debt of gratitude for forcing him to look into their sister's death. After all this time he had finally got an explanation of sorts for why their parents had shown them so little love. Although he would never be able to prove his theory, their old neighbour's story was illuminating. It seemed their parents had simply never recovered from the loss of their daughter.

Hjörvar bent down and straightened the crooked cross. There was nothing on the white plaque but his father's name and dates. When the brothers had purchased the cross two years ago, the person who took their order had asked whether they wanted to add something, like '*In loving memory*' or '*R.I.P.*', but they had said no. It would be hard to find another funeral that had cost as little, but that had nothing to do with tight finances or the desire to save money. Their father had left behind a considerable legacy. He'd hardly spent anything over the years, as you might expect of someone who was constantly away at sea, so it wouldn't have dented the brothers' inheritance much if they'd splashed out on an extravagant funeral. But that would have seemed almost like a mockery in the circumstances.

The settlement of their father's estate had been dealt with as quietly as his funeral. His assets and shares were sold and the profit split between the brothers, along with the balance in his bank accounts, which was substantial. Hjörvar had paid off the mortgage on his flat in Reykjavík, then given his children the rest. But however generous the amounts involved, he knew they would never be enough to placate his daughter or get his son back on the rails. Money was an inadequate plaster when it came to patching up emotional wounds.

The grave looked a little better once the cross had been straightened. But any sense of grief failed to materialise, or indeed any kind of sentimental response to his father's death. If anything, Hjörvar had found the grave more touching when the cross was crooked.

There was no point lingering. He hadn't been able to form any connection to his father in life and there was no hope of doing so now that he was dead. No doubt the same would be true of the sister he had never known. Yet, as Hjörvar walked towards Salvör's grave, he expected to be moved by it. Unlike his father, she had never failed him. Perhaps, he thought cynically, because she'd never had the chance.

When he found it, Hjörvar thought at first that he'd got the wrong grave. But the position fitted the information he'd found online, so he bent down and brushed the snow from the stone until he could read the inscription. There was his sister's name. The dates of her birth and death were right as well. Underneath them, there was a Bible reference: Luke 23:34.

Hjörvar stood at the foot of the grave, examining it, puzzled. He hadn't been mistaken. It was strangely well tended and there was even a vase sticking out of the snow by the headstone. Although it contained no flowers, clearly the vase couldn't have been there since Salvör was buried. She had died more than half a century ago and a china vase would have been broken or blown away at some point in the intervening years.

His mother hadn't put it there. After the divorce, she had moved to Reykjavík with him and Kolbeinn and never returned to the east, even for a visit. The only explanation was that his father must have tended to the grave until his own death. The vase could easily have been put there two years ago. But it was harder to account for the Christmas decoration planted in the middle of the plot: a cross with a string of light diodes, intended to illuminate the grave during Advent, according to Icelandic custom. Two Christmases had passed since his father had died and the cross looked too flimsy to have withstood the elements that long.

Hjörvar noticed that there was an identical cross on the neighbouring grave. He wondered for a moment if they were placed on all the graves in Höfn churchyard as a matter of course. Then he remembered that he hadn't seen this kind of decoration on any of the other plots, so that was unlikely to be the explanation. Unless they had just forgotten to remove these two once Advent had passed.

Hjörvar was so deep in thought that he failed to notice he was no longer alone until someone tapped him on the shoulder.

He didn't jump, perhaps because he was becoming inured to surprises after his recent peculiar experiences. Turning unhurriedly, he found himself face to face with a young man in a down jacket. The man explained that he was the vicar. Hjörvar introduced himself, and they shook hands.

This was a different vicar from the one who had officiated at his father's funeral. That man had been considerably older, and definitely past his sell-by date, judging by his hoarse voice and tuneless singing. This must be his replacement.

'I hope you'll excuse my curiosity but I was on my way to the church when I spotted you here. I thought I'd come over and say hello as I don't think I recognise you. I wanted to welcome you to our congregation if you've just moved to the area – only if you're interested, of course. I know from personal experience how difficult it can be to move to a new place. I've been here nearly two years myself but I'm still a bit of an outsider.'

Hjörvar sidestepped having to refuse the invitation to attend church by telling the vicar his reason for moving east to Höfn. He also told him about his links to the town and that his father was buried in the churchyard. He was saved from having to mention his sister by the vicar asking when his father had died. It turned out that it was just before he had taken over from his predecessor, as Hjörvar had suspected.

Their conversation soon dried up and Hjörvar prepared to make a move. But before he could say goodbye, the vicar changed the subject: 'Do you mind my asking what your connection is to this grave? Only, it's a long time since anyone's visited it.'

Considering that the man had been vicar here for less than two years, Hjörvar found this rather an odd thing to say. After all, many of the people resting there must have died decades ago and it was unlikely that they got many visitors. 'This is my sister. She died very young, so I'm just paying my respects. I can't say I really remember her.' There was no need to tell the truth, that he didn't remember her at all. It was none of the vicar's business.

The man nodded. 'Ah, I see.' He pointed to a neighbouring grave, just beyond the one that was also decorated with a diode cross. The headstone looked recent. 'The woman who's buried there tended to your sister's grave for many years, from the time her husband was buried next to Salvör until she herself passed away. I've never known a grave looked after with such loving care. Apparently she used to come here faithfully every week. I'm sorry you never got to meet her. Especially as you didn't miss her by much. She died in the autumn.'

Hjörvar studied the three graves belonging to Salvör and the couple. He couldn't see their names from where he was standing but knew he was unlikely to recognise them. 'Did the woman know my father or mother? To be honest, I know virtually nothing about my family in these parts or about any friends my parents had when they lived in Höfn.'

The vicar shook his head. 'No. I started chatting to her one day and we became good friends after that. She told me it was no trouble for her. It was just that her husband's grave was so well tended that she found the comparison sad. So she took care to keep them both equally tidy. She said she'd been feeling a lot better since she started doing that. According to her, the spirit had changed and become much more peaceful.'

'The spirit?' Hjörvar didn't immediately grasp what the man was talking about. He hoped his question wouldn't prompt a religious answer. He didn't know much about that sort of thing and wouldn't have a clue how to respond.

'Oh, she claimed there had been a bad atmosphere around the grave – before she started looking after it, that is. She didn't explain, just said it had made her uncomfortable whenever she visited her husband.' The vicar smiled. 'I expect it had more to do with her husband dying before his time. Grief's particularly acute when death comes unexpectedly. But the bereaved gradually adapt to the change in their circumstances and start to feel better. Perhaps the neglected grave was an uncomfortable reminder of how quickly people forget. That would explain why she felt more at ease once she had started taking care of it.'

'So you're saying that my father didn't look after the grave?' While this didn't surprise Hjörvar, it didn't sadden him either. On the contrary: if his father hadn't felt any obligation to visit his daughter's grave, that let Hjörvar off the hook for neglecting his father's.

'Apparently not. But your mother used to tend to it back when she lived here – according to the woman I mentioned.

After she moved away, though, no one bothered. The woman's husband died some years after your parents' divorce and by then she said the plot was looking a bit scruffy.' The vicar's gaze wandered away from Hjörvar, back to the three graves. 'There's no one right way to honour the memory of the dead. Not everyone does it by visiting cemeteries.'

'No. That's true.' Hjörvar hoped the man wasn't under the impression that he was the type to fuss over graves. If so, he would be disappointed, as Hjörvar had no intention of coming back. While they were standing there, chatting, he'd been aware of a creeping sense of unease that had grown more and more unsettling until he felt a powerful urge to leave. He could understand only too well how the woman had felt.

The vicar was still contemplating the graves. 'The saddest part of all is that there's nobody now to look after the woman's grave. Or, of course, the other two.' He bent down and plucked the diode cross from Salvör's plot, then the one from the husband's. 'That's probably the last decoration either of these will ever see. She put the crosses there early last autumn and died shortly afterwards. She was so ill by then that she knew she was unlikely to last until Advent.'

Hjörvar couldn't take any more of this. If the vicar went on any longer, there was a risk he would feel guilt-tripped into taking responsibility for all three graves.

Pretending he had to be somewhere else, he said a hasty goodbye and headed to the gate. During the short walk, his spine prickled with the awareness that he was turning his back on his sister's grave. He could almost hear her screaming at him. He could have sworn it was the same anguished screeching that had echoed out of the past when he'd spoken to the old man from the retirement home.

It was as if a cork had been popped out of a tight bottle-neck. Hjörvar was deaf to the squeaking of the gate as he opened it: it was drowned out by the memory of his sister's screams; by the memory of him clasping his hands over his ears. No image of a face came back to him. Clearly that hadn't left such a strong impression. But the screams reverberated in his head as loudly if his sister were standing beside him, her mouth a gaping black hole.

Hjörvar quickened his pace, hurrying away down the road. How would he cope if he couldn't shake off this ear-splitting noise? He knew a man who'd been so tormented by chronic tinnitus that he'd actually considered having the hearing destroyed in that ear just to be free of it. At the time, Hjörvar had thought he must be crazy even to consider such a thing. Now, he could understand him.

He needn't have worried. The further he got from the cemetery, the fainter the screeching became until in the end, mercifully, it stopped. But he was left with the question he would probably never be able to answer: what the hell had been wrong with his sister? Surely no child would scream like that without good reason.

Chapter 21

The beauty of the day was in stark contrast to the grimness of the occasion. Not a hair stirred on their heads and the sun shone down from a sky of brilliant blue. Helpful though the mild conditions were, Jóhanna thought heavy cloud and gloom would have made a more fitting backdrop to their search. But the weather wouldn't be governed by the needs of mere humans. It cared nothing for their plans. In summer, it got its kicks from ruining garden parties and outdoor festivals with rain and gales, taking particular pleasure in targeting the National Day celebrations on 17 June. Now, it was mocking them by wasting a beautiful winter's day on an occasion of unmitigated horror.

Jóhanna adjusted her snow goggles. Wherever she looked, the glare hurt her eyes. It was a good thing she had abstained from the booze yesterday evening, as the conditions were perfect for a splitting headache. It was bad enough being physically tired, achy and short on sleep, not to mention oppressed by the mental strain associated with the search. A hangover would have been the final straw.

Geiri had refused to discuss yesterday evening's uncanny incidents. He'd rubbished the idea that he'd felt icy fingers touching him under the duvet, saying dismissively that she must have been dreaming and should go back to sleep. She hadn't pursued the matter last night; he'd needed his rest and she had thought it could wait until morning. But when she'd woken up, she had no longer been so sure of herself. In the night, she had been positive that they had both experienced the same sensation, but by the time she'd got out of bed doubt had begun to erode her certainty. As the day wore on, she became increasingly convinced that the icy fingers had been nothing but the damaged nerves in her back sending a confused message to her brain, and that Geiri had been dreaming. The whole thing had been pure coincidence. This made the day much easier to bear and they had both headed to work as if nothing had happened.

At the factory, Jóhanna had immersed herself in her duties, sparing little thought for the rescue operation. She wasn't expecting to be called out. Since the location had already been pinpointed by the drone, a minimum of volunteers would be needed. They were planning to send a small advance party to check that the suspicion was correct. If it was indeed a body, the big guns would be summoned from Reykjavík, along with further searchers. When, towards midday, she'd heard the throbbing roar of the helicopter, she had known what it meant.

Shortly afterwards she had received a text, sent to all members of the rescue team, notifying them that their services were required. It didn't specify what they were looking for but she assumed the team would be needed to fine-comb the area around the most recently discovered remains. If further bodies were out there, it would be better to find them straight away than to have them turn up one by one as they had in recent days. Of course, their search couldn't guarantee that there was nothing else out there; it would only reduce the likelihood. A united effort by all the rescue teams in the world wouldn't be enough to scour three hundred and twenty square kilometres of rough terrain. Even if they had a whole year. Even without the snow. Too many people had vanished without trace in the Icelandic highlands over the centuries.

It should have been a far simpler matter to locate the car the trekking party had used to reach the area. Not only were there relatively few routes it could have taken, but the drifts weren't deep enough to have buried a big four-by-four. Yet repeated aerial sweeps of the reserve had revealed nothing resembling a vehicle. The only conclusion was that the party must have been given a lift to Lónsöræfi by an unknown person.

Geiri had told her over breakfast that the police were going to appeal for the driver to come forward. During her coffee break she had seen the notice appear on the online news sites, and she had also read a report in which the journalist had managed to produce two whole paragraphs on the accidental death of the four individuals found so far, despite a total absence of solid facts. She was impressed by the writer's skill. If she herself had had to produce an item about the case, it would have read: *Four people from Reykjavík have been found dead in the Lónsöræfi wilderness. There is no information at present about their movements or how they died.*

According to Geiri, it wouldn't be long before the media got their hands on more details. As soon as the final post-mortem had been completed and the deceased had all been formally identified, their names would be released. The pathologist had not returned to Höfn for the latest discovery. Apparently he still had to perform an autopsy on the body of the man that Jóhanna and her companions had come across. The hope now was that the names of the victims would prompt somebody to come forward, who might be able to tell the police more about what their plans had been.

Jóhanna saw no reason why the appeal for the driver shouldn't be successful. The person in question had nothing to fear as they weren't suspected of any wrongdoing. There might even have been more than one driver. If the trekking party had consisted of five people, they would either have required a very large vehicle with room for five plus a driver and all their gear, or else two smaller vehicles. In which case, there was double the chance that someone would get in touch.

Jóhanna trudged on, poking her avalanche probe into the deep snow. It slid through with ease. She took another step forwards and repeated the action. Beside her, several of her fellow volunteers were spread out in a row. The turnout had been good; everyone who could had responded to the callout. They were all eager to do their bit to bring an end to this agonising process. The sooner all the bodies were found, the better for everyone.

It was partly this that had motivated Jóhanna herself to answer the call. But her main reason was more selfish. The instant she'd heard the helicopter, the thought had flashed through her mind that Geiri would be home late. That would mean another evening alone in the house, perhaps until the early hours. Far better to spend that time with the rescue team and have something to keep her occupied, even if it was something as depressing as searching for dead bodies.

Her boss had released her, albeit grudgingly. His reluctance was evident from the delay before he answered. He was expecting a large amount of fish and her new colleague in quality control wasn't yet experienced enough to cover Jóhanna's job as well. Her boss had clearly wanted to say no, they couldn't spare her today, but his sense of social responsibility had been too strong. By delaying his answer, he had given her a chance to change her mind, but Jóhanna didn't take it. She reflected yet again on how much she missed the competent presence of her Polish colleague who had left. Eventually, her boss had ended the awkward silence by saying that she could go.

On the way home, Jóhanna had rung her friend Dísa to wish her happy birthday. She'd been meaning to call that evening, when there would be time for a leisurely chat, but now she would be back late. And calling from the mountains wasn't an option as there was no mobile phone signal unless you had a Tetra radio. Dísa didn't pick up, though, and Jóhanna had to be content with leaving her a message on voicemail. Her attempt to sound upbeat wouldn't fool Dísa. Jóhanna had never been any good at acting and her friend would immediately intuit that something was wrong. Still, it couldn't be helped. Jóhanna had left her message, then started walking faster, in a hurry to get home and change into her snow gear.

Geiri hadn't been particularly pleased when she appeared on the scene. That morning he had remarked on her limp and warned her not to overdo it at the factory. She had promised not to. But he hadn't vetoed her joining in the search because it hadn't even crossed his mind that she would volunteer. So, strictly speaking, she wasn't breaking any promises. She would have a chance to explain that to him later.

The man in charge of transporting the rescue team to the search area must have noticed her limp too, though he didn't comment on it. Once the vehicles had gone as far as they could, he had assigned her to ride the rest of the way on the back of one of the snowmobiles. There was a time for pride but this wasn't it: Jóhanna had accepted the lift gratefully. The pains in her legs weren't really that much worse. She would only have to walk a short distance with the team, just around the area where the body had been found. And she had been assigned to the group searching closest to the remains, presumably for the same reason as she had been given the lift.

While she was tramping the snow and probing it with her stick, she shot occasional glances at the people who were at work uncovering the body. It was rumoured to be a woman. That would mean two men and three women dead. So much loss of life would have an impact far beyond their next of kin. It would be a stark reminder to future visitors to the highlands that they should take more care, ensure they were properly equipped and notify people in advance of their plans. That would work for a while. Sooner or later, though, the tragedy would be forgotten, except by the families and close friends of the departed, whose lives would never be the same.

A woman further down the line called out that she had found something and everyone stopped moving while it was investigated. When it turned out to be a rock rather than something more grisly, the searchers moved off again with their patient rhythm: one step forwards, prod; another step, prod.

When they reached the end of their designated sector, their group leader proposed taking a coffee break before embarking on the next. No one objected and they walked over to the large tent that had been erected as a base.

The hot coffee was welcome. They cradled their mugs in both hands, thawing their numb fingers. It seemed ironic, Jóhanna thought, that the human race should be preparing to send people to Mars, but still couldn't invent a pair of gloves that truly kept your fingers warm.

Geiri appeared in the doorway of the tent and nodded to her as a sign that he wanted a word. Leaving the others, she followed him outside, braced to have to explain what she was doing there.

But it turned out he wanted something quite different. 'Are you doing OK?' His voice contained no hint of accusation that she wasn't looking after herself, no over-anxious solicitude of the kind she could do without.

'Yes, perfectly fine,' Jóhanna replied firmly. It was true: she was feeling pretty good. There was nothing wrong with being physically tired or having aches and pains. Both were a temporary state, unlike the loss of a loved one.

'Then I was wondering if you could do me a favour.' Geiri's eyes were fixed on hers and she couldn't help noticing the dark circles under them, and the reddened skin of his face. 'Don't hesitate to say no if it's too much. You promise?'

'Sure. What do you want me to do?' Jóhanna couldn't begin to guess what he was going to say next.

'We've uncovered the woman. They're about to lift her onto a stretcher and take her back to Reykjavík in the chopper.' Geiri glanced over at the place where the body had been excavated. Among the group of people standing there were their dinner guests from the previous evening. 'I need you to take a quick look at the body for me.' Geiri was standing very still, waiting for her reaction.

Jóhanna was momentarily speechless as she tried to get her head round his request. After a pause, she echoed: 'Look at the body?'

'Yes. Just for a moment.'

'Why?'

'I want to know if you recognise her.' Geiri wiped a drip from the end of his nose with the sleeve of his coat. 'Just say if you'd rather not. There's no pressure.'

Jóhanna felt a sudden sympathy with her boss's dilemma earlier that day. All her instincts were screaming at her to say no: the last thing she needed right now was to come face to face with another dead woman. But at the same time, she wanted to oblige. Geiri wouldn't have asked her to do it unless he thought it was important. After a moment's hesitation, she said: 'Yes. I'll do it.'

'Are you sure?' Geiri shifted awkardly as if expecting her to change her mind. 'The body's in a bit of a bad state.'

Jóhanna took a deep breath. 'Quite sure. But tell me something.' Her gaze shifted to the group standing around the unseen corpse. 'Who do you think it is? Do I know her?' Against all common sense, she found herself praying he would say no. But he would hardly ask her to make an informal identification of a woman she didn't know. If the face was a well-known one, those standing by the hole would have no trouble identifying it themselves. The images of friends, relatives and acquaintances flew through her mind. She didn't want to see any of them staring up blindly from a snowy grave. If that's what she was going to be confronted with, she wanted to be mentally prepared. Immediately she started wondering who had disappeared off social media in recent days. Why hadn't her friend Dísa answered the phone that morning? She could feel her heart beginning to race. 'Who is it, Geiri?'

'I can't tell you that. It could influence your reaction – and I may be wrong. It's better if you take a look at her without me putting any ideas into your head. It's too easy to get confused and see what you're expecting to see. The face is a bit of a mess.'

Jóhanna inhaled deeply, through her nose this time. This information had made her even less eager to set eyes on the corpse. 'When do you want me to do it?' She read the answer in his expression. 'Now?'

Geiri nodded. 'Finish your coffee. It doesn't have to be this very minute.'

Jóhanna raised the mug to her lips with shaking hands. The tremor had nothing to do with the cold. When she took a mouthful, the coffee had lost all its flavour. Since there was no point waiting, she'd better get it over with. 'OK, I'm ready.'

Geiri sent her a reassuring look. 'It'll only take a moment.'

They walked over to the hole together. Jóhanna could see from the expressions of those standing there that they knew Geiri thought she might recognise the dead woman. They watched her coming, then stepped aside to make room for her. She wished Geiri hadn't told them, though she knew it had been necessary. One of the Reykjavík contingent was bound to have raised objections if the local policeman had brought his wife over to view the body for no good reason.

Her greatest fear was that it would turn out to be someone she loved. That she would have to conceal her shock and grief in front of all these people. The four dinner guests from the night before were studiously avoiding Jóhanna's eye. She was grateful for that at least. It would have been wildly inappropriate for them to start thanking her for yesterday's meal or asking for the salad recipe.

Clenching her jaw, she took a step closer, and Geiri did the same, sticking close to her side. Neither reached for the other's hand, though she longed to cling to his. She took another deep, steadying breath, then looked down into the hole.

A shudder ran down her spine and she could feel the skin prickling all over her body. For an instant, she closed her eyes to recover from what she'd seen and steel herself to take another, longer look. Then she exhaled and opened her eyes again.

At her feet were the remains of a woman, lying on her back. One of her arms was propped at a right angle against a boulder, as if reaching up to the sky. The curled fingers made the hand look like a spider. It was this that the drone operator had spotted protruding from the snow.

The woman was slim and appeared to be young. She was wearing more clothes than the other bodies Jóhanna had glimpsed: a thin long-sleeved top, jeans and trainers, which hadn't yet been entirely brushed clean of snow. But the clothes were still totally unsuitable for the conditions, even if she had originally been wearing a coat over them. She had no jacket, scarf, hat or gloves. She might almost have fallen from a plane.

Jóhanna forced herself to examine the frozen face and the mousy-brown hair hanging down beside the cheeks in icy locks. The mouth was wide open, as if the woman had died in the middle of screaming for help. Jóhanna found it hard to tear her eyes away from the seemingly bottomless black cavity. There was a dark, dirty-looking crust around the mouth too, as if the woman had been cramming chocolate cake into it like a toddler during her death throes. The cold shudder down Jóhanna's spine intensified. But the woman's mouth was nothing in comparison to her eyes, which were gaping black holes in her ashen face.

Jóhanna felt a dizzying sense of unreality, as though she wasn't actually standing there beside an icy grave, staring at this horrific death mask. Closing her eyes again, she mentally counted up to ten to steady herself. It worked and she opened her eyes. She was here to identify the body. Did she know this horribly transformed woman? She forced herself to study the gruesome sight more carefully. No, she didn't know her. She had just begun to shake her head when suddenly she saw beyond the contorted features to the living person. She blinked, then turned to Geiri. 'I do know who it is. It's Wiktoria – who used to work with me at the factory.' She wrapped her arms around herself to ward off the shivers. 'I didn't think she was the outdoor type.'

Chapter 22

Lónsöræfi, the previous week

Agnes had fallen asleep at last, worn out by anxiety and the pain in her wrist. She was swaddled in Tjörvi's sleeping bag, still wearing her coat, with the hood pulled up over her head. She looked almost unrecognisable as she lay there, flat on her back to protect her arm, her eyes puffy from weeping, her face haggard with grief, even in sleep. Upsetting as it was to see her in this state, Dröfn couldn't avoid it, short of closing her own eyes, as the three of them were squashed into the two-man tent in their bulky outdoor clothes.

It had been a huge relief when Agnes had finally dropped off. Dröfn had been trying, in spite of her own distress, to comfort her friend, but words had failed her and she kept falling back on the same platitudes: *It'll be all right. Haukur knows what he's doing. He'll find shelter for them both. And Bjólfur's a tough nut.* She filled her voice with all the conviction she possessed, not only for Agnes's sake but for her and Tjörvi too.

Words had no power to comfort Agnes, though. The only sign that they were having any effect was when Dröfn came out with reassuring nonsense like: *The weather's only this bad here by the tent. There won't be any wind where Haukur and Bjólfur are. There are loads of huts around the glacier. They'll have taken refuge in one of them. They'll have found a cave – an ice cave. The glacier's full of caves.*

If they had been alone, Dröfn would have stuck to this kind of foolishly optimistic rambling, since it seemed to help Agnes. Dröfn even found it comforting herself, though she knew there was no truth in what she was saying. But every time she trotted out another implausible suggestion, Tjörvi caught her eye and shook his head. If Agnes was aware of his scepticism, she didn't show it.

Tjörvi turned his head a fraction now to look at Agnes. After studying her for a moment, he closed his eyes and sighed. 'They're not coming back.'

Dröfn hushed him, hissing at him to keep his voice down. She didn't want Agnes to wake up or, even worse, for Tjörvi's fatalism to filter into her dreams. The roaring of the wind drowned out any whisper but they kept their voices as low as they could. 'Don't be so pessimistic,' she said fiercely. 'You made it back. How do you know they won't as well? She's got to hold on to that belief. And so have I.'

'They're not coming back.' Tjörvi uttered these words with the finality of someone who has given up all hope. His face was an even grimmer sight than Agnes's. Although the icicles caking his beard and eyebrows had melted, his angry-red nose and cheekbones seemed to be darkening and acquiring a bluish tinge. The skin was flaking from his lips, turning them almost white. And the ghostly torchlight only made things worse, giving him a zombie-like appearance.

When he'd first crawled into the tent, Dröfn had brushed most of the snow off him, taken off his hat and given him hers to wear instead, then unzipped her sleeping bag and draped it over his shoulders. He was shaking too violently to do anything for himself. In fact, it was a miracle he'd managed to unzip the tent flap in the first place. When Dröfn pulled off his gloves, his fingers were so swollen that they wouldn't fit into her warm, dry pair, but she had a spare pair of mittens and managed to force his hands into those. To her consternation, he didn't wince at all during this painful operation. When she asked if she was hurting him, he denied that he was being brave, saying he was just too numb to feel anything.

It was the same when she'd tugged off his boots. They were frozen so hard that there was hardly any give in the material, and it took all her strength to work them to and fro until she could prise them off his feet. When she pulled off his socks, his skin felt shockingly cold to the touch. The sales assistant who'd sung the praises of the super-pro boots had clearly been exaggerating. Tjörvi's feet looked even worse than his hands and she averted her gaze in horror from his frostbitten toes.

She wrapped his feet in some thin woollen underwear she found in the backpack, then sat on them. They were so icy that even through her thick, padded trousers she could feel the cold radiating into the backs of her thighs. Nevertheless, the sleeping bag round his shoulders gradually helped ease his shivering. After that, she helped him off with his outer clothes, which were cold and wet, now that the warmth inside the tent had melted the ice on them. Luckily, however, since he didn't have a change of clothes, the thick jumper he wore underneath was dry.

'Tell me again how you lost sight of each other.' Dröfn hadn't liked to question him while Agnes was awake. At first, it had been difficult to understand what Tjörvi was saying through the chattering of his teeth. He had been incoherent with shock as well, made worse by Agnes's constant interruptions with panicky comments or questions. Had Bjólfur definitely zipped his coat up to the neck? Had he and Haukur been intending to stick together or split up? Bjólfur didn't feel the cold, Agnes insisted. He had his phone, she kept repeating.

But while this might have helped him survive somewhere else, of course it would be useless out here.

Agnes had kept saying wildly that they should go out and search for Bjólfur and Haukur. That was the only time Tjörvi had intervened – with a flat refusal. As long as the storm was raging outside, they weren't moving an inch. Perhaps it was because he was having such difficulty talking through his chattering teeth, but he didn't point out the obvious: that neither he nor Agnes was in any fit state to walk. If anyone went out to look, it would have to be Dröfn. She was eternally grateful to him for vetoing the idea.

Now that Agnes was asleep and he had stopped shivering, Tjörvi could tell his story without interruption. His voice heavy with sadness, regret and gloom, he gave a bald account of what had happened. Because his head was lowered, Dröfn couldn't see if his eyes were open. Instead, she focused on his painfully cracked lips, hoping against hope that some part of his story would give cause for optimism. It didn't.

Having failed yet again to find Haukur's measuring instrument, they had persevered, going a bit further, then a bit further. When, belatedly, they realised they would have to start back, they had split up in one last-ditch attempt to locate the equipment. It was then that the blizzard had struck. At first the snow had come down so thickly it had been difficult to see. Then a gale had blown up and that was when things had gone disastrously wrong. Totally disorientated by the whirling maelstrom of flakes, Tjörvi had lost contact with his companions.

After a brief attempt to look for them, he had given it up as hopeless. Blinded by the whiteout, clueless about which direction they had taken, he'd realised he was completely lost. The roaring of the storm had snatched away his voice when he called their names, and drowned out any possible reply. Abandoning the attempt, he had started back towards where he thought the tents might be. Confused, groping through the unrelenting whiteness, he had struggled on until in the end, against all the odds, he had stumbled on the camp.

When Tjörvi finished his story, they sat there in silence, listening to the wind howling outside. The canvas cracked and billowed wildly, and in the worst gusts Dröfn was afraid it would be torn to shreds. What the hell were they supposed to do then?

She shuddered. Her train of thought had exacerbated the chill that was slowly creeping into her bones. She was the only one who didn't have a sleeping bag to keep her warm. Noticing that she was shivering, Tjörvi met her eye and said: 'There's something you've got to do, Dröfn.' His tone warned her that she wouldn't want to hear what he had to say. She remained stubbornly mute, hoping he wouldn't continue. He laid his numb hand in its too-tight mitten on her thigh as if he wanted to squeeze it but didn't have the strength. 'You've got to get over to Agnes and Bjólfur's tent and fetch their sleeping bags and torch. And grab anything else we can use to keep warm. Including the stuff from Haukur's tent.'

Slowly, Dröfn shook her head. 'I can't. I can't go out there.'

'You've *got* to, Dröfn. And you've got to do it now. I'm afraid it's only a matter of time before the other tents are blown away. Then it'll be too late.'

As if drawing power from his words, the screaming of the wind outside grew even more savage. Dröfn had the feeling it was just waiting to pounce on her the moment she ventured out. 'What if *I'm* blown away? What if I get lost too?'

'You won't be. But if you're afraid, stay down on your hands and knees. You won't get lost. The other tents are right beside us. I wouldn't ask you if I thought it was dangerous. You can do it.'

'But—'

'*Now*, Dröfn.'

There was no alternative. Swallowing the lump in her throat, Dröfn zipped her coat up to the neck, pulled on her gloves and, as she didn't have a spare hat, took hers back from Tjörvi. After that she was ready to go, as she was already wearing her boots and protective trousers.

'Take the torch.' Tjörvi jerked his chin towards it. 'Agnes and I can manage without a light. You can't.'

Dröfn reached for the torch, refusing to acknowledge to herself that its beam had dimmed since she'd switched it on. She groped her way to the door of the tent and took hold of the zip. Before opening the flap, she turned back to Tjörvi. 'There's something I need to tell you. Just so you don't think I'm being totally pathetic. You see, it's not only the storm I'm frightened of.' And now it all came pouring out: the horror that had seized her in the hut; how she was far from convinced that it had been the reindeer she and Agnes had heard outside the tent when they'd been alone. As she started to apologise and say that of course this was rubbish and probably just a reaction to the extreme conditions, Tjörvi cut her off.

'You don't need to make excuses.' His eyes on the weak beam of the torch, he added: 'There's something out there. I don't know what the hell it is – but it's not the reindeer.'

This was absolutely the last thing Dröfn wanted to hear. She'd been expecting reassurance before she braved the wild night alone. 'Did you see something?' she quavered, her voice threatening to break. Grimly, she fought back her tears. Any she did shed would freeze on her cheeks the moment she opened the tent flap.

'Yes. There was something following me. And it wasn't Bjólfur or Haukur.' Tjörvi looked into her eyes. 'And it sure as hell wasn't the reindeer.'

'Following you where? All the way here?'

Tjörvi didn't answer this. 'I came across blood in the snow. Twice. A lot of blood. Not a trail. Just big patches of it.'

'Blood? Who from? Bjólfur? Haukur?' Dröfn could feel the last tiny spark of hope being extinguished. 'Whose blood?'

Tjörvi dropped his eyes, shrugging almost impercept-ibly. 'You need to get a move on. You'll be back before you know it.'

There was no point trying to press him for an answer when clearly he didn't have one. Dröfn unzipped the door, took a deep breath, then squeezed her way outside. It was a battle to stand upright as she tried to close the flap behind her; the wind seemed bent on knocking her off her feet. Hard pellets of snow lashed her from all sides, getting under her hood and stinging her eyes. She screwed them up, shielding them with one arm, but it made little difference.

It was only a few steps to Agnes and Bjólfur's tent. A few big steps and she'd be there. She would go in, grab what she needed, then hurry straight back to Tjörvi and Agnes. What-ever she found there would have to do. There was no way she could bring herself to venture any further from safety, all the way to Haukur's tent.

It should be easy. Yet it felt insurmountable. She couldn't make herself take that first step. But the wind, seemingly tir-ing of her dithering, now took charge, shoving her forwards like a playground bully. She staggered two steps, then fell onto her hands and knees. Once down, she decided to crawl. That way there was no danger of being caught by a violent gust and hurled away into the blinding whiteness.

Being on all fours wasn't as bad. Dröfn felt a little steadier and the snowflakes constantly blowing into her eyes didn't sting as much. She moved as fast as she could to the neighbouring tent and rose on her knees to undo the zip. Succeeding without too much effort, she pushed her way inside.

After giving herself a moment to catch her breath and allow her madly galloping heart to slow down a little, she set to work, gathering together all the things she reckoned she could lug back to the other tent in one journey. Rolling up the two sleeping bags, she crammed them into their thin stuff sacks, sticking the torch into one of them, then dragged over the two backpacks. Wasting no time going through them, she forced the contents of one into the other until it was overflowing. The food in the plastic bag at the back of the tent would have to stay there. Hunger wasn't a primary concern – not yet, anyway.

Just as she was hoisting the pack onto her back, she thought she heard a noise outside, caused by something other than the storm. Tensing, she strained her ears. Over the moaning of the wind and the crack of the canvas, came a sound that froze the blood in her veins. She had heard that spectral voice before. In her panic, her senses became super keen, making her hyper-aware of her surroundings, as if anything that might interfere with her concentration had been switched off. Oblivious to the cold and to her physical discomfort, all her attention was focused on those bloodcurdling repeated pleas to be let in.

Shrieking to Tjörvi for help was out of the question. She had to keep quiet. How she knew this was immaterial; the instinct was so strong that it didn't occur to her to question it.

As she crouched there, breathing without the slightest sound, she was able to pinpoint the source of the voice. It was coming from the side where Haukur's tent was. In addition to the horrible muttering, she heard a clatter she recognised: the noise of someone moving around in a tent full of stuff.

It might be Haukur or Bjólfur. Supposing they were in such a bad state that they'd dragged themselves into the first tent they'd reached? But the same instinct that had warned her to stay quiet now told her that this wasn't the case. No one could have entered Haukur's tent – at least, not since she'd left Tjörvi and Agnes – or she would have heard the telltale sound of the zip. And it was unthinkable that the pleading voice could belong to Haukur or Bjólfur. It was a woman. Or a child. Impossible to tell which. Maybe neither.

A sudden sharp tearing sound from the direction of Haukur's tent almost gave Dröfn a heart attack. The door zip. But this time, instead of being immobilised by fear, she was galvanised to grab the two sleeping bags and fling herself at the door. Keeping her head resolutely turned away from Haukur's tent, she set off at a fast crawl, without pausing to close the tent flap behind her or put both her arms through the straps of the backpack. She dropped the torch, then snatched it up again but, as she did so, the backpack fell off and dragged along in the snow beside her.

Moving as fast as she could, she screamed to her husband at the top of her voice: 'Let me in! Let me in!'

But when she got there the tent flap was still closed. 'Let me in, Tjörvi! Let me in!' she shrieked.

'I'm trying!' he called back. The mittens must be hampering his poor, maimed hands.

Dröfn flung a look over her shoulder as she reached for the zip. The beam from her torch could barely penetrate the curtains of snow but it was enough to show her what looked like a dark shape crawling towards her. Then the light went out. Instead of screaming or making a run for it into the blind darkness, she braced herself and turned back to the zip.

Hauling it up, she forced her way inside. 'Shut it! Shut it!' There was no need to yell but she couldn't help herself. Something had touched her ankle.

Tjörvi had managed to drag off one of the mittens. Clumsily, he zipped the door shut behind her, then sat staring at her, open-mouthed and panting. Agnes, woken by the commotion, sat up a little, moaning at the pain in her wrist. 'What? What's going on?'

Dröfn turned to the closed tent flap, opening her mouth to answer, but couldn't force out a single word.

Outside she could hear that ghastly, pathetic muttering. It sounded so close now, almost as if someone was sitting just the other side of the thin sheet of canvas.

Chapter 23

Erlingur was talking but Hjörvar could barely take in a word. Although he tried to listen, his thoughts kept drifting in another direction, like iron filings being drawn to a magnet – the magnet in this case being his sister. He couldn't stop thinking about her. What had been wrong with her? What in God's name had his father been thinking of to take her for a walk on the rocks? Although his dad wasn't a native of Höfn, he had lived there long enough to be aware of the blowhole and how dangerous it was. There had been no need to drive the twenty kilometres out to Stokksnes to take his daughter for a walk when there were so many beaches around the town that were not only scenic but much safer.

It was unlikely that the police files would shed any light on the matter, or that Hjörvar would even be allowed to see them, let alone Salvör's medical records. But he was pinning his hopes on these official documents. They offered the only chance of getting to the bottom of the story. His parents, the only people who could have told him what he wanted to know, had died leaving no explanations behind. In fact, they had gone out of their way to destroy any reminders of their daughter.

'Did you know about the little girl who fell down the blowhole?' Hjörvar had been burning to ask this question but had restrained himself until now, when, momentarily forgetting himself, he blurted it out.

Erlingur shot him a look of surprise. Frowning, he put down the list of jobs and sat back in his chair, turning his head to the window. 'I have to say, that's a bit of an odd question.'

'I know.' There was no point pretending it had anything to do with what Erlingur had been telling him about the shift handover. The other man had no way of knowing about his connection to the little girl since Hjörvar had never mentioned that he'd lived in Höfn as a child. Quite frankly, he hadn't thought it was any of Erlingur's business where he was from, nor did he want to have to explain why he had seen so little of his father after moving to Reykjavík – perhaps because he didn't understand it himself. So it was no wonder Erlingur was taken aback by his question.

Erlingur shrugged and brought his gaze back from the window. 'Yes, as a matter of fact I have heard about the accident. I grew up in Höfn, remember? All the kids here knew the story. I was about twelve at the time and the accident scared us off cycling out here. I suppose you could say it made sure we didn't suffer the same fate.'

Hjörvar put down his coffee mug. Now that he had raised the subject, he might as well pursue it. 'Why didn't you mention the accident when you told me about the blowhole?'

'Why?' Erlingur shrugged again. 'To be honest, I didn't know you were that interested. But since you are, you might as well know that the kid and Ívan weren't the only people to die that way. One of the soldiers who worked here fell down the blowhole too, and there must have been others over the years. But the simple reason I didn't tell you about the girl is that a load of daft stories have grown up around the incident and I don't have any patience with that kind of nonsense. You know the sort of thing: people claiming they've seen the girl on the rocks at night or by the house where she used to live. They didn't tell those tales when I was young, so you can't blame my generation for them.' Erlingur locked gazes with Hjörvar. 'If you ask me, it's a bad idea to encourage that kind of rubbish. We all have odd experiences at times. Me included. A while back, I thought I saw a yellow parrot outside the window here.' He nodded at the glass. 'Totally crazy, of course. I didn't see any reason to tell you because I thought we ought to stay grounded. Stick to what's real. You know what I mean.'

Hjörvar, who knew exactly what he was implying, dropped the subject. He didn't want to be reminded that he'd been prey to some odd delusions himself recently, nor did he like the idea of seeing his sister out there on the rocks. The chopper was due back today, which meant he'd be taking the evening shift again, and if it arrived as late as it had the last couple of times, he would be in for another long wait, alone in the dark.

Erlingur turned the conversation back to practical matters, ending all talk of the blowhole. He didn't so much as glance out of the window. After running through the list of outstanding jobs, he finished his coffee and rose to his feet. Then he paused to scratch Puss behind the ears as if he had something on his mind but didn't know how to say it. Hjörvar had got to his feet to accompany him to the door. He hovered awkwardly, wondering if something was expected of him. Their mutual social awkwardness meant this kind of situation wasn't uncommon.

The silent impasse was broken when Erlingur finally stopped stroking Puss, said 'Right,' and made for the door. Hjörvar hurried after him, dreading his imminent solitude and keen to make the most of his colleague's taciturn presence as long as he could.

It was a pity the remaining tasks would take him next to no time. He'd make some phone calls, Hjörvar decided. He'd ring his brother. Maybe even his children. However stilted any conversation with them was bound to be, anything would be better than sitting here alone, waiting for the helicopter, gazing into the blackness outside the window. He couldn't shake off the churning fear that he'd hear his sister's screams again, echoing in his head in the silence.

'Don't forget to call HQ when you're leaving.' Erlingur stopped by the door, fishing his phone from his pocket, as if reminding himself as well. 'And feel free to give me a bell if you pick up any news from the chopper crew. One of the pilots radioed earlier and I got the feeling from what he said that the latest body was a local. A woman. That got me worried that it might be someone I know.'

'Will do.' Hjörvar doubted he'd be given any inside information. Last time he'd serviced the chopper, the crew had been in no mood for a chat. He could just picture their faces if he started trying to winkle out the victim's name. He had no intention of bringing up the subject unless they mentioned it first.

Erlingur left, closing the door behind him, leaving Hjörvar alone once more with only Puss for company. In a bomb-proof building, he reminded himself. Inside a security fence, surrounded by antennae, with every available instrument for communicating with the outside world. In spite of the isolated location, surrounded by the merciless sea and sheer, inhospitable mountains, he had nothing to fear. Absolutely nothing at all. Apart from his own thoughts. The worst thing about those was that there was no escaping them. Everywhere he went, his head went too.

Telling himself to snap out of it, Hjörvar got down to work, spinning out every job as long as possible, but he was still finished in no time. Puss followed him from room to room, sitting there, watching intently as he worked. Nice though it was to have his company, by the end Hjörvar was beginning to feel uneasy under the cat's unblinking gaze.

Now there was nothing to do but wait for the helicopter to announce its arrival. The only places to sit in the station building were the chairs in the office and the canteen. Over in the staff accommodation, there was a sofa and beds; the only problem was that he wouldn't be able to hear the radio from there. That left him with a choice between standing up, sitting on the floor – or rearranging the furniture. None of these options were particularly appealing but he opted for the one that involved the least physical effort or discomfort. If his mind began to play tricks on him, he reasoned, it would happen regardless of where he was on the site.

So the canteen it was. He filled Puss's bowl, though Erlingur had told him when he arrived that he'd only just fed the cat. At least Puss wouldn't be able to stare at him while he was busy crunching up his food. Hjörvar emptied the dregs from the coffee jug into his cup, indifferent to the grounds. After all, it wasn't like they'd kill you.

Before getting out his phone, he took the precaution of drawing the curtains across the window, releasing clouds of fine dust into the air as he did so. Clearly, they hadn't been touched for years. The material was barred with lighter and darker stripes where the folds had been unevenly faded by the sun. Yet however mottled, ugly and dirty they were, the curtains did their job. The moment the black void outside was hidden, Hjörvar felt his tension easing.

Kolbeinn answered on the third ring, his familiar voice instantly reassuring. Suddenly Hjörvar no longer felt alone in this godforsaken spot. He wondered why he hadn't called his brother more often over the years. Kolbeinn was the only person in the world he was close to. Usually people had a range of friends and relations to fall back on, but Hjörvar only had Kolbeinn. Which was much better than no one, of course. As he listened to his brother telling him that he had finally got round to taking the camera film to be developed and would pick up the pictures tomorrow, Hjörvar vowed to make more of an effort to stay in touch with him from now on. Though only time would tell whether he'd keep his vow. He knew himself too well: there was no guarantee.

When Kolbeinn stopped talking, it was Hjörvar's turn to relate what he had learnt that morning. He tried to sound normal but his brother obviously wasn't fooled, and asked if everything was OK. Hjörvar used the Lónsöræfi disaster as an excuse, explaining that he was a bit depressed about the tragic events that had been playing out in the highlands not far from where he lived. As he said this, it occurred to him that it might actually explain why he had been feeling so off recently. News of the fatalities wasn't exactly cheering. That, combined with the bizarre story of his sister, was a poisonous cocktail for the imagination.

Once the brothers had exhausted the subject, they ran out of things to say. Hjörvar longed to keep Kolbeinn on the line, but he just couldn't think of any way to do so. He stammered something and paused, but by then it was too late: Kolbeinn had said goodbye.

Hjörvar became conscious again of the silence. Of the cat's unblinking gaze.

Rather than putting the phone down, he hesitantly selected his daughter Ágústa's number. The green symbol of a telephone receiver appeared on the screen and his finger hovered over it for a moment while he wondered again whether this was a bad idea. Just then a gust of wind blew something against the window pane with a muted thud, making him jump, and removing all his doubts. He pressed the symbol.

Ágústa left the phone to ring for a lot longer than Kolbeinn had. Hjörvar could picture her gnawing at her lower lip as she stared at the screen, trying to decide whether to pick up. In the end she did, just before it rang out. On the rare occasions he called his kids, it was always touch and go whether they'd deign to answer. While they were making up their minds, he used the time to count the rings, which is how he knew how many there were before it would disconnect.

'What?' As always, Ágústa sounded angry and petulant. He missed the bright, cheery voice she'd had as a child and wondered whether she only resorted to this aggrieved tone when he called or if she sounded like that with everyone. He hoped for her sake that she reserved it for him. Life was so much harder if you were morose rather than naturally upbeat, as he knew to his cost.

'I just wanted to hear the sound of your voice. It's ages since we last talked. I gather you've been trying to get hold of me.'

Ágústa snorted, which told him all he needed to know. Still, it was better than listening to her customary reeling-off of his failings. He was beginning to know that speech by heart.

When it became apparent that Ágústa wasn't going to say anything to fill the silence, he began to tell her about Salvör. The story of his sister was so unexpected that she forgot her bad mood and even interrupted him with questions, sounding much less hostile than she had at the beginning of the call. The trouble was, he knew so little himself that he couldn't really supply any more details, though he did his best. He was prepared to make something up to fill the gaps in his knowledge, if it meant her voice would sound like it used to before everything had gone wrong.

When Hjörvar had finished his tale, it was Ágústa's turn. Instead of berating him, she volunteered the information that she was starting a new job on Monday. She sounded as excited as anyone who was on the threshold of something new. Even a miserable sod like him knew what that felt like: hard though it was to believe now, he'd actively looked forward to starting work at Stokksnes.

While Ágústa was talking, Hjörvar noticed that Puss was no longer staring at him but had turned his attention to the curtains. Without warning, the cat leapt onto the table, his spine bristling, his tail like a bottle-brush, then began stalking warily towards the window.

Hjörvar frowned. It occurred to him that the noise earlier might have been a bird crashing into the glass. Perhaps it was lying outside, injured, and the cat could sense it somehow. There was another faint thud. It wasn't loud, like knocking or something being flung at the glass; it sounded more like someone patting it with the flat of their hand.

Puss was right by the curtains now. He poked his head between the dusty folds.

Ágústa was in mid-flow when Hjörvar felt a stabbing pain in his chest as though he was having a heart attack. The cat had parted the curtains enough to allow Hjörvar to see out and he gasped as he made out the shape of a hand on the glass. There was somebody out there. Some unwelcome intruder. It couldn't be anyone he was expecting because he would have noticed if the helicopter had landed, even if the pilot had forgotten to radio ahead. Helicopters couldn't exactly sneak up on you.

If he drew back the curtains he would be face to face with the person outside. The fact that he'd only made out the dim shape of a hand did nothing to diminish the creepiness; it made it far worse.

Belatedly, Hjörvar became aware of the silence at the other end of the line. His daughter had sensed his distraction.

'Did the connection go?' she asked.

'No, I'm still here.' Hjörvar kept his eyes fixed on the wall in front of him to resist the temptation of sneaking a sideways glance. He could see the curtains in his peripheral vision and that was quite enough.

'Tell me, then, what was I talking about?' His daughter's voice was teetering between happiness and fury. 'What was I saying?'

Hjörvar hadn't a clue. But right now he had bigger worries on his mind than disappointing his daughter. 'Listen, Ágústa, I'll have to call you back later. I'm at work and something's just come up.'

'Of course. Of course you're at work.'

Hjörvar didn't hear what she said next because he had hung up on her. Their delicate relationship had just been smashed once again, but it couldn't be helped. He was in no state to carry on a conversation now. It would be a job for another day to pick up the pieces and glue them back together.

Puss hissed, retreated from the window and jumped down onto the floor, then shot out of the room and fled down the corridor, still fluffed out to almost double his normal size.

Hjörvar swallowed and rose slowly to his feet. Reaching out, he twitched the curtains shut again. Then he took the two steps into the office, went over to the screen showing the security footage and chose the CCTV camera that pointed out to sea, angling it round to show the window of the canteen from the outside. It was the only way to rid himself of this horrible fear; he had to see in black and white that it was nonsense. His eyes must have been deceiving him. Nobody had any business out here after dark.

It wouldn't even be worthwhile for burglars to break in here. The instruments might be priceless but they wouldn't be able to sell them. There was no black market in Iceland for equipment from a radar station, as any thieves would surely know.

As the camera slowly tracked round, Hjörvar prepared to experience a flood of relief. He knew the screen would show nothing but the outside wall and the window. Except maybe a dead or stunned bird lying on the ground below. Or a starfish thrown up against the window by the wild surf. Yes, he could imagine how it would be possible to mistake a starfish for a hand.

The image on the camera was still turning when the entry-phone in the corridor started ringing. Hjörvar's head shot up. He stared out into the corridor. This wasn't happening.

The entryphone rang again, with a long, insistent shrilling. Hjörvar heaved a deep breath, then released it. He turned back to the screen. He could only deal with one thing at a time. Once he had seen for himself that there was no figure standing outside the window – that it was just his imagination playing tricks on him – he could give his attention to the auditory hallucinations. This madness had to stop.

But the screen didn't show him what he had been hoping for. Outside the wall of the canteen, a child was standing. As plain as day. A little girl who could only just reach the window. Her arms were hanging down by her sides now but her face was pressed close to the glass. Her hair and floral-patterned dress appeared to be soaking wet.

And she was wearing only one shoe.

Chapter 24

There was a police car parked outside the rescue-team head-quarters, with a light on inside and a shadowy figure behind the wheel. Apart from that, the car park was deserted. There were countless vehicles but their drivers were all up in the search area and wouldn't be back until later. Jóhanna had been sent home early, accompanied by one of her team-mates, who had volunteered to go with her, not because people doubted her ability to find her way back but because it was against team policy to allow anyone to travel on foot through the highlands alone.

Jóhanna's companion had seemed as glad to get away as she was. Once they'd reached Höfn, he had offered to take care of all the gear they had brought back to town with them, and Jóhanna had been too weary to protest. She would have preferred to stay and help, even if that meant sitting on a hard plastic chair, watching him work – anything to avoid a long, lonely wait at home until Geiri got back.

Jóhanna stepped out into the dusk. She had walked to the team headquarters earlier, fuelled by a vigour that had helped her forget the pain in her back and legs. It wasn't the first time a rescue operation had had that kind of galvanising effect on her. But coming face to face with the corpse of her former colleague, Wiktoria, had robbed her of her last reserves of energy. Since then, every step she took had hurt. And, short though it was, the last stretch home would be an ordeal.

The driver of the police car rolled down the window, calling her name and waving to her. Jóhanna returned the greeting with an inward sigh. She was in no mood to linger in the cold, passing the time of day with the young policewoman behind the wheel. Much as she longed for another human presence, she couldn't face a conversation. There was nothing she wanted to say or hear. Dropping her arm, she started walking away.

'Jóhanna!' The policewoman was still waving. 'Geiri asked me to give you a lift home.'

Jóhanna turned and stared dully at the young woman, her brain slowly processing what she had said. The woman seemed to interpret Jóhanna's silence as a sign of disbelief. 'He radioed me earlier. Don't you want a lift?'

The offer was welcome, and accepting it would be easier than opening her mouth to refuse. Jóhanna nodded and went over to the car. She racked her brains for the young officer's name but all she could remember was that it was short and began with D – Dísa or Dóra. Despite the effort she was making to disguise her limp, Jóhanna caught the look of concern on the young woman's face.

'Have you hurt yourself?' She was staring at Jóhanna's legs.

The passenger seat proved much softer than the hard bench in the old ice truck in which Jóhanna had been given a ride back to town. Sitting proved such a relief that Jóhanna finally felt able to speak. 'An old sporting injury.'

'Oh.' The policewoman smiled. But instead of starting the engine, she gestured at Jóhanna's right shoulder. 'Belt.'

While Jóhanna was strapping herself in, the young woman kept her eyes on the windscreen. 'It's terrible what happened up there. I don't know what to say. I'm so sorry about the woman you used to work with.'

Although Jóhanna's physical pain was no longer quite as acute, she was still in no fit state to discuss the discovery of the body. 'Thanks for collecting me,' she said instead.

'Oh, no problem. There's absolutely zero happening this evening. It's good to have something to do.' The young officer drove off, one hand on the wheel. She seemed to have understood that Jóhanna didn't want to discuss Wiktoria. 'One question: are you hungry? I was going to grab a quick bite to eat and you're welcome to join me. It would save you having to cook at home.'

Jóhanna had no appetite at all. She was wearing her bulky snowsuit too, so not exactly dressed for eating out. But it would mean company. It didn't bother her that the invitation had almost certainly been Geiri's idea. 'Yes, please.' Realising she couldn't sit down to dinner with this woman without knowing her name, she asked her, adding that unfortunately she was terrible at names. It turned out that the policewoman was called Rannveig. Which was neither short nor began with a D.

There were few other diners at the restaurant as people tended to eat supper early in Höfn, and the two women took a seat by the window that looked out on the parking spaces and the police car. Jóhanna couldn't tell if this was a deliberate choice on Rannveig's part, but she decided not. After all, who would be stupid enough to break into a police vehicle? Unzipping the top half of her snowsuit, she pulled it off down to her waist and it bunched uncomfortably behind her back, the sleeves dragging on the floor. Too bad, she thought.

A young waitress took their order and disappeared into the kitchen. Jóhanna had decided on a burger, though she wasn't hungry. She had to eat something if she didn't want to wake up starving in the middle of the night and have to go downstairs and brave the kitchen alone. Rannveig, meanwhile, ordered the smallest starter on the menu. That settled it: the idea that they should eat together had definitely come from Geiri.

'Can I ask you something?' Rannveig took off her police cap and laid it on the table. 'You don't have to answer.'

Jóhanna nodded. 'Sure.' She knew the question was bound to concern the body. What else could it be about? But now that she was sitting in a comfortable chair and enjoying the company of another human being, she felt a bit more capable of talking. Not with much enthusiasm, but she could at least answer a few simple questions. If they related to Wiktoria, there was no risk of her breaking down or otherwise embarrassing herself – she'd emptied her tear ducts on the way back to town. She felt too numb and drained now to show any emotion.

'Geiri asked us to find out what we could about Wiktoria to speed up the investigation tomorrow. But we aren't getting anywhere. A lot of the people she associated with have left town and the ones who are still here say they haven't heard from her since she quit her job. Everyone says she moved to the East Fjords but no one seems to know where exactly. I spoke to the fish factory and they said the same thing. All they know is that she'd met a man and was planning to move in with him. I get the impression they were a bit pissed off when she handed in her notice.' She paused while the waitress brought them their non-alcoholic drinks. After she'd gone, Rannveig continued: 'Did she tell you anything about her plans?'

Jóhanna ran a finger down the condensation that had formed on the outside of her cold glass. 'She was in love. With the captain of a fishing boat from the East Fjords. I have a feeling he lived in Neskaupstadur. Or Eskifjördur. I can't quite remember, I'm afraid. It all happened so fast.' Jóhanna corrected herself. 'From my point of view, anyway. She turned up to work one day, handed in her notice, then dropped by my office to say goodbye. That was about two months ago.'

'Did she mention his name or how they met? It would help us a lot. There are quite a few ship's captains registered in the eastern region, as you can imagine. Even if we just had his first name, it would save us an awful lot of phone calls.'

Jóhanna searched her memory. Wiktoria had told her. The trouble was, she hadn't taken it in, but then it hadn't occurred to her that she would ever be asked about it. 'Oh, God. Like I said, I'm terrible when it comes to names. But I think he was called Einar. Or Eidur. Maybe even Einir. Something short, beginning with E. Though for all I know he could have been called Játvardur or something completely different. I can't remember his patronymic either. I don't think she ever told me. We only really talked about work and occasionally about Poland. I liked hearing her talk about her homeland. But we hardly discussed private stuff at all, so I have no idea where they met or how long they'd known each other.' Suddenly Jóhanna was struck by a thought. 'She was living with another man for a while – a Polish sailor. She moved out some time before she left Höfn. I know because she was looking for a room to rent, as she didn't want to fork out for a whole flat. She was saving up. To earn money faster, she worked shifts at the hotel on top of her day job.' Jóhanna blew out a breath. Realising she had lost the thread, she added: 'Maybe the guy she used to live with knows something. I got the impression their break-up was amicable.'

'Or not.' Rannveig smiled faintly, trying to hide her disappointment. She had obviously been hoping that Jóhanna would be able to supply the captain's full name, address and maybe even his ID number. The information about Wiktoria's ex-boyfriend didn't seem to be news to her. 'We're trying to track him down. His former employer says he found another job shortly after he and Wiktoria split up. The employer doesn't know where but assumed it was on a boat, possibly registered abroad. We'll trace him eventually but it'll be a bit trickier than if he still lived here.'

A silence fell. When the food arrived, they picked at it with an equal lack of enthusiasm. After eating barely half of her starter, Rannveig pushed her plate aside. 'I know you said you two weren't that close, but do you have any idea what Wiktoria can have been doing with those couples from Reykjavík? Could she have known them? Or been their guide?'

Jóhanna swallowed a bit of dry burger. 'I simply don't know. She rarely visited Reykjavík, so I doubt she can have had many friends there. She mostly hung out with other Poles, as you might expect. And I never heard her say anything about wanting to work as a guide.'

Rannveig's questions seemed to have dried up. Jóhanna took this as a sign of how unexpected it was that one of the victims should have been a former employee of the largest fishing company in Höfn. And from Poland, too. But there was no getting away from the fact that the others hadn't had any obvious reason for being in the highlands either.

While Jóhanna was forcing down a few more mouthfuls of burger, Rannveig confided that there had been no response to the police appeal for the group's driver to come forward. None of the tour operators specialising in jeep trips had given the party a lift up to Lónsöræfi. The police had also spoken, she said, to the handful of people who'd hired super-jeeps from car rentals in the area, but they had drawn a blank there too. The Reykjavík police were currently ringing round rental companies in the capital area, so it was still possible they might find a lead. So far, though, their enquiries hadn't produced any results.

As Wiktoria's car didn't even have four-wheel drive, it was thought highly unlikely that this could have been used to transport the party, though there was an outside chance that they had all crammed into it somehow and managed to nurse it over the rough track into the highlands. If the car wasn't large, there was a faint possibility that it hadn't been spotted because it was buried in a snowdrift. Or had rolled or slid into a ravine or a dip in the ground. First, though, the police were going to check whether Wiktoria's car could have been left in one of the fishing villages in the East Fjords where the unidentified ship's captain supposedly lived. They would get onto that tomorrow. Having shared this information, Rannveig lapsed into silence again and neither of them spoke as Jóhanna finished the food on her plate.

Jóhanna insisted on paying the bill. The meal had done her good. She was feeling calm now and was confident that she'd fall asleep the instant her head touched the pillow – before she'd even turned off the lights. The thought of going home and waiting alone for Geiri no longer filled her with dread.

When the police car pulled up outside her darkened house, her eyelids still felt heavy. She opened her mouth to say goodnight but Rannveig interrupted her. 'That's funny.' She leant forwards over the steering wheel to get a better look at Jóhanna and Geiri's house. 'A man came in this morning about a historical incident. I wasn't on duty at the time but I noticed it in the log when I got to work. He used to live here as a child.'

Jóhanna glanced at the house. Like the other properties in the street, it was a modest building. A very ordinary home, built for a family in the days when people were less demanding about storage space and floor-to-ceiling windows, and when wall sockets for landlines had still been considered indispensable. 'We bought it from a couple of brothers whose parents had built the house, so I'm guessing it must have been one of them. What's he doing in Höfn? They both live in Reykjavík.'

This time it was Rannveig's turn to be at a loss for a reply. 'I've no idea. It said nothing about that in the log. Just that he'd requested to see some old files.'

'Old files?' Jóhanna turned to look at Rannveig. 'What sort of files?'

'About an accident. A fatal accident.'

Jóhanna was instantly aware of a tingle in the small of her back that she knew was psychosomatic. The words 'fatal accident' had a particular significance for her. When she'd woken up in hospital, cut to pieces and sewn back together, she had been told that she was lucky to be alive: the accident could so easily have been fatal. During her convalescence and rehabilitation, she had been forced to listen to the same lecture more than once: if she'd landed on a rock, if she'd ended up under the car, if she'd been thrown over it or the driver had been going any faster, there could only have been one outcome. They never pointed out how lucky she'd have been if the car had been travelling more slowly, the brakes had worked properly, she'd landed on a traffic island rather than in the road, or had managed to dodge out of the way. Let alone if she hadn't gone out running late that evening in the first place. Or had taken a different route.

Of course they never said that. It would only have been rubbing salt in the wound. She had to focus on life, on the future. She was lucky. She had avoided a fatal accident. Hurrah.

'Who died?' Jóhanna felt compelled to ask, despite feeling she never wanted to hear about another death again.

'A little girl. Hardly more than a toddler. Her name was Salvör and she was his sister.' Rannveig continued talking, moving on to the question of whether he had any right to see the files.

Jóhanna listened but didn't take in the words. She didn't want to. It was hard enough processing her reaction to the five fatalities in Lónsöræfi. She couldn't face thinking about a small child as well.

She interrupted Rannveig: 'How awful. Anyway, I think I'd better say goodnight. I'm completely shattered.' She managed to squeeze out a smile. 'I hope you find that ship's captain. And, by the way, thanks for everything.'

'It was nothing.' Rannveig's answering smile was much more genuine than Jóhanna's. She leant forwards over the steering wheel again, studying the house. 'Just one thing – your front door appears to be open. Not a very good look for a policeman. Or, I don't know, maybe it's a great sign – no criminals around here!'

Jóhanna followed her gaze and saw that she was right. The front door was ajar.

Her dreams of bed evaporated. To her surprise, her voice was fairly steady as she replied: 'That's strange. It was open the other day as well. We probably need to get it fixed.'

'Do you leave it unlocked?'

'No.' Jóhanna didn't want to lie. 'I'm pretty sure I locked it when I went out. Last time too.'

Rannveig was still staring at the door, her expression serious now. 'Did you change the locks when you bought the house?'

Jóhanna shook her head. 'No. I don't think so. All the keys were handed over to us.'

The policewoman turned to her. There was no need for her to state the obvious: they could never be sure that they'd been given all the keys when they took possession. 'It's a bit of a

weird coincidence that the door should suddenly start opening of its own accord just when the son of the previous owner
happens to be in town.'

Jóhanna's vision of bed, rest and sleep slipped through her
fingers. 'You know, if it's all right with you, I'd be grateful if I
could wait for Geiri at the station, after all.'

'Of course. But I'd like to take a quick look around inside
your house if you don't mind. Just to be on the safe side. You
can come with me if you like or you can wait here.'

Jóhanna chose to wait. Rannveig got out of the car and
went in through the open door. After a minute or two, she
reappeared, closed the door behind her and got back in the
driver's seat. 'The house is empty. I can't see any signs of a
burglary but you two should still take a good look around this
evening.'

As the police car slowly moved off, Jóhanna kept her eyes
on the house until she couldn't twist her head round any further. She didn't see anything out of the ordinary. No movement, no lights, no unexplained shadows. It was only as they
drove past the neighbours' place that she spotted their black
Labrador, Morri, standing stock still in his garden, staring
fixedly at her house. There was a glint of white teeth.

She didn't need to open the car window to realise that he
was growling.

Chapter 25

Lónsöræfi, the previous week

It wasn't yet morning in any meaningful sense of the word. It wasn't even five o'clock. Dröfn and Tjörvi never set their alarms that early – not unless they had a flight to catch. There was no need. Neither of them was the type to get up with the lark for a session at the gym or to arrive at the office before anyone else. Now, though, they were driven by pure desperation; the survival instinct. The wind had dropped but they couldn't rely on the temporary lull to last. They needed to get moving as soon as possible, before the next blizzard blew up.

Dröfn had woken to find herself lying in a tight huddle, sandwiched between Tjörvi and Agnes. To fit into the two-man tent, they'd all had to turn on their sides and sleep pressed together like sardines. Such was the heat generated by their bodies that in the end they had all removed their outer clothes and slept in nothing but their woollen underwear. Agnes had needed help to get out of her coat and jumper. Clearly, her wrist wasn't going to mend on its own, any more than the damage to Tjörvi's face, fingers and toes.

Normally, Dröfn's transition from sleep to waking was a gentle one. She surfaced and dozed off again, surfaced and dozed, until her alarm clock went off. But this time the change had been instant, from sleeping to wide awake. With a single thought in her head: to get out of here.

There was a peculiar, foul smell tainting the air in the tent. It took her a moment to realise that it was coming from Tjörvi's wounds. Dröfn felt her throat tightening and had to concentrate hard on breathing to stop herself from whimpering aloud. She had to be strong. If she gave up the fight, there would be no hope of rescue. This thought worked, and she managed, somehow, to hang on to her self-control.

The spine-chilling muttering outside the tent had fallen silent in the end, cut off as abruptly as Dröfn had woken. One minute they could hear it, the next it had stopped. Afterwards, they had sat there for a long time, their eyes fixed on the tent flap, no one saying a word. Strong though the impulse had been to cry out in fright, they had all stayed quiet. Like small creatures faced with a larger predator, they had obeyed their instinct to make themselves as inconspicuous as possible.

Don't move, don't make a sound.

It was better to be on the safe side. When they'd finally allowed themselves to relax, Agnes had broken down in tears while Tjörvi had started rooting around in the stuff that was strewn all over the tent. It was typical of him to react to a difficult situation by engaging in some kind of displacement activity – tidying up the garage, sorting out his wardrobe – though the contents of the tent didn't offer him much scope. Dröfn, in contrast, tended to freeze into immobility at such moments, as her reaction yesterday evening had shown. She had sat there, unable to tear her gaze from the door of the tent, shaken by the ragged pounding of her heart.

Afterwards, they had spoken little and eventually settled down to sleep, trying to push away all thoughts of what had happened. Oddly enough, they had succeeded and all three had soon drifted off.

'We've got to get going.' Dröfn shook Tjörvi gently. He was still lying in his sleeping bag, staring blankly at the roof of the tent. He hadn't said a word since waking. Above them hung the torch Dröfn had retrieved from Bjólfur and Agnes's tent. When the strength had belatedly returned to her limbs after the horrible noises outside had stopped, she had hung the torch from the roof and left it on all night. Its beam was now as weak as the one she had lost in the snow. In the dim yellow light the three of them looked even more ghoulish than they did in reality. As if they had already crossed the great divide.

Dröfn was the only one who was dressed and ready to go. Agnes and Tjörvi were still in their sleeping bags. Once she had got up, creating more room for them, they had both seized the opportunity to roll over onto their backs. 'Get up,' she said urgently. 'We've got to make a start.' The need to leave this place was so powerful that her body literally ached with it. Every bone, every muscle, every nerve was screaming at her to get out of there. But it was a different story with Tjörvi and Agnes. Although they were as wide awake as she was, they seemed unable to move. She assumed their physical sufferings were to blame, the pain of their injuries sapping all their energy. If she had hurt herself too, all three of them would lie there to the bitter end. What a slow and horrible way to die.

'Please. Get up.' Surely they must at least be experiencing some normal bodily urges. Dröfn tried to appeal to these. 'Even if it's only to pop out for a pee.'

Her words seemed to work. Agnes sat up with a moan of pain. She shook Tjörvi as Dröfn had done. 'Up you get. We've got to hurry,' she said weakly. 'We've got to find Bjólfur.'

Dröfn groaned under her breath. She wanted to go back to the car, not head into the unknown on a hopeless cause. Instinct warned her not to start that argument straight away, though. Her first goal was to rouse them out of the tent to empty their bladders. After that she would persuade Agnes that it would be much more sensible to walk back to where they could get a phone signal and call out the rescue teams. It was the only sensible course of action. The only thing to do. She realised that she was screaming the thought inside her head.

In the end, Dröfn succeeded, through cunning and a great deal of gentle coaxing, to persuade them to leave their sleeping bags and put on their coats over their long woollen underwear. She kept her face carefully expressionless as she helped Tjörvi into his shoes and mittens. His frostbite urgently needed medical attention. It was looking worse than it had last night, his toes and fingers even darker purple and more swollen. She had to loosen the laces before she could cram his poor feet in their woollen socks into his shoes. The worst part of all was that he didn't even wince. Dröfn had to swallow the constriction in her throat before she could raise her eyes to his face again. Somewhere, she found the strength to give him a watery smile, though all she really wanted to do was curl up in a ball and howl.

Dröfn would have to open the tent door. Neither of the others was capable of it, any more than they had been capable of dressing themselves. Reminding herself sternly that they had no choice but to leave the safety of the tent if they were to escape from here, she took hold of the zip. There was no alternative. Heaving a deep breath, she closed her eyes and pulled it up as fast as she could. She waited. When neither Tjörvi nor Agnes emitted a yell, she knew it was safe to open her eyes.

Outside it was pitch black. Everything was perfectly still. The warm air from the tent escaped in a billow of vapour, lending a dreamlike atmosphere to the scene. Then the coils of moisture evaporated and the surroundings became more real. In the faint corona of torchlight, which extended about a metre from the tent, Dröfn saw that the drifts were considerably deeper. Deep enough to alter the appearance of the landscape. That was bad. Now it would be even harder to find their way back. If their tracks had been completely obliterated, they would have no chance of retracing their steps.

Dröfn tried to summon up her courage by kidding herself that they would find the way. It was the only thing that would force her out of that tent. She had to cling to the belief, however foolish it was, that they would find their way back. Of course they would.

She clambered out and straightened her cramped legs, telling herself to breathe steadily. At first her breaths came so fast and shallow that she was almost hyperventilating, but when no sinister noises reached her ears, it became easier to get a grip. Once she was sure it was safe, she bent down to help first Agnes, then Tjörvi, out of the narrow opening. All three of them stood there for a long moment, peering into the surrounding gloom, before working up the courage to move.

There was no need to go behind the tent to pee but they did so anyway, as if they all felt the need to pretend things were normal. That nothing had changed. That they were as polite and civilised as they always had been and there was no reason to behave like wild animals just because they were facing an icy death. This gave them the strength to pretend that the end was not as inevitable as Dröfn feared.

As Dröfn watched Tjörvi hobbling the few steps around the tent, the last vestiges of her optimism drained away. He would never be able to walk all the way back to the car. Agnes seemed no better off, though it wasn't her feet that were the problem. However much Dröfn tried to support her, every step Agnes took jolted her wrist. Like Tjörvi, she felt worryingly hot to the touch as well. Dröfn told herself it was just the heat from their sleeping bags but the truth was that, despite having been wedged between them, she herself wasn't burning up like they were.

Next to their tent was an empty space where Agnes and Bjólfur's should have been. It must have been snatched away by the storm during the night. There wasn't so much as a tent peg left. In their race to pitch it, they obviously hadn't hammered them in securely enough. At first, Dröfn thought Haukur's tent had gone as well, but as her eyes adjusted to the dimness, she saw that it was still there. Collapsed and half buried in snow, but there. She tensed as she made out a bulge inside, then realised it must be his rucksack and sleeping bag.

'Maybe Bjólfur's in Haukur's tent. Maybe he couldn't make it all the way to ours. He must have been too exhausted to drag himself any further.' Agnes had spotted the bump too. 'He could be asleep.'

'That's just Haukur's stuff, Agnes. The bump would be bigger if it was a person.' But the moment she'd said it, Dröfn began to wonder. It wasn't entirely far-fetched to think that it might be Haukur or Bjólfur lying under the canvas. Maybe the deep snow made the size of the bulge deceptive. But no one could be asleep in there. Not unless it was his final rest.

If it was Bjólfur, Agnes would be distraught, incapacitated by grief, but at least she would stop this madness about going to look for him. Slowly but surely, they would be able to shepherd her back to the hut and then to the car. Or at least in the direction they thought the car lay in. On the other hand, if Bjólfur wasn't inside, Dröfn could use the opportunity to hunt for painkillers in Haukur's backpack. They had already used up the small supply they had brought along. If she could persuade Agnes and Tjörvi to take a hefty dose of them, it would increase their chances of making it out of here on foot. And if all else failed, she could always pour the rest of Tjörvi's brandy down their throats.

Then there were the car keys. They might be in Haukur's rucksack. So far, her rescue effort was focused on reaching the car. She hadn't thought any further than that. But it occurred to her now that they would need the keys in order for that plan to mean anything. Dröfn said in a voice that was deceptively brave: 'I'll check, all the same.'

She braced herself, resolutely pushing away the memory of yesterday evening. The bloodcurdling muttering had started near Haukur's tent. Whatever it was that had made those noises, it had crawled out of his tent and pursued her back to Tjörvi and Agnes. What if that shape under the canvas was the horrible thing? But, no, it couldn't be. It couldn't be that.

Dröfn left Agnes and Tjörvi and waded the short distance through the drifts to the collapsed bundle of canvas that was Haukur's tent. Hurriedly, she started scraping snow away from the door to find the zip. Then, before opening it, she glanced back to check that the others were still standing there. They were. Yet although they were so close, they looked like two shadow beings, like people who are dead but haven't yet realised the fact.

Dröfn didn't know why her mind should have produced that image but she guessed they must be seeing her in the same way. Their chances of making it out of here alive were vanishingly small. They might as well be shadow beings. She felt as if she was the only one refusing to acknowledge the fact. Agnes and Tjörvi were becoming resigned to their fate.

She unzipped the door of Haukur's tent, lifting up the canvas so most of the snow slid off. Then she took a deep breath. There was nothing for it. What might be waiting for her inside? She realised there was no point trying to peer in as the darkness was even blacker in there than out here. She would just have to stick in her arm and fumble around.

Dröfn gritted her teeth. She knew she would scream her head off if her hand encountered a foot or a head. Judging by the total silence inside, if she did touch a body part, the person in question would be dead. Despite the gloves she was wearing, she knew that the feeling in her fingers would stay with her all the way back to the car. As for an encounter with something worse, something that was alive – but not . . . She knew what would happen in that case: she would go out of her mind with terror.

But she didn't experience anything of the sort. Instead, her groping fingers touched something that could be Haukur's backpack and she dragged it towards her, causing the bulge at the front of the tent to shrink. When she stuck her arm further inside, all she could feel was something soft – either a sleeping bag or clothes. She couldn't reach all the way to the back without burrowing inside the collapsed tent and there was no way in hell she was doing that.

Backing out with the rucksack in her arms, she stumbled over to Agnes and Tjörvi. 'There was no one inside, Agnes.'

Dim though the torchlight was, it couldn't hide the agony in Agnes's expression. 'Then we'll have to go and look,' Agnes said. 'We'll have to search for Bjólfur. I can't leave him behind here. He needs help.' She didn't say a word about Haukur, but then that was understandable. When the going gets tough, you put your loved ones first.

Dröfn answered as gently and steadily as she could, as if she was trying to persuade a child: 'I really think it would be better to head back to the car, Agnes, and phone for help.

Neither of you can walk far and if we go out of our way to look for Bjólfur, you'll never make it all the way back. The men went off in the opposite direction to the one we came from, remember?'

'We're not going to look for anyone, you're right about that. But I'm afraid we're not walking to the car either, Dröfn.' Tjörvi's voice was matter-of-fact and unemotional. He sounded as if he had just made coffee and noticed that they were out of milk. Clearly, he wasn't merely on the verge of accepting his fate; he already had.

'Of course we are.' Dröfn hugged the backpack as if it was a life-belt and she was adrift, far from shore. 'We've got to.'

Tjörvi listened, then said: 'We don't know the way and, even if we did, I can't walk. It's no good, Dröfn.' As if to emphasise the fact, he had to pause for a moment before finding the strength to add: 'Our only hope is to hunker down here and wait for someone to come and rescue us.'

Dröfn turned to Agnes for support. They had always stuck together in a crisis. But Agnes was a shadow of her former self. She was staring dully at her injured wrist, still muttering that they had to find Bjólfur.

So it was up to Dröfn to talk them round. 'Nobody's coming to rescue us,' she pointed out patiently, 'because nobody knows we're here. And there's no one else travelling in the area, so the chances of a search party finding us here are nil. Zero, Tjörvi. Our only hope is to make our own way back.'

'It's too far, Dröfn. We'll die of exposure. All three of us. If we wait it out, we'll have a faint chance. Not much of one – but a chance, all the same.'

Agnes suddenly rallied enough to say: 'I'm not staying here. I can't cope with another evening like yesterday. What the fuck was that?' When neither Dröfn nor Tjörvi spoke, she answered herself: 'Whatever it was, it means us harm. It's horrible, evil. I just want to find Bjólfur and get out of here. Maybe we'll be able to get a phone signal. Maybe we won't have to go very far.'

They all knew this wasn't going to happen, but Dröfn pounced on this feeble declaration of support. 'Yes. Let's find a phone signal.' Seeing that Tjörvi was about to weigh in, she forestalled him: 'I'll go and look for Bjólfur. And check for a phone signal on the way. I can't go far, Agnes, because we've got a long trek back to the car. But I'll have a look around here. By the time I get back, you two will have had a chance to rest a bit more. Then we'll set off.' It had hit home that she would have to make a sacrifice herself if she was going to get them on side. The thought of heading off into the darkness alone terrified her, but if that was what it took to make them go back with her, she was prepared to do it. She simply couldn't face cowering in that tent for days, waiting for the dreaded muttering to start up again. 'Agreed?'

Agnes's barely audible 'yes' clashed with Tjörvi's 'no'. Dröfn grabbed his coat to keep him outside with her, then told Agnes to go inside the tent and lie down. As soon as she had vanished through the flap, Dröfn whispered in his ear that she wouldn't go far. She'd walk in a straight line and turn back at the point where the men had turned east to follow the edge of the glacier. It wasn't snowing any more, so she couldn't get lost – all she had to do was follow her own footprints back to the camp. She would be an hour at most. His job was to make sure that Agnes fell asleep. That way she would lose track of time and Dröfn could claim she'd been gone for longer than she had.

Dröfn paused, her gaze fixed on Tjörvi's face. 'I've never been so frightened in my life. I promise to be careful. Trust me.'

'Then walk in a straight line and turn round the instant you reach the glacier. Don't you dare deviate from that line. And come back quickly. Promise me.' He stooped and kissed her on the forehead. His lips were flaking so badly that it was like being brushed by dry straws. 'I'll wait for you here. Take the torch. Your need is greater than ours.'

Dröfn wrapped her arms around him and hugged him as tight as she dared. Then she poked her head through the tent flap and freed the torch that was hanging from the ceiling. As she did so, she was careful not to tread on Agnes who was lying on her back, staring up unblinkingly, her face stiff. 'I'm afraid I've got to take your light, Agnes. I'll try and find Bjólfur. If I don't manage, it'll mean he's dug himself into a drift. At least he'll be safe there. The rescue team will find him later.'

'OK. But try anyway. Please.'

'I will, Agnes. I'll do my best.' Dröfn had the torch now and nothing remained except to leave. But she couldn't go without saying something. 'Take care of yourself, Agnes. I'll see you in a bit. You get plenty of rest in the meantime, so you're ready for the walk.'

As she said it, Dröfn realised it was a bad idea for Agnes to lie down in her coat. It would be dangerous if their outer gear was damp or sweaty when they set off. Reminding Agnes of this, she bent down to help her friend off with her coat. Despite being as careful as she could, Dröfn knocked Agnes's wrist, making her whimper. In the end, though, she got the coat off, then helped Agnes zip herself into her sleeping bag.

Before standing up again, Dröfn tipped the contents out of Haukur's backpack in the hope of finding some painkillers. When a pill bottle rolled out, she exclaimed in relief. Picking it up, she peered at the label in the torchlight. It was a strong anti-inflammatory painkiller and the bottle sounded almost full when she shook it. She clutched it to her chest with both hands for a moment before opening it and making Agnes swallow three pills.

After that, Dröfn stuffed Haukur's belongings back into his pack to make more room for Agnes and Tjörvi in the tent. Among the contents she had spied a pocket knife and kept hold of it. To her dismay, there had been no sign of a car key. She tried not to think about that. They would just have to hot-wire the jeep, like in the movies. It would be the least of their problems. She stood up, crouching under the low tent roof.

Before stepping outside, Dröfn said: 'We'll go for that sauna this evening, Agnes. Like you said. I remember now that there *was* one at the hotel, after all.' She blew her friend a kiss and said goodbye.

Although Dröfn had so much she wanted to say to Tjörvi, she made do with hugging him again, kissing him and telling him how much she loved him. That would have to do. If she said any more, she wouldn't be able to go. Her courage and resolve were no more than skin deep. She helped him into the tent again, staying outside herself, aware that if she didn't, she would never make herself leave. Bending down and leaning in through the opening, she helped him out of his coat and shoes, then pulled the mittens back onto his hands. She didn't want him to have to see his damaged fingers. Then she opened the knife and laid it in his palm. 'Just in case.'

She kissed him one last time and tore herself free before he could see the tears that had started to slide down her cheeks.

Then she started walking, into the infinite darkness.

Chapter 26

'Is everything OK?' The helicopter pilot was looking at Hjörvar, his brow furrowed with concern. He'd asked if he could dash into the station to use the toilet and Hjörvar had escorted him inside. While the man was busy, Hjörvar had hurried into the canteen to check the window again. He couldn't resist the urge. But when he warily parted the curtains, his eyes met nothing but darkness. The little girl hadn't come back. She had vanished immediately after he'd seen her on the screen – the moment he'd looked away. One minute she was standing there as still and straight-backed as a toy soldier, her nose almost pressed to the glass, the next she was gone as if the night had swallowed her up.

He had spent the time until the helicopter announced its arrival alternately checking the screen and peering out between the curtains, unable to stop himself – though he knew the security cameras were on, recording his bizarre behaviour.

Now one of the pilots had witnessed it too. He had taken Hjörvar by surprise, without even trying to sneak up on him. Hjörvar had simply been so intent on the window that he hadn't heard when the man returned from the toilet.

'Yeah, sure. Everything's fine.' Hjörvar straightened up, trying to appear normal. 'I just thought a bird might have flown into the window.' It reminded him of the time when his mother had caught him red-handed, pinching the Christmas biscuits, and he'd pretended to be looking for the remote control in the larder. As an excuse, the bird was about as plausible.

'A bird?' The pilot's expression was as sceptical as his mother's had been then. 'I thought they only flew into windows that reflected the light or that you can see inside. Not at night, with the curtains closed.'

'Oh, really? Well, there's no bird there, in any case. So you may well be right.' Hjörvar obeyed an irresistible compulsion to peer out again. 'I expect the wind blew something against the glass.'

The man nodded doubtfully, then lost interest in the subject. 'Thanks, anyway. Right, best be heading off.'

'Yes. Of course. Will you be back this way tomorrow?' Hjörvar hoped it wasn't too obvious that he was praying the answer would be no. He just couldn't face another late shift. He didn't even feel up to taking a morning shift alone. At this time of year, the early mornings were as black as the evenings.

The man zipped up his jacket. 'The less said about that the better. But I doubt it. I mean, for Christ's sake, surely there can't be any more bodies up there?'

'No. Let's hope not.' The man needn't doubt his sincerity; with all his heart, Hjörvar wanted this to be true.

They started walking towards the exit. Hjörvar was about to do as Erlingur had asked and enquire about the dead woman when Puss appeared by the end of one of the big containers that housed the radar sensors. This was most unusual as the cat generally fled into hiding when he heard the chopper approaching and didn't reappear until it had taken off again. He must have got confused.

'Is that a cat?' The pilot was regarding the animal in surprise. Puss stopped dead and stared back at the unexpected visitor.

'Yes.' Hjörvar tried to play it down. 'It's a stray that pays us a visit from time to time.'

The pilot bent down to scratch Puss behind the ears, but the cat dodged away. As the man straightened up again, he glanced around. 'Isn't this place full of sensitive equipment? Is it safe to have a stray cat wandering around in here?'

Hjörvar was in no fit state to come up with a clever answer, an answer that would ensure that the cat's presence at the station didn't turn into a big issue. No one had commented on it so far, but it wouldn't take much for Coast Guard HQ to change their mind and insist that Puss must go – if only because the guys at NATO might take a dim view of him. Whenever they were expecting visitors from abroad, he and Erlingur shut the cat in a room in the staff accommodation, and up to now they had got away with it. But Hjörvar thought he'd better say something now or their precautions would have been wasted. 'Nothing's happened. And he's absolutely no trouble.'

'I see.' The pilot looked down at Puss, then back at Hjörvar and smiled. Hjörvar didn't know him well enough to interpret the smile. He just hoped it meant the man wasn't going to take it any further.

They went outside with Puss on their heels. Thanks to the cat, Hjörvar had missed his chance to make enquiries about the dead woman on Erlingur's behalf. The pilot said goodbye and jogged over to the waiting chopper, which was one of the two big Coast Guard machines, capable of carrying a five-man crew and nearly twenty passengers. It defied belief that this blue-and-white colossus could actually take off. Hjörvar had given up trying to understand how it was possible but he always felt a frisson in his stomach when it lifted off the ground.

Puss sat down beside him and mewed. It had a melancholic sound, Hjörvar thought. He couldn't help wondering if Puss knew instinctively what was on board. Cats had a better sense of smell than humans, didn't they? So it wasn't inconceivable that the animal could pick up the odour of death from inside the machine.

Hjörvar waved goodbye to the other pilot, who raised a hand in farewell. The passengers sitting in the back kept their eyes to the front, not even glancing out of the windows when the helicopter finally took off. It couldn't be much fun being cooped up in a tin can like that with a body bag. As if to underline these thoughts, Puss emitted a loud yowl. His gaze was fixed on the helicopter, his body poised as if to leap after it. But instead, he followed Hjörvar back into the building.

Hjörvar had no intention of sticking around. The sooner he got out of here, the better. He would do one more circuit of the station to assure himself that everything was on that should be on and off that was supposed to be off. Then he'd fetch the keys and his laptop and hightail it home. His main fear was that he would be in such a hurry to leave that he would take the dirt track back to the ring road too fast. If the car rolled, he would be in an even worse predicament than he was here at the station.

Inside, all was quiet. The only sounds were the familiar hum of the radar antenna. And Puss's pathetic yowling. Wasting no time, Hjörvar set off on his tour of inspection, almost running from room to room to check that everything was in order, leaving the canteen and office till last. That way, as soon as he had grabbed his laptop and made sure the coffee machine was off, he could dash straight for the exit.

Like everywhere else in the station building, all was in order in the canteen. The curtains were still closed and this time Hjörvar resisted the impulse to look outside. What good would it do? Seeing a small hand or the girl's face outside the glass wouldn't make him feel any better. If anything, it would be much worse. The short walk from the front door to the car would seem endless.

Hjörvar grabbed the laptop from his desk, shoved it in its case and zipped it up, all in record time. While doing so, he kept his back to the screen relaying recordings from the CCTV feed. The camera was still angled towards the outside wall of the canteen and, as with anything he might spy through the curtains, he felt it was better not to know.

But just as Hjörvar was hurrying out of the office, he gave in to the temptation and paused to look at the screen. It showed nothing out of the ordinary. Only the wall, the window and the snow beneath it – unmarred by footprints. He emitted a heavy sigh, unaware that he had been holding his breath.

It would be OK.

Of course it would be OK.

There was nothing outside the window. There never had been anything there. He'd imagined it, like the ringing of the entryphone. The news of his long-dead sister had come at the worst possible time. And it didn't help that his only memory from those days was the noise of her terrible screaming. Of himself clasping his hands over his ears.

Had he failed his little sister in some way? Had something happened that he wasn't aware of? Or hadn't wanted to get involved in? Was he conjuring up her image out of some kind of guilt at his own cowardice as a child? Of course, it was absurd to think that a mere kid could have had any influence on the actions of adults. But a small child wouldn't know that. Perhaps he had felt bad about it at the time and this had left him with a sense of guilt associated with the suppressed memory – guilt out of all proportion to how little he could have done to change the course of events if his parents had betrayed his sister in some way.

That was it. He had an intuition that it was. Yet the cause of her screams remained a mystery. Like the manner of her death. Was it an accident or could his father have deliberately done away with his daughter? And if so, why, for God's sake?

Their father had been a cold, ill-tempered man. But it was one thing to have a surly temperament, quite another to murder one's own child. Hjörvar couldn't picture it. But then he hadn't actually known his father that well. Perhaps that was no coincidence. If this completely unsubstantiated suspicion had a basis in reality, perhaps their mother had wanted to keep the brothers as far away from their father as possible. Think about it: if he had been responsible for their sister's death, how could she have trusted him with the two of them? The answer was simple: she couldn't.

It still didn't quite add up. Why would their father have killed their little sister? Yes, she had been difficult, but he was rarely home, spending most of his time at sea. The burden of caring for her had fallen squarely on their mother. Hjörvar had never been under the impression that his father was a bad man. But supposing he was wrong? Could Salvör's screaming have been connected to something their father had done to her? Something he was afraid she would tell people about when she was older?

There was no point standing there brooding on the past. The fact was, he couldn't remember anything from those days, so he was in no position to get to the bottom of it. Unless he went to a shrink. Maybe an expert could help him recover the memories that must be locked inside his head. It would probably take a crowbar to prise them loose, but if he found a good practitioner, it wasn't impossible. There was a lot to be gained. If he could put his past in order, his future would be free. Then he could concentrate his energies on becoming a better person.

Hjörvar was conscious of feeling a little calmer. He was no longer on edge and his heartbeat was slow and steady. There was nothing wrong at the station apart from the inventions of his tortured psyche. There was nothing to be afraid of. No need to leave the light on in the canteen and lie to Erlingur that he had forgotten to switch it off.

Puss wound himself around Hjörvar's legs, still mewing, still being a nuisance. The fact that Hjörvar was feeling better seemed to make no impression on him.

At that moment, the phone in Hjörvar's pocket started ringing and he saw that it was his son, Njördur. For once, he answered immediately. It must be because he was feeling almost drunk with relief. They exchanged polite greetings but Hjörvar didn't ask how his son was getting on with finding a job. He was in too good a mood to put up with any of Njördur's bullshit. If he'd found a job, he'd tell his father – there was no need to interrogate him about it. Whether he'd be telling the truth was another matter. But it turned out that he wasn't ringing with news of that sort. The purpose of his call was to ask about Salvör. Clearly, his sister had been in touch.

Njördur seemed sceptical about Salvör's story and Hjörvar had to refrain from reminding him that if anyone was an expert in making stuff up, it was Njördur, not him. Hjörvar wasn't in the habit of lying to his kids. Come to think of it, maybe always telling them the unvarnished truth was a mistake. Because it was rarely what they wanted to hear. But now he merely repeated what he had told Ágústa, adding nothing more. He had no intention of sharing his suspicions about Salvör's fate.

In the darkened canteen, the screen showing the revolving radar antenna was suddenly very conspicuous. Hjörvar's eyes were drawn to it against his will. Noticing that the interference was out of sync with the revolutions again, he felt himself break out in a cold sweat.

His conversation with Njördur was winding down. Before saying goodbye, Hjörvar impulsively offered to take Njördur and his sister out for a meal next time he was in Reykjavík. His son's delight at this invitation was touching.

Hjörvar was left standing there with the phone in his hand, watching the massive antenna rotating, and feeling the familiar sense of dread. When he saw a small hand reach up into the image, the fear tightened around his heart.

Instinctively, he bent down and scooped up the cat, then made for the exit as fast as he could, trying desperately to ignore the trail of small wet footprints that ran along the corridor, prints that hadn't been there a moment earlier.

When he entered the large space housing the two radar containers, he couldn't help noticing that the footprints disappeared by one of the spiral staircases leading up into the radome. Momentarily rooted to the spot with terror, he raised his eyes with slow reluctance up the metal steps. On the top stair, a small foot appeared, without a shoe. It was Puss who broke his trance. The cat started struggling so frantically that Hjörvar had to tighten his grip. Still clutching the animal in his arms, he made a run for it, the laptop trapped under his elbow.

Once he was safely outside the door, he had to put Puss down in order to activate the alarm. His hand was shaking so badly he could hardly punch in the numbers. The whole time he was wondering how fast someone could run down the stairs, but he managed to control his panic long enough to enter the code.

The moment Hjörvar slammed the door, the handle was grabbed from the other side and began to turn. He staggered backwards, almost losing his balance, then recovered and set off at a sprint for the gate. As he opened it, he snatched a nervous glance over his shoulder for Puss. The cat was nowhere to be seen, although the black markings of his coat should have been visible against the snow. Hjörvar called him but the cat seemed to have gone into hiding. Going back to look for him was out of the question. Puss had survived in the open air before they'd taken him in. He'd just have to fend for himself again now.

Hjörvar exited through the gate and closed it behind him, pausing to scan the area inside the perimeter fence one more time in the hope that Puss would emerge from his hiding place. There was no sign of him.

Hjörvar tossed the laptop onto the passenger seat of the car, stuck the key in the ignition and started the engine. He didn't waste time putting on his seat belt and the warning bleeps went off, reminding him to think better of it. He ignored them.

He reversed out of the parking space and turned the car to face the dirt track that led to the main road. Beyond the glow of the headlights, it vanished into the gloom. He undipped his lights to see a bit further, then cast one more glance out of the side window and, seeing no sign of Puss, accelerated away.

The steering wheel felt icy to the touch but he gripped it for dear life as if fearing he would be ripped out of the car. He had to fight against the urge to put his foot to the floor.

When he reached the gate that closed off the area to unauthorised traffic, he was forced to stop. He took a deep breath. Then, counting up to ten, he leapt out, opened the gate, drove through it, then went through the same motions to shut it behind him, holding his breath the whole time he was outside. By the Viking Café, he had to stop again to open the barrier in order to continue along the straight track. All the lights were off in the low wooden building and there wasn't the faintest glow from the riding stables on the other side of the road. Hjörvar had to summon up his nerve to roll down the window and reach out an arm to hold his access pass to the card reader in the darkness. Out of the corner of his eye, he glimpsed the car that had been sitting on the side of the road for weeks, the car that got so badly on Erlingur's nerves. Hjörvar had never been bothered by its presence; it hadn't irritated him or roused any other feelings. Now, though, in his agitated state, he could have sworn there was a figure sitting in the driver's seat, watching him. Total bullshit, of course – but he couldn't shake off the impression.

For the first time, it struck him how agonisingly slowly the barrier was going up. The instant he was sure it would clear the roof of the car, he stamped on the accelerator, not bothering, for once, to check if it had lowered behind him.

Not until he was out on the main road with the tarmac reassuringly solid under his wheels did he feel a slight easing of his tension. Pulling over to the side of the road, he took out the radio and informed HQ of his departure. This wasn't quite by the book, as he was supposed to radio them before leaving the site, but that was the least of his worries.

The man who answered didn't seem to notice anything amiss, though to Hjörvar it sounded as though his voice was trembling and breaking on every other word. The moment he'd reported in, he said a hasty goodbye, then put down the radio and turned to look back across the lagoon to the radar station.

The giant white golf ball was dimly visible. Hjörvar shifted his gaze back to the road. He would be in Höfn in no time. Until then, he would just have to discipline himself not to look in the rear-view mirror.

Only when he took the turning into town did the crushing weight of his fear lift a little. He felt like a man lying trapped under a stack of timbers – after two planks have been removed. But it was enough to let him think clearly. Or more clearly, at least.

It wasn't a shrink he needed. Or not only a shrink. What he needed above all was to find out what had happened to his sister. Only then would he be able to forgive himself for having failed her, for having clamped his hands over his ears when she needed him most. And accept too that he'd only been a child.

Until then he would have no peace, regardless of what was causing these delusions or bizarre experiences. Regardless of whether she could hear him. Of whether this was all psychological or else some strange version of reality, as unlikely as a helicopter that could defy the laws of gravity and rise into the air.

Hjörvar parked in front of the shabby industrial housing unit where he lived and went inside. Instead of taking off his shoes at the door as was his custom, he marched straight into the kitchen, got out a bottle of gin and took a hefty swig.

Chapter 27

Jóhanna's wait for Geiri at the police station was beginning to feel like an endurance test. She yearned to soak her sore muscles in a hot bath, then climb into bed. Of course, she could have showered at the station and gone for a lie-down on a couch in one of the cells, but it wouldn't be the same. Still, on the plus side, at least here she had Rannveig's company.

The young policewoman had gone out of her way to be kind. In between taking care of her duties, she regularly put her head round the door of the little interview room where Jóhanna had settled down to wait. Suspects were provided with a small sofa to sit on instead of a hard chair at the table; presumably the intention was to create a relaxed atmosphere. While the sofa was an improvement on the unyielding plastic chair in the kitchen, unfortunately it was only a two-seater, with hard wooden armrests which made it impossible to stretch out. Jóhanna had tried various positions; every sofa or chair offered at least one comfortable option, she told herself, except this one.

Every now and then, Rannveig would pop by to offer her something to drink or eat. Apart from that, Jóhanna killed time with her phone. It was nearing the end of its life and the battery didn't last long. In the end, it shut down without warning, although according to the screen display there had been about twenty per cent of battery power left. That was when the time really began to drag. Jóhanna found herself trying to engage Rannveig in conversation whenever she looked in, but soon ran out of things to say. So few topics seemed remotely appropriate in the circumstances.

'How does coffee sound? Too late, maybe?' The young woman appeared in the doorway again. 'By the way, it only just occurred to me that I should have offered you some pain-killers. We've got anti-inflammatories, both tablets and topic-al gels. They're pretty indispensable in our line of work.'

Jóhanna swallowed her pride and accepted the pills. She also decided to heave herself off the sofa and follow Rannveig into the kitchen. There was no call to make the young woman run around like a waitress with coffee and pills. Besides, it would do Jóhanna good to stretch her legs and have a change of scene. It wasn't exactly cosy in the interview room, in spite of the police's creditable attempts to create a pleasant atmosphere in there.

Jóhanna lowered herself into a chair at the kitchen table, unable to hide a wince as she encountered the hard plastic. She appreciated the way her companion pretended not to notice. Rannveig merely shook another pill out of the bottle and gave her three instead of the two she had asked for. Jóhanna swal-lowed them at once.

Next, Rannveig brought their coffee over in two pastel-coloured Moomin cups that seemed incongruously cheerful.

'Out of interest, I rang my colleague who handled the request for the old files I mentioned.' Rannveig handed Jóhanna a small carton of long-life milk. While Jóhanna was pouring a generous splash into her coffee, Rannveig took a seat herself and continued: 'I just wanted to hear his opinion of the man, because of this business of your open door – you know, whether the guy had struck him as a bit weird or cap-able of anything dodgy.'

Rannveig didn't explain what she meant by 'dodgy' in this context and Jóhanna thought it better not to ask. She didn't want to know what the police thought the man might be capable of. 'Did he remember him?'

Rannveig smiled. 'Yes. Thankfully, we don't get many people coming in. Anyway, the good news is that my colleague didn't get any bad feelings about the guy. He said he was just a very ordinary middle-aged bloke, a bit shy and quiet. I don't think you need have any major worries about him. Still, it's strange about your door. You two should hurry up and get the locks changed.'

'I'll call a locksmith first thing tomorrow morning.' Jóhanna cradled her coffee cup in both hands to warm them. She was still feeling chilled to the bone after her trip into Lónsöræfi. 'Stupid not to have done it when we first took possession. It never crossed my mind.'

Rannveig dismissed this oversight. 'I didn't change the locks either when I bought my flat. It's not like you don't have enough else to do when you're moving.' She sipped her coffee, then added with a smile: 'I bet the neighbours in your street were pleased when you bought the place. You know it had been standing empty for a while – two years, I think? That's quite a long time by the standards of the Höfn property market. The previous owner was such a miserable old git that it was like he infected the house. As kids we used to be terrified of him, even though he was hardly ever there. We never went anywhere near his garden when we were playing. We used to say it was haunted.'

'Haunted?' It was the first Jóhanna had heard of such a thing. Geiri hadn't said a word when they were arranging to buy the house, but she supposed that wasn't surprising. Some superstitious nonsense dreamt up by kids had no place in the serious business of house-buying, even though Geiri, who had grown up here himself, must have heard the tale. 'Haunted in what way?'

Rannveig's smile faded. Jóhanna had probably sounded too serious. 'Oh, sorry. I shouldn't have mentioned it,' she replied. 'Honestly, it was total nonsense. I expect it started because of the fatal accident the owner's son was asking about. It happened long before my time but somehow the story lived on among the locals, especially among us kids. Probably because it involved a child. They used to say the place was haunted by a little girl who would try and trick us into playing with her. But anyone who fell into her trap would die young. Total nonsense, like I said.'

Jóhanna forced a smile. 'Yes, of course. Total nonsense.' But her thoughts flew to the small blonde girl next door with her innocent desire to make friends, and then to the icy fingers she believed she had felt touching her spine. She felt sick.

'And let's not forget that the theory about it being haunted doesn't make any sense – the child didn't die in the house or the garden. The accident happened out at Stokksnes. So it's not like anyone actually passed away on your property.' Rannveig gave Jóhanna an apologetic look. 'I shouldn't have brought it up. I just assumed you must have heard about it.'

'Don't worry about it.' Jóhanna let go of her mug and waved her hand dismissively, as if she wasn't remotely concerned. But it wasn't true. Her unsettling suspicion that the rumour had some basis in truth was mingled with irritation at Geiri. He should have told her. But the feeling passed immediately, because, the fact was, the old story wouldn't have changed their minds about the purchase. The price had been too good to refuse. They'd both wanted a house rather than a flat and there were only a limited number of properties available in a small place like Höfn. Neither of them earned a particularly good salary, and, in contrast to so many rural towns in Iceland, there was enough work here, which meant demand for property was high. The house had seemed like a godsend. It would have taken more than a ghost to put them off.

Rannveig carried on apologising. 'Between you and me, I reckon the story started with our parents. They probably used it to deter us from hanging around the old man's garden. He had a bad reputation in town as a grumpy old recluse and they didn't trust him with their kids. But because he was away so much, I suppose people tended to forget what was behind it. Anyway, I believe that's the explanation.'

The awkward silence that followed their conversation about the girl and the house was only broken by the sound of the front door opening. Hearing voices, Jóhanna realised, to her dismay, that Geiri wasn't alone. She'd been hoping they could go straight home together when he turned up. Clearly, she could forget that idea.

But Geiri was alone when he appeared at the kitchen door. He smiled wearily at Jóhanna and nodded to Rannveig, who shot to her feet as though she'd been caught slacking. She disappeared in the direction of the front desk and Geiri lowered himself into the seat she had just vacated.

Jóhanna expected him to ask what she was doing there, why she wasn't at home, but he didn't. He seemed even wearier than yesterday, much more so than he had been this morning. 'I can't come home just yet. I'm sorry.'

'Don't worry about it.' Jóhanna was aware that she had said exactly the same to the young policewoman earlier and that her words were no more sincere now than they had been then. 'I can easily wait.'

She proceeded to tell him why she was there, adding that they needed to change the locks. Geiri listened, nodding, but didn't seem interested. She might as well have turned up at the station in the middle of summer and hung around merely to tell him that they needed to mow the lawn. But then what had she been expecting? He was tired and distracted by work.

'We've still got a few things we need to go over. It won't take long. In fact, this should be the last long day. For now, anyway. Everyone's leaving tomorrow. We should be able to handle the rest of the stuff at our end without any back-up. No one else has been reported missing and we've done a thorough search of the area around the bodies. If we hear that someone else was out there, we'll mount another search, but for now we're assuming that's all of them.'

Geiri met her gaze with a heavy sigh. 'The case is as good as over. I checked my email as soon as we got a phone signal and the results of the post-mortems on the first four bodies have come through. There are no suspicious circumstances surrounding their deaths. So, as far as the pathologist's concerned, it's not a criminal matter. It'll be up to other people to work out what went on up there, if that's ever going to be possible. Your mate Thórir has offered his assistance with that. He says he might be able to get some foreign experts he knows to compile a report. Anyway, I'll be free from tomorrow, apart from simple follow-up jobs which can be done in normal working hours. Unless anything unexpected comes to light during Wiktoria's post-mortem.'

This was the best news he could have given her. Now the dark evenings would be spent the way they were supposed to be, in cosy togetherness. There was no place in that picture for icy fingers creeping up either of their spines. Everything would return to normal and the events of the last few days would recede until they were nothing more than a bad memory. A memory that would come back to haunt her less and less often with the passing of time.

'Do you want to come and say hello to the gang? It's the same lot who came to dinner. If they know you're waiting for me, I reckon we'll finish up sooner.'

They got up and Jóhanna put her head round the door of the meeting room to say hello. The people in there looked as dog-tired as Geiri. She said she'd leave them to hold their meeting in peace, adding – just to exert a bit of pressure – that she would wait outside in the meantime. The fact was that if she didn't get to bed soon, she'd have to call in sick tomorrow – either that or turn up to work in a wheelchair.

Jóhanna returned to the little sofa and her frustrating attempts to find a comfortable position. She still hadn't succeeded when Thórir appeared and told her the meeting was just drawing to a close. Then he asked where the toilet was and she pointed him in the right direction, but instead of immediately leaving, he hovered awkwardly in the doorway, as if something was troubling him. When he finally spoke, the cause of his discomfort became clear. 'I just wanted to offer my condolences. For the woman you used to work with. An awful business. Awful.'

'Oh, right. Thank you. Yes, such a tragic, strange thing to happen. But the people I'm most sorry for are her family back in Poland. It must be terrible to lose a loved one far from home. It seems so wrong somehow.'

'God, yes. I'm just glad it's not my job to break the news to them.' Thórir folded his arms across his chest, apparently in no hurry to find the toilet.

'Same here.' Jóhanna wondered who the job would fall to, now that the investigation was no longer the business of the local police in Höfn. Possibly the pathologist. Then again, possibly not. Who would want to hear about the death of a loved one from the person who had just been carving up their body? No, it would probably fall to someone in Selfoss or Reykjavík CID.

Thórir looked both ways as if making sure there was no one within earshot. Then he leant his head into the room and whispered: 'I can tell you one thing, if you'll keep it to yourself – for now, anyway.'

Jóhanna nodded, her eyes wide. She was too tired to conceal her curiosity.

'I reckon the woman you used to work with died some time before the others. Of course, they'll need a post-mortem to confirm the fact, but I'm pretty confident. The body showed signs of having been frozen for much longer than the others. In my opinion, at least. The effect of freezing temperatures on the human physiology, both living and dead, was part of my studies.'

'You mean she was the first to die?' Jóhanna didn't think to whisper and Thórir shot a nervous glance down the corridor. Then he put his head back into the room, keeping his voice down.

'Yes, I mean she must have died quite a considerable time before the others. Long before the two couples arrived in the area. Maybe even a matter of months before.'

Jóhanna hesitated before posing the question she couldn't help but ask. 'You mean because of the state her face was in?' With horrifying clarity, she saw again the hollow, black eye sockets and gaping mouth. When Thórir appeared reluctant to answer, she added: 'What actually happened? Was it connected to the pool of blood they found by the hut?'

Thórir shook his head. 'No, I don't imagine so. The most obvious explanation is an animal of some kind. A fox or raven. Probably a raven. Birds tend to eat the eyes and tongue first because they represent the most easily accessible soft tissue. They find it harder to tear through skin or hide to get at the flesh beneath. No doubt they'd have eaten more if the body hadn't been buried under a layer of snow—' Thórir broke off, as if belatedly realising that those weren't the kind of details Jóhanna had been after.

Reluctant though she was to hear any more, she had to get one thing clear before she went to sleep that night: 'This did happen after she was dead, didn't it?'

Thórir was quick to reply: 'Oh God, yes. Unquestionably.'

Jóhanna lapsed into silence. She couldn't think of anything else to say. And she couldn't bear to hear any more details about the state of the bodies – whether Wiktoria's or the others'. Besides, the fact that Wiktoria had died long before the rest of them was so unexpected that she needed some time to digest the news. No doubt a load of questions would occur to her after Thórir had left. Not that it mattered, since he was unlikely to have the answers.

'Keep the information about Wiktoria's time of death under your hat, will you? It's only speculation – at present. Though I'm afraid the post-mortem is likely to confirm my theory.'

Having got this off his chest, Thórir vanished in the direction of the toilet, leaving Jóhanna deep in thought. If Wiktoria had no connection to the couples from Reykjavík, there was no need to waste any more time puzzling over that aspect. But this begged a new question: what on earth had Wiktoria been doing out there in the wilderness in the middle of winter, all on her own?

When Thórir passed the door again shortly afterwards, Jóhanna pretended not to notice him. She needed peace to think and, anyway, she'd already heard more than enough.

By the time the meeting finally ended she still hadn't come up with any theories about what Wiktoria might have been doing in Lónsöræfi. The visitors filed out of the room first, and once they had set off back towards their hotel and guest-house, Geiri and Jóhanna were able at long last to go home. She had rarely been so grateful to pull on her snowsuit. Heavily though the garment weighed on her, it didn't matter. In no time at all she would be tucked up in bed.

Geiri put an arm round her shoulders after they had gone a few steps from the police station. Although this additional weight was the last thing her poor, maimed body needed, it was worth it for the comfort it gave her. She didn't want to destroy the mood by bringing up the subject of the house, the open front door or the ghost story. Nor did she want to betray Thórir's confidence by asking about Wiktoria. All that could wait.

As they walked along the path below their house, she noticed that the light was on in their neighbours' sitting room, although all the other lights were off. As a result, the window was as bright as a computer screen.

Framed in the rectangle of light was the neighbours' small daughter. It must be long past her bedtime and the other darkened windows suggested that her parents were asleep. Jóhanna thought the little girl was wearing pyjamas. She had both hands pressed to the glass and appeared to be saying something. Then she waved. Jóhanna and Geiri raised their hands in return. Until they realised that she wasn't waving to them but to someone in the garden. Jóhanna sensed Geiri tensing beside her. He moved swiftly to the garden fence and looked over.

Jóhanna went to stand beside him. There was no one in the garden. But the little girl in the window carried on waving.

Chapter 28

Lónsöræfi, the previous week

The thin veil of cloud was dispersing. Now and then there was a glimpse of stars, one or two at a time, never enough for Dröfn to be able to recognise the constellation. Yet she looked up at regular intervals, holding on to the hope of seeing something familiar. She needed that so badly, even if only for a fraction of a second before the clouds closed over again. She wasn't asking for much, just a brief vision of something comfortingly familiar, something other than this endless snow, this harsh, alien landscape.

Dröfn didn't know how long she had been walking, or how far she had come. It was a good while since she had been able to make out the shape of the tent when she looked back, yet she couldn't stop herself from casting frequent glances over her shoulder. She needed to reassure herself that the way back was still there. It wasn't like she was following a marked path; all she could see was the line of her footprints unravelling behind her as far as the darkness allowed. Which wasn't far.

She believed she had been walking in a straight line but it was hard to judge. There were no landmarks to go by, so for all she knew she could have been walking in a circle. One thing was sure: she hadn't yet reached the place where she would have to make a ninety-degree turn. The place where she had promised to turn back. There was nothing to stop her doing that here and now, of course. Nothing but her conscience. She just couldn't look Agnes in the eye and lie to her.

That wasn't the only reason, however. The truth was that she couldn't face returning to the others. Not yet. Horribly exposed though she felt, walking alone out here in the presence of God knows what, at least she didn't have to confront the fact that neither of them was capable of walking back to the car. As long as she was alone, she could keep kidding herself, keep closing her eyes to the state they were in, keep imagining that the three of them all had a realistic chance of making it home alive.

It helped that she hadn't been aware of anything frightening. No menacing noises or voices or deeper shadows in the lightless gloom. The instant she heard or saw anything uncanny, she would hightail it back to the tent as if it were a fortress. Even a thin sheet of canvas seemed better than no protection at all.

She reminded herself that she had spotted a dark patch in the snow while she was walking. The light had been too dim for her to discern the colour but she'd had a horrible premonition that if she were to walk over and shine her torch on it, she'd discover that it was red. Tjörvi had spoken of patches of blood, but this couldn't be one of the ones he had seen: too much fresh snow had fallen since then. Hastily looking away, she had quickened her pace. There were some things it was better not to see.

A shape loomed up in front of her and instinctively she slowed down, her strides becoming shorter. Once she had approached a little closer, her straining eyes made out a slope, so steep it resembled a wall. At least that's how it appeared to Dröfn, from a distance, in the poor light. This had to be it: the turning point.

She pictured herself retracing her steps, returning empty-handed to the tent, with no news of Bjólfur or Haukur's fate.

She hadn't come across a single trace of them, nothing to suggest they could be anywhere nearby. But that was to be expected. The blizzard had erased their footprints, blowing them away or filling them in with snow. The only hope of finding the men now would be if she were to run into them on the way back to the camp. And that was unthinkable. Judging by the state Tjörvi had been in after a much shorter time out there in the freezing cold, neither of them could still be on their feet.

The only real hope was that they might have acted fast and dug themselves down into a snowdrift or resorted to some other survival trick that Haukur might know of. If Bjólfur had been alone, she doubted he would have sought shelter in time. He was the type who refused to quit and would struggle on for as long as humanly possible. That sort of behaviour might not matter in the city, but in these conditions it could mean the difference between life and death.

Dröfn came to a halt. She had decided to make a wish. She felt she should focus on that and that alone, which she couldn't do if she was wading through snow at the same time. Surely she had the right to make three wishes? That's how it worked. You got three at a time and it wouldn't do to squander them. Squeezing her eyes shut, she wished, first, that Tjörvi would recover, that he would be better by the time she returned. Her second wish was that Agnes's pain would have improved enough for her to feel up to walking to the car. Her third, and last: that Bjólfur had found Haukur and followed his advice. If he hadn't, Dröfn didn't want to come across him. Since it was unlikely she would find him alive, she would rather return with the news that his fate was still uncertain. She didn't want to break it to Agnes that he had gone to join his ancestors, alone and bewildered, in that brutal storm.

Dröfn opened her eyes and started moving again, closer and closer to the slope, until she could no longer take another step without climbing it. For a moment she couldn't work out her right from her left. It wasn't something she normally had any problems with, but she felt disorientated by the unchanging whiteness and the silence. Eventually managing to ground her thoughts again, she turned to the right and peered in the direction Tjörvi said they had taken.

The route was demarcated on the left by the steep slope and on the right by a jumble of large boulders. Most of the rocks were buried under the snow but here and there one jutted out, thrown into sharp relief as, without warning, the moon shrugged off its veil of cloud. Dröfn's torch was dying, its feeble glow illuminating no more than a couple of metres in front of her feet, but the sudden brightness allowed her to see some way along the path Tjörvi had described. This wouldn't last, though: the moon was bound to disappear again in a minute, judging by the luck she'd had so far.

She was too tired even to flinch when a movement caught her eye, some way off. Dröfn squinted towards it, berating herself for having used up all her wishes. She could have done with one now, a chance to wish that the shape coming towards her was Bjólfur, rather than something evil.

The thing, staggering ever closer, wasn't Bjólfur. Or Haukur either. It was the reindeer cow. She was moving as if every step was her last and Dröfn felt a pang at not having thrown her those crusts of bread when she'd wanted to. The poor creature was starving to death before her eyes.

Was there no end to the wretchedness and cruelty of the world? Dröfn felt her tears brimming over and slowly rolling down her face. At first they felt pleasantly hot on her frozen cheeks but by the time they reached her chin they had turned icy and stung her jaw. Yet she couldn't stem the tide. She didn't howl, just wept silent tears for Tjörvi, Agnes, Bjólfur and Haukur, for the reindeer, and for herself.

When the well of tears eventually dried up, she felt as bad as before, if not worse. There was no point standing there, waiting for some kind of miracle. The time for those was over. She would have to work up the courage to return to the tents. Once there, she would have to force more painkillers and brandy down Agnes and Tjörvi's throats, then head off again.

Just as she was about to turn back, she saw the reindeer lower its head to sniff at something in the snow. At first she thought it must be some vegetation uncovered by the wind, and felt briefly glad for the animal. She took a few steps nearer to see what it was, shining the wavering torch beam at the thing protruding from the snow. To her horror, she saw that it couldn't be a plant. That bright orange colour didn't belong to any species outside a botanic garden or a greenhouse. As if to confirm this, the cow looked up and stumbled away. Sticking her head forward, she stared at Dröfn as if waiting for some kind of reaction from her.

Full of a horrible suspicion of what she would find, Dröfn walked slowly forwards. The cow retreated, step by step, in feeble rejection of her presence. When Dröfn reached the place where the orange colour formed a stark contrast to the white snow, she fell to her knees. Not to get a better look but inadvertently, as if her body was telling her all hope was lost, that surrender was all that remained. Her grief was too heavy for her legs to support.

Dröfn had recognised the object. It was Bjólfur's colourful shoe. He had bought it to match his and Agnes's Tinni coats, on that shopping expedition to town when they had all kitted themselves out with new footwear for the trip, including Tjörvi's useless boots. Dröfn stared at the heel that, according to the salesman, provided such excellent ankle support. She reached out her hand to touch it but could hardly feel anything through her thick gloves. Propping her torch on the ground to illuminate the shoe, she began gingerly to scrape off the snow. She wasn't going to clear away any more than necessary. Terrible sights were more bearable if seen a little at a time.

But no ankle appeared. When Dröfn had dug out the upper part of the shoe, she saw that it was empty. Digging more frantically, since there was no longer any need for care, she scraped away enough to get a proper purchase, then prised the shoe out of the snow.

The laces had been deliberately loosened far enough down to make it easy to remove, so it wasn't as if it had simply fallen off because Bjólfur hadn't laced it tightly enough.

Dröfn turned it over in her hands, examining it as if she thought the shoe held the clue to what had happened. Then, putting it down, she began rooting around in the snow nearby. She found the other shoe almost immediately and it told the same story: Bjólfur seemed to have undone the laces and pulled it off.

If she hadn't witnessed Tjörvi's badly damaged feet, this would have presented more of a riddle. But Dröfn could almost understand the urge to drag off one's shoes in a misguided attempt to spare agonisingly swollen toes. It occurred to her that Bjólfur couldn't have got far with frostbitten feet, in nothing but his socks. She stood up again, leaving the shoes where they lay. They were of no use to anyone now. At first she stood still, scanning her surroundings, then, seeing nothing of interest, she decided to move. She put her feet down tentatively, aware that at any minute she might tread on Bjólfur, who couldn't be far away. He must have been at the end of his strength and utterly confused at the point when he'd taken off his shoes.

She didn't have to search for long. A few metres away from where she stood, something that looked like hair was showing above the snow. Puzzled that she couldn't see a coat or protective trousers, she clung to the hope that it was just the corpse of some small creature. But when she got closer, she shrank back in horror. Next to the hair, the smooth whiteness had a different texture: it wasn't snow but bare skin. So much for the hope that it was an animal. There were no hairless creatures in these parts.

Dröfn fell to her knees again. She scraped away enough of the snow to see that Bjólfur wasn't wearing his coat or his jumper or trousers. He appeared to have taken off almost all his clothes. She brushed the snow from his hair. She had to make sure it was Bjólfur, not Haukur. Both were dark and she couldn't tell them apart from their hair alone. She would have to dig deeper and expose what she didn't want to see.

The man was lying face down. She tried to turn his head but his neck was stiff and unyielding. His body must be frozen solid. The thought was too horrible to contemplate. She braced herself to exert more force, then realised that she couldn't bring herself to do it. What if his neckbones cracked? Dröfn raised her eyes to heaven, then lowered her head and cried helplessly over the body. She couldn't do any more. The shoes had belonged to Bjólfur. She didn't need to see her dead friend's face to be sure that it was him. She was afraid that, if she did, the sight would rob her of the last of her courage.

There would be nothing left but to lie down beside him and give up the fight.

She forced herself to her feet again, leaving the torch lying on the snow. It flickered, then went out. As if ordained, the clouds closed up, obscuring the moon and intensifying the darkness. Dröfn looked at the body for the last time, only now registering what she hadn't wanted to see: Bjólfur was facing in the wrong direction. As if he had been crawling not towards the tents and safety, not towards Agnes, but away into the wilderness. Dröfn couldn't even shudder; she was too cold for that. She had been standing still too long and would have to move if she wasn't to share Bjólfur's fate.

She had a horrible suspicion of what he had been fleeing.

Dröfn sent up a silent prayer that she wouldn't hear that muttering voice on her way back. There was no point making a wish, since it had become cruelly obvious that wishes didn't work. She simply turned and started walking back in the direction of the camp. When she came across what might have been Haukur's coat under the snow, she didn't even slow down. Bjólfur was dead. Haukur was dead. She couldn't cope with seeing any more bodies.

Just like on the way there, she lost all sense of how long she had been walking. The one compensation was that the going was a little easier, treading in her own footprints where she had already trampled down the snow. In places, though, they were as deep as post holes and provided no help, but she stuck to her tracks without deviating an inch, afraid that otherwise she might stray from the path.

Dröfn's feet were aching when the moon peeped out from behind the clouds again and she finally made out the dim shape of the tent ahead. The pain had begun as a cold sensation but had gradually become sharper, more excruciating.

Trying not to think about what had happened to Tjörvi's feet, she resolved not to take off her boots when she got back to the tent. If her toes looked like his, she would rather not know.

Just outside the camp, she paused. She needed to compose herself before facing Tjörvi and Agnes. It would take all her strength not to break down.

The pause became drawn out. Aware of the throbbing in her poor, frozen feet, she blew out a breath. She couldn't wait any longer. It was only then that it occurred to her there was no sound coming from inside the tent. Neither Agnes nor Tjörvi had uttered a word since she'd got back. There was an ominous hush and everything was almost perfectly still. The only sign of the wind was the occasional gentle puff of air, hardly stronger than a sigh, though much colder. If Tjörvi was asleep without snoring, it would be a first. Licking her lips, Dröfn discovered that they were dry and cracked.

She took two steps towards the tent. 'Tjörvi? Agnes?' No answer. Moving closer still, she noticed the canvas stir and flap idly on the side facing away from her. Hardly daring to breathe, she picked her way around the tent and saw the canvas billow slightly again, revealing a large tear. It felt as if her heart was being crushed. She couldn't see any figures inside. Again, she called out, in a faltering voice this time: 'Tjörvi? Agnes?' The only answer was silence. Steeling herself, she took hold of the torn canvas and peered inside. The tent was deserted.

Dröfn straightened up, bewildered. Going back round to the front of the tent, she unzipped the door to double-check. But it only confirmed what she had seen. Sleeping bags, rucksacks, outdoor clothing and other stuff were strewn around inside. But the tent was empty of people.

Unable to face the sight, Dröfn took hold of the zip and slowly, mechanically, pulled it shut again. Then she studied the snow at her feet, seeing the tracks they had made when they'd all got up to empty their bladders that morning and her own line of footprints leading away and back again. But she couldn't see any prints telling her which direction Agnes and Tjörvi had taken after they'd left the tent. Then again, she did notice some strange marks in the snow, which she traced back to the rip in the canvas. Someone had apparently climbed out of the hole and dragged themselves away from the camp behind the tents. As if in a daze, Dröfn followed the marks further and further across the snow until finally she stopped and fell to her knees. Not quietly this time. The hush was broken by a howl that started in her abdomen and burst from her mouth as if she had been hit in the stomach with a baseball bat.

There they lay, Agnes and Tjörvi, a few metres apart. Like Bjólfur, they were lying face down, virtually naked; Agnes in only her long-sleeved thermal vest and Tjörvi bare-chested but wearing his long johns. Tjörvi's head was turned to one side. Dröfn noticed that Agnes was facing towards him, as if their eyes had met in their final moments. She let out another howl – a deafening, animal cry. She'd never have believed herself capable of producing such a sound. Both were unquestionably dead. No living person would look like that. Or lie there, motionless, in the snow's deadly embrace.

Still on her hands and knees, Dröfn shuffled towards them, still producing those terrible, animal cries. Her face was wet with tears, her nose running, the salt stinging her raw lips. Reaching Tjörvi's side, she rose up on her knees and buried her face in her hands, sobbing so convulsively that her whole body shook. She wept for the future that would never be, for the love that was now turned to grief, for the warm body that was forever cold, for his voice that had been silenced, and all the things they would never now do together.

After a while, she raised her face from her wet gloves. Taking one of them off, she stroked Tjörvi's cheek with her bare fingers. It felt icy and rough to the touch, quite unlike the cheek she had known. Trying not to look at his maimed hands, she searched for a place to stroke. In the end, she laid her hand on his head. His hair was the only thing that still felt like him.

And now, for the first time, her ears picked up the dreaded muttering she had been so afraid of hearing when she was alone in the dark. Turning as if in slow motion, Dröfn saw a movement in the canvas of Haukur's collapsed tent. Perhaps it was just the gentle breeze stirring the material, but she couldn't push away the thought that it might be something worse. That there was something under there, crawling towards where the door must be. Her grief giving way to terror, Dröfn scrambled to her feet. She had to get out of there.

Yet, in spite of her terror, she couldn't simply abandon Agnes and Tjörvi, couldn't leave them lying there like carrion. There was no time to bury them but she had to do something. Dragging off her scarf, she laid it over her husband's face, then covered Agnes's cheek with one of her gloves. She couldn't spare anything else.

At that moment she caught sight of Tjörvi's phone and the knife lying in the snow between the bodies. She snatched them up, shoving the phone into her coat pocket. Maybe, just maybe, she would find a signal and then it would be good to have some battery left. Her own phone was pretty much out of juice. She meant to hold the knife in front of her. It was open, and although Dröfn could have wished the blade was bigger, it was at least a weapon. Gripping the hilt in her gloved hand, she felt a faint sense of reassurance, although the knife hadn't saved Agnes or Tjörvi's lives. Then she set off at a stumbling run, in the direction she believed the hut lay in. She didn't stop to worry about what would happen when she became less sure of her surroundings. The only thought in her head was to put as much distance as possible between herself and that thing in the tent. As long as her whole mind was focused on that aim, no other thoughts need trouble her.

Her progress was slowed by frequently twisting round to look over her shoulder. But perhaps it made no difference in the end, because every time she glimpsed what looked like a shape following her, she stumbled along faster. She didn't need to get a better view; she already knew who it was. The frozen woman with the lightless black eyes, who had been standing outside, staring fixedly at the door of the hut when Dröfn was in the hall.

When she caught a flicker of movement ahead of her too, Dröfn thought her last moment had come. Then she noticed that this was something bigger, and after a minute or two she realised it was the reindeer. The cow had her back to her and was moving slowly over the frozen snow-crust. Completely disorientated now, Dröfn decided simply to follow the animal. It was no worse an idea than any other. The reindeer had been shadowing them for much of this nightmarish journey. For all Dröfn knew, the cow might now be heading back the same way. Yet slowly though the reindeer was walking, her stride was longer than Dröfn's, and it took every ounce of Dröfn's strength to keep up with her.

There came a point when Dröfn knew she was close to giving up. Her feet felt as if they were bursting out of her shoes and she could no longer feel her toes at all. The fingers of her gloveless hand were numb too. She had buried it in her coat pocket, but the pocket wasn't lined and the cold, shiny fabric didn't retain any heat.

By now, Dröfn was shivering uncontrollably. In some part of her mind, she knew she mustn't drop the knife and she concentrated hard on gripping the hilt. But her thoughts seemed to be slipping away from her and she was no longer entirely sure whether she was awake. Perhaps this was all a nightmare. She was so confused that she couldn't always remember why she was walking or where exactly she was. The only idea that remained clear was the need to keep up with the reindeer.

Suddenly, the animal fell forward onto its knees and tried in vain to get up. Dröfn seized the chance to stop walking for a moment, hoping she could take a short breather while the cow was struggling to her feet. But her teeth were chattering uncontrollably now and she could feel herself losing heart.

The reindeer collapsed onto her side. Raising her big head, she lowed feebly at the dark sky. Dröfn, on the brink of surrender herself, realised that the animal had given up the fight. She crept closer. As she reached the beast, its head fell back onto the ground. The reindeer tried to lift her head once more as Dröfn loomed over her but she was too weak. Dröfn could see the whites of the cow's brown eyes as the poor creature tried to look away.

Dröfn fell to her knees again. Not from grief this time but because she couldn't stand upright any longer. She stayed like that for a while, shaken by spasmodic shivers. In front of her was the reindeer's furry belly. The animal must be warm. And soft. With a final effort of will, she dragged herself over to it.

Everything would be OK if she could just rest for a moment or two. She wrapped her arms protectively around her body, being careful not to stab herself with the knife. Then she lay back against the thick pelt, feeling the animal's ribcage rising and falling, hearing the heart beating through her hood. She was struck by the thought that they were both caught in the same predicament. Here they lay, the cow that hadn't had the sense to go down to the lowlands when autumn came, and the woman who hadn't had the sense to stay away from the highlands in winter. Dröfn's eyelids grew heavy and she was just drifting off to sleep when the heartbeat stopped and the reindeer's big body grew still.

Dröfn opened her eyes. Only now did she register that the sky had turned pale with the late winter dawn. Then, to her astonishment, she saw the hut. She was looking down on it, so she must be at the top of a slope. Her mind cleared enough for her to realise that she was saved. The reindeer had brought her back to where she wanted to be – at the first attempt. All she had to do now was make it to the car. And if she had managed to get this far, she ought to be able to walk the last stretch. The logic seemed convincing, but there was a strange fog clouding her mind and she was becoming confused again.

Dröfn hugged herself tighter. She had to get to her feet, walk down to the hut and get the heat going inside. Then she could rest until she was ready for the next leg of the journey. However much she might dread entering that place, she had no other choice. She'd got to stop herself shivering.

It was a good plan. Dröfn gazed at the hut, feeling vaguely pleased with herself. But before getting up and walking down the slope, she just needed to rest for a little while longer.

Just close her eyes for a moment.

For a moment.

A moment.

Her eyelids drooped, and just before they closed Dröfn saw the door of the hut open. Yet even that couldn't stop her from sinking into sleep. Shortly afterwards she stirred. Someone had shaken her. The adrenaline began coursing through her veins and suddenly her mind was clear. She tightened her grip on the knife, ready at last to face up to the thing that had been terrifying her ever since that night in the hut. Forcing her heavy lids open, she looked up.

When her eyes met a familiar face, Dröfn smiled. Her fingers relaxed on the knife and it dropped into the snow beside her. She was going to be all right. She was saved.

But it was only a matter of seconds before she began to regret having let go of that knife.

Chapter 29

Jóhanna collected up the cushions from the garden sofa that were lying scattered around the deck. The wind had knocked over the box they were stored in and if she didn't rescue them now, there was a risk they would be blown not only out of the garden but out to sea. Every time she stooped to pick one up, she let out an involuntary groan. Still, she consoled herself, her muscles weren't as sore as they had been yesterday. They would be even better tomorrow, until in the end the pain was nothing but a bad memory. Until the next time she overdid things.

Having chucked the last cushion into the box, she rested her hands on the lid and cautiously stretched her back. It had been a long, gruelling day at work, as she'd had a lot of catching up to do. In addition to her normal jobs, she had been left with a list of tasks that her new colleague hadn't managed to cover when taking the shift alone yesterday. Jóhanna had pulled out all the stops, despite her aching body and lack of sleep. It had been a difficult night. She had woken up repeatedly, convinced that someone had opened the front door and come in. In the end, she had got out of bed, careful not to disturb Geiri, and propped a kitchen chair under the handle of the front door. After that she had finally succeeded in dropping off and slept through to the morning.

Tonight would be different, she was sure. She had arranged for a locksmith to come, and popped home at lunchtime to let him in to change the locks. From now on, no one would be able to get in except her and Geiri.

Jóhanna straightened up, her back feeling better after a bit of a stretch. She decided to fetch a rock from the garden to weigh down the lid of the box. The wind was forever blowing it over and it was getting to be a nuisance.

She stepped down off the deck and went over to the fence, kicking lightly at the snow in the flowerbeds where she remembered having seen some big stones.

A child's voice reached her from the other side of the fence. Glancing up, Jóhanna saw the golden head of her neighbours' small daughter peeping over the top. The fence was much taller than her, so she must have climbed onto one of the rails. 'Careful you don't fall off,' Jóhanna warned.

'I won't. I can climb.' Only the child's eyes and nose were visible. 'I like climbing up here. To talk to the girl.'

'What girl?' Jóhanna's voice emerged more shrilly than she intended. 'There's no girl here, sweetheart.'

'Yes, there is. But you're not her mummy. She lives in your garden. Sometimes she comes round to my garden. But only sometimes.'

Jóhanna's throat felt suddenly tight. 'There's no one in the garden but me. Anyway, it's late. It's nearly suppertime. You'd better hurry up and go inside.'

The golden locks swirled as the child shook her head. 'I'm not hungry. I want to play outside, with my friend. Mummy said I could. And she *is* there.' A small hand reached over the fence to point. Next moment the little girl lost her footing and nearly fell, clinging on by only one hand. But she managed to right herself and a chubby finger pointed to the garden behind Jóhanna's back. 'There. She's only got one shoe on.'

Jóhanna didn't look round. Instead, she shot a glance at the garden door to make sure Geiri wasn't standing there. She didn't want him to hear what she was going to say next. 'You're not allowed to play with the girl in our garden,' she said sharply. 'It's not allowed. You must find yourself a different friend, at nursery school. Promise me.'

The little girl frowned. 'Why?'

'Because. No one's allowed to play with the girl in my garden. No one at all. And you're not to climb on the fence either. It's dangerous and you're not to do it.' If Jóhanna sounded angry, she had good reason. Although she had no personal experience of bringing up children, she had been a child herself once, and angry grown-ups were something she remembered going out of her way to avoid. She just hoped her words would have the same effect on the kid next door.

'You're mean.' The little head disappeared and Jóhanna heard the child running back to her house. Jóhanna was left standing there, with no interest now in searching for a suitable stone. All she wanted was to hurry back inside.

She walked quickly up the steps to the deck. Once she had closed the door behind her, the conversation with the girl next door began to seem unreal. Had she really lost her temper with the neighbours' child? Because of some ghost story the kid had obviously heard, though apparently in a more innocuous form than the one Rannveig had shared with Jóhanna. Jóhanna doubted the child would play with her imaginary friend if the other children at her nursery school still believed the girl in the garden would drag her into the grave.

Jóhanna couldn't resist the impulse to peer out into the garden. She switched off the inside light, so she could see better. The garden was empty. Of course it was. Of course there was no little girl out there.

'Geiri!' Jóhanna called into the kitchen where her husband was cooking. 'You remember when we took down the flagpole and found that shoe?'

Geiri called back: 'Of course I do. Why?'

'Do you happen to remember whether the little girl next door was watching at the time?' Jóhanna was still staring outside. When he asked why she wanted to know, she didn't reply.

Geiri didn't seem to mind her lack of response. 'I don't think so. But it's always possible. We hired a crane, after all, and kids tend to be interested in that sort of thing. She could have been watching and seen the shoe. Climbed onto the fence and looked over, maybe, like she's always doing. Which reminds me, we need to get somebody in to reinforce it, or it could come down in the next storm.'

Jóhanna didn't comment. She knew they wouldn't find anyone to repair the fence until next spring. But the moment Geiri mentioned the crane she felt better. That must be what was behind it. The child next door had been watching when they found the shoe and invented an imaginary friend for herself. It was a coincidence, that's all. Her claim that there was a little girl in the garden had nothing to do with the ghost story that used to circulate among the local kids. Jóhanna was flooded with relief and chided herself for having been so silly.

She didn't say a word about it to Geiri and he didn't comment on her interest in the shoe. They ate supper and cleared up. Afterwards, they settled down in the sitting room to watch the news. For the first time in several days, the discovery of the bodies in Lónsöræfi was no longer the lead story. That honour went instead to a fatal road accident in which two people had died. As always with car crashes, Jóhanna felt sympathetic twinges all over her body as she listened to the report. But this time they didn't immediately subside, perhaps because she'd had enough of tragic accidents recently to last her a lifetime.

When the newsreader got to the Lónsöræfi story, Geiri turned up the volume. Nothing emerged that they didn't already know. Lowering the volume again, Geiri said: 'By the way, the knife turned out to be clean, according to the lab. Assuming it hadn't been carefully washed, it's clear it can't have been used for anything more sinister than cutting up food. And presumably the tent canvas too. How it ended up with that woman, Dröfn, is anyone's guess. It wasn't linked to any of the deaths, though. And the big stain they found in the snow by the hut wasn't blood after all. Not human blood, anyway.' Geiri stretched his legs and propped them on the coffee table. Resting his head on the back of the sofa he stared up at the ceiling. 'It was reindeer urine, mixed with blood or myoglobin, caused by some disease. Which explains the colour. I don't know if they're actually planning a post-mortem on the reindeer cow but they're pretty sure she was sick and that the urine was hers. Apparently an infection like that can prove fatal to animals when conditions are severe – and I think you could safely describe the weather conditions up there as severe.'

Jóhanna certainly wouldn't disagree with that. She propped her legs on the table beside his, then rested her head on his shoulder. 'Have they found out yet what Wiktoria was doing up there?'

'No. She seems to have had no connection to either of the couples. I gather the pathologist believes her body had been there longer. Possibly ever since she left Höfn. It shows signs of having been lying in above-zero conditions for a while. And as the weather has been freezing hard ever since the other party went missing, it seems likely that her presence there had nothing to do with them.'

So Thórir had been right. Jóhanna merely nodded. There was no need to betray Thórir's confidence by mentioning to Geiri what he had told her. It wouldn't make any difference now.

'They've not had any luck tracing that captain, so they're beginning to wonder if she could have invented him. Then gone into the highlands to kill herself, maybe. She wouldn't be the first. But the question remains: how did she get there? And the walking party too. There are no vehicles abandoned in the area. We'd have found them by now if there were.'

To Jóhanna, this didn't seem right. Wiktoria had never struck her as depressed, in fact quite the opposite. For example, she had been busy planning her summer holiday just before she handed in her notice. She was going to Poland and wanted to make sure she and Jóhanna wouldn't both be away at the same time. Jóhanna just couldn't make this fit with the idea of Wiktoria deliberately heading into the highlands to end it all. Though, of course, she knew that suicide could be a spur-of-the-moment decision, taking people completely by surprise, not least those who killed themselves. 'Has her car turned up?' she asked.

'Yes, it has. They found it today. It had been left out at Stokksnes, near the Viking Café car park. Apparently, it's been there for ages but no one gave it any thought. The car's full of her belongings, so it seems she was serious about moving. How she got from there to Lónsöræfi, though, is anybody's guess, but hopefully we'll find out one day. And as for who gave the two couples a lift up there, no one's come forward to solve that yet either.'

The newsreader had moved on to lighter matters. On the screen was a fat seal that had become a regular visitor to Reykjavík's hot-water beach at Nauthólsvík, to the delight of the sea bathers. The seal blinked slowly at the camera, then looked away, obviously fed up with humans.

Jóhanna knew how it felt. She looked at Geiri. 'Did you get a chance to talk to the man we bought the house from? Did he have a key?'

'Yes, I had a word with him. He doesn't have a key and swore he hasn't been anywhere near the house since he and his brother cleared it out. He was telling the truth, I'm certain of it. I've listened to so many people lying to the police that I reckon I can tell. Anyway, even if he was lying, we needn't worry about it now that we've changed the locks.'

It was hard to trust other people's instincts. After all, instinct wasn't based on logic, which made it impossible to convince others of its value. People either trusted it or they didn't. And this time Jóhanna wasn't convinced. 'What's he doing here, then? Don't you think it's a weird coincidence that the business with the front door should start just when he happens to be visiting Höfn?'

Geiri leant over and kissed her on the forehead. 'He works for the Coast Guard. Out at Stokksnes. He's been there for months, so he's not here to rob us. Besides, nothing was missing. We must have just forgotten to lock the door.'

Jóhanna noticed that he said 'we', though she had been the last one out of the house on both occasions. She pulled his hand towards her and dropped a kiss on his knuckles. Then she told him what she'd learnt about the man's sister's death and how he'd been trying to find out information about it. But she left out the bit about the ghost story. Geiri didn't need to know that she had heard it. 'Did he get the files he wanted?'

'No. But he will in the end. It all has to be done by the book, so Selfoss will take care of it. I got permission to tell him the details, though. The case was closed long ago and it's not a confidential matter. It didn't end up on our desk because there was anything suspicious about it, but just because the police have a duty to investigate all accidents. They concluded that the girl's death was accidental. An awful tragedy, but there was no more to it than that.'

Jóhanna shuddered. 'Did she drown?'

Geiri shrugged. 'Either drowned or died from being bashed against the sides of the blowhole as she fell down it to the sea. The post-mortem couldn't establish which. There were a lot of smashed bones, including her skull and limbs. All pretty grim. I can't understand why the man's so desperate to get hold of the files.'

Neither could Jóhanna, but she tried. 'Maybe his parents refused to talk about it. And now it's too late. You can understand why he'd want to find out exactly how it happened.'

'It's quite clear how it happened. But sometimes people need to see things in black and white before they can accept them.'

Jóhanna had no wish to discuss the matter any longer. She had to banish the accident and the stupid ghost story from her mind. The whole thing only made her miserable. The house was her and Geiri's home and would be for the foreseeable future, and she had to feel at ease here. There were quite enough distressing things going on in the outside world: she needed these four walls to be a sanctuary. She and Geiri had started to touch on the subject of children, not very seriously so far, but every time the subject came up, they were a little more committed. When they did start a family, she didn't want to have to feel anxious every time her child went out into the garden.

The Prey

'I could really do with watching a comedy.' Jóhanna reached for the blanket at the end of the sofa and spread it over their legs. 'Something silly.'

Geiri changed over to the streaming service and they agreed on a film they normally wouldn't even have considered. When it began, she realised it was intended for children but at least that meant it wouldn't involve any gory deaths.

Seeing that Geiri's eyes were closing, Jóhanna nudged him. Although she was as bored by the film as he was, rather than feeling sleepy she was bursting with questions. 'I've been thinking about the two couples from Reykjavík. Are there any theories about why they were all half naked or at least under-dressed? And why their bodies were found in different places? Why they didn't stick together?'

Geiri jerked, then pretended as usual that he had been awake all the time. Jóhanna repeated her questions, knowing that he'd been asleep. When he answered, his voice was low and husky as if he was speaking out of the remnants of his dream. 'We know why the two who were found side by side weren't in their outdoor clothes. The IT unit in Reykjavík managed to unlock the man's phone, which was one of the two we found in the coat in the hut. It contained a short video he'd recorded for his wife just before he died. It's pretty unhinged, which suggests they must have completely lost it. We know they weren't high because there were no traces of any drugs in their blood-stream. They just seem to have freaked out, but while they were stone-cold sober.'

'What was in the video?' Jóhanna tried to imagine what it would be like to record a farewell message to Geiri. If she had to do it unprepared, while dying of cold, it was bound to sound pretty crazy to anyone watching it later.

309

'He was in such a state that it's hard to understand him. But he does say clearly that he and Agnes – the woman with him – had to get out of the tent because someone was opening the door. He says they had to cut their way out. Then there's some confused stuff about the voice begging them again and again to let it in.'

'The voice? What voice?'

Geiri shrugged. 'Your guess is as good as mine. It sounds like he assumed his wife would know what he was talking about. Mind you, that doesn't mean anything, as the stuff about the voice makes no sense at all. The general consensus is that he must have lost his grip on reality as a result of hypothermia. His bodily functions were slowing down – his brain too. They think he must have been hallucinating that someone was trying to get into the tent – someone who meant them harm. The upshot is that they rushed out into the snow in their underwear, which was presumably what they'd been sleeping in. And we all know how that turned out.' Geiri paused, shaking his head sorrowfully. 'When he recorded the message, Agnes was still alive too. The technician says you can hear her muttering faintly in the background. She seems to have lost the plot as well. The technician needs to clean up the sound, but as far as he can make out, she's begging Tjörvi to let her in, whatever she meant by that. It's clear from the video that they were both out in the open at that point.'

Jóhanna shuddered. 'Awful, just awful.'

Geiri nodded. 'You're telling me. But the last bit is the worst. The video ends with the man saying goodbye to his wife. It's like he's suddenly recovered his right mind, because what he says then makes perfect sense. Christ, what a business.'

Jóhanna shuddered. 'Do they know if his wife ever saw the video? The phone was found in her pocket, wasn't it?'

Geiri shook his head. 'According to the guy who examined the phone, no one had watched it. So she never got his message.'

They were both silent for a while, watching the farcical antics on the TV screen without really seeing them. Geiri yawned. Before he could nod off again, Jóhanna quickly slipped in another question. 'What about the purpose of their trip? Do you know any more about that? About what exactly they were doing up there?'

'No, not for certain. But after their names were released, a friend of theirs contacted the police to say he'd introduced them to a geologist who was doing a research project on the Vatnajökull ice cap. Maybe it had something to do with him.' By the end of this speech, Geiri's voice was beginning to slur.

Jóhanna nudged him gently as his breathing grew heavier. Starting awake, he continued from where he had left off. 'We'll get to the bottom of it. Don't you worry.'

'Just one more question, Geiri. It's not about bodies or anything like that.'

'What?' Geiri, who had stopped even trying to pretend, didn't bother to open his eyes this time.

'Wiktoria was a big animal lover. I know she'd never have killed herself without making arrangements for her pets. Do you have any idea what happened to her parrot? Or her cat?'

Chapter 30

Puss was staying out of sight. Hjörvar had stuck his head out of the car window several times to call him, shouting louder each time. He wasn't worried about being overheard because there was nobody here. He was alone in the dark on Stokksnes.

He rolled up his window and leant back against the hard seat. Instead of feeling his usual annoyance at how uncomfortable it was, he was reassured by its solid familiarity. He sat there for a while, gazing out to sea. Although the new moon was no more than a nail paring in the cloudless sky, its light glittered on the choppy surface as the black tops of the waves gleamed and disappeared in turn.

Hjörvar was faced with a dilemma: should he turn round and drive home or get out and search for Puss on foot? It was the whole reason he was here. The idea had seemed like a good one when he'd got in the car, but his enthusiasm had begun to wane the moment he turned off onto the dirt road that led out along the causeway to the radar station. It was only when he reminded himself how stressed he had been feeling alone at home that it had begun to feel like a better idea. A storm was forecast and he felt responsible for his little friend – his only friend. He wouldn't be able to sleep, worrying about the poor creature vainly seeking shelter where there was none to be had.

When he and Erlingur had turned up to work that morning, Puss was nowhere to be seen. Hjörvar had told Erlingur that the cat had slipped out of the door and vanished when he was leaving to go home the previous evening, which was true enough. Hjörvar also told him he had searched for Puss unsuccessfully before going home, which wasn't true. There was absolutely no way he could admit to Erlingur that he had fled the station in a panic.

The day had worn on, with no sign of the cat. Hjörvar had hardly left Erlingur's side. It was the only way he could survive the shift. He'd even had to fight the impulse to wait outside the door while Erlingur was in the toilet. The one time he did step into another room was when he got the phone call from the police, but then his attention had been so focused on the conversation that his fear had temporarily receded.

To his intense gratitude, the day had passed without any strange incidents. But also, sadly, without any sign of Puss.

The two men had driven home together and on the way Hjörvar had surrendered to the compulsion to look back. Just to be on the safe side. That was when he'd thought he'd caught a glimpse of Puss's small figure darting round the corner of the station building. But when he'd opened his mouth to ask Erlingur to stop, the other man had forestalled him by pointing out that the abandoned car had finally been removed. When Hjörvar had glanced back again, Puss was nowhere to be seen, so he had decided not to say anything.

He hadn't been sitting in his flat for long before he began to regret it. He couldn't stop thinking about the poor little creature, alone, abandoned and hungry. It didn't help that there was nothing in the flat to distract him. He didn't have any books and there was nothing on TV. All he could think of was to go online but he'd soon scrolled through all the main news sites without finding anything of interest.

It was then that he'd recalled the inscription on Salvör's cross and decided to look up the quotation. His search immediately took him to an online Bible site where he called up the Gospel of Luke. If he remembered right, the reference had been to Luke 23:34, but rather than enlightening him, the verse left him nonplussed.

Then Jesus said, 'Father, forgive them, for they know not what they do.'

It was hard to fathom why these words should have been chosen for a child's grave. But since the answer to the riddle wasn't to be found online, he closed his laptop and made himself something to eat. As he sat at the little table in his open-plan kitchen, munching his toast, his thoughts flew again to poor Puss, starving out there in the cold and dark. The toast tasted like ashes. It was then that he had stood up, fetched his coat and got in the car, determined to rescue the cat.

Hjörvar blew out a breath and closed his eyes. Then he opened them again and got out into the unrelenting darkness. The slam of the car door echoed in the silence. He stood without moving for a moment or two, in the hope that Puss would come running. No such luck. Still, he shouldn't have been surprised as the cat didn't like the car. Hjörvar would have to use cunning to get him into the vehicle – if he ever found him.

When he found him, Hjörvar corrected himself. He was damned if he was leaving without the cat.

He walked over to the perimeter fence and opened the gate, telling himself sternly that there was nothing to be afraid of. If there was anything untoward about his sister's life or accident, he wasn't to blame. The information from the police had removed all doubt of that. Well, more or less. They had confirmed that there had been nothing suspicious about her death, which was consistent with what Hjörvar already knew. But at the same time he had learnt more details about what had happened.

According to the officer Hjörvar had spoken to, his father had taken Salvör out to Stokksnes for a walk on the beach. But she had soon got tired of the beach and wanted to go on the rocks. His father had carried her in his arms for safety's sake, as witnesses confirmed. At the time, there had been a large number of people working at the radar station and they'd had a good view of father and child from the window of the canteen. His father's account of what happened next was that his shoelace had come undone and he'd been forced to put Salvör down for a moment while he was retying it. He'd no sooner bent over than a wave had exploded out of the blowhole. Salvör had started running towards the hole, drawn by the thrilling sight, too young to have learnt caution. As the wave crashed back through the hole, it had snatched her with it. The whole thing had happened in a matter of seconds.

The report also revealed that the girl had been suffering from various problems as a result of her late development. When Hjörvar enquired further about these problems, the police officer had told him the files didn't include any more detailed description. It seemed unlikely she had ever been taken for a formal diagnosis, judging by the absence of any reference to one in the papers in the police archives. The post-mortem report had simply glossed over the question of her mental development.

The policeman had sounded so relaxed that Hjörvar had got the impression he was perfectly satisfied by the facts of the case. Initially, this was reassuring but, after he had rung off, Hjörvar began to have his doubts. He was only too familiar with the view from the canteen. Familiar enough to know that there was no way the witnesses could have seen what happened after his father had put Salvör down to tie his shoelace. A small child would have been invisible from the window, and so would a crouching man, because the shore ridge rose up in between, blocking the view of the rocks themselves.

Of course, that on its own wasn't enough to disprove the story. Accidents could happen without any witnesses. You didn't have to look any further than the recent tragic events in Lónsöræfi for an example of that. No, what troubled him more had been the policeman's answer to the question Hjörvar had asked next. What had Salvör been wearing when her body was found? The officer had been a bit taken aback but had nevertheless provided a rough description of the child's clothes. A flowery summer dress, a yellow hand-knitted cardigan, thick white tights and a pink leather shoe. On her right foot.

That was the problem. A pink leather shoe – on one foot.

The police officer turned out to be the man who had bought the brothers' childhood home, the very person who had found the shoe buried in his garden. But he wasn't aware, as Hjörvar was, that the dirty brown shoe had originally been pink. A pink shoe for a left foot.

How was it possible that one shoe had vanished down the blowhole on his sister's foot while the other had remained in the garden? Surely his father wouldn't have taken his daughter for a walk on the beach wearing only one shoe? Of course, it was conceivable that Salvör had owned two pairs – Hjörvar sincerely hoped that was the case. He had decided not to jump to any conclusions until he had received all the paperwork. It was bound to include photos of Salvör's body and therefore of the shoe, so if it was identical to the one that had turned up in the garden, Hjörvar knew what he would believe.

In the meantime, he didn't want the idea to become prematurely fixed in his mind that his father had, whether deliberately or not, killed his daughter in the garden, then covered up the deed by throwing her down the blowhole. The blowhole where he knew the sea would smash her little body repeatedly against the rocks and eventually return it, so battered that it would be impossible to determine the cause of death.

Hjörvar began calling the cat again. 'Puss! Here, Puss.'

There was no movement anywhere. Hjörvar thought he could hear the antenna revolving in its dome, though that could only be an echo in his head. But he couldn't hear any mewing or creaking of the frozen snow-crust to indicate that the cat was on the prowl.

It was so hard to see anything that Hjörvar decided to switch on the outside lights. Then at least the area closest to the station would be lit up. He doubted Puss had gone far, though he couldn't be sure. Perhaps the animal had decided to wander further afield. If so, Hjörvar would be going home alone. No way was he going to drag himself round the whole peninsula, with its alien landscape of black sand and grass-crowned hummocks, rendered even eerier by the snow, hunting for Puss. But there wasn't much conviction behind this decision. That was probably exactly what he would end up doing.

Hjörvar unlocked the door of the station building and went straight to the light switch. His visit would show up on the security system but that couldn't be helped. He wasn't sure he wanted to work here any longer. He would probably ask his manager in Reykjavík for a transfer. He just hoped they wouldn't use this as an excuse to get rid of him.

The lights came on outside and Hjörvar hurriedly left the building again. With the site illuminated, he'd expected to feel less jumpy, but the lighting had the opposite effect, merely intensifying the wall of darkness beyond, making it seem an even denser black. As if it would swallow up anyone rash enough to stray beyond the glow of the lights.

At that moment the phone rang in Hjörvar's pocket, the sound so sudden and shrill that he nearly jumped out of his skin. He fumbled for it frantically, assailed by a horrible feeling that the ringing would draw the attention of the watchful darkness.

It was Kolbeinn on the other end, and he came straight to the point, saying he was sending Hjörvar the photos he'd picked up from the developers. Apparently the film had been rewound after only half the frames had been used. Nevertheless, it had contained several pictures, including some of their sister.

Kolbeinn didn't comment on Hjörvar's silence, he just rang off without any attempt to conclude their conversation on a sentimental note. It was how their phone calls normally ended. Clearly, the brief period when they had been able to have more in-depth conversations about their sister and parents was over. Salvör's existence was now old news to Kolbeinn, finished business that required no further attention.

This couldn't have been further from how Hjörvar felt.

A miaow reached him from round the corner of the building. It sounded like the plaintive noise Puss made when he was hungry, which was hardly surprising, given that he hadn't been fed at the station since the day before. It was a good sign, too, since it would make him easier to catch. Hjörvar followed the noise, grateful now for the glow of the outside lights as he was heading towards the side of the building that faced onto the sea and the rocks. Just then, the phone in his pocket started emitting a series of bleeps and he assumed that this was Kolbeinn sending him the photos.

Puss was standing by the wall of the building, staring out to sea. He was clearly visible against the snow, his black-and-white coat making him look like the puzzle of a black cat that was missing several pieces. He glanced round at Hjörvar and miaowed again. But as Hjörvar approached him, the cat slunk away, unwilling to be caught. He had a tendency to do this and, when he did, there was no point chasing him. Hjörvar decided to stand still and ignore him. See if that would make the cat come trotting over.

Reluctant to look at the rocks as he stood there, pretending indifference to the cat, Hjörvar turned his head east towards Vestrahorn and the dramatic mountains beyond, but they were barely visible in the gloom. The little he could make out of their faint outlines reminded him of the fangs of some predator. Of course, he could turn the other way and look at the lighthouse, but then he wouldn't be able to see Puss out of the corner of his eye. There was a risk he'd lose sight of him and have to start the search all over again. He took out his phone instead.

One after the other, he opened the pictures Kolbeinn had sent. The first was of himself as a little boy with his younger brother beside him. They were sitting on the sofa that had still been there in the living room all those years later when they'd cleared out their childhood home. He felt a hairline crack forming in the dam that was holding back his memories. The trigger was the white football shirt he was wearing in the photo; on the front of it was the good old crest of a cockerel standing on a football. He recalled how it had smelt when he'd taken the shirt out of the plastic. It was a gift his father had brought him back from England.

Hjörvar scrolled to the next picture and saw that it was of his father. This time he was the one sitting on the sofa beside Kolbeinn. Judging from his brother's clothes, the photo had been taken on the same occasion. His father looked pleased and proud, with longer hair and a more impressive beard than

Hjörvar remembered him having. The crack in the dam began to grow.

It split even wider as he studied the next two snapshots.

The first showed him outside in the garden in his Tottenham shirt, playing with a football. The space he had to play in was limited by a big hole that had been dug in the middle of the lawn for the flagpole.

The second picture was of a little girl who had to be Salvör. She looked angry, her face fixed in a scowl, her mouth turned down. Her straight, dark hair was cut short and someone had tried to liven it up with a cheerful bow. But the ribbon couldn't offset the aura of unhappiness emanating from the child. Although the photo was in black and white, it was quite clear that she was wearing a flowery dress and a light-coloured cardigan that could well have been yellow.

The photographer seemed to have tried again in the hope of capturing a better expression, maybe even a smile, but to no avail. This time Salvör had her eyes tight shut and her mouth wide open in a scream.

Hjörvar didn't need any soundtrack. He could hear that ear-splitting screech as if she were standing right beside him. It was the scream he had already heard in his memory – but now he could see the gaping mouth too.

He scrolled to the next picture. It had also been taken in the garden, like the photo of him with the ball, and he was wearing the same shirt. But this time Salvör was there too. She was wearing the flowery dress and pale cardigan. Hjörvar zoomed in on the photo to see her shoes. As far as he could tell, they matched the one that had been found under the flagpole. The laces were undone on one of them – on her left foot.

Judging by the picture, he was not pleased to have his sister there. He had his hands over his ears and his face was contorted in a grimace. Not without reason, because she was still shrieking. It looked as if she had been put out in the garden in the hope that she would calm down.

The crack split wider. The dam quivered. It was ready to burst. Hjörvar opened the last picture. And then it happened: the dam cracked wide open. But the memories of Salvör didn't flood over him like an unstoppable torrent, rather they appeared one by one, grainy, in fits and starts, as if they were being streamed over a bad internet connection.

The trigger was yet another attempt by the photographer to capture a memorable moment – a moment guaranteed to warm the cockles of his parents' hearts when they were older and the children had left home. *Oh, do you remember this?* That was the magic of photographs: they conjured up long-ago moments – often forgotten ones – bringing them vividly back to life.

But not all moments captured on film deserve to be remembered. Some are better forgotten.

This snapshot showed one such moment. Salvör stood there, still screaming, her mouth a gaping O, like in the previous two pictures. But it was something else that froze the blood in Hjörvar's veins. On the grass beside the little girl lay a baseball bat and ball. Probably the very ones mentioned by the old man at the nursing home. Hjörvar could recall now the heft of the bat in his hand, the smoothness of the wood. The memory of the bat wasn't sweet like the one associated with the football shirt. It made him shudder.

And he knew why.

He was with Salvör in the picture. Although he was blurry, which made it hard to see his features, it was him. There was no doubt. He was in the act of bending down to pick up the baseball bat from the lawn. The bat he would then raise in the air, swing behind him, and bring down with all his might on the head of his unbearable, noisy little sister. The sister who always ruined everything.

The phone fell from Hjörvar's nerveless fingers and sank into the snow. The screen briefly lit up the white crystals in its shallow hole, then went dark. He didn't bend down to retrieve it.

Puss mewed loudly but instead of coming to Hjörvar, as he had been hoping, the cat had moved away. He was now over by the high fence between the radar station and the shore. Puss leapt up, climbing the wire mesh. Then, poised on the top, he turned briefly to look at Hjörvar and mewed again, before jumping down on the other side.

Hjörvar stood there, staring after the cat. He felt like a man who has just recovered consciousness to find himself handcuffed to a hospital bed with a police officer sitting in the visitor's chair. Had he really done it? Smashed the baseball bat down on his sister's head so hard that it had killed her? Had the force of the blow knocked her backwards into the hole in the lawn? Had he remembered it right? It would explain the shoe.

Did people's memories of the past really record what happened? Weren't they inevitably distorted by wishful thinking, on the one hand, and on the other, by dread of what might have happened? These thoughts must all be stored in the same part of the brain: what happened, what ought to have happened and what definitely shouldn't have happened. They must be governed by some kind of retrieval system.

Instinct told him that in this instance his memory wasn't deceiving him. The sequence of his father running over was too sharp; of him lifting Salvör out of the hole and vanishing with her into the house. Then his mother's loud weeping and screams of horror. His father disappearing with Salvör. Hjörvar had never seen her again. And now he recalled how everything had changed after that: how his parents had stopped hugging him, stopped kissing him goodnight, avoided all physical contact with him; how they had seemed to shudder whenever he spoke to them or tried to touch them.

He understood the Bible quotation on the cross only too well now: it was directed at him. He was the one Jesus was supposed to forgive; he was the one who didn't know what he had done.

Hjörvar felt somehow dislocated from his own body. No longer cold, in spite of the freezing temperature. No longer afraid, in spite of the darkness. He was totally numb.

Turning on his heel, he walked steadily towards the gate and out of it, without returning to the building to switch off the lights. They didn't matter. For all he cared, they could stay on forever. He left his phone where it was lying. There was nobody he wanted to call. His sister's tragic death and his part in it weren't something he wanted to share with any other human being. Not with Kolbeinn and certainly not with his own kids. Of course, he ought to confide in them. They deserved an explanation of why he had been such an uncaring, useless failure of a father. It would help them come to terms with themselves and hopefully allow them to achieve a better life one day.

But it wasn't to be. Not this evening.

He walked along the fence in search of Puss. There was a strange inevitability about it when he saw the cat out on the rocks. Their eyes met. Hjörvar kept going, climbing over the shore ridge but stopping well short of the blowhole. The black opening reminded him of a rotten mouth cavity. He said Puss's name in a low, gentle voice. The cat turned away and sat down. Right by the blowhole.

Hjörvar took two steps forward. He had to get the cat. He couldn't go home and lie there alone and unsleeping. He had to have Puss there with him. The cat wouldn't judge him for what he had done. Cats were used to killing things without an iota of shame. It was in their nature.

But when Hjörvar bent down to pick him up, Puss darted away. He wasn't quite sure whether the animal was fleeing him or alarmed by the tremendous roar of surf echoing up the shaft. It made no difference. Hjörvar knew what to expect. As he straightened up, he saw her standing there on the other side of the hole: a little girl in a rose-patterned summer dress, a yellow cardigan and one shoe. She was staring at him from under knitted brows, her mouth half open to reveal her tiny milk teeth. There was no sign of forgiveness in her face.

The blowhole exploded. When the column of seawater toppled back, it snatched Hjörvar with it. As he was sucked down the shaft, the little girl watched and smiled.

Puss watched too. While Hjörvar was discovering for himself what it was like to die in the rocky hole, the cat let out a single mew, then turned away.

His life in this place was over. Just as Hjörvar's life was now over.

But unlike Hjörvar, the cat still had several lives to spare.

He padded past the radar station and out onto the gravel track leading to the main road. Would he head towards the bright lights of Höfn or in the other direction, through the Almannaskard tunnel into the Lón district beyond?

Only time would tell.

Chapter 31

A new day, a new opportunity. Countless possibilities to invent a new self. Tinker, tailor, soldier, sailor, rich man, poor man, and all that: there was no shortage of identities to choose from.

Thórir didn't need to make up his mind right now. The opportunities would turn up, as experience had shown him. All he needed to do was keep his eyes and ears open. He was good at reading people, which made it easy for him to identify the gullible, the unsuspecting, the type without an ounce of paranoia in their make-up. Of course, he couldn't just spout any old crap, it was a little more complicated than that, but more often than not he could pose as whatever or whoever he liked. People weren't in the habit of suspecting that the person they were talking to was lying about his profession. Particularly if he was convincing and spoke fluently, without any sign of hesitation. And Thórir possessed a natural talent for acting. When he threw himself into a role, he managed to forget himself to the extent that he became the person he was playing.

That wasn't his only useful skill. After just a few minutes chatting to a stranger, he could suss out exactly what would win them over and what their life was lacking, and so work out which role would fit in perfectly with their expectations, their attitudes and dreams. Having identified what was missing from their life, he would set out to plug the gap. Sometimes the person in question wouldn't even have realised the hole was there. Or else they were achingly conscious of it. That made things even easier for him. The more powerful the unfulfilled need, the easier his role. After all, the person who was floundering didn't stop to examine the life-belt when it was thrown to them.

Thórir was driving along the coast. The view was magnificent, the freezing temperatures lending the air a crystal clarity, the sky a cloudless blue. He gazed at the glacial tongues spilling down from the ice cap to sea level, at the small islands dotting the lagoon close to the town. He might as well make the most of the incredible scenery since he was unlikely ever to return. His flight was leaving shortly and he would be saying goodbye to Höfn for the last time. It was best not to stay too long in one place and he had already been here far longer than originally intended. It had never been part of the plan to join in the rescue effort and he had taken a big risk in doing so.

The temptation had been irresistible, though. After returning to civilisation, he had spent several nights at a hotel further down the coast, near the Jökulsárlón glacial lagoon with its picturesque icebergs, while he was recovering from his ordeal. As a result, he had been feeling rested and full of renewed vigour as he stood, freshly shaven, at the airport, about to head home, when his eye was drawn to a group of search and rescue volunteers who had just arrived. Overhearing the reason for their presence in Höfn, he had acted on impulse. Instead of checking in for his flight to Reykjavík, he had gone to the service desk and changed his ticket. It had been easy. Then he had gone to the little car rental booth and asked if he could keep his vehicle a bit longer. Again – no problem. After that, he had simply walked up to the group and introduced himself as a fellow volunteer. The National Association had advised him to meet them at the airport, he explained, as he had decided to come by road instead of flying. No one had questioned his claim and by the time they left the airport together, he had become part of the group.

The follow-up was easy. The locals had assumed he was part of the back-up contingent, like the policemen from Selfoss and the representatives of the Identification Commission. And he believed he had been genuinely useful to them. That was his general intention, though he wasn't always successful. He yearned to help.

Occasionally things went badly wrong. Not often – but occasionally. Up to now, the most serious cock-up had been the car crash he had unwittingly caused. That had been a while ago, when he had still been feeling his way in his attempts to become somebody else. A beginner's mistake, you could say. He had gone onto a Facebook page where people were advertising for tradesmen, and found a request from a woman he liked the look of. The rest had been simple: he had phoned her, posing as a car mechanic, and offered to come round to her house and sort out her brakes on the spot. She had welcomed his offer, especially when she heard the price he was proposing, cash in hand.

After a bit of googling and watching a few YouTube videos, he had gone round to the woman's place and done a pretty good job, he reckoned, based on what he had learnt from his online research. And that wasn't all; he'd also managed to charm the woman into agreeing to a date. But this had come to nothing because she had rung him that same evening in a terrible state. It turned out she had knocked down a young woman who was out running, and she was claiming it was his fault. He'd sworn he hadn't a clue what she was talking about – he hadn't been anywhere near her car – then he'd hung up. When the police called him the following day, he admitted he'd talked to the woman on the phone about mending her brakes but explained he hadn't yet found time to do so. They'd believed him. After that he'd changed his number and never heard from the woman again.

So it had been a pretty wretched reminder of his beginner's mistake when he'd bumped into the very woman he believed had been the victim of that accident. He had kept his head, though, by telling himself that he hadn't been behind the wheel that day. It hadn't been his fault. Anyway, she seemed to have made a decent recovery. Sure, she limped a bit, but not all the time. The damage couldn't have been that bad. And seeing as she had got over it, there was no point in his dwelling on the accident.

It had been yet another sign, though, that he needed to be more careful. He had got away with it for too long and this had made him reckless. His recent run of bad luck meant it was time to take a short break. Not for too long. Just enough to get his bearings. Because he was confident that his luck was about to turn and there were good times ahead. The past was just water under the bridge; it couldn't be changed. Whereas the future awaited, full of promise. He just needed to pause and catch his breath before resuming the game.

And, it went without saying, he would have to be more careful next time. Because mistakes, he had learnt, tended to snowball. But this latest snowball seemed to have completed its run down the slope.

The pushing-off point for the snowball had been a visit to Höfn on private business about six months previously. He'd got talking to the woman working behind the bar of his hotel. Like the rest of the staff, she was a foreigner. Her name was Wiktoria, she was Polish and she had two jobs as she was saving up to buy a flat. Thórir had taken to her straight away, admiring her drive. He discovered that she had just split up with a guy as their relationship hadn't worked out, and he could hear in her voice that she was on the lookout for a good man. Well, he could play that good man. No problem.

He was a ship's captain, he told her, and could boast some of the best catches in the whole eastern region. They'd ended up talking until the bar closed and she finished her shift. The following day he had cancelled his business in Höfn and extended his stay at the hotel. That evening, he had lain in wait for her at the bar. This time she'd accepted his invitation to go on an outing with him the next day to the Jökulsárlón lagoon, as part of a sightseeing drive around the south-eastern corner of the country. The success of the trip had exceeded his expectations, as it turned out that it was the first chance she'd had to explore the area since moving there.

Eventually, he'd had to head home to Reykjavík, but they'd stayed in touch. He'd continued to play the role of the fairy-tale prince she so obviously deserved, inviting her on the odd weekend break to different parts of the country, when she didn't have a shift at the hotel and he wasn't 'stuck out at sea'. She was very keen to see his home in the village of Neskaup-stadur in the East Fjords, but he made excuses, explaining that his house had burnt down while he was away on a fishing trip. At present he was living in a small rented flat but he was planning to build himself a new place. Getting carried away, he'd asked if she would like to help him design the new house, adding that money was no object. She had been full of ideas and suggestions, and he had agreed to them all.

Before he knew it, he was trapped. Cornered. Wiktoria wanted to move in with him. She wanted to oversee the construction and didn't mind if they had to live in a rabbit hutch until the house was ready. As it was, she was living cooped up in a bedsit with nothing but a bed, a wardrobe, a toilet and a shower, so she wasn't fussy.

Originally, he had told her that his wife had recently died of cancer, so he didn't want news of their relationship to get out.

She mustn't post any pictures of them together on social media or mention to anyone in Höfn that they were seeing each other. If she did, the news was bound to spread to the East Fjords and there hadn't been a decent enough interval since his wife had passed away. Now, though, this excuse had run out of steam and Wiktoria had set him an ultimatum. Her landlord had got wind of the fact she was keeping pets in her room and she wanted to hand in her notice before she was kicked out. He would have to make up his mind: it was now or never.

He'd had no alternative but to agree to her moving in with him: he couldn't bring himself to end their relationship.

When the big day arrived, he said he would drive from the east to meet her halfway, as the road conditions were bad and her car wasn't reliable enough. Then he had jumped on a plane to Egilsstadir in east Iceland, where he had hired a large four-by-four. Since he drove faster than her and had set off earlier, they had met not halfway as planned but in the Lón district, close to Höfn.

At that point he had tried to buy some time by saying he wanted to explore a bit while they were there. She hadn't been too pleased about that as she had her cat and parrot in the car, along with her modest collection of belongings. But in the end she had let herself be persuaded and had parked her car in a gravel lay-by beside the ring road. Leaving her pissed-off cat, and the parrot squawking in its cage, she'd got into his jeep.

The problem was that he hadn't a clue what he should pretend he wanted to see, so in the end he had turned onto a dirt track leading into the Lónsöræfi nature reserve. Having driven along it as far as possible, he had insisted on continuing on foot, dragging Wiktoria along with him, though her shoes were totally unsuitable for winter hiking. By then she had begun to suspect that there was something amiss, though she hadn't said anything. So they had walked and walked, and he had pretended to admire the spectacular scenery, his brain working all the while on some way of getting out of his predicament. But his mind had been blank.

Eventually, they had come across a hut that turned out not to be locked. He'd rather not dwell on what had happened there. Basically, she had demanded to know what was going on and he had ended up admitting the truth: that he wasn't a ship's captain, he didn't live in the East Fjords and he certainly wasn't planning to build his own house.

He was rarely forced to confront the consequences of his actions when the game was up. Usually, when the truth came to light, the reckoning happened over the phone. And it didn't come without warning but after he had got bored of the role and had started actively avoiding the person he had been putting on an act for.

Putting on an act was a good description of what he did, in his opinion. He wasn't lying. Not exactly. He was acting and doing a good job of it. He was living the best version of his life, which wasn't the life he had been allotted. He felt it was up to him to compensate for that.

The hut hadn't provided the same safe distance as the phone, though. The situation had got out of control. In the end, he had pushed Wiktoria out of the door as she was standing in the hall, pulling on her outdoor clothes and insisting that he drive her back to her car. Then he had shut the door on her, locking it from the inside. At first, she had hammered on the door and screamed at him angrily, but before long she was begging him to let her in. Finally, she had gone quiet. While all this was going on, he had been sitting on the floor in the hall, staring into space. These transitions often proved very difficult for him. He was no longer Hafthór, captain of a successful fishing boat in the East Fjords. Nor had he yet become the character he would assume next. In between roles, he was forced to be himself. And that was hard to bear.

Quite a long interval had passed between her falling silent and his opening the door. Wiktoria had vanished, but it hadn't been difficult to follow her trail from the hut. Having clearly abandoned all hope of getting him to open the door for her, she had gone in search of alternative shelter. Of course, she had failed in this, though she had managed to cover a surprising distance, considering that she wasn't even wearing a coat. It had been left behind in the hut in all the commotion. When he'd thrown her out, she'd had her mittens in her hands and had already put on her hat and scarf. Presumably that was what had enabled her to make it as far as she did. He'd found her lying in a motionless huddle in the snow. Without realising it, she had been walking in the opposite direction from the car.

He had apologised to her then, saying that he hadn't intended for things to end this way. He'd only wanted to help. Wiktoria hadn't answered. So he had decided the right thing to do would be to speed up the process by removing the rest of her outdoor clothes. The damage had already been done and there was no reason to prolong her suffering. So he had unwound the scarf from her neck and pulled off her mittens and hat.

He wasn't worried about being implicated in her death. After all, she might never be found. Although she wasn't that far away from the hut, she'd wandered off the path and it would take an organised search effort or extreme bad luck for someone to stumble on her. Besides, it would be difficult to link them. There was no digital trail, as he'd avoided communicating with her via email or text messages, and he steered well clear of social media, which was fatal for people in his position. The funny thing was how little suspicion this seemed to arouse. If anything, people seemed to admire his decision. If the police examined Wiktoria's phone records, they would see that he'd been in frequent contact with her, but he would have no trouble talking himself out of that. He'd say he had been pursuing her after meeting her at the hotel, which was true. But unfortunately she'd fallen for the captain of a fishing boat instead, he'd say ruefully. He could explain away his trip to Egilsstadir by claiming that he'd been looking for work in the east. The case would be dropped, as there would be no evidence of anything criminal.

While he was struggling to pull off Wiktoria's jumper, she had twitched and he had recoiled in shock. After a few moments' indecision, he had resumed the task of undressing her. As a precaution, he had also taken her mobile phone from the back pocket of her jeans. Not long afterwards, she had twitched for the last time and her breathing had finally stopped. The whole thing had taken far longer than he'd expected but he hadn't left her. He'd remained at her side, keeping her company to the bitter end, though freezing himself. He hadn't wanted her to die alone. He wasn't a bad man.

On the way back to the car, he had thrown her phone off a steep crag and let the wind whip away her clothes, one after the other: jumper, mittens, scarf and hat were swept away over the frozen snowfields. He wasn't worried that they would ever be found. The nature reserve was large, drained by countless rivers and streams. Most of the clothes would be washed down into the watercourses sooner or later and end up in the sea, pausing here and there en route, as in the case of her hat.

He had taken the keys from Wiktoria's pocket, with the intention of moving her car to a location well away from the turn-off to Lónsöræfi. When her absence was eventually noticed, it wouldn't do for anyone to guess that she might have gone there. Leaving his rental jeep in the lay-by, he had got behind the wheel of her car and driven through the Almannaskard tunnel with the cat mewing plaintively in the back and the parrot shrieking in its cage on the passenger seat. He had parked the car out of sight of the ring road on the dirt track leading out to Stokksnes. Before abandoning it and embarking on the long trek back to his jeep, he had let out the cat and released the parrot from its cage. He was a bit miffed when neither animal had appeared particularly grateful to be set free, but in the end they had moved away. The parrot had flown off towards the sea, and the last he'd seen of the cat, it had been padding along the track in the direction of the radar station. No doubt both creatures would survive and in time learn to be grateful for their freedom.

He had never intended to return to Lónsöræfi. Absolutely not. But a new role had been born on that long hike to retrieve his jeep and it had taken over, eventually leading him back there. He had become Haukur, a PhD student doing research on glaciology. The idea had been born out of the circumstances. The nature reserve and the Vatnajökull national park had been much on his mind during his lonely trek.

This role had turned out to be the biggest mistake of his life. There was no way he could have foreseen the tragic repercussions it would have.

At first he'd been quite pleased to be going on the trip with the two couples. He'd felt compelled to return to the hut to double-check that he hadn't left behind any incriminating evidence that could be traced to him. For the last couple of months he had been sleeping badly, constantly starting awake in the middle of the night to the sound of Wiktoria's weeping and pleading to be let in. The problem was, her anorak had got left behind at the hut in the panic, and awareness of this fact had stopped him getting back to sleep after his bad dreams. But there was no way he could bring himself to return alone to dispose of her coat. Travelling out there with company would be quite a different matter, though. The expedition would provide him with the perfect opportunity to rectify his mistake.

It was only supposed to be a short trip: one night in the hut, another in a tent, then home again. But fate had intervened with a vengeance.

The two men had insisted on coming with him to take readings from the equipment – an eventuality he hadn't foreseen. There was no equipment, of course. His plan had been to walk along the edge of the glacier for a while on his own, then return with the imaginary readings. Instead, he'd been forced to pretend he couldn't find the instrument. But that had backfired too, because he hadn't been prepared for the stubbornness displayed by one of the men. Really, it was the two men's pig-headed refusal to give up that was to blame for what had happened afterwards. It wasn't his fault. He had been just as much a victim of fate as the rest of them. It was only by sheer luck that he had got off more lightly.

It had been a close call when the three of them had gone out to search for the instrument and got caught in a blizzard. It had been touch and go whether he'd make it back alive himself. What had saved him was being able to take the others' protective clothing as, one by one, he came across them. First Bjólfur's, when he found him absolutely done for on his way back to the camp. By stripping off Bjólfur's clothes, he had shortened his death struggle – really, it had been an act of mercy.

As Bjólfur's coat had been far superior to his, he had let the gale whisk away his own shabby anorak, just as it had Wiktoria's clothes two months previously. But he'd had the presence of mind to take his car keys and wallet out of his pockets first. He'd chucked Bjólfur's phone down beside him and emptied his pockets of everything else. Then he'd wrapped the rest of the man's clothes around his own waist and neck. With the added layers to protect him from the elements, he had managed to make it back to the camp.

There had been no way he could bring himself to get into the tent with the waiting women. How was he supposed to break it to them that their husbands had given up the fight and wouldn't be coming back? That would have to wait until morning. So he had crept into his own tent, right to the back, where he had curled up in a ball to keep warm and had fallen asleep. Admittedly, he hadn't come across Tjörvi at any point but he assumed the man must have suffered the same fate as his mate Bjólfur.

In spite of his exhaustion, he had slept only fitfully, repeatedly disturbed by the same nightmare as he'd had in town. He'd thought he heard Wiktoria begging for help outside the tent and at one point he'd thought she was inside with him. The dream was even more potent than it had been in town because of what that woman Dröfn had experienced in the hut. He had managed to shut down the conversation by making up some tale about a woman who had been murdered there by her lover long ago. Dröfn had fallen for this lie, but the incident had left him feeling badly rattled. How could she have experienced the same thing as him? It wasn't as though she had been there to witness the deed and was being haunted by the same memories as he was. So it was no wonder that he'd been badly spooked in the tent, especially when it blew down on top of him in the storm. There had been no way he could go outside and put it up again.

Early the next morning, he'd been woken by noises outside and, hearing the three of them talking, realised that Tjörvi had made it back after all. He overheard Dröfn saying she was going out to look for Bjólfur. While this was going on, he had lain low, still curled up in a ball at the back of his tent. That had turned out to be lucky, because before Dröfn set out she had stuck her arm into his tent and taken his backpack. He had huddled there without moving for a long time, waiting for her to leave, and still hadn't made up his mind how to reveal himself to the others when he'd heard Wiktoria's voice again. The nightmare that had repeatedly disturbed him in the night had started up once more.

Only this time he was awake.

The extraordinary thing was that Agnes and Tjörvi seemed to be aware of her too. He'd heard cries and the sounds of bodies tumbling about as if they were clambering out of the tent. Then the sound of their voices had seemed to be coming from further away. He'd waited until their cries had fallen silent, together with the nonsense Tjörvi was pouring out for Dröfn's benefit, it seemed, though she was nowhere near. When he'd finally dared to go out himself, he'd found them some distance from the camp, wearing nothing but their underwear. They were as far gone as Bjólfur had been, though Tjörvi was in an even worse state, judging by his fingers and face. At least, he'd been too weak to reach for the knife when he realised what was happening. Though he had tried.

He had stripped them of what seemed most useful. Tjörvi's woollen vest and Agnes's long johns, which he could use as an extra scarf. He'd also had a look in their tent and retrieved his rucksack, which he took back to his own tent, where he stuffed in his sleeping bag and pulled on the extra clothes before heading off back to the hut. There had no longer been any need to work out how he was going to rejoin the group because the group no longer existed. Or at least it wouldn't for much longer, judging by the feeble moaning Agnes and Tjörvi had been making as he set off.

In the end he had made it back to the hut and gone inside for a brief rest. Just long enough to gather his strength for the next stage. The less time he spent in there, the better, because the place gave him the creeps.

When he had recovered sufficiently, he had gone outside and, to his astonishment, spotted Dröfn lying near the top of the slope, half on the body of the reindeer that appeared to have given up the ghost. The last thing he knew, she had headed off towards the glacier. He would never have expected her to find her way back to the hut. Instead of embarking immediately on the final leg of his journey, he had climbed up the slope to where Dröfn was lying and stroked her head in its woollen hat. He had liked her best of all the party. At this, she had emitted a feeble croak, like a baby bird that had fallen from its nest – straight into the jaws of a cat. For some reason she was holding his knife but she was too weak to use it.

He took pity on Dröfn, as he had on Wiktoria. Mindful of how unnecessarily drawn out Wiktoria's death throes had been, he had removed all Dröfn's clothes apart from her underwear, before laying her down again near the reindeer. Then he had stayed beside her until it was all over. It hadn't taken long.

Looking away from Dröfn, he had stared at the knife lying on the snow. It belonged to him and he'd wondered whether he should take it with him or leave it there. In the end, he'd decided to leave it. The knife would only remind him of all these deaths and he wanted to put them behind him as soon as he could. Nevertheless, he picked it up and wiped the handle to remove any fingerprints he might have left on it, before dropping it back onto the snow.

Afterwards, he had chucked Dröfn's clothes in a heap in the hall of the hut, removed Wiktoria's anorak from the peg and closed the door behind him. It didn't matter if Dröfn's clothes were found, because he had no fear of anyone linking him to the two couples. He hadn't stayed at the same hotel as them, since they had chosen the one Wiktoria used to work at. He hadn't wanted to risk being recognised there, though he had a full moustache and beard now, in keeping with his role as a geologist. In addition, he'd taken the precaution of keeping his phone switched off on the journey to Lónsöræfi, so he was fairly confident that it wouldn't have connected to the same masts as the others'. Lastly, he wasn't worried about being caught on any of the photos on their phones, as they'd been too egocentric to take anything but selfies.

He'd got away with it. The police had actually called him to ask what he'd been doing in Höfn. By then, though, he was posing as the rescue-team member, Thórir, and had inveigled his way into the inner circle of those organising the search. As a result, he'd known that the police were going to contact all travellers who had spent a night in the area or hired a four-wheel drive there. Forewarned, he had managed to answer the call without any of those around him discovering what it was about. He'd had no difficulty inventing a reason for his presence in the east, and after that he had been eliminated as a suspect.

The dashboard clock showed that it was time to get himself to the airport. The sightseeing trip was over. He gazed out over the lagoon, saying a silent farewell to the little town. As he drove along the ring road to the airport, he watched the small plane making its descent and put his foot down. He still had to return the hire car and he didn't want to miss his flight. He had already spent an extra night in Höfn and needed to make himself scarce – the longer he stayed, the more risk there was of exposure.

If that happened this time, it would be very different from on previous occasions. The consequences would be far more serious. Lives had been lost, even if in each case it had been an accident. Normally, he left behind a trail of furious people who were too ashamed of having let themselves be taken in to pursue him or go to the police. He chose to believe that in spite of their seething rage, they understood on some level that he had meant well. There were limits, though, to what he could achieve. In the end his efforts always came up against a brick wall. And then it was time to find himself a new role.

Thórir parked at the airport, fetched his bag from the back, went inside and dropped his keys into the return box marked with the name of the car rental company. He walked past the new arrivals from Reykjavík, who were standing in the area by the check-in desk, waiting for their luggage. Pausing, he pretended to look at something on his phone while eavesdropping on a conversation between two men who seemed to be there on official business. As he wasn't intending to stay on, what they were saying was of no relevance to him, but it was hard to wean himself off the habit.

What he heard sparked his interest, he had to admit. As far as he could gather, the men were from the Occupational Health and Safety Authority, there to investigate a fatal accident. It sounded as if it had something to do with the sea; at least, the plan was apparently to comb the beaches. Then they changed the subject and started discussing another recent accidental death, though it seemed it wasn't their job to investigate that. Thórir thought it involved a small girl. Apparently the child had gone out into the garden to play that morning, only to be crushed by a fence that had collapsed on top of her.

It took all Thórir's self-discipline not to strike up a conversation with the men. He could introduce himself as a representative of Fisheries Iceland, who had been sent to the town in connection with the accident. But it was too risky. He'd already been in Höfn too long. So he turned aside. Thórir had come to the end of the road as a character. He would have to be himself until a new opportunity crossed his path.

There was a woman ahead of him in the check-in queue. He waited patiently for his turn, using the time to come up with a new name. Adam was good. Styrmir too. Either of those. Or perhaps just Adam Styrmisson. Or Styrmir Adamsson.

Perhaps he would be a doctor this time. A surgeon. It was a profession that had always appealed to him. The new name and new role would have to wait, though, until he could find someone to act it out for. Until then, his old name would have to do.

The passenger in front of him took her boarding pass and he moved forward to the desk. The young woman smiled. 'Name?'

He smiled back. He had to resist the urge to use his new name, as he had bought his ticket and rented his car in his old one, which matched his ID.

'My name's Njördur. Njördur Hjörvarsson.'

Icy little fingers suddenly slipped under his jacket and touched his back, making him jump and spin round. There was no one behind him.

With a puzzled shrug, Njördur started walking out to the waiting plane. He must have imagined it.

Like the sound of Wiktoria's weeping that he could have sworn he heard echoing inside the plane just before he stepped aboard.

A figment of his imagination. Nothing more.

Acknowledgements

Special thanks for assistance are due to: Sigurjón Björnsson and Gudmundur Ólafsson from the radar station at Stokksnes; Detective Jóhann Hilmar Haraldsson in Höfn; Laufey Gudmundsdóttir at Glacier Journey; Ásgeir Erlendsson and Ásgrímur L. Ásgrímsson from the Icelandic Coast Guard; Bryndís Bjarnarson from the Municipality of Hornafjördur, and Gunnar Ásgeirsson and Hjalti Thór Vignisson from Skinney-Thinganes Ltd.